G. A. Johansson was born and grew up in Sweden. She came to England in her late teens to study English, intending to stay for only a year. Still here, she now lives on the south coast, near Chichester. "The House on the Lake" is her first adult novel, although she is the author of five children's books: two in the series, "Alice's Magical Adventures" and three in the series, "The Adventures of Tula and her Troll". These books are available on Amazon.

To find out more, visit her at www.briarfieldpress.com

Happy Birthday Jan!

Love Cherie

xxx

The House by the Lake

G.A. Johansson

BRIARFIELD
PRESS

ISBN: 978-1-9162027-0-2

Book design by The Art of Communication www.book-design.co.uk
First published in the UK 2020

Dedication

I dedicate this book to the memory of: Catherine King,
successful novelist and dear friend,
whose friendship gave me the inspiration for this book.

Acknowledgements

I owe my thanks to my family: Paul and Suzie for their patience and understanding and, as ever, to my friends Lorna and Hilary for their constant help and support, also to my colleagues at Portchester Writing Group.

A special thank you to Linda March, of The Good English Company, whose help has been invaluable in creating a finished novel.

To Christine Hammacott of The Art of Communication, for producing a splendid cover and book design.

All of you have made the writing of this, my first adult novel, an enjoyable experience.

Chapter 1

Bristol, September 2005

Ellen stared at the Georgian building in the painting. Her body tightened as she fought against the feeling of being sucked into the frame. The sensation of standing on the damp grass, close to the lake, was becoming overwhelming. Uneasy and shaken, she took a step back. A moment's panic set in: the lake was behind her…

A slight nudge at her elbow broke the spell. Surprised, she turned towards the man standing next to her. He was casually dressed in an open-necked shirt, with dark, greying hair, but his stone-coloured eyes unsettled her. He smiled, 'Do you like it? It was one of my earlier works.'

Ellen glanced around, glad to avert her gaze from his. A few people were studying the other paintings in the room. When she had come in, she hadn't noticed this man, the artist; she had only looked straight ahead drawn to this painting as if by a magnet. Every day for the past week on her way to work, she'd stopped by the gallery window to look at the house.

It was a three-storey mansion with decorative stone mouldings above the many large windows. Four steps led to the porch, which was held up by two pillars. A short distance from the building, an ornate water fountain stood in front of a copse of trees. The painting was in oil, with heavy bold brushstrokes, making the house the main feature with lawns sloping down to a lake.

Today the painting had disappeared from the shop window. Had it been sold? She hoped it had been moved inside. On an impulse, she had entered the gallery.

Ellen pulled herself together and prepared to return his smile but was startled by a change in him. The smile had gone and the tension in his face was unmistakable. His fixed gaze held her attention – she had never seen such dark grey eyes before. She hesitated before answering.

'Yes, I like it very much.' Guess he's anxious to sell, she thought.

'Perhaps you know this place?' His penetrating eyes searched hers for an answer.

'Is it the Lake District? It's vaguely familiar, but I've never been there.' Ellen blushed slightly.

'Yes, a corner of Lake Windermere.'

'I'd like to have it.' She was surprised to hear her own voice. She hadn't intended to buy it and now she had, without even asking the price. She was pleased to find that it was only sixty pounds, she could afford that, it was reasonable. The artist showed his relief, the tenseness left his face and a smile played at the corners of his mouth. He also gave her directions to find the house, although she hadn't asked for them. His voice was relaxed when he said, 'I believe it has been waiting for you.'

Ellen had arranged to pick up the painting from the gallery after work. When she arrived, it was ready to close for the day. Looking around, she was relieved to find that the artist wasn't there. She had been unnerved by him and this bothered her.

At home she removed the mirror from above the fireplace and hung the painting in its place. Pleased she took a step back; yes, it looked all right there. She poured herself a glass of wine, lit a candle and leaning back on the settee, turned on the television. After a minute or two, she realised that she hadn't seen or heard a word of what was being said. Her eyes were on the painting. She turned off the TV and walked over to the fireplace. Why did this house fascinate her? Now that she owned the painting, she thought that her interest would fade. Why had she bought it, when it had made her feel uneasy? She couldn't answer that. It was bought on an impulse; there was something about the house she couldn't explain.

The next day her unease became anxiety. She felt her frown grow deeper with concern as her eyes constantly wandered to the painting. The book she had picked up to read rested on her lap, and she had to force herself to finish a page before allowing her gaze to return to the picture. When she came home from work, in the days to follow, she often found herself standing in front of it, and the feeling of being pulled into the frame remained. One day she took a deep breath, 'All right, you win.'

In the morning she woke with a start, remembering what she had decided to do. Pulling the jeans up over her slender hips, she glanced in the mirror, pleased with what she saw. She hesitated before picking up the phone. Could Annie manage the shop on her own? It was Friday after all. What should she tell her? The truth? Perhaps not… she would go and see for herself first.

Three years ago, thanks to money left by her grandmother, she'd been able to invest in the half-share of a business. Struggling at first, it was now doing well. Ellen had the talent to make and sell her own designs. Annie, her business partner, was an accomplished dressmaker. It was down to their hard work that the shop was a success, and luck had also helped them on the way. One client had been pleased with their work and recommended their designs to her many friends. At the age of twenty-eight, Ellen had reasons to be pleased.

She nervously ran her hand over her long auburn hair, which fell loosely around her shoulders, then touched her temples, as she listened to Annie's soft Welsh accent over the phone.

'Sure, I'll manage. And Moira will be in tomorrow. See you Tuesday. Another headache?'

Not this time, she thought, although there had been many lately.

The car keys were not on the ornamental plate on the sideboard, where she always left them. Searching for them irritated her; finally she found them in her coat pocket. Her mood had been brought on by her guilty feelings and she shook them off. Annie had said she'd manage, so why feel bad about it?

It was a four-hour journey to the Lake District; after a couple of hours of heavy traffic, Ellen's stomach was starting to rumble and she decided to pull off at Crewe Services. She estimated that, if she didn't take too long over lunch, she'd arrive at Lake Windermere about three in the afternoon. Before leaving home, she had booked a room for the night close to her destination.

The journey took her an hour longer than anticipated, but, thanks to the information the artist had given her, she was confident that she'd find the house. He had told her that the turn off from the main road was easy to miss. Because of this, she slowed down to look out for it and came off onto a narrow and uneven road leading through woodland. Five minutes later after a sharp bend she could see the lake, and at the top of the slope stood the house in the painting.

At the sight of it Ellen inhaled sharply, taking another deep breath, and full of apprehension, she got out of the car. What had brought her to this place? What was waiting? Standing still, she took in the scene before her. In spite of the goose bumps prickling her skin, she decided to walk closer.

The driveway had not disappeared completely; a barely distinguishable path led up to the house. What once had been a lawn, now overgrown, swept down towards the lake. She walked through the high and yellowing grass and as she came closer she could see signs of neglect: broken windows and damage to the walls. It was evident that the house had been empty for many years.

Was the orchard still behind the house? The thought had popped into her head, and startled her so much that she stopped abruptly. What orchard? There must be an explanation. She tried to convince herself that she was being stupid and to shake off the feeling of unease, but it remained. She knew that the slightest irritation would bring on a headache.

By the time she reached the house and stepped onto the porch, her head was throbbing. The door was ajar. Her hand rested on it, ready to push it open. A strong sense of foreboding told her not to enter. But her brain wasn't in charge and, before she knew it, she'd moved over the threshold. A cry escaped her. The large hall was familiar, she had been here before. Blood rushing to her head, she slumped against the doorframe. With her heart thumping, she took several deep breaths to calm herself. She wanted to run out of the house but she was no longer in control.

In a trance she crossed to the other side of the hall, ignoring the impressive but broken staircase leading to the upstairs landing. Her eyes were fixed on a door. Opening it, she entered the room, knowing it would be the drawing room, with the magnificent marble fireplace taking up a part of one wall. She wanted to speak, to protest at what was happening, but she couldn't utter a sound. Her legs buckled beneath her and she slumped to the floor. Trembling, she scrambled onto her knees, a deep sob escaped her and she hurriedly pulled herself up.

The room was empty except for one piece of furniture: an old chair covered with stained red velvet and much faded.

Her eyes were drawn to this chair; she recognised it. With her heart hammering, she made a huge effort to turn to flee, but stopped abruptly at the sight of footprints on the floor behind her. Then she realised the prints were hers, left by her shoes damp from the grass, and she giggled nervously. She wiped her forehead with the back of her hand, hardly registering that it was clammy. She felt detached. Was she dead? Get a grip, she told herself, you're getting hysterical. It's a bad dream and it will end. You'll find that you have never been to this wretched house, never set eyes on it. As if to confirm her thoughts, she dug her nails into her forearm and felt a sharp pain. It wasn't a dream: this was real, it was happening. On unsteady legs, she decided to explore the house. She had to know what had brought her here, whatever it was.

In the kitchen, she opened the old baking oven and peered inside, letting her hand run across the dusty black iron cooker. A name was struggling to come to her mind: Molly? Or was it Millie? The effort made her headache intensify and she dismissed the thought.

Confused and exhausted, she made her way back to the drawing room, where she gratefully sank down on the dusty velvet chair. By now her head was ready to explode and she reached for the painkillers in her bag. She took more than she should have, but she had to get rid of the headache. She couldn't cope with it, not now.

What was happening? Too many thoughts were whirling around at once. Annie was a sensible, no fuss person – she'd make sense of this. Ellen took out her mobile to call her, but the phone remained dark, no signal.

As she sat there slowly regaining her composure, her eyes caught the peeling wallpaper and absent-mindedly, she pulled at it. Although her head was throbbing, her brain registered that she recognised the much-faded paper. It revealed an intricate pattern: a flower head, resembling that of a tulip in a soft pink colour, surrounded by swirling moss-green leaves, and carefully dispersed amongst the leaves, dashes of blue.

She'd been particularly fond of this wallpaper. Was it because she liked tulips?

As she admitted this, her shoulders slumped and her eyes filled with hot tears. This house was familiar, but there was no other memory telling her why that should be.

Her gaze wandered to the tall window, where a pane was missing. She glanced up at the high ceiling with its attractive mouldings. The remains of a bird's nest balanced, where the picture rail met the corner. Feathers and bird droppings littered the floor. It was cold in the house and her fingers began to feel numb; she'd left her gloves in the car.

When the tablets had taken effect and the pain subsided, she raised herself from the chair and walked over to the window. There she could see what was left of the orchard, not much. The sky was rapidly getting darker and a mist was settling amongst a few overgrown trees. Through the broken windowpane, she could feel the chill in the wind.

The floor creaking under her feet brought back a memory. On an impulse, she bent down and lifted the loose board. A few letters lay beneath, bound together with a purple ribbon. She was not surprised. Somehow, she had known they would be there. Had she been sent to find them?

She shook the bundle gently and let her hand run over it, dispersing a cloud of dust. Did these letters mean anything to her? Her muddled brain told her that they must be important, but feeling empty and drained she knew they had to wait. There were shadows in the room already, too dark to stay in the house. Although the letters excited her, she wanted to be in a comfortable place when she read them. With the bundle safely tucked away in the inside pocket of her wax coat, she made her way out of the house and walked back to the car.

The pub where she had booked for the night was a low whitewashed building, with a slate roof, old fashioned and quaint, just how she liked it. Inside it had black beams on the ceiling and a roaring fire in the huge grate. Several old photographs were displayed on the wall to the side of the bar counter. Her excitement rose, as her eyes strayed to one in particular: a photo of the house. Ellen's skin tingled.

The landlord came up to her, 'Can I help you?'

'Yes please, a glass of the house red. I rang earlier and booked a room for tonight, I'm Ellen Kerry.' Her eyes strayed back to the photo.

'Yes, I can show you the room when you're ready.'

'I'll drink my wine first. What can you tell me about that old photo – the one with the house? I've bought a painting like that. I'm sure it's the same house.'

'Ah, so you bought it. It's called "Lakeside House".' The landlord unhooked the picture and handed it to her. 'An artist came in here and showed a lot of interest in this photo. He said he'd painted a picture of the house.'

Ellen stared at the photograph. She had seen the dilapidated fountain and the trees at the house today and they were on her painting. But they were missing from this photo. How did the artist know about them?

Her thoughts were interrupted when the landlord spoke again. What he said made her head spin. With a quick movement, she handed the photo back. Her fingers were burning. With his last sentence hanging in the air, she leaned heavily against the bar. She grabbed it with both hands, her nails digging into the counter.

'What did you say?' she asked loudly. 'Can you repeat it, please?'

A concerned look replaced the smile on the landlord's face and he nodded reassuringly at a young couple, whose heads had turned towards them.

'Are you all right?' he asked.

'I'm sorry, I didn't mean to shout. It's just that I didn't quite catch what you said.' But she had. She had heard every word. Her hand shot to her inside pocket, where she could feel the letters. 'Are you sure we're talking about the same house?' she stammered, her face flushed, her mouth dry.

'No doubt about it,' was his answer. 'It was pulled down over seventy years ago. Just as I said. Totally demolished: nothing left.'

Chapter 2

The landlord's face blurred and Ellen's grip on the counter tightened.

'But I've come from there. I saw it…' She stopped. The letters! Less than an hour ago she'd been inside. She had proof that the house was there. 'What else did the artist say?' She tried desperately to compose herself and managed a weak smile.

'I asked if the painting was for sale. I thought since it was local history, it would have been nice to have. But he said it was for a lady. That must have been you then.'

'No, I had never met the man before.' A chill ran down her back and she shuddered.

'You don't look well. Can I get you a cup of tea?' The landlord put down the tea towel and looked at her, 'It wouldn't be any trouble.'

'That's kind, but no thanks. I'm fine really.' Ellen picked up the glass of wine and put it down again; she needed a clear head. 'So, you're absolutely sure about the house?' she insisted.

The concerned look returned to the landlord's face and he turned to an old man, who was limping towards the bar.

'Albert, help us out. You were a young man at the time. This house...' He pointed at the photograph, 'This lady is under the impression it's still there.'

'Naa.' Albert shook his head. His wrinkly face broke into an appreciative smile when he turned towards her, 'Razed to the ground it was, nothing left 'cept a brick or two.'

'But the fountain and trees, I saw them today. They're not on this photo.' Ellen realised that she sounded incoherent and steadied her voice, 'But they're on my painting.'

'Well, I've heard someone local took that picture just before it was pulled down. He admired the building and wanted a memory of it. A bit of vandalising had gone on before that. Guess the fountain had been removed and the trees cut down for firewood.' Albert smiled, 'Don't you fret, young lady, they were there all right, just as on your painting.'

Her head started to throb again and although she knew it wouldn't do her headache any good, she grabbed the wine and gulped half of it down. It made her cough. She touched her temples, she couldn't collect her thoughts and merely nodded a 'thank you' to the old man. Nothing added up.

'I'll go to my room now for a rest. Bit of a headache,' she added. Her hand trembled as she accepted the key from the landlord's outstretched hand. If she couldn't make sense of what had happened, it would drive her mad.

In her room she closed the curtains, the nights were drawing in and soon it would be pitch black outside. In the morning she would see the full autumn colours of the Lake District. This she'd always longed for, but now she had no enthusiasm for it.

She took the letters out of her coat pocket and held them with both hands. The writing on the first one was fine and precise. She held it to her nose, did it have a smell? No, only dust and old paper. Was the name familiar? No, nor the name on the envelope underneath, but it was in a different hand. The writing was heavier and bolder. Before she went down to dinner she would read them. They held the key. But first she would freshen up. She placed the letters on the bedside table.

Stepping out of the shower, Ellen wrapped the bath towel

around her. She was more relaxed, but the headache was still there. Before she stretched out on the bed, she took a couple of painkillers. A few minutes of rest would do her good. Albert, the old man, might have some more information. She would go back to the bar and talk to him.

She sat up with a jerk, she must have dozed off. Her watch told her that she'd slept for fifteen minutes. She dressed in a hurry and went downstairs, picking up a menu from the bar counter as she passed.

Albert sat by the fireplace cradling an empty beer glass. Without asking if she could join him, she sank down on the chair next to him.

'Can I buy you a beer?' Her voice was anxious, almost pleading.

'Thank you. It's not every day a young lady asks for my company. Are you feeling better now?'

'Yes, much,' Ellen answered, which wasn't true. 'Can I ask you a few questions about the house?'

'Might've known it wasn't my charm that attracted you,' Albert sighed and touched his beard, but a smile showed on his wrinkly face. He held up his glass and nodded towards the bar. The landlord came over with a fresh pint.

'I'll pay for it,' Ellen said. 'I'd like to order a rump steak, chips and a glass of red wine. But not right now, in about an hour, please.'

'I'll put it on your bill.' The landlord took the menu. 'Headache gone?'

She nodded absent-mindedly and turned to Albert, 'What can you tell me?'

'The house by the lake?' He looked thoughtful, 'Not much, I wasn't born when it happened. And a teenager by the time it was pulled down.'

'What was it that happened?'

'Well, that's just it. Nobody knows why the owners left and never came back. They disappeared under strange circumstances. All I know is what I heard my parents say at the time of it being pulled down. They knew a relative of the servants, who stayed on to look after the house, but those people couldn't stay forever. Anyway, nothing came of it. Although all sorts of rumours were bandied about, nobody could prove any wrongdoings. After that, no one lived there and the rest you know.'

'What was the owner's name?'

'I don't know. Guess my parents mentioned it, but I can't remember. You might find some information in the archives of the newspaper,' he volunteered.

Ellen looked past Albert into the burning fire; the heat was warming her trouser legs. The flames were leaping and dancing in front of her eyes and for several moments she was mesmerized. She became aware of Albert looking at her curiously.

'A mystery,' she said flatly.

'Indeed. It was.'

'Another pint?' she offered.

'Naa thanks, must be on my way.' Albert stopped at the bar counter and exchanged a few words with the landlord. Both glanced back at her. Pretending not to notice, she continued to stare into the flames.

After the meal, Ellen's headache had gone, and she felt relaxed. There had been ten diners in all, not many for a Friday evening. Most were locals, too cold for tourists this time of year, she guessed. It was the last day of September and it had been a rainy month, so perhaps not surprising. A young couple were also staying at the inn and she kept up a conversation with them. Still early in the evening, she would have liked to chat a bit longer, but in her rush to come downstairs she had forgotten the letters. She felt the urge to read them now.

Ellen unlocked the door to her room and headed straight for the bedside table. She stared. They were gone. Falling to her knees, she searched the floor. Nothing. Her hands flew to cover her mouth. 'I'm sure that's where I put them,' she whispered. Still on her knees, she pulled away the bedside table, in case they had fallen behind it, but the area under the bed was scrupulously clean: no dust, no letters.

'I've put them somewhere else,' she mumbled, 'they must be here.' She started a systematic search of the room.

They were not to be found. Impossible! Had someone been in her room and stolen them? Who and why? No one could have known about them. It didn't make sense. Was anything else missing? She checked her belongings but could account for everything, and she remembered locking the door.

She sat down, rubbing her temples. Were the letters real? She had found them, hadn't she? Or had she imagined it? The landlord and Albert had said that the house wasn't there. With clammy hands she touched her cheeks, which were radiating heat. Was she running a temperature? A sob escaped her, 'What's happening to me?'

'No,' she protested, and sat up sharply. No, the letters were real. The names on the envelopes, what were they? She vaguely remembered a woman's name, but with her head throbbing at the time... There were no addresses or stamps on the envelopes, that she did remember. The letters had been hand-delivered.

Tears burnt her eyes, 'I *did* find them,' she whispered.

Was she going mad? She'd been inside a house, which wasn't there and discovered letters which were nowhere to be found. Perhaps they didn't exist either? With her head in her hands, she slowly rocked to and fro.

Had a chambermaid been in her room? To do what? Why would she steal the letters? The bedclothes had not been turned down. In the bathroom, the towels had not been touched. Nothing had changed and she wanted to scream in frustration.

She decided to talk to Jones, the landlord. As she locked the door of her room, she rattled the handle to make sure.

A middle-aged woman was serving behind the bar and moved over to Ellen with a smile, 'Good evening. What can I get you?'

'Good evening. A glass of red, please. Is Mr Jones about?'

'He'll be back shortly. Can I help you? I'm Mrs Jones.'

'Pleased to meet you. I'm staying here, Ellen Kerry.'

'Yes, I know,' Mrs Jones nodded.

'Tell me, does anyone come into my room in the evening?'

'No, we do all the necessary in the morning.'

'Just wondered. By the way, I've lost a bunch of letters. Have any been found? It's possible that I dropped them here.'

'Sorry, I would have known. It's only me and my husband working.'

'OK, but if they should turn up...'

'Yes, of course. Are they important?'

'I guess they could be.' Ellen frowned and wrinkled her forehead, 'Can I stay another night? Possibly two?'

'Yes, no problem. We're quiet this time of year.'

'Thanks.' She picked up her glass and moved to a table by the fireplace. She was in doubt about everything. Why had she asked if the letters had been found? She'd left them on the bedside table, but it was possible that she was wrong. Wasn't it?

Letting her thoughts wander, she stared into the flames. Tomorrow, she would go back to the house. It must be there. Why did these people tell her that it wasn't? She glanced over to the bar, where Mr Jones stood next to his wife. She eyed him suspiciously. What reason could he have to lie to her? Had he stolen the letters? He must have done. Who else? Had he been absent from the bar earlier in the evening? But she had enjoyed her chat with the young couple and wouldn't have noticed. And then there was Albert.

Nothing added up, she shook her head. Tomorrow she'd go back to the house, and then she would know.

Ellen slept late the next morning and when she came down after ten, she had missed breakfast.

'I can get you coffee and toast but no cooked food,' Mrs Jones offered.

'That's kind. I don't often have a cooked breakfast anyway. That'll do fine.' Ellen jumped at a loud rattle of glass behind her. Mr Jones had put a heavy crate of beer bottles on the floor.

'How are you today? Better I hope.'

'Thanks, I'll live.' She smiled back, feeling guilty about her suspicious thoughts from the previous evening.

'Off exploring then?' Mr Jones asked later, as she got ready to leave.

'Yes, you could say that.'

'There's some stunning scenery here and you're in luck today: clear blue skies and sunshine – a beautiful day for a drive. Wish I could come with you.'

'No, you don't.' Mrs Jones laughed and gave her husband a playful slap.

Ellen gripped the steering wheel harder. After the next bend, she would see the house.

If it was there. It would be – of course it would. She wasn't imagining this; nor was she going mad.

She drove around the corner in second gear, taking it slowly, to prepare herself for what she was about to see. Triumphantly she slammed on the brakes and laughed out loud. She'd been right all the time. *The house was there, and it looked exactly the same.* Nothing had changed. She wished that she'd brought her camera. Pity, she'd wanted to show Mr Jones that he was mistaken. How could he have got it so wrong? He must have meant another house, that was obvious. Lakeside House was definitely there.

Ellen closed the car door behind her and strolled purposefully up to the front door. Today there was only one thing she wanted to check on. She made her way directly to the spacious lounge, where she lifted the floor board.

Nothing.

Had she expected the letters to be there? She didn't know, but she would dismiss them and everything else about this house. It meant nothing to her. Go home and forget about it – for her sanity, that was the best thing to do. It felt good, she sighed with relief. She might even get rid of the painting.

She didn't linger, she was in a hurry to get back to the car and leave. Then she turned to take a last look at the house and a cold sweat engulfed her, as suddenly the knowledge hit her with force. She was deluding herself. This house had a hold on her, it wasn't going to let her go that easily. At the next petrol station, she stopped and bought a map of the local area.

Back at the inn, Ellen placed the map on the bar counter.

'Mr Jones, can you show me the exact location of the house on the picture, please?'

The landlord pulled the map towards him and studied it for a few seconds, 'There! Can I mark it with a small cross?'

Ellen nodded, but she'd already seen where he had placed the tip of the pen.

'Thank you,' she pursed her lips, not looking at him.

'Is something wrong?' Mr Jones asked. 'You do seem concerned about this house.'

'Well, no, just wanted to make one hundred percent sure that we were talking about the same house.'

'And are we?'

'Yeah, we are,' Ellen answered slowly.

Chapter 3

'Annie, I need you. You must come!' Ellen pleaded over the phone.

'You're asking me to drive for more than four hours, to look at a house that might be there and then again it might not! Can't you hear how crazy you sound?'

'But it *is* there.'

'You don't make sense.'

'That's just it. I have to find out if I'm going mad. You're the only person I can ask. Please, Annie!'

'I thought you took time off because of a headache, not to go swanking off to the Lake District.'

'Sorry, I'll explain later. I'll book you in for Sunday night and I'll pay for the room. We don't open on Mondays anyway, so you can go back Monday morning.'

'I must be mad too, but OK, I'll come. If I set off first thing, I'll be there about lunchtime.'

'Thanks, you've no idea what this means to me. I'll treat you to lunch first and then we'll drive to the house.'

'OK. See you,' Annie sighed.

On Sunday morning Ellen sat by the window in the bar, impatiently waiting for her friend. Annie had called to say that she was half an hour away. As her car pulled up, Ellen ran out and hugged her.

'You're an angel. I've got a G& T waiting for you in the bar. I'll drive later, only water for me.'

'Now, tell me the whole story again. Slowly, so I can take it in. I know you told me over the phone, but it was a bit of a ramble.' Without interrupting, Annie listened carefully, leaning with her elbow on the table and resting her head in her hand. She didn't take her eyes off Ellen for a single second. Her face grew increasingly concerned as the story unfolded.

'Say something!' Ellen pleaded.

'Order us soup and bread, that's quick, and I'll think about it while we eat.'

Ellen finished her mushroom soup first and sat quietly watching her friend until she put her spoon down and looked up at her.

Annie pulled a face, 'It's all so strange. I don't know what to say. This is the house in the painting you bought?'

Ellen nodded.

'Well, let's go and look at it.'

Twenty minutes later Ellen steered the car off the main road and onto the woodland track, which would take them to the house.

'After this bend, we're there,' she glanced at Annie. The next second she stood on the brakes so hard, that the car swerved, narrowly missing the ditch.

Annie flew forward, only restrained by her seat belt.

'For God's sake, are you trying to kill us? Why in heaven's name did you brake? There was nothing there,' she shouted angrily.

Ellen was gripping the steering wheel, her knuckles showing, her forehead resting on the wheel. Her face was ashen when she looked back at her friend, her body trembling uncontrollably.

Annie leaned forward to catch her words, which were barely audible.

'That's it.' Ellen pointed up the grassy slope, 'Up there.

That's where it was. That's where the house should be.' At that moment her mind clouded over.

She became aware of a gentle touch on her arm and slowly the fog which filled her head lifted.

'Here, have a drink of water. You've had a shock.'

Ellen brought the bottle to her lips with shaking hands but didn't drink.

'I need help, Annie.'

'Take it easy. We'll talk this over. It'll be OK, you'll see. You've had a lot of headaches lately. You should check it out.'

Ellen nodded reluctantly, she pulled her coat closer and folded her arms across her chest.

'I suppose you're right. Now that we're here, come with me. For my own peace of mind, I need to see what's up there. There's no house of course, but it's hard to accept.'

'Sure, let's go.'

Ellen led the way up the slope and became more downhearted the nearer they got. She walked over to where she'd seen the fountain on her previous visits. She got down on her knees and let her fingers run through a yellowing tuft of grass, a small tea rose should be growing here. The clump of trees was also gone. The only sign that an orchard had ever existed were two overgrown trees covered in grey moss. Ellen jumped as a pigeon broke free from the branches. A few pieces of rubble lay around, and one or two crumbling bricks were scattered on the ground where the house should have stood.

Moving over the grass, she picked up a brick. She turned it over in her hand and with a sigh let it drop again. Tears blurred her eyes and she turned from Annie before brushing them away. Her friend watched her from a short distance.

Ellen walked up to her.

'OK. Annie, we can leave now. There's nothing more to be seen here. Thanks for putting up with me.'

Annie stroked her shoulder, 'We'll go back to the pub and talk this over. There's bound to be an explanation. You'll be fine, you'll see.'

Ellen shook her head, 'Will you drive? I don't feel up to it.'

'Sure, I'll just check my mobile before we leave.'

'No point, you can't use it here. No signal,' Ellen said.

'Mine is OK.' Annie held up the phone for her to see.

'Odd.' Ellen got hers out and found that it too was working.

Neither Ellen nor Annie spoke on the drive back to the pub. Ellen saw Annie glancing at her several times, but she was grateful that her friend left her to sort out her muddled thoughts.

'Sit down,' Annie told her when they arrived back in the bar. 'I'll order. How about a cream tea? I'll find out if they do them. Or would you prefer something stronger?'

'No, tea is fine.' Ellen sank down onto the armchair by the fire, as Annie walked over to the bar.

'We're in luck, cream tea it is,' Annie exaggerated the cheerfulness in her voice, but dropped the pretence when she saw her friend. 'Oh Ellen, you look awful.' Annie bent down and put an arm around her.

'Thanks, is that supposed to cheer me up?'

'Sorry, I didn't mean to…'

Ellen waved a hand at her, 'It's OK. I know what you mean. But I can't stop thinking about this. There're so many unanswered questions. It's hard to accept that all this is in my imagination. Why did the picture affect me so much?'

'That's a good starting point. Go back to the gallery and talk to the artist and if he's not there anymore, find out what they can tell you. That should help.'

'You're right, I'll do that. And as I'm here anyway, I'll call in at the newspaper office in Kendal on my way home tomorrow. They might have records about the house. It's worth a try.'

'I thought you were supposed to forget the house. It's not there!'

'I can't. It was so real. It might help to settle my mind.'

'If it makes you feel better,' Annie looked thoughtful, 'but promise, no more talk about the house. It's not there.'

Ellen nodded.

'Let's have a relaxing dinner. If you'll be all right on your own, I'll leave after breakfast. I have a couple of dresses to finish. I left them for tomorrow, as we're closed.'

'Yes, that'll be fine. What did Ken say about you dashing off, leaving him behind?'

'Oh, he'll get over it. He's the understanding type.'

Unlike, Pete, she thought. Four long years living together and then it was all over. Her mother had proved to be correct when she'd said that Pete wasn't right for her. The heartache had been overwhelming. She had believed that they were soon to be married, but Pete had met somebody else and it had happened so quickly. It was only five months ago and she still missed him. The strain had driven her to the point of a breakdown.

⚜

The next morning, Ellen waved Annie off and then drove to Kendal. It was easy to find the office of The Courier. The reporter in charge was helpful and gave her access to the archive. But with so little information at hand, it wasn't easy. With no firm dates or years to go by, she was only guessing. The name, Lakeside House, wasn't enough. It was going to be a fruitless search, or so she thought.

Ready to give up, she found a small article published in 1935. She was elated, now she had a year.

It read: *The property known as Lakeside House has been demolished after having been left deserted for nearly twenty-five years. It has an interesting history. Documents detailing the maintenance of the house were deposited with the law firm of Holden & Son. The instructions were that it should be maintained in good order until the owners returned. What happened to Edouard Villiers and his young wife, twenty-nine years his junior, has remained something of a mystery. According to Holden & Son, the couple had gone abroad. However, they could not explain their lengthy absence. Eventually, the money for the upkeep had run out and the owners never returned to claim the property, which, finally, was pulled down.*

Ellen read the article again and again.

'Edouard, Edouard,' she repeated the name several times. Did this name mean anything to her? It was French, of course, and it rolled off her tongue easily. She took a copy of the article to show Annie.

On her way back to Bristol, she pondered what had happened to her this weekend. It was hard to accept that it was unreal. In the house, she'd touched doors and felt the hardness of the wood on her palms, she'd sat on a chair covered in red velvet. She'd felt the coldness of the black iron cooker and wiped the dust off her hands. Finally, she'd found the letters. If only she hadn't lost them again. Was it possible to imagine all this?

Ellen parked the car in her allocated place, outside her small terraced house in the Clifton area of the city. Inside she tossed her wax coat onto a chair and rang Annie.

'Hi, just got back. What about you?'

'Fine, just the usual Monday morning hold-up, but it didn't take too long. How did you get on at the newspaper office?'

'I'll show you what I found tomorrow. You'll be surprised.'

'Are you making an appointment at the doctors?'

'No hurry, headache gone.'

'Come on, Ellen, you promised.'

'OK, OK, I will.' Ellen ended the call. Before putting down the phone, she called her mum and then the surgery. She got an appointment for Wednesday, in two days' time, thanks to a cancellation.

That done, Ellen wandered around the room, she adjusted the cushions on the easy armchair and stuck her finger into the earth of the house plants, which were all dry and needed water. She sighed. Her small terraced house was comfortable, consisting of two bedrooms upstairs, the guest room smaller than hers but large enough for a double bed. Downstairs, the kitchen had a small table and a couple of stools. Her lounge was spacious and also served as a dining room. She liked to be surrounded by many things, and every surface had an ornament. Today she couldn't relax. She picked up a vase, wiped off imaginary dust, replaced it and picked up a porcelain figurine. She didn't like it, it was out of fashion, but it was a gift and held a memory of the person who had given it to her, so she didn't want to get rid of it.

Fed up, she threw herself back onto the settee and continued to stare at the painting; the feeling of being sucked in was gone. What did it want from her? In the morning she'd call in at the gallery to find out more about the artist. The belief that her unwillingness to let go, was somehow controlled by the house, gave her extreme feelings of anxiety and dread. She knew with certainty that this was only the beginning...it hadn't finished with her yet.

Chapter 4

'We've very little information about the artist.' Mrs Clarke the owner of the gallery, a smartly dressed woman in her late fifties, smiled apologetically at Ellen. 'He paid a small fee, which is customary to display the painting. You paid us with a credit card, which is perfectly acceptable, and we gave him the cash. We do insist on a contact number of course, but we never used it. I should have it here somewhere.'

'Can I have it, please?'

'It wouldn't be correct to give it out without permission. But I'm happy to call him for you.'

'Thanks, that would be helpful,' Ellen nodded.

Mrs Clarke turned over the pages in a ledger and let her finger run down the list of names.

'Ah, here we are, Henry Allen, looks like a mobile.' Ellen watched as she punched in the number, frowned, disconnected and tried again. 'Sorry, but the number doesn't exist,' she said uneasily. 'I don't understand why that should be.' She appeared uncomfortable.

'Have you had dealings with this artist before?'

'No, and normally we wouldn't take a single painting, but he was so persuasive. I could tell it wasn't a recent painting, and when I said so, he told me that he'd painted it some time ago.' A slight blush appeared on Mrs Clarke's face.

'Well, that's what I thought too, the frame is old.'

'Yes, he said he'd found this old frame and it suited the painting so well.'

Ellen nodded, 'Yes, it does.'

'Perhaps I shouldn't say this,' she hesitated, 'but I got the impression it was to you he wanted to sell. I could be wrong of course.' Mrs Clarke dropped her eyes and stopped abruptly.

'What made you think this?' Ellen felt her cheeks warming.

'I'm so sorry. I really shouldn't have said.' Mrs Clarke moved to the front door and held it open, 'But he could have sold the painting twice before you came in...,' she stammered.

Ellen glanced over her shoulder as the door closed behind her. That woman couldn't get rid of me fast enough, she thought.

It pleased Ellen that Annie was alone in the shop as she walked in. She needed to talk.

'I can't let this go,' she said.

'Can't let what go? Oh no, you mean the house! Please, you must.'

'Listen to this, Annie!' She held up the copy of the newspaper article and told her about the visit to the gallery, not leaving out anything that had happened since they left the pub in Cumbria.

'I agree that what the gallery owner told you is odd. But she said it was only her own thoughts; it doesn't necessarily mean anything. This isn't doing you any good. Get rid of the painting!'

Ellen shrugged her shoulders and changed the subject.

'I'll be late in the morning. I've got a doctor's appointment.'

'Oh, good, I'm so pleased to hear that.' Annie's face lit up.

The shop bell rang and Ellen showed a customer some of her latest designs, but the woman left without placing an order. In the workroom at the back, Annie was busy finishing off a dress.

'Mrs Hall will be in for this one today. She had a fitting on Saturday and I've had to do a small alteration.'

Ellen nodded and picking up her sketch book, she quickly drew the outline of Mrs Shepherd's slender body and added her short expertly styled hair, which she coloured in black. She continued to sketch the velvet dress; the image had just popped into her head, and she could see it clearly. By the time the doorbell rang again she had finished.

'What did the doctor say?' Annie asked on Wednesday morning.

'Oh, he said to come back again if the headaches become more frequent.'

'What? Did you tell him what you saw? About the house? Or rather what you *thought* you saw?' she corrected herself. Annie was leaning over the cutting table, in her hand she held a pair of tailor's scissors. She stopped her work and glared at Ellen.

'No, I didn't,' Ellen answered reluctantly.

'Why on earth not? That's why you went to see him.'

'I went because of my headaches. I don't want him to think I'm mad.'

'But, Ellen, you said you needed help and you meant professional help. Remember? The headaches could be the cause of it.'

'Could be, but I'm not sure. First I want to see what happens when I go back.'

'Please, don't tell me you mean the Lake District!' Annie's eyes widened and she stared at her in disbelief.

'Yes.' Ellen turned away and picked up a drawing.

'Sit down and listen very carefully.' Annie was unable to hide her anger and the scissors hit the table with a loud bang.

Ellen swung round and stared at her.

'If you want to remain my friend, you do not go back there. Please, do this for me, wait a month. Let this settle down and if it still bothers you after that time, go then. But I don't think it will.' Annie spoke fast, the words tumbling out. Her face was taut as she continued with a tremor in her voice, 'For me, please, Ellen.'

'Oh, I hate to see you upset. You've got tears in your eyes!' Ellen bit her lip. Annie's words left her downhearted and somewhat annoyed, but she realised she couldn't cause her friend this much unhappiness. She made up her mind in an instant. With a few quick steps she was by Annie's side, putting an arm around her shoulders. 'I'm sorry it's disturbing you so much. I had no idea. OK, I'll stay away. I'll do as you ask, if it means that much to you?'

Annie's face was deadly pale as she answered, 'It does, Ellen. It scares me.'

Chapter 5

Cumbria, late October 2005

'Nice to see you again!' Mrs Jones, the landlady, exclaimed when Ellen walked into the bar a month later. 'You're in the same room as before. You must have been quite taken with our little pub. I'm pleased you like it here.' Her face had lit up in a broad smile and there was sincerity in her voice.

Ellen nodded, if only you knew, she thought. Inwardly, she sighed, taken, that could be right, but by what?

Annie had made her swear not to go back for a month. The month had gone and the urge to return had remained, Ellen had been counting the days. Annie had been frantic and had spent hours trying to talk her out of it. When her pleading had fallen on deaf ears, she'd done the opposite and sulked for several days, refusing to speak. Ellen had ignored her. As far as she was concerned, she'd kept her promise. It had been hard. There had been times when she'd picked up her car keys ready to jump into the car and drive to Cumbria.

'Thanks, Mrs Jones, it's good to be here again.' She didn't say it with much conviction; in truth, she wondered if it had been wise. Perhaps Annie was right? But the pull of the house was as strong as ever. *She'd had to come back.*

Their shop closed early on a Saturday, so there had been no need to take time off. But it was late when she arrived at the pub, and she decided to wait until morning to drive to the house.

After dinner she spent the next hour in the bar, hoping that Albert, the old man, would show up, but there was no sign of him. In the end, with nobody to talk to, she decided to have an early night.

The next morning, Ellen stopped the car before the bend, which would reveal the view of the lake. Her heart hammered and her breath came in short bursts; I'm having a panic attack right now, she thought. 'Start the car, drive around the bend, and see once and for all that the house isn't there. Then go home and never come back to this place,' she spoke the words aloud, pausing after each one to get her normal breathing back.

When she had calmed down, she turned the ignition key, slowly, she put the car into gear and released the clutch. The car moved forward, until her foot on the break brought it to an abrupt halt.

For a long time she sat there, her hands gripping the steering wheel until her fingers ached. Her body frozen, the blood in her veins not flowing, she was void of all thought. Slowly her head cleared and she had to accept that the house standing at the top of the slope was in its prime, exactly as it appeared on her painting. It would have been easier, if it had been abandoned like before.

Everything about it was fresh and cared for. The window frames were not stained by mould, nor the stone work, as she'd seen on earlier visits. The lawn had been trimmed recently and a wisp of smoke rose from the chimney. A path leading up to the house was wide enough to drive a car up to the front door.

With an effort she swung her legs out, they felt numb; she was unsure they would carry her. It was several moments before she let the soles of her shoes touch the grass.

Go inside, a voice urged her. *Don't delay. It's imperative that you do. Go now.*

Was she dreaming? Not aware of moving, she floated up the slope towards the house, not feeling the weight of her feet on the ground.

Another voice brought her to a stop.

Go back to the car.

But she carried on.

Don't go there, it commanded.

I must.

You don't have to.

Yes, I'm expected.

Ellen kept on walking; she had to obey the stronger voice. As she got to the door, all her doubts vanished. Without hesitating she entered the house.

Lakeside House, Cumberland, late October 1902

In the entrance hall, a huge painting of a horse faced her. It took up a large proportion of the wall, and she vaguely remembered seeing it before. Where? Was it in the National Gallery in London? Or was it here? On the other walls hung paintings featuring landscapes, with wrought iron sconces holding candles on either side of the frames.

Ellen untied the ribbon which held her bonnet in place and removed it from her head. She felt a moment of dizziness. A bonnet?

Why was she wearing it? Yet she had removed it as if it was the natural thing to do. She clasped the woollen bonnet to her chest, afraid that it would vanish at the next moment, and moved up to the large mirror on the wall.

To steady herself, she gripped the armrest of the chair next to her. A face gazed back, with cheeks coloured pink by the chill of the outside air. Her own face, yet changed. Her auburn hair was draped over her ears and fashioned into a bun at the top of her head. She stared at the image.

'I'm Ellen,' she whispered. 'Who is that? What's happened to me? Why am I wearing these clothes?' She looked down and briefly touched the brown flannel blouse and then pulled at the green woollen skirt. She hesitated before pulling the heavy cloak off her shoulders and dropping it onto the high-backed leather chair, as she knew was her custom. That knowledge added to her confusion. But somehow it was right to be here; this was where she lived. Slowly, she began to accept her surroundings. Other thoughts took over her mind. Memories of the previous days in this house came to her and she knew that she'd just been for a walk in the wood.

Ellen fought these other thoughts. This wasn't right. She didn't belong here.

The voice in her head said, *Yes, you do now. Don't leave.* She wanted to fight this voice but felt her will drain away. All would become clear. She acknowledged that someone was waiting for her in the other room and everything was apparent in her mind from that moment on.

She glanced up at the huge chandelier, which hung from the ceiling. George lit it every morning when he arrived for work. Her eyes followed the polished mahogany staircase leading up to the first-floor gallery landing, where another but smaller chandelier hung above the stairwell. Nothing of this surprised her.

Her feet took her across the floor, which was patterned with white and black tiles, towards the door leading into the spacious drawing room. She entered and stopped inside; her attention was immediately drawn to the wallpaper and it startled her, she remembered pulling at the faded remains on her first visit. It was beautiful, it had the soft pink tulip motif interwoven with moss green leaves. The room was tastefully furnished, heavy velvet drapes hung at the windows. Several armchairs, with high back rests, stood a safe distance from the leaping flames in the fireplace. On a small table by her side was a large bouquet of white chrysanthemums in a porcelain vase. Dotted around the room were a number of smaller tables. An ornately carved display cabinet, filled with china and ornaments, took up most of one wall.

'Lenora, is that you? I heard the door opening. Why are you standing there? Come here.' The voice came from the depths of a chair.

'Yes, Edouard, it's me,' Ellen answered and moved over to a green armchair, picked up the embroidery which rested on it and sat down.

'You've been a long time. Where have you been?'

'I've only been for a short walk.'

'You've been gone for some time, be careful not to get lost.'

Ellen leaned forward and rested her hand on her husband's arm. She knew he was half-joking and half-serious, she could find her way around anywhere in these woods. She gripped the sleeve of his dark suit firmly and looking directly into his unseeing eyes, she answered, 'Edouard, I am sorry if I'm late for lunch. Have I really been gone that long? It feels to me that we've just had breakfast. Are you hungry?'

She heard a voice which belonged to this person, who was called Lenora, and she was taking over. Her awareness of being Ellen was diminishing, becoming distant. She would be leaving, going somewhere else. She couldn't keep her here, soon she would be gone. Lenora was in her place. Ellen was slipping to the back of her mind. She wasn't fighting it. That was as it should be.

Her hand remained on her husband's arm, while she regarded him thoughtfully. His dark hair was peppered with grey, his features were strong with a firm chin, but fine lines were showing on his face. She most admired his gentle, understanding eyes, which were a dark grey and before he became blind could be so penetrating. But his kind face and eyes could be misleading. It was a face that didn't reveal the unbending will he possessed. It belonged to a man of strong character and in control.

She had been seventeen years old when she came to live at Lakeside House. As her family's oldest and most trusted friend, Edouard become her guardian when tragically she'd lost her parents in quick succession. He had employed a lady tutor, who had also served as her companion; she had much to thank him for.

Edouard enjoyed painting and for her twenty-first birthday he had painted her portrait. She'd worn a floral organza dress, with a white rose tucked into her long hair. For the picture she was seated on the red velvet sofa, with one arm elegantly resting on the backrest, the other relaxed by her side. At one point, towards the end of the many sittings, he'd put his brush down and regarded her intently for minutes. He had often done so and had then usually asked her to move an arm slightly or to increase her smile, so she had not found this strange. This time had been different. He had walked across, taken her hand and stunned her with a proposal of marriage. Lenora had stared at him in his paint-splattered coat and at first thought he was not serious. Edouard had repeated his question and, although the proposal had appeared spontaneous, she knew that he never acted on impulse. He had given it much thought and explained that he wanted to offer her the security that being his wife would bring. She had accepted, although he was twenty-nine years her senior. Lenora had waited for Edouard to come to her bedroom on their wedding night, but he did not come. She was soon to realise that theirs was a marriage in name only. Edouard had never made demands on her but treated her as a daughter.

Before their marriage, she had spent her days with her companion and had hardly missed Edouard on the times he had gone out and returned late or in the early morning. There had been rumours amongst the servants that he had a mistress, but from the day of their wedding his nights away had stopped. Had he known that he was going blind at the time of their marriage? Could it have been his mistress who ended their relationship for the same reason? No, this she could not believe. She felt ashamed to have this thought in her head. Edouard was an honourable man. He'd done what he thought was correct at the time.

He spent days painting. The fells and the lakes offered beautiful views and he became reasonably accomplished. Some of his pictures were considered good enough to be hung on the upstairs landing and in the bedrooms. The painting of Lenora, however, was to be found in the library, where he could see it every day. Edouard had put much effort into this portrait and was pleased with the result. He had continued to paint after he became blind, which had brought some interesting results. But gradually he spent less time at the canvas. Perhaps he should try again. Lenora made a mental note to encourage him.

'Dear, what are you thinking of? Why are you not speaking to me?'

'Oh, I'm sorry, I was lost in thought.' She turned her attention back to her husband. 'I haven't been gone long. You must be more patient.'

'My dear, I didn't mean to upset you.' Edouard lifted his face up to hers, his grey eyes unblinking.

'Don't fret so much. I'll always be back.' Lenora bit her lip, she hadn't meant to sound impatient. To make amends, she patted the soft wool of his sleeve. Edouard was always smartly dressed, his suits carefully tailored of fine cloth and his shirts impeccably starched. She had made sure that it continued after he had become blind.

She swiftly removed her hand, 'I'm going to check with Molly about lunch. I'll be back directly.'

Once she'd closed the door behind her, she leaned against it to steady her breathing. This kind man had trapped her. This house held her prisoner. There had to be more to life and she wanted more. His kindness was choking her. Lenora's thoughts wandered back to the early days when servants lived in the house. There had been a housekeeper, cook, maid and George, of course. He was the only one of the old servants still with them. He saw to the garden and carried out the maintenance.

George had brought Molly to them. They hadn't been married then. Molly had been widowed at an early age and George had helped by finding her employment at Lakeside House. Eventually they had married, more for convenience Lenora believed, than out of love for each other. But the marriage worked. Both preferred to live in their own home rather than in the servants' quarter, which now stood unused except for storage. Their hours became flexible as the couple grew older, an arrangement which suited both them and Lenora.

George had gained much weight in his later years; he was now quite portly, whereas Molly, small and skinny, was blighted with a face that always appeared unhappy. In the winter there was less work for George, but he kept the fires burning and the lamps lit and he fed and groomed Gladys, the old mare. Molly kept busy with all the usual household chores. However, Lenora often took over the cooking.

As the mistress of this big house, she enjoyed the responsibilities it brought. She had been married to Edouard for eight years and, until recently, had been happy. In her youth, her naivety had led her to believe that what he had to offer would be enough. Her husband loved her as a daughter and for her, he was the father she had lost.

But as the years had gone by and Edouard's sight had started to fail, she had become more impatient. Why was he always so even-tempered and dependable? He had had to learn to cope with his blindness, and their days had been fully occupied. She'd been the dutiful wife and spent time by his side, assisting him until he had learnt to look after himself and find his way around the house. At first it had been a struggle, and no one knew that she'd often gone to bed full of resentment.

Lenora shook her head, she must rid herself of these

thoughts – they made her anxious; irritated, she flung the kitchen door open.

'Molly, why isn't lunch served?'

'Sorry, Miss Lenora, but you asked for it to be set back by half an hour.'

'I did no such thing.' She hesitated, 'If I did, I've changed my mind. What are we having?'

'I've made a shepherd's pie. It's ready.'

'Please, serve it now.'

'Yes, Miss Lenora,' Molly's thin face turned pink.

Lenora jerked to a halt as she slammed the door shut behind her. What was she doing? It wasn't like her. Perhaps later she would apologise to Molly.

'Is everything all right? Is there a problem in the kitchen?' Edouard stood facing her in the open doorway of the drawing room. He was leaning on his stick.

'A misunderstanding, it was my fault.'

'Dearest, this came for me today. Will you read it, please?' Her husband held a letter in his outstretched hand.

'Of course, let's do so while we are sitting at the table.'

Lenora studied the envelope, 'This comes from Canada. Who do you know there?'

'It's my brother.' Edouard sank back in the chair, his cheeks flushed, 'I haven't heard from him in years. Please, hurry and read it. I hope all is well.'

She discarded the envelope and read in silence.

'It appears to be. At least no one is dead. Your brother has a son. He's coming to England and would like to stay with us.'

Edouard nodded, 'Of course, of course, that's good news. What else does Henry say?'

'He apologises for not having written before. He is well and has a comfortable life. He hopes that your disagreement is now forgotten and that you'll be able to welcome your nephew.'

'Of course!' Edouard hit the floor with his stick. 'We'll be delighted, won't we, dearest? Does he say how old my nephew is?'

'His name is Charles. He doesn't give his age, but if he's old enough to travel on his own he must be grown up.'

'We'll send a reply to my brother at once. Fetch the pen and paper!'

Lenora took her eyes off the letter, 'Edouard, this has been travelling for weeks. There's no time for a reply. Charles is due here tomorrow.'

'I say, we must have the guest room ready for him.'

'Yes, I'll ask Molly to start this afternoon. We'll have the room aired and the bed made. I am sure we have enough provisions to give him a good welcome lunch.'

'How long does he intend to stay?'

'It doesn't say, dear. I will read the whole letter for you now, from the beginning.'

Edouard rested his hands on his cane while he listened. When she had finished, he spoke.

'I haven't seen my brother for more than thirty years. He wasn't married then, so I guess that Charles is about your age, Lenora. He will be company for you. I sometimes feel it was selfish of me to keep you here. It is lonely for you with just the two of us.'

'Yes, a little,' she answered. More than a little, she thought. Life was easier before Edouard had lost his sight. At least they used to often entertain and with that came visitors. But now it happened only occasionally and then it was mostly the Edmondson family, their nearest neighbours. She shook off the thought with a shrug of her shoulders.

A knock on the door interrupted them and Molly entered carrying a large silver tray. She glanced over at Lenora before putting it down on the table with a slight thud.

During the lunch, Edouard enthusiastically made plans for his nephew's visit. Lenora realised by his rosy cheeks that he was indeed excited to have news about his brother.

'I do wonder what Henry has told my nephew about me.'

'Why so? Is there anything that worries you?'

'Well, there was some acrimony, enough to make Henry leave the country.'

'Do you care to tell me about the disagreement you had with your brother?'

'It was significant, but not my fault. Henry was always stubborn, like a terrier. He wouldn't let go if he thought he'd been wronged. You can't help who you fall in love with, and we fell for the same woman.'

Edouard leaned forward, both hands clasping the stick. He sighed and turned his head towards Lenora, 'Yes, it was my late wife and your godmother. She chose me over Henry.'

'Oh, I see,' Lenora took a deep breath, 'I can't remember her well.'

'No, you were a small child.' Edouard paused and then his voice rose, 'Henry seemed to think that because he saw Victoria first, he should have her. But it doesn't work like that. After all, it's not as if they were stepping out together, he'd only danced with her at various gatherings. But Victoria told me that she'd been smitten by him, so he might have had some encouragement and assumed that would continue.'

'Did you part on bad terms with Henry?'

'Well, we never came to blows. But when Victoria and I let our feelings for each other be known, Henry wouldn't speak to me.'

'Oh, but Victoria loved you.'

'Yes, that's right, but Henry couldn't accept it.' Edouard looked up in a fluster. 'In the library there's a photo album, please, fetch it for me. I can show you photographs of Henry and also of Victoria.'

Lenora searched the library and found the album hidden under several volumes of heavy books. She had looked at it before and got lost in the pages of beautiful ladies dressed in flowing gowns and gentlemen with top hats, but she didn't know who they all were. Years ago, Edouard had shown her photos of Victoria, his late wife, but none of Henry. Victoria had died when Lenora was young. As a consequence, Edouard had spent more time at Lenora's parents' home as a welcome guest. Years after his wife's death, she'd overheard her parents speak about Edouard and a lady friend. But their conversation had ended as soon as Lenora had entered the room.

She returned with the heavy brown album, the thick leather covers embossed with gold leaf, and placed it in Edouard's lap. He rested it there for a moment and his fingers traced the motif on the cover, before handing it back to her.

'Here, you take it. I can't remember exactly where they are. Look at the first pages and tell me what you see.'

She opened the album with care; it was old. The photos were mounted in openings cut in oval and square shapes. Now her interest was in the early photos; she found several of two young boys. They were standing side by side, wearing school uniforms, with an impressive building behind them. Lenora paid special attention to the photos of the boys at an older age. The very last ones showed two young men, in their twenties.

'Well, what have you found?'

'I see the ones of you and Henry. You were both handsome young men.'

'Henry is three years younger than me and better looking, I believe.'

'Kindness is more important than looks, Edouard. You've taken good care of me.'

'Thank you, dear, and have you found Victoria?'

'I am looking for her now. Oh, yes, this is her. She was a lovely lady, Edouard. What beautiful hair, and she's wearing the most becoming of dresses.'

'Yes, and her eyes, Lenora, I loved her eyes. They were so kind; they made her face light up and she was always smiling.'

'You still miss her, don't you, dearest?'

'Victoria was the love of my life. I love you too, Lenora,

but it's a different love I have for you.'

'I know that.' She closed the album. Being married to Edouard, she would never experience this other kind of love. She couldn't stop a sigh escaping as she turned to her husband.

'What about tomorrow? Will you send George to Kendal with the trap to fetch Charles?'

'Yes, there is only one train at twelve o'clock to meet.'

'Now I'll go and help Molly to get everything ready. I'll make sure she has used the best linen. We do want to give your nephew a good first impression. I'll join you in the library after you've had your afternoon nap.' Lenora placed a light kiss on her husband's forehead. In reply, he reached out and stroked her cheek.

Chapter 6

Ellen found herself in the car staring up at the house. No light was to be seen in any of the windows.

'I remember,' she whispered. Later that evening, Lenora and Edouard had walked upstairs together, on the first landing, Edouard had turned left to his bedroom and she'd turned right to the first room in the corridor on the other side. She had begun to remove her dress, no, Lenora's dress and then… nothing, until now.

She had no memory of Lenora leaving her and Ellen coming back, anxiously she rubbed her forehead. She shook her head in disbelief as she acknowledged that she was wearing her jeans and jumper, what she'd had on when she left the pub this morning.

How had she found her way back to the car in this darkness? For how long had she been sitting here?

Lakeside House was a menacing shadow and blackness surrounded her. Lights could only be seen in the distance on the far shore of the lake. Fear gripped her.

Panic-stricken, she fumbled with the ignition key. The car lights cut through the darkness and she thought she saw a shadow move. This made her press down too hard on the accelerator and the car jumped forward; she swerved to avoid the ditch. Every nerve in her body jingled, she was icy cold. Her hands shook on the steering wheel and she held onto it hard, afraid that she might let go. She greeted the lit-up village and the welcoming sign of the inn with tears of relief; she was safe.

She stayed in the car unable to calm herself.

'Please, please, can someone explain to me what's going on? I am so scared. I need to know. I can't understand this,' she whimpered. Her head throbbed, with a pain that intensified as soon as she tried to make sense of what had happened. She was someone else. She was Lenora. How could she be? Why was this happening to her? She used both her fists to beat the pain and the thoughts out of her head, but to no avail.

After a long time in the car, Ellen knew she had to go to her room, but she couldn't face the people in the pub. Without greeting anyone, she hurried past the bar and fled upstairs, leaving a surprised landlady staring after her. In her room she ran up to the mirror by the dressing table, she looked the same but it was also the pale face of another frustrated woman. Lenora stared back at her. She tried to control her shaking body by gripping the armrest of the chair next to her. Her head was throbbing.

A loud knock on the door brought her back, and with her voice breaking, she asked, 'Who is it?'

'It's me, Mrs Jones. Can I come in, please?'

'Oh no, not now,' she mumbled and hesitated before opening the door. She leant on the door frame and forced a smile, 'Yes …?'

'Can I help in any way? I became worried when I saw you arrive. You were white as a sheet. Have you been in an accident?'

'Thank you, but no. No accident.' She held her head with both hands, 'I have the most awful migraine.' When she saw Mrs Jones' concerned face, she added, 'I'm sorry if I worried you. I have painkillers and I was just going to take some. I won't be down for dinner by the way.'

Mrs Jones raised her eyebrows, 'It's gone ten, and we've finished serving.'

'Is it really?' Ellen glanced at her watch.

'Well, if you're sure. I'll say good night. Hope you're well for breakfast.'

Ellen shut the door and leaned against it for a few moments, she was exhausted – and no wonder after the day she'd had. She stumbled across the room to her bag with the headache tablets, shook one out in the palm of her hand, hesitated and added another. Fully clothed, she slumped onto the bed and fell into a restless sleep.

An hour later she woke, cold. She undressed and dropped her clothes onto a chair. At four a.m. she woke again, her mouth dry and her head thudding. She slid out of bed, searching for more painkillers and the water bottle she always carried around. She couldn't find the bottle, so cupped her hands under the tap in the bathroom.

Sleep wouldn't come, she stared at the white ceiling and every scene of what had happened at the house repeated itself in front of her eyes. What did it mean? Edouard was her husband? No, he was Lenora's husband! But she was Lenora! She lived there. The thoughts whirled round, and she couldn't find relief, 'I'm Ellen. I'm Ellen,' she moaned.

At six in the morning, she switched on the TV to watch the news but immediately turned it off. The noise which filled the room was too much. It mingled with the words in her mind, which she wasn't in control of. To calm down, she counted to six, breathing in from her stomach and then exhaling slowly, continuing to count to eleven. This should work. She wished that she had a paper bag to blow into, she'd heard that was supposed to help. Strangely, she was smiling at the thought.

'Mrs Jones, that was lovely, the smell of the bacon was heavenly,' Ellen pushed the plate away, 'I was ravenous. Can't remember the last time I enjoyed a cooked breakfast.' Although she was still ridiculously tired after a sleepless night, she had to eat to regain her strength.

Without knowing what made her ask, she called out to Mrs Jones as she was leaving the table, 'I've decided to stay tonight as well. Is that OK?'

'Yes, of course. Not feeling well enough to drive back today?' Mrs Jones' face was serious.

'No, not that. But there's something I need to do here.' Ellen surprised herself by adding, 'I might be late again tonight.' Her subconscious mind had made the decision for her; she was going back to Lakeside House.

Before getting into her car, she sent a text to Annie: Staying another night. See you Tuesday after lunch. This time she didn't bother to ask if it was OK. As she pressed send, she imagined Annie's response: If you've any sense, leave and come home. Please, don't stay there. That's what she would have said. That's why she hadn't called her.

It was easy for Annie. This was happening to her, Ellen, and she couldn't let it go. Yes, it scared her, but she was held here by a force, and she had to find out what it was. A force, which controlled her mind and was too strong to fight. It gave her no choice.

Chapter 7

Lakeside House, Cumberland, late October 1902

Ellen began to sense Lenora's presence as she walked up the slope towards the house and she made her welcome. By the time she'd reached the front door, Lenora was in control.

Edouard greeted her in the hall, 'Did you enjoy the walk, dearest? I hope you've wrapped up warmly. It's chilly today and the days are growing shorter.' He waved a piece of paper, 'I've received a telegram from Charles. I asked the courier to read it for me. He arrived on the train, which came in just after twelve. He'll be in time for lunch. By now George will be on his way back from Kendal with him.'

She removed her woollen bonnet before answering, 'Molly has got his room ready and prepared a substantial lunch. He'll be hungry after his journey. We'll have a light supper tonight instead.'

'Just as you say, my dear. I'm excited to meet my nephew and to have news of my brother.' He put a hand to his ear, 'I can hear the trap pulling up, they have arrived.'

She saw the flush on her husband's face and was filled with a sudden tenderness, this must mean so much to him.

'Come on! Let's meet your nephew on the porch.' She gently took his arm.

Outside they were greeted by Gladys, the grey mare,

shaking her head, with steam coming from her nostrils. George's helping hand was brushed aside by a smiling young man as he jumped down from the carriage. He wore a heavy dark wool jacket over a slender body, broad shouldered and with an open boyish face. His head held high, his eyes immediately found Lenora's and held them.

She met his stare, her cheeks warmed, and she lowered her eyes. With a firm grip on Edouard's arm, she guided him down the remaining steps.

'Charles, welcome to Lakeside House, I'm pleased you've chosen to visit us. My home is yours for as long as you wish to stay.' Edouard fumbled for his hand.

Lenora saw the surprised look on Charles' face change to understanding as Edouard's eyes didn't directly meet his.

'Thank you, Uncle. I'm delighted to be here. I've always wanted to come to England and in particular Cumberland. Father speaks of it often.' He turned to Lenora, 'And this is your charming daughter.' His eyes twinkled as he brought her hand to his lips.

He is holding on for too long, it's not proper, she reflected and carefully tried to loosen her fingers, but his grip firmed. She remained silent, her hand imprisoned in his.

'No, Charles, you have the pleasure of meeting my dear wife, Lenora.'

Charles pulled back, straightened his shoulders and slowly let go of her hand, 'I apologise.'

'Think nothing of it, Charles. We differ many years in age. You're not the first to make the same mistake. Now, we shall have liquid refreshments and something to eat. George will take your luggage to your room.'

Lenora lowered her eyes, what should she say to this man? She had stayed silent for too long, but she found his stare unnerving. She had blushed, and she was sure he had noticed.

She cleared her throat, 'Let's go inside, I think it will soon rain. It does quite a lot here you'll find.' Realising that she'd spoken too hurriedly, she managed to smile back at him and continued at a slower pace, 'I'll send Molly to unpack your cases. You may wish to freshen up and rest after your long journey?'

Charles' eyes held hers, 'Thank you, Lenora, but I'm more than pleased to have lunch. I don't wish to hold it up, should it be ready. And I prefer to unpack my own cases.'

'Then we shall go directly to the dining room.' She could see him restrain a smile and she hurried ahead, warmth creeping up her neck.

'Lenora, you may wish to show Charles to his room,' Edouard suggested after lunch.

Molly knocked on the door at that moment, 'Oh Molly is here. Will you take Mr Villiers to his room, please,' Lenora tried to hide the relief in her voice.

'Yes, Miss Lenora,' Molly nodded. 'I've left your light supper ready to go on trays. I'll just show the gentleman upstairs and I'll be off.'

'Thank you, I can manage the trays. We'll see you in the morning.' Lenora noticed the surprised look on Charles' face and explained, 'Molly and George still call me Miss Lenora, as they did when I first came here many years ago. It's what I'm used to, and I like it that way.'

After the door had closed behind them, Edouard spoke, 'Charles is an excellent young man, eloquent and well mannered. Don't you think so, Lenora?'

She didn't answer immediately, at lunch she'd been more relaxed. This is my husband's nephew she told herself. But she didn't know how to behave towards him. She had not met many men her own age and wasn't used to their company. The way he'd looked into her eyes and held her hand was surely how every young man would behave? But would you do so to your uncle's wife? She wasn't sure.

'Yes, dear, he's most pleasant company,' she answered at

length. 'He's kept us entertained throughout luncheon with his stories about life in Canada and the amusing incidents which took place on his journey here.'

'Yes, it was quite emotional to have news of my brother, and to hear that he is well was such a relief. What does my nephew look like?' Edouard asked.

'Remember the photographs I looked at last night, of your brother as a young man? Charles resembles his father. His hair is not as dark and I don't know the colour of your brother's eyes, but Charles' are green.'

'Quite handsome then?'

'Yes, you could say so,' she answered, pleased that her husband couldn't see her blushes and somewhat surprised that she'd noticed the colour of Charles' eyes.

Chapter 8

Charles looked around the comfortable room and closed the door behind him with a satisfied smile. He'd arrived at last, the journey had been long but his welcome warm. His father had described his brother as an agreeable man, so he was sure he would be well looked after. He had also realised that his uncle was well off, so there would be no need to spend much money. This thought was of comfort to him. Charles knew that Edouard had stolen his father's sweetheart and this had caused the rift, which resulted in him emigrating to Canada. But that was a long time ago and his father had arranged for his visit to Lakeside House.

It seemed that Edouard had done well as far as women were concerned, he was married to a much younger wife a desirable woman at that. There must be life in the old goat yet, if he could satisfy her. Charles frowned, he supposed that she had no choice but to share her old husband's bed, but it seemed such a waste, with her healthy complexion and young skin. He'd admired her long auburn hair and willingly got lost in her deep blue eyes, she was attractive in a serene way. He even believed that he had embarrassed her, Charles smiled to himself.

It had been quite a shock to find that his uncle had lost his sight. However, his wife was attentive to his needs and he appeared well able to manage most tasks on his own.

He had looked forward to exploring England and leaving life in Canada behind for a time. He would return once things had settled down. He had planned to stay away for at least a year, perhaps much longer if the opportunity arose.

Charles opened the first of his suitcases, he'd better unpack. He wasn't used to servants doing that for him and detested the idea of strangers rummaging about in his luggage. There was ample room for his clothes in the huge mahogany wardrobe, and having finished, he opened the window overlooking the orchard. He quickly closed it as the cold autumn wind hit his face and his hostess had been right, it was indeed raining. Charles smiled, 'Lenora,' he whispered.

He felt the crisp linen on the bed and bounced onto it, before lying down and closing his eyes. Yes, he was going to like it here, he just knew he would.

Chapter 9

Edouard pulled the chain hanging out of his breast pocket and held out the watch for Lenora to see.

'Please, tell me the time. Charles is late. Shall we start supper without him?'

She looked at the ornate china plate, where the pheasant was cut and arranged in thin neat slices.

'It's only just gone five past seven. The meat is cold, it won't spoil. Let's wait a few minutes.' It amused her that Edouard insisted on carrying his watch, although he was blind.

A discreet knock was followed by Charles entering the dining room, he had changed out of his travelling clothes and was dressed in a casual jacket and flannel trousers.

'I apologise. I was more tired than I realised, and I fell asleep. It's the time difference, I'm not yet used to it. In Canada it's now lunchtime, I believe.' He took his seat opposite Lenora and his eyes found and held hers. 'You look lovely tonight, Lenora, your hair is most becoming dressed that way.' He stopped abruptly and glanced at his uncle. 'Oh, I hope it's all right for me to say so and I'm sorry, I didn't know that you change for dinner.' He indicated the casual clothes he was wearing.

'Don't worry, Charles...' Edouard stopped and turned a surprised face at his wife when she interrupted him.

'We don't normally, but as it is your first night here...'

Lenora paused, she'd been too eager to explain. She could feel her cheeks warming at his steady gaze, as if his intention was to memorise her features. Charles had guessed that the reason for her elegant appearance was to impress him. He took the plate from Edouard's outstretched hand and helped himself to slices of cold pheasant, only then did he reluctantly look away.

'Quite so, Charles, you dress whichever way you feel most comfortable. I tend to stick to my suit, that's become a habit.' Edouard patted the lapel of his black jacket and smiled, 'I expect that Lenora has welcomed the opportunity to dress up.'

Edouard had given his full attention to his nephew but now turned his sympathetic face towards her. He reached out and took her hand for a moment, expertly avoiding the crystal glass by his side.

Charles observed this, raising an eyebrow. When his eyes once more sought hers, she kept her resolve of not looking away. But she was disturbed by the way she felt. She found that he appealed to her senses, she was flattered and this confused her.

This evening, she'd taken extra care with her appearance. Her hair was arranged softly on top of her head in a loose bun, and she was dressed in her favourite blue velvet gown. She didn't often wear it and it had seemed a pity to leave it in the wardrobe tonight. This was her excuse. When Charles turned to her husband, she drew a breath of relief.

'Forgive me for asking, Uncle, but how did you lose your sight? Please, don't answer if you find my question impertinent. However, my father doesn't know, and with your permission, I'll write and inform him of this.'

'Of course, you may, I was going to tell you myself. It's now three winters since I became totally blind. I lost my sight gradually, over a number of years.' His voice was relaxed, 'I've humbly accepted that I'll never get it back. But I am at ease with my situation; I have much to be grateful for.' He smiled at Lenora.

'You do cope very well, Uncle, you handed me the plate just now.'

'Yes, the table is always laid in a certain manner. I know where the plates and glasses are positioned. I also find my way around the house perfectly well on my own, as long as nothing is moved. All the furniture must remain in the same place.'

'Ah, very clever!' Charles nodded. 'I see that this can work.'

'It does. To start with, I needed Lenora's help but not now.'

Lenora reached out and placed a hand on her husband's arm, 'You manage as well as if you can see, and your hearing has improved to compensate. You hear things, which I don't.'

'That's because you're not listening, my dear,' Edouard laughed, 'but tell me more, Charles, about my brother. I was delighted to hear that he is well.'

'He is indeed, and he'll be pleased to have news of you. Obviously, your blindness will distress him, but I'll tell him that you're coping well and your delightful wife is such a credit and help to you.'

'Yes, that's very true. What has your father told you about us growing up together?'

'You had a happy childhood, he said. He hasn't got many memories of his early years in France; he was only six when your parents brought you to England.'

'I was nine, but we did go back to France on holidays to visit family. Surely he remembers that?'

'He talks mainly about your life in Cumberland, he loved the countryside here. He has prepared me for the beautiful views of the fells and lakes, which he grew up with and took for granted.'

'You'll be able to see them for yourself soon.'

'Tell me, Uncle, how do you remember my father?'

'He was my best friend throughout our early years. Henry had a strong personality, I suppose he still has. He didn't want to give up if he thought he was right. I have never known anyone to be so stubborn,' Edouard sighed.

'Yes, he told me about Victoria. I wasn't supposed to mention her, but now I have. She was his first sweetheart.'

'I don't think Victoria saw it that way, but that's in the past and best left there. Henry took the rejection to heart and left England. An overreaction, everyone thought so at the time.'

'I know that father will always want to put right what he thinks is wrong, he is unbending in his principles. He can be aggressive if he's in a temper. I'm like mother, she has more liberal thoughts and is not too serious-minded.'

'You must tell me about her later. Are you ready for another glass of this excellent claret?' Edouard asked and handed Charles the decanter.

'Thank you, Uncle.' Charles turned to Lenora, 'I should call you, Aunt.'

'Please, call me Lenora, as you've done. It's much better. Would you like more pheasant?'

'No thank you, but it was delicious.' Even so, he took the plate out of her hand, a smile played on his lips as he gently eased her fingers off the rim, before putting it down on the table.

'Do help yourself to more wine whenever you wish.' Lenora said the first thing that came into her head, making a desperate effort to keep her voice normal, but the touch had sent a tremor up her arm.

'Of course, you must feel at home. Unfortunately, I cannot see when it's empty.' Edouard raised his hands in a despairing gesture but smiled.

To Lenora's surprise, Charles drained his glass of wine and stood up from the table, 'Thank you, Uncle, you're making me most welcome. Now, if you'll excuse me, I'll go to my room. I have not yet fully recovered from the journey and I must write to Father and tell him that I've arrived safely.'

Lenora's chest rose, and she took a deep breath as Charles winked at her.

Where was she? Ellen stared at the full moon; startled, she turned to either side. It took her a few seconds to realise that she was standing on the lawn outside Lakeside House. How did she get there? In the moonlight, she could see the outline of the house clearly, last night it had been a dark shadow. The panic of the previous night had vanished, and she walked calmly towards her car. It was time to leave: for now. Who had made that decision? She didn't know.

She had another life here and she was intrigued by it. Edouard was a kind man, and she was beginning to like the attention Charles paid to Lenora. Why was this happening to her? One day she would find out. That was her reason for coming back.

Chapter 10

Bristol, November 2005

Annie sat with her back to her when Ellen walked into the workroom at the rear of the shop, 'I'm here!'

'So you are.' Annie's answer was short, and she didn't look round. She continued to sew, the machine making whirling noises as her hand moved over the slippery pink material in front of her.

'Sorry, have you been busy?' Ellen raised her voice to be heard.

'Not run off my feet exactly, but you had an appointment with Nora Shepherd at eleven. I had to dream up an excuse.' Annie turned in the chair.

Ellen felt a stab of guilt when she saw the disappointed look on her face, 'Oh God, I forgot. I intended to reschedule her. What did you say?'

'I said you had a message this morning and rushed off to a sick aunt.'

'But if that really had happened, we should still have called her.'

'I know, that's what she said. It wasn't a good excuse, but all I could think of in a hurry.'

'OK. I'll make it up to her. I'll ring and apologise.'

'Good!'

'Annie, stop sulking! I want to tell you what happened at the house.'

'I'm not interested, it's...' Annie stopped in mid-sentence, her voice sharp, 'What house? We've agreed it isn't there, Ellen.'

'What if I told you that it is? Only now it's not derelict, Edouard lives there and he's my husband. I have another life, I'm Lenora!'

Annie flew up and was by Ellen's side in an instant; her nails dug into Ellen's shoulders, as she pushed her down onto a chair, 'It's OK, just sit there for a minute. Calm down, you're too excited. I'll come with you to the doctor, I'll see if we can go immediately.'

'Annie, I like this other life, it doesn't scare me anymore. Someone or something has called me back to this house, and I have to live there to find out why. It's a good life. I'm not in danger.' Ellen smiled reassuringly, but her smile faded when she saw the expression on Annie's face.

'Wait a minute!' Annie ran out and placed the 'closed' sign on the door, turning the key in the lock at the same time. She sat down with a thump in front of Ellen, 'Tell me all!'

Ellen told her about the house, about Edouard and Charles and didn't leave out Molly and George. Annie listened intently; her red cheeks gave away her anxiety.

'Where were you when you became Ellen again?' Annie was unable to hide the concern in her eyes.

'In the car, both times, I think.'

'There you are, you fell asleep and dreamt it.'

'Asleep! All day, in the car? No, I wasn't.'

'I'm worried, but we can get help. I'm sure Moira will put in more hours until you're better. With the right treatment, you can be back here in months.'

Ellen's eyes widened as Annie's words began to sink in. Her friend meant what she said. Annie didn't believe her. Why should she? The story sounded crazy, she knew that, but she'd been sure that Annie was the one person she could tell.

She felt her throat constrict, when she realised that she was wrong. Annie thought she was unhinged. Before getting up, she swallowed hard several times and with her back to her friend, she took a deep breath, 'You're easy to fool, I've made it up.' With a smile, she turned to face her, 'You must admit it was a good story. I'm a bit disappointed you thought I'd gone mad. You know me so well. But your suggestion about Moira putting in more hours is good.'

'Oh, Ellen, why did you say it then? That wasn't nice. I was worried stupid. Are you telling the truth now?'

Ellen held up her hand, 'Scout's honour. It was silly. Sorry!'

Annie's face was a picture of frustration, 'But you shouldn't have scared me like that. You sounded so convincing. I would be very, very angry, if I wasn't so relieved.'

'Sorry!' Ellen looked up from her diary, 'You're right. I have overdone it, with the break up from Pete and all the upset. I'll take a couple of weeks off.' She scanned her diary, 'This week is busy, and I need to be back for the Christmas rush, but I could take the next two.'

Annie nodded her head with enthusiasm, 'Oh, Ellen, it'll do you good.'

Ellen had remembered the 'For Rent' sign outside the whitewashed cottage, three doors down from the pub in Cumbria. 'Yes,' she said with a distant look in her eyes, 'I'm looking forward to it. Can't wait.'

*

Ellen switched off the phone and rubbed her nose; it always itched when she was unsure about something. She was pleased, although worried at the same time. Had she just done something incredibly stupid? She'd agreed to rent the cottage for six months; it would be available from the first of December. The agent had told her the landlord had reduced the rent for the winter months: five hundred pounds for the first four months. After that, April and May would cost six hundred a month. The cottage was furnished, but she hadn't been inside and had only seen the interior on the agent's website. She bit her lip, it was more than she could afford. It meant she would have to cut down on other things and use the money she'd saved for the wedding. Well, there wasn't going to be one now. What's more, no summer holiday either. She frowned, was it worth it?

The agent had promised to check with the owner if she could have it from the twenty-first of November. This was when her two-week break started and she'd made this a condition. When he called back she could say she'd changed her mind, or that she wanted to think about it. But if she dithered, she might lose it, he'd said there had been another inquiry.

When the phone rang ten minutes later, she'd made up her mind.

'Miss Kelly, the owners have agreed to speed things up, you can have it from the twenty-first. We just need to sort out the deposit and I'll e-mail the contract.'

As she put down the phone, a feverish excitement rose in her, any doubt had vanished. She knew that she'd made the right choice. 'Yes,' she shouted, hitting the air with her fist, 'I've done it!'

She was going to live a life, which she wasn't sure was real but had become a necessity. A life she craved. Now she could take full advantage and spend as much time as she liked at Lakeside House, and no inquisitive questions to answer from Mrs Jones.

The agent had assured her that the paperwork would be sorted by the time she drove up on the twenty-first, all she had to do was pick up the key. She slumped down on the sofa. Her body was limp and her mind drained: all the anxiety and uncertainty before making her decision had exhausted her.

Ellen had to work hard that week; she had let things slip and it wasn't like her. She stayed on late to finish off two sketches of business suits. An important client of Annie's had found Ellen's designs to her taste. Annie was a good seamstress and a perfectionist. She wouldn't let anything go until completely satisfied and now Ellen had delayed her by keeping her waiting for these sketches. Everything had changed since she had seen the painting.

Next, she sorted out the bills to be paid, then spent time on the phone, rescheduling appointments. She was pleased that Nora Shepherd had called in, at first agitated about the missed appointment, but when she had seen the fabulous blue velvet dress Ellen had made for her, she had accepted the apology.

After that every spare minute had been spent making an identical dress for herself. She'd been able to match the colour and although the quality of the velvet wasn't quite the same, the result was stunning. The gown had long tight sleeves and the bodice clung to her with a v-shaped décolleté, it had a defined waist, with the material hugging her hips and flowing to the floor.

'When are you going to find an occasion to wear it?' Annie asked. 'It really is a lovely dress.' She couldn't tell her that Lenora had a dress just like this and Ellen had decided to wear it as soon as she got home. Perhaps every evening, but she didn't tell Annie that either.

Instead, she answered, 'Oh, for something special, I guess.'

'Why have you made it? You don't spend ages on a dress like this if you haven't got a date planned to wear it.'

Later, Ellen looked up to see a tense Annie observing her, 'What's up Annie? You OK?'

'I can't stop thinking about what you said, about the house, you know.' Annie's worried eyes held hers. 'And now you're going back there.'

'Honestly, I am not going to the house.' Ellen lied and

walked over to her friend and gave her a hug, 'I promise!' To reassure her, she did her best to appear cheerful and smile a lot and gradually, as the day wore on, Annie relaxed.

Oak Tree Cottage, Cumbria, November 2005

Ellen opened the door to the cottage with some apprehension. She'd seen pictures of the interior, but they didn't always give an accurate description. The cold hit her as she stepped over the threshold. The agent had promised that the heating would be turned up before she moved in. She would check on it, but she had her doubts.

The furnishings were pleasant enough, she thought, as she moved about the room, she could live with them. She might buy a few cushions and a couple of colourful throws but nothing major. A few logs were left behind, enough to make a fire tonight, she'd have to get more in the morning. The bedding felt cold so she turned up the thermostat, grateful that the cottage wasn't damp.

She removed the blue gown from her case and felt the softness of the velvet. A dress looking exactly the same hung in the huge mahogany wardrobe in Lenora's bedroom. It was Lenora's favourite dress: she only wore it for special occasions. The image of the dress had popped into Ellen's mind, before she had even seen it.

She unpacked the groceries, she'd bought enough for a couple of days, but tonight she'd eat at the inn.

As Ellen walked into the pub, Mrs Jones greeted her with a cheerful, 'Good evening! It's good to see you again. How are you?'

'I'm fine, thanks.'

'You haven't booked, but we do have a room.'

‘Guess what, Mrs Jones? I’ve rented Oak Tree Cottage down the road.’

‘Well, I never! How long are you staying?’

‘Only two weeks this time, but I’ve taken the cottage for six months, so I’ll be back for Christmas.’

‘Good, then we’ll see more of you. I hope you’ll pop in for a drink.’

‘Yes, of course and I’ll have dinner here tonight.’

Ellen found it difficult to sleep, the unfamiliarity of the cottage and the anticipation of going to the house in the morning kept her awake. She’d not been to Cumbria for a month. It was Annie’s fault, she had been more traumatised by Ellen’s experience than she’d been herself, so staying away had served an important purpose. For the sake of her peace of mind and the business they were running together, she’d agreed to Annie’s demand. Her friend had wanted what she thought was best for her.

At least once a week during the past four, Annie and Ken had taken her to the cinema or out for walks, as well as asking her over for meals. Because of their thinly camouflaged questions, she’d realised that they were keeping an eye on her, making sure that she wasn’t going insane.

When she’d told Annie that she’d rented the cottage, her suspicion had flared. Ellen had told many lies since her first trip to the Lakes and it had bothered her enormously. It wasn’t in her nature but lying came easily to her now; “I love the village and the surroundings, it’s so beautiful and restful,” she’d said. “I won’t go anywhere near Lakeside House. Why should I? It doesn’t exist.” Annie obviously didn’t believe her, and in desperation, Ellen had added, “I swear on my mother’s life, I won’t go there.”

Why had she said that? It had slipped out and she’d immediately regretted it. It made her feel uneasy. What if anything happened to her mum? Would it be her fault? Oh, dear God, please don't let it, she'd never forgive herself.

Her thoughts drifted to the house, and that always made her feel better. She longed for this other world, to which she was allowed access. She knew that life there continued in her absence. She thought about it constantly. When she entered the house, Lenora took over her mind, her body and soul, and she became part of it.

Chapter 11

Lakeside House, Cumberland, November 1902

Ellen opened the door to Lakeside House and Lenora slipped into her mind that very moment. She shrugged off her heavy cape and without looking down, she knew that she was wearing Lenora's long brown woollen skirt and the red flannel blouse with the upturned collar.

Charles greeted her in the hall and took a step towards her, but she put out a hand to stop him. When they were alone in a room, it worried her to be close to him. She brushed past him with only a nod of her head.

The tension between them was apparent to Ellen and she frowned when Lenora's memories came flooding back. Charles' attention had continued unchecked because she'd done nothing to stop him and wasn't sure if she ought to. Were his actions to be considered improper? They took the form of small but deliberate touches; sometimes he rested his hand on her shoulder, before he let it brush down the length of her arm onto her hand, which he held for the merest moment. It sent a tingle through her body, which wasn't unpleasant but... not knowing what her eyes told him, she'd always looked down. Charles did this in the presence of Edouard, which made it impossible for her to speak out. How could she, when she wasn't sure of his intention? Perhaps this was his way of being friendly? She didn't want to jump to conclusions that would embarrass him and her as well.

'Lenora, may I speak to you?' Charles took her arm.

'No, I must go to Edouard directly.' She shook her arm free and caught the surprised look in his green eyes.

To her relief, he didn't follow her and she found her husband in his favourite chair. She noticed that he hadn't changed the collar and cuffs on the shirt he was wearing. It annoyed her, as he always cared about his appearance.

'Edouard, your collar is not clean.' Her voice had an edge to it.

'It will do for another day.'

'You can't see the condition of the ones you've worn. I do put out a fresh collar and cuffs for you every night for a reason.'

'I am well aware of that, dear. I thought it would be less washing for Molly.' Edouard's puzzled face showed that he was taken aback by her remark.

'Molly doesn't mind,' her voice was strained.

'What's the matter, Lenora? You're displeased.'

'Nothing is the matter. Why do you think something is wrong?'

'I sense that you don't enjoy Charles' company, you don't speak freely around him. You do not engage yourself with him but seem to distance yourself. Why is that? He is our guest.'

'I would have enjoyed playing chess with him, but he can't,' her answer was deliberately evasive. 'Edouard, we haven't played since you lost your sight.'

'Teach him!'

'I have offered, he's not interested. You can see that I've tried. But I'll suggest a card game before lunch.'

'Excellent! However, I do hear you refuse his company on your walks.'

'My walks are precious to me. Please, don't ask me to share them with him.'

'Of course not, dearest. I do enjoy having Charles here and

I was hoping that you would find him good company too.'

'To be honest, I don't know how to behave around him. He unsettles me.'

'Unsettles you!' Edouard's frown showed his deep concern and he remained quiet. A moment later his face lit up, 'We'll have a lunch party on Sunday and invite Jenny and Jonathan. Charles will be pleased to meet them and if they bring Emily, there'll be someone else your age.'

She sighed deeply, that wouldn't change anything. It would be a temporary distraction, but that would be all. Still, it would be nice to see Emily.

'You don't have to do this for me…' She was interrupted by Charles entering the room.

'Nonsense, that's agreed. We'll send George over with the invitation this afternoon.'

'Charles, will you have a game of cards with me now before lunch?'

'I'll be delighted. Let me set up the table.'

Minutes later the table was ready and the cards were dealt. Lenora glanced over at Charles. His head was bent forward in concentration, his eyes on the cards in his hand. Perhaps I've been too harsh in my judgement, he's behaving impeccably, she thought.

She tried a smile, 'Charles, it's your turn.' Her voice was pleasantly cheerful.

A smiled lurked at the corner of his mouth as he tweaked his cards. His eyes locked into hers, 'I shall enjoy playing this game, very much indeed, Lenora.' The tone of his voice was silky smooth and she raised her eyebrows. He seemed excessively satisfied, she wondered if he was referring to this game, or did he have another in mind?

In her room, Lenora stepped out of her dress, the full skirt left standing stiffly on the floor. This evening she'd worn her green satin gown, the bodice low cut, the long sleeves trimmed with brown fur. How she loved wearing beautiful gowns but so seldom had anyone to show them off to. Except tonight, Charles had told her that she looked lovely but not in a flirtatious way. He'd behaved like a gentleman throughout the evening and at times like this she found his attention agreeable.

Preparing to call on Edouard for her nightly visit to his bedroom, she put on her white linen nightdress and dressing gown. It saved her time to be ready for her own bed and as he couldn't see what she was wearing, it couldn't embarrass him. For the first few years of their marriage, she'd always gone to his room fully clothed.

Her husband was propped up in bed and she leaned in pulling at the cushions behind his back, 'Is that better?'

'Thank you, dear.'

She laid out clean clothes for him to wear the next day and proceeded to stoke the fire in the small grate and then returned to sit by his bedside, a book in her hand.

'Edouard, you might be right. I have been more attentive to Charles and he has responded in a pleasant way. I will enjoy his company after all.' She'd certainly do her best, she thought, if it made her husband's life brighter. Charles was his only close family.

'I'm pleased to hear it.' Edouard reached out and gave her hand a squeeze.

'I've come to the last chapter tonight. You'll have to choose something else for tomorrow. Shall I read, "The Pickwick Papers"?'

'"The Pickwick Papers" will do well, thank you.'

Lenora closed the book and ended her visit with a light kiss on her husband's forehead, which he acknowledged by bringing her hand to his lips, 'Good night, dearest.'

The next morning she found Charles standing in the hall at the bottom of the staircase. He was dressed in his dark winter coat and woollen trousers. He didn't speak but his face, which was turned up towards her, was calm in anticipation and his eyes bright.

It had an immediate effect and Lenora warmed to him, she had a change of heart, 'Do you care to accompany me on my walk?' She had spoken the words spontaneously, but it was what she wanted.

'I'll be delighted. I've already dressed warmly for my own walk, but with you it will be more pleasant.' His face showed relief.

A thought crossed her mind. Had he planned this? Probably, but she didn't mind.

The air was icy cold and the frost remained on the ground, it covered the grass and melted under their boots as they walked down the slope. She pulled her winter cape closer and looked down, watching her step carefully, so not to slip. Charles placed a hand under her elbow to steady her.

She smiled gratefully, 'Let's walk down to the lake. I usually follow the path by the boathouse and then go home through the woods. I love the smell of pine.'

'You lead, Aunt.'

She didn't like being called aunt, but she let it pass.

The sky was a clear pale blue and the wind coming from the north smarted as it hit their faces, Charles rubbed his cheeks with his knitted woollen gloves. They walked past the boathouse and moorings. There wasn't much movement in the green water, but the path running along the lake was wide enough for them to walk side by side.

'How big is this lake?'

'Oh, it's enormous, Charles, like a small sea.'

'And how big is that?'

Lenora laughed, 'I don't know to be honest. But look, you can barely see the other side. It's far away.'

Charles stepped closer to the edge and removing his

glove, tested the water, 'It's freezing! I wouldn't want to take a dip in that.'

'If you're here in the summer, you might enjoy it.' Lenora blushed as soon as she'd said it.

'And would you like that?'

'Edouard has invited you to stay as long as you like.' Her voice was casual and in a hurry to change the subject, she added, 'In the summer there are pleasure boats on the lake, but they don't come near our shore.'

The path through the wood took them on a longer route. They followed an uneven and barely visible mud track, now dried up, avoiding stones and tree-stumps. It was warmer in the wood, the rays from the sun were melting the frost and water drops fell onto their faces as they brushed under the rustling leaves.

'Are you sure this is the right way?' Charles asked laughing, and took hold of an overhanging branch to let her pass. 'It doesn't seem suitable for a lady.'

'I agree, but it's *my* secret path and I like it,' Lenora turned a happy face towards him. At the end of the walk, both were laughing as they entered the hall of Lakeside House.

Lenora removed the cape and adjusted her hair in front of the large mirror, her face was rosy from the cold and her eyes shining. With a smile she turned to Charles, 'I'll be pleased if you care to join me tomorrow as well.'

Charles' lips briefly brushed her hand, 'I'll be delighted.' His voice was polite and without any trace of familiarity.

Lenora nodded, she felt so much happier, a cloud had lifted from her mind. This was a Charles that she could cope with. He had changed, he was different now. This was surely how it should be.

Chapter 12

Charles smiled, he could be agreeable, particularly when it resulted in getting his own way. Lenora was definitely warming to him. Perhaps it would result in his achieving his goal? Well, why not? His uncle had not played fair with his father; time for payback.

Of course, this wasn't why he'd been despatched to England. No, he'd been sent with instructions to be gone for a year. He had 'ruined', so he was told, the seventeen-year-old daughter of family friends. He smiled at the memory, she'd been a little beauty, but the consequences had not made it worth the experience. He had tried to tell his father the truth, that Charlotte was already 'ruined' and he wasn't to blame. His father had exploded in a rage, believing that he was lying.

After a year, when Charlotte reached the age of eighteen, he would have to return and marry her. But she had rejected him. He hoped that would still be the case, unless their parents forced the marriage. Luckily for him, he hadn't made the girl with child.

Have sense boy! You shouldn't do your philandering so close to home, his father had roared. He would have to be more careful next time.

Well, now he was far from home. His uncle was blind, that should make it easy, what you don't know won't hurt you. There was an English rose right here, not quite ready for plucking but soon would be.

Charles had left his door ajar, there was only one other room between his and Lenora's and her footsteps could be heard on the landing. He caught her disappearing down the corridor into Edouard's bedroom, as he'd seen her do on previous nights. As always, she was wearing a dressing gown over her nightdress and she stayed for a considerable time. He was sure he could give her more satisfaction than this old man. But his clumsy approaches had been rejected, she had become shy and wary of him. However, now he could see a way forward. From the moment he had applied his new method, he'd found that it was working. He would have to tread carefully, or the bird would fly. He smiled, this was a game he intended to win.

Chapter 13

Oak Tree Cottage, Cumbria, November 2005

Ellen woke early, she was frozen. She'd returned to the cottage late last night and only then had she realised that she'd been at Lakeside House for two nights. The cottage had been stone cold. 'Damn, I forgot to buy wood, must get some today,' she muttered. The supposed central heating didn't work well, she thought, as she huddled into her clothes. What she needed was a hot cup of tea.

She brought the cup to her mouth but stopped dead in the middle of the floor as the memory of what had happened at the house came flooding back. Charles was up to no good, she didn't trust him. But however much she'd like to, she couldn't impose her will on Lenora. Every decision was made by her alone. Ellen had no say in what Lenora did and she was falling for Charles, only she didn't know it.

Why was she going back? It was the only way to find out where this was taking her. She was intrigued by the life; she was actually enjoying it. It was the most exciting thing that had happened to her.

Perhaps she was mad.

Could she be? No, she shook her head, of course she wasn't. When this started, she had thought about that possibility, but she wasn't imagining this.

She closed her eyes, her fingers running in circles over her temples, and let her thoughts drift. She believed that she entered time warps, which she could pass into and leave, not always at her own will. Lenora lived this life when she wasn't there. Lenora took over her mind when she came back to the house, and only then did she know what had been going on in her absence. That was the only explanation she could come up with. Was she right? It would have to do for now.

A chill ran down her back and she sat down with a thud. Oh God, she liked that life better! It was taking over. However much she liked being Lenora, she couldn't let that happen. With an effort she swept the thoughts aside, desperate to replace them with others. She had to do something to take her mind off Lenora and the house.

But what? Oh yes, she could shop and buy wood, but then what would she do?

There had to be something else, she must think hard, must think... Oh, this was ridiculous!

She knew! It wouldn't hurt to clean the cottage and later have lunch at the pub. It would be good to speak to a human being. Were the people at Lakeside House human? She truly didn't know. Was *she* human when she was there? Oh no, this had to stop; she was thinking about the house again.

She dressed quickly and hurried out, the questions still ringing in her head.

'Ellen, how do you find Oak Tree Cottage?'

'Oh fine, Mrs Jones, a bit chilly, that's all,' she'd nearly answered that she hadn't spent much time there.

The pub wasn't busy, so she stood by the bar talking to Mrs Jones, who told her about a funny incident with a customer which made her laugh. She relaxed, she hadn't laughed for a while and it felt good. During their conversation, she decided to stay away from Lakeside House for a day or two. This, after all, was the world she belonged to. Once her mind was made up, the anxiety she had felt during the day vanished and she became calm.

The evening was spent in front of the fire and she checked her e-mails, several were from Annie and a text from her mother, asking why she hadn't let her know she was on holiday.

She picked up her phone, 'Hi, Mum, thought I'd better give you a ring.'

'I'm glad you did, I've called you several times. Don't you check your messages? Annie told me you're on a break. Why haven't you come home?'

'I needed to be on my own, Mum.'

'You're not with a man then?'

'No, no more men. I've lost interest after Pete.'

'Oh dear! What a pity, I would have been happier if you were. How are your headaches by the way? I worry about you.'

Ellen was taken aback by the question, in fact she was stunned. They had vanished, and she hadn't missed them for a second.

'Hello, are you still there?'

'Mum, they're gone,' she answered, at the same time trying to remember when she'd had the last one. It was soon after she'd known Lenora.

'That's wonderful, darling, but are you sure you're all right? You would tell us wouldn't you, if something is wrong?'

'Everything is absolutely fine, Mum.' Ellen ran a hand through her hair, here we go, she thought. Why does she have to ask questions?

'We are here to help. And it is a bit strange you spending all that time alone.'

'Mum, you know the break-up from Pete upset me, being here is doing me good. I wish you wouldn't go on about it.'

'You must admit it's not like you to go off like that.'

‘Mum, I’ve got my dinner in the oven. I need to see to it.’

‘All right, darling. Now do remember to keep in touch. Dad sends his love and we’ll see you at Christmas.’

Ellen finished the call with a deep sigh. It was going to be difficult to explain why she wasn’t coming home for Christmas. She’d decided to spend it at Lakeside House.

Oh Mum, she thought. If you knew, you wouldn’t sleep at night. You and Dad would have me locked up. But she had to go through with this; she would have an explanation in time.

⁂

The next morning, Ellen ate breakfast in a hurry, not quite knowing why she’d rushed until she found herself by the door. With a semi-conscious movement, she picked up the car keys. She was going back to the house.

No, she wasn’t.

Immediately she dropped the keys back onto the table. It was against her earlier decision, she had vowed to stay away for a while. But life had become exciting now that Lenora got on well with Charles. What would happen next? She had to be there to know.

The next second the keys were in her hand again, she pressed her lips hard together and ran out to the car. She had tried, the pull was too strong.

Ellen stood in the hall at Lakeside House, waiting for Lenora to take control. It had become easy for her to do so. To feel her own memory slide back and be replaced with Lenora’s had been unnerving at first. Although she craved this life which had become a necessity, she had been unsure and frightened. Once she had even tried to stop Lenora from taking over her mind, by concentrating hard, but she had failed. Now she didn’t fight her anymore, she longed for it.

‘Lenora, where are you? Don’t keep me waiting, I’m here,’ she whispered.

Chapter 14

Lakeside House, Cumberland, late November 1902

Charles' chair was empty, this was the first thing she noticed as she entered the dining room, 'Is Charles not down yet?'

'Oh, he's been and gone.' Edouard reached for the marmalade, 'He's out for the day.'

'Oh,' Lenora felt a pang of disappointment, 'where?'

'George has taken him to Kendal to look around. I asked George to show him the lakes, so they'll be out all day.'

'Charles didn't mention it to me.'

'No, dear, it was a spur of the moment decision and George wasn't busy today.'

'Jenny Edmondson has sent me a note to thank us for the luncheon invitation and they are pleased to accept. Molly is happy to cook and serve, she'll take a different day off instead. We're lucky that she's willing to fit in with our arrangements.'

'It suits both her and George.' Edouard nodded. 'What will we eat, my dear?'

'I've asked her to prepare jugged hare, it's her speciality, as you know. I expect Charles has never tried it.'

'Ah, one of Molly's best. I'm sure he'll like it.'

'I had planned a lemon sorbet for dessert, but our freezing pot needs replacing, so we'll have a trifle instead. I'll be busy for the next three days helping Molly with the preparations.

I'll have to miss out on my morning walks.'

'Charles will be disappointed. He's come with you several mornings this week. You were quite adamant that you should spend them on your own. What made you change your mind?'

'Charles is polite and pleasant, since I became more agreeable. I believe I like having him around after all.'

'Excellent, excellent, you don't know how happy I am to hear this.'

Lenora entered the kitchen where Molly was in the process of skinning the hare, 'George should have done this for me, but I can't find him.'

'It's not a pleasant job. Well done, Molly. I believe George has taken Charles out for the day. Do you have enough of the juniper berries and the redcurrant jelly?'

'I have plenty of berries, you picked a lot and they dried nicely. Can I have some port for the gravy, Miss Lenora?'

'Of course, I'll fetch some at once,' Lenora nodded.

'It's the port and the hare's blood that makes the gravy so rich and tasty.'

'You're quite right. It wouldn't be the same without it. I'll get sherry as well for the trifle. I'll make that if you don't mind, Molly. I really enjoy doing it. I know yours is excellent, but you have plenty to do without it.'

'If you say so, Miss Lenora, not that I can't manage,' she sniffed.

Lenora sighed as she left the kitchen one had to be careful with Molly, who was easily offended. Perhaps she should let her do the trifle and she could start preparing the dining room by bringing out the crystal glasses and the cutlery.

Lenora had a huge bunch of roses on the table in front of her when Charles entered the dining room the next day. He picked up a single flower and brought it to his nose.

'Where did they come from? Their fragrance is strong enough to fill the room.'

'George has been to Kendal to fetch them. They are for our lunch party tomorrow.'

'I say, you do it in style. I'm impressed.' He bowed deeply, and with a sweep of his arm, held it out. 'May I present a beautiful rose to another, equalling its beauty.'

'Thank you,' she stammered, her cheeks burning hot. It had been so unexpected, she didn't know what else to say. Still blushing, she frantically searched for words, 'Well, we don't often entertain so we like to do it properly when we do. This lunch is for you to get acquainted with the Edmondson family, our nearest neighbours.'

'I'm looking forward to meeting them. I'll be on my best behaviour. I hear they are bringing their daughter, Emily.'

'Yes, you'll like her. She's a few years younger than we are.'

'Not too young, I hope.' Charles winked.

Lenora felt uncomfortable, 'No, she's not too young to converse with in a pleasant manner.'

'Let me help you. Do you want the stems cut like this?' Charles changed the conversation; he had noticed the coldness in her last remark.

Moments later he was called away by George, who told him that his uncle requested help with a small matter.

When she had finished the table looked elegant, with the well-polished silver cutlery and crystal glasses. The roses were displayed as a centrepiece in the middle of the table, all except one.

Jenny and Jonathan Edmondson arrived at one o'clock on Sunday, accompanied by their daughter, Emily. Lenora and Edouard greeted them in the hall.

Jonathan looked serious and austere in his suit and waistcoat, he repeatedly ran his finger under his starched collar and fingered the gold chain of his pocket watch, which shone against the black cloth. In contrast, the ladies' dresses were colourful. Lenora felt dull in the maroon gown with a lace collar reaching her chin; she wished that she'd worn a brighter dress. Fully aware of Jenny's strict taste in clothes, she had avoided her favourite décolleté. But she found comfort in the rule that the hostess should not outshine her guests. Jenny's full figure and high bosom were elegantly gowned in violet, the upright pleated collar held together with a cameo brooch. Emily was pretty in her pale blue silk gown, blond curls arranged on top of her head.

'Emily, where did you find this exquisite lace?' she asked.

'Oh, my grandmother worked it for me. It would be impossible to find the like in a shop.' She held her sleeve closer to Lenora for inspection.

Lenora let her finger run over the finely worked lace and nodded, 'I do so agree.'

Sherry was to be taken in the lounge, where Charles was waiting to be introduced to the Edmondson family. He bowed his head slightly to Jonathan Edmondson but brushed his lips over the two ladies' gloved hands.

Presently Molly announced that luncheon was served. Lenora sat at one end of the table with Edouard opposite. Charles was seated next to Emily.

Lenora had Jonathan on her right and after he'd consumed the main course, he rested his cutlery on the plate and announced in his deep voice, 'I must remark on the jugged hare, it's superior to that of Rosa, our own cook; the gravy is excellent.'

'Jonathan, don't you dare to repeat this in front of Rosa, or we shall have a crisis on our hands,' his wife didn't smile, her face taut, she gave her husband a disapproving stare. The prospect of this was obviously of some concern to her.

Lenora laughed, 'Molly will relish the compliment, but I will not tell her about the comparison, as we know they do meet occasionally.' Jonathan had surprised her, he was a serious man and seldom took to paying compliments.

Now Jonathan turned to Edouard and held out his glass to him, 'This is a good vintage. I think it has an excellent nose.'

'Thank you, Jonathan. I am glad you appreciate my wines. As you know, I take them seriously and care about them.'

'You keep the best cellar in the district.'

Edouard didn't answer just nodded his head in quiet satisfaction.

'Did you make the trifle, Lenora?' Emily asked, after the dessert had been served. 'I know how much you enjoy cooking. I so wish I could, but I'm hopeless...'

'There's no need for you to learn; we have a cook to do this,' her mother interrupted.

Lenora let the comment pass, Jenny was a forthright woman and not afraid to speak her mind.

Emily blushed, embarrassed by her mother's remark, her light blue eyes opened wide and she stammered, 'Yes, I know, Mother.' She fell silent and fidgeted with her napkin.

Charles broke the awkward silence, 'This dessert wine is also good. May I have a refill?' Of the two decanters placed by his side, Edouard found the one containing the sweet wine, by letting his hand follow the contour of the crystal.

Charles divided his attention between the ladies admirably. Emily was brighter now, her blond curls bobbing on her head as she got into conversation with him.

She is normally so shy, it's good to see her enjoying herself, Lenora thought. From the appreciative glances Jenny and Emily gave him, she felt sure they found his company pleasant. He had managed to bring Jenny out of her shell, her face was softer and had lost its sternness.

When the ladies retired, Charles chose to accompany them to the drawing room, instead of accepting Edouard's offer of a glass of port. 'It's an excellent vintage, you'll be missing out,' he enticed him.

'Thank you, Uncle, but I will try it another time.' Charles

rested his hand under Jenny's elbow to escort her out of the room and was rewarded by a delightful smile.

In the drawing room, Charles took a seat next to Emily and Lenora watched them closely. What was Charles whispering? She would have liked to know, when Emily blushed and waved a fan in front of her face. Why had she brought a fan in the midst of winter? Lenora couldn't imagine the reason for this. She frowned, Charles' manners were not impeccable, she thought, he should know that you do not whisper in the presence of other people. Had he not been taught this? Life in Canada was no doubt freer than here. Why did it matter? He could speak to whom he liked, it was of no concern to her, but he was giving Emily a lot of attention – it wasn't really necessary to be so very polite. However, tomorrow she'd resume her walks and she wished that he would join her. Lenora suddenly realised that at her side, Jenny was speaking, and she turned to face her with a smile.

'Uncle, may I take Gladys to Kendal on my own?' Charles asked the next morning. 'I passed by the stables as George was grooming her and he's willing to get her ready for me. With your permission of course,' he added.

'When are you thinking of doing so?'

'Well, today actually.'

'Can you handle the carriage and horse?'

'Yes, in Canada, we have no driver, we do it ourselves. Life is different there.'

'Well, if you're sure, of course you may.'

'Thank you, Uncle.'

Charles returned ten minutes later, his face like thunder, 'I told George to bring Gladys out for me. He had the audacity to tell me that he only takes orders from you. Your servant should behave with respect, this really won't do.' He looked expectantly at his uncle.

'Come, come, Charles. George knows what he is doing, he's merely following orders. And only I will decide if it's necessary to reprimand him. In this case, I think not.' A smile lingered on Edouard's lips as he rose from his chair, 'I'm taking a breath of air, so I'll tell George.'

He was by the door when he turned, 'Gladys will be expecting her carrot, Lenora. Can you find one and bring it out to the stables?'

'Of course, and I'll join you for a walk in the orchard.' Lenora lowered her head; like Edouard, she had found Charles' indignation amusing, and she bit her lip to stop herself from laughing. That would certainly add to Charles' bad mood.

'Your carriage will be awaiting you very soon.' Edouard's cane tapped the floor.

Without a backward glance at Lenora, Charles followed his uncle out of the room.

Later, she learnt that Charles had stopped by Greenwood House to collect Emily. They hadn't been alone, the maid had supervised their day. Lenora smiled with satisfaction; Charles wouldn't have expected this.

When Lenora opened the curtains in the morning, she was delighted to see that it had snowed overnight. Exhilarated, she ran to Edouard's room in her nightgown. Her husband was sitting up in bed; his eiderdown pulled up to his chin, he was shivering.

'It has snowed, Edouard! I'm so excited.' She was clapping her hands and taking small leaps of joy.

'That's why George is late then. I have no fire lit.'

'I'll do it. Who knows when George will be in, and it's very cold in here.' Lenora pulled up a rug in front of the fireplace and fell onto her knees; it didn't take her long before a fire was burning in the grate. She laughed excitedly and wiped her hands on her white gown leaving smears of soot, 'If it snows more, we can get the sledge out.'

'You're like a child at Christmas, Lenora.'

'Wouldn't it be marvellous if we have a white Christmas this year? We can go to church with jingle bells. Oh, it would be so wonderful!'

'It makes me happy when you are. Having Charles here has made a difference, as I thought it would.'

His words made her pause, her smile died and she looked thoughtful before she spoke, 'I'm feeling the cold. I rushed in here without my dressing gown.' She rubbed her arms, 'I'll see you at breakfast.'

'I want it to get warmer in the room before I dress, so don't wait for me. I'll be down in my own good time,' Edouard answered.

In the corridor she ran straight into Charles. He grabbed her arm to stop her from stumbling, 'Lenora!' He held her at arm's length, smiling, 'You have soot on your nose.' His eyes strayed down her body.

'Charles!' Her hand went up, but not to her nose. Embarrassed, she placed it at the deep v-shape of her nightgown, where her breasts heaved in time with her increased breathing.

Charles' eyes lingered, and his hand brushed lightly against her gown as he let go. Without a word she ran past him into her room, where she leaned on the closed door for several minutes, waiting for her breath to return to normal.

Chapter 15

When Lenora stepped out into the cold air, she hoped it would clear her mind. Her cheeks blushed at the memory of this morning; it had affected her in a curious way. Instead of being angry, she'd been confused at the warmth she'd felt creeping up inside her. She'd tried and failed to untangle her muddled thoughts. This had dampened the joy she'd felt earlier when she'd seen the snowflakes fall outside her window. Gone was the childish excitement, which had filled her, in anticipation of a walk in the snow.

Deep in thought, she walked on and found herself by the side of the lake. Her thick headscarf slipped, and she pulled it up, brushing away the wet flakes from her hair. At that moment she saw a rowing-boat drifting some way out in the lake.

'Hello! Hello,' but her voice was lost in the wind. 'Oh no!' She gasped and stared in horror. It was difficult to see in the driving snow, but there appeared to be a person slumped over the side of the boat. Something was wrong. She turned and ran towards the house, gathering up her long skirt in both hands, slipping several times on the snow. By the time she thrust the front door open, she was panting and out of breath.

Charles was waiting in the hall, 'Lenora, don't let this spoil…'

But she brushed past him on her way to the lounge, 'Please, Charles, not now. I must speak to Edouard, it can't wait.'

Charles followed her, 'You will not tell him about this morning…?'

'No, of course not, there's nothing to say.'

'Dearest, will the snow stay with us, do you think?' Edouard was leaning back in his armchair, eyes closed, as they entered the room.

'Yes, dear, but I have seen a boat drifting on the lake. There appears to be a person in it. We must send George out to help. Where is he? It's snowing and very windy, the sky tells me there's more to come.' She moved restlessly up to her husband's side and turning to Charles, she added, 'You'd better go with him. It needs two of you.'

'I agree, but George has gone to Kendal.' Edouard sat up straight.

'Then I must go on my own,' Charles volunteered.

'Can you handle a boat?' Edouard asked.

'I can row if that's what you mean.'

'I'll come with you. You'll need help and I'm dressed for the weather.' Lenora was already walking towards the door.

'What about you, Charles?' Edouard turned his head towards him.

'I will fetch my coat.'

'Lenora, lend him my heavy coat, it's in the hall. It'll be quicker,' Edouard suggested.

As they reached their own boat by the moorings, Lenora pointed, 'There! Can you see it? It's moved further away.'

'Yes, I can just about make it out. Here, let me help you.'

Lenora waved his hand aside, 'I can manage.' She pulled her woollen skirt up above her ankles, revealing her sturdy leather boots, and climbed in.

Charles rowed with purposeful strong strokes against the force of the cold wind, but to Lenora it seemed to take a long time to reach the boat. She shielded her face against the snow, which blew into her eyes. She strained to look ahead through the driving wet flakes and only when they got alongside did she sigh with relief.

'Oh, it's just the cover, which has blown about,' she called out to Charles. She pulled at it, peering underneath, 'The upright shape, made me think it was a person.' The boat was empty, the oars rested in their sockets, there was no sign of it having been occupied recently.

Charles removed his gloves, before leaning over the side to pull the torn rope out of the water, he wiped the wet snow from his face with the sleeve of his coat, 'It has broken loose from its moorings.'

'This boat belongs to Jonathan Edmondson, we'll have to tow it to shore.' Lenora pointed to the name painted on the side. 'He has named it "Emily".'

Charles tied the rope to the stern, his fingers turning red from the icy cold water, and he had several goes until he successfully tied a secure knot.

'It will be harder to get back, towing that one, but at least we'll have the wind with us,' Lenora said to encourage him.

'I'll manage.' Charles blew warmth into his freezing hands.

'It's lucky for you that Edouard always leaves them in his coat pocket.' Lenora picked up the gloves, which had fallen down by her feet, and handed them to him. As Charles gripped the oars, she pulled her cloak closer and huddled down.

It was still snowing heavily as Charles jumped out by the boathouse, his feet in shallow water, they had not quite reached the mooring. He attempted to pull the boat up onto land, 'I can't get it any closer. Not with the weight of the other boat. You'll have to jump. I'll catch you.'

Lenora balanced at the front of the boat and shuddered at the thought of stepping into the icy water. She had that choice or to do as he'd asked. She hesitated only slightly before leaping into his outstretched arms.

He stumbled with the weight of her body and fell backwards onto the snow-covered ground with her on top of him. His eyes flew open and his grip around her back tightened, the next moment she tasted the snowflakes on his wet lips. His arms pressed her body down harder onto his own. For a moment she let herself be kissed...

Charles' gloved hands gripped her face and this brought her to her senses.

'Charles,' she stuttered, 'don't do this.'

'Lenora, from the moment I stepped off the coach and saw you, I've wanted you. I adore you. I know how you feel, I can see it in your eyes.'

She struggled and as his grip loosened she scrambled to her feet. Her hair had come undone and got into her mouth and was smothering her face. She brushed it away and only bent to pick up her headscarf before turning to run. Charles leapt up and grabbed her from behind. He held her firmly with one arm, with the other he lifted her auburn hair and kissed the nape of her neck, his lips moved slowly from side to side and she felt his warm breath on her skin. She wanted to move but she couldn't, she tingled with a sensation which was running through the full length of her body. She stood still, her eyes closed, inhaled, and her deep breath was followed by a low moan.

At this her cheeks burnt hot, the spell broke with a jolt and she struggled to pull away.

With a sharp movement, Charles twisted her body round and pressed her hard up against him, so that her face was close to his, and kissed her. She brought her free arm up and hit him fully in the face with the palm of her hand. She cried out in tears, mixed with frustration, 'You fool! You've spoilt it all.' She lifted her hand as if to strike him again.

Charles pulled back and glared at her, his eyes unbelieving. He rubbed his cheek, where already a red blotch had emerged, overshadowing the redness of the cold.

'Tie up the boats,' she shouted. Sobbing and not stopping to put on her headscarf she ran towards the house, angrily brushing away the hair blowing wildly in her face.

'Lenora?' Edouard was standing in the hall.

'Yes, dear,' she took a deep breath, relieved that he couldn't see the state of her. She swept back her hair and lifted her wet skirt to look at it. Her husband was the one person she had not wanted to see at this moment.

'What happened? Where is Charles?'

'He is seeing to the boat. It belongs to Jonathan. The storm had broken its moorings. I was wrong, there was nobody in it.' The words tumbled out as she hurried towards the stairs.

'Are you all right? You sound upset.'

'No, it's just that I'm cold and wet. I must change. I'll see you presently.'

That evening at the dinner table, Charles' eyes searched hers repeatedly. Lenora couldn't bear the sight of him and stubbornly looked away. She'd carefully avoided him all day, overwhelmed by the heavy feeling of embarrassment which filled her, and the guilt, which tormented her. There had been moments when she'd felt her breathing increase rapidly, putting pressure on her chest.

When she left the dining room she was alarmed to find that Charles had followed her out, 'We must talk.'

'There's nothing to say.'

'Yes, there is, I love you Lenora. I know you feel the same. You can't hide your feelings.'

She glanced towards the dining room door, 'I don't

know how I feel, so how can you? You must consider that I'm your uncle's wife.'

Charles stepped closer, forcing her up against the wall, his hands on her waist, his lips seeking hers.

Lenora turned her face away and his kiss landed on her cheek. She suppressed a cry, Edouard was blind, but his hearing was excellent, 'You must leave this house. You can't stay.'

Charles' face expressed his shock, 'You can't mean that!'

'I do. I can't betray Edouard.'

'So, you admit that you're attracted to me.'

'I've never said that,' she blushed.

'Not in so many words. My uncle need never find out.'

'You must leave. Let go of me.' She pushed him away.

'I can't. What excuse do I have to give him? He's expecting me to stay for a considerable time.' Charles had hold of her wrist.

'You're hurting my arm.' His grip loosened slightly but he still held on.

Why does he make it so hard for me? she thought. If only he would listen. She was trying to do what she knew was right. Forcefully, she shook her arm free, 'You'll have to think of an excuse. I won't tell your uncle about this, it would upset him too much. Now go to him. Please!'

On her return to the dining room, she placed the cheeseboard on the table without a glance at Charles, her hand trembling slightly. She handed the port to Edouard, who poured a glass and passed the decanter to his nephew.

'This is your chance to try this vintage. It's the bottle from last Sunday, but you didn't want it then. One shouldn't keep port too long once it has been opened. Let's toast you being here!' Edouard held up his glass. 'It's pleasant for Lenora to have someone her own age around. Don't you agree?' He turned towards his wife and although she didn't answer, he continued, 'You must stay as long as you like, Charles.'

Charles did nothing to hide his amusement, his eyes twinkled as he stared back at her.

Lenora looked down at her plate. Please, don't make it difficult for me, Edouard, she thought. You couldn't have chosen a worse time, Charles has the nerve to take pleasure in this. She was aware that her expression was one of disdain as she lifted her head and returned his stare, her port glass remained on the table, as she'd no intention of toasting Charles' stay, 'Haven't you got something to tell Edouard?' she asked.

'Oh yes, Uncle. I did mention this to Lenora earlier. I do want to see Edinburgh. You and father have a cousin there. I would like to go and see him and his family. I thought I would leave in a couple of days.'

'Cousin Frederic! I doubt he's still alive.'

'Maybe not. But he'll have family and I intend to seek them out.'

'I won't stand in your way of course, but you must spend Christmas here.'

'I'm not sure, Uncle, I don't want to overstay my welcome.' His eyes strayed to Lenora.

'Nonsense! At Christmas, you must be here. I won't hear of anything else. Now that's settled.'

Charles threw an inquisitive glance at Lenora, who looked away. She knew to her dismay that she wouldn't be able to change Edouard's mind, once it was made up. And what excuse did she have to do so?

Chapter 16

Lakeside House, later that evening, November 1902

The dressing gown slid off her shoulders and crumpled into a half circle on the floor by her feet. The flickering candles sent light across the pale skin of her naked body and gave it a sheen, which reflected back at her from the full-length mirror. She lifted her hair and touched, with her finger tips, the places on her neck where Charles' lips had caressed her. Her touch made them burn again and a ripple surged through her body. She cupped her full breasts in her hands and let her fingers move down to her waist, still feeling Charles' firm grip. It startled her for she realised that what she had most wanted was for him to hold her close.

In just over a week's time it would be her twenty-ninth birthday. What would it be like to have a man's body against hers? Would it happen to her one day? It was something she had yet to experience. A voice whispered to her, Charles wants you. You can have it. Why wait? Charles wants you...

What possessed her to have these thoughts? She stooped down and picked up her dressing gown, sweeping it around her shoulders. She'd never looked at her body in this way before. She blushed and nervously looked around the room, as if expecting to be found out doing something she should not, and embarrassed stepped back from the mirror. All this was Charles' fault, he was putting these thoughts into her head. She was glad he was leaving, if only Edouard hadn't insisted that he should come back for Christmas.

Charles must be punished for what he'd done, she couldn't allow this insolent behaviour to continue. Edouard had always behaved as a gentleman and such was his devotion that he had given up his mistress to offer her his home and security. It would have been against his principles to continue the affair, even though his marriage to her was in name only. A mistress and a wife would not have been acceptable in the circles in which he moved.

When her attitude towards Charles had changed and she'd treated him with greater kindness, he had at first responded like a gentleman and she'd enjoyed his company. But after the boat trip he'd dropped all pretence. All along it had been a charade, she was sure of that now. She was a lady and his uncle's wife and he didn't show her respect. He treated her like a loose woman. Was that what she'd become? Anger rose in her. She'd behaved properly at all times, except when she had jumped out of the boat. Charles had kissed her and, for a second, she'd kissed him back. But that was all and only because she'd been taken by surprise. What was it he'd said that he could read in her face? When the answer became clear to her, she whispered, 'This madness has to stop.'

Lenora held on firmly to the banister as she made her way downstairs, she'd spent most of the following day in her room to avoid Charles, but now she would have to endure one more evening with him. He was due to leave in the morning after an early breakfast. George would take him to the station in Kendal.

In the dining room, Edouard and Charles were already seated. She knew that her face betrayed her anger and merely gave Charles a slight nod before taking her seat. Edouard had insisted that Molly should cook a special farewell dinner, giving Lenora more time to spend with them; she would have preferred not to.

'We're sorry to see you go, are we not, Lenora?' Edouard frowned as he turned his face towards her. From his demeanour, she could tell that he had sensed a change in her.

She avoided answering directly, 'I'm sure Charles will enjoy his visit to Edinburgh and change of scenery,' she replied.

'I shall be sorry too,' Charles looked straight at her. 'I've enjoyed my visit here more than you can imagine. I'll be back to spend Christmas with you.'

'No need to hurry back, if we see you here on the twenty-third of December, that will suit very well,' Lenora said.

'Lenora!' Edouard's voice rose. 'What do you mean, dearest? Charles is welcome back when he so wishes.'

'Of course, dear, I meant no offence. I want Charles to know that if he finds his stay in Edinburgh agreeable, there's no need for him to return sooner.'

'Forgive me, it was your voice that misled me,' Edouard frowned.

'No offence taken. I do understand perfectly.' Charles stared back at her with a wry smile on his lips.

Lenora remained silent for most of the dinner. The conversation was kept up by the two men. Her husband did his best to draw her in but failed. As soon as Molly had removed the dessert plates, she made her excuse, 'I'm so sorry but I do have a slight headache. If you will excuse me, I shall retire now.'

'That explains it, my dear. I was worried about you,' Edouard said.

She turned to Charles, 'I may not see you in the morning, so I will say good-bye now. I wish you a pleasant journey and stay in Edinburgh with your cousins.'

Lenora crossed to her husband's chair and leaned over to kiss his forehead, 'I'll not come and read for you tonight, dearest. George is here to collect Molly, I'll ask him to see to your fire before they leave.' She left the room.

As she moved up the staircase, she found that Charles had followed and was a few steps behind her. She turned around in alarm, 'Charles!'

'Please, Lenora,' he begged. 'I cannot leave you like this. Your face is hard and your eyes are cold, I cannot bear to see them so.'

Lenora's eyes widened when she saw tears in his eyes and genuine sorrow on his face. She was too stunned to stop him when he reached out for her hand. He gently turned it over to show the palm and let his lips brush her fingertips. His voice was soft as he whispered, 'Forgive me, Lenora, for what I saw in your face is no longer there.'

'What did you see in my face?' she asked stiffly.

'I thought I saw love in your eyes.'

'You were wrong, Charles.' Without another word, she turned and with a straight back climbed the stairs. On the landing, she paused for a moment and looked down to where he stood, his head bowed.

By the time she'd closed the bedroom door, her heart was beating hard. Had she been wrong about him? She had to admit that she could be. After much agony, the answer came to her; deep down, she wanted to believe him. His apology had been sincere and the look in his eyes couldn't be faked. What was she to do? In frustration, she threw herself on the bed, beating her pillow with her fists, tears streaming down her cheeks.

Chapter 17

5th December 1902

'Lenora, I worry about you; another headache last night. But your steps seem lighter this morning. Am I right?'

'Yes, I'm well now.' She kissed Edouard's forehead, and to her surprise he gripped her hand firmly and didn't let go.

'I'm pleased. I wonder what your thoughts were about Charles leaving; he's been gone almost a week and you haven't mentioned him. I'm not at all sure that you two got on?' He lifted his head up to her.

She looked into his eyes, they were not focussing on hers. It made it easier to lie. 'We'll have to do without his company for a while. Of course, it's a shame, but it was his wish. Charles has come all the way from Canada, so naturally he wanted to visit his relations. And he'll be back for Christmas, as you requested.'

'Don't you?'

'I want what you want, dearest. But now, I find it's good to be the two of us, like it was before he came.'

'Come closer,' Edouard pulled her towards him, 'I have something I must say to you.' He paused and his grip on her hand remained firm, 'I love you with all my heart, and it does me good to hear you say that. I gave my word to your parents to take care of you and I intend to keep it. But

I wonder if it was right to marry you. You should have the company of younger people and a husband your own age.' Edouard sighed deeply, his shoulders slumped and his face drawn.

'Dear, dear Edouard, you must not have regrets.' Lenora fell onto her knees and rested her head in his lap, 'Hush! Don't fret, I am content.'

'Content! But are you happy?' He stroked her hair with his free hand.

'Yes, I want for nothing.'

'If you're sure, dearest?'

She stood up and nodded absent-mindedly; she had meant every word she'd said. She was pleased to be alone with him, relieved that now she needn't worry about what Charles would whisper or his touch, which would send tremors through her and to be free of the pressure his closeness brought. It would give her time to sort out her mixed feelings. She was fighting Charles but at the same time drawn to him. She had to do what was right for her husband and giving in to Charles was not. She would have no peace until she'd sorted out the confused thoughts which filled her head.

She swallowed hard, Edouard had sensed her unhappiness, he was an intelligent man and sensitive to her mood. She vowed to reassure him that she loved him and was happy as his wife.

Edouard took hold of the armrests and heaved himself out of the chair, 'It's your birthday tomorrow. I've not forgotten. We shall celebrate and go to Kendal for the day.'

'I would like that very much, but I'll be just as happy if we spend it at home quietly. We can celebrate next year, when it's my thirtieth. We could invite our friends.'

'Too many quiet days! I've already arranged it with George.'

Lenora's gaze followed him as he made his way across the room, his cane making no sound on the huge carpet, only heard as it hit the wooden floor. A wave of tenderness swept over her.

When the door shut behind him, she felt her smile fade and she stared vacantly in front of her. He can't see me smile, but he can sense it. But she had lied and lied.

'Could he sense that as well?' Her stomach churned as she asked the question out loud, as if she thought the walls would answer. 'Could he?' But she received no reply.

Oak Tree Cottage, Cumbria 6th December 2005

Ellen whispered, 'I lied about Charles, I lied.' She sat up with a jerk; these were not her words! Oh my God, an inner voice was filling her head: Lenora's words. She opened her eyes. She was at the cottage, and above her was the white ceiling of her bedroom. She glanced at the clock on her bedside table, it was morning. Oh my God, what was she doing here? Why had she left Lakeside House? Lenora was still with her. This was a horrible mistake, she shouldn't be here. Lenora's voice was in her head, her thoughts blending with her own. She couldn't separate them.

'Calm, Lenora, calm, I can't help you with your thoughts. They must be yours alone, I can't have them!' she wanted to scream, but it stuck in her throat, the words came out in a whisper. Touching her temples, she tried to channel her thoughts. Please take them back, Lenora! Please take them back.

Ellen threw herself onto the pillow, she closed her eyes and took several deep breaths to calm down. The events of the past few days passed in front of her. She felt *sure* that there was a message for her. If so, it wasn't clear. What could it be? It was all too much! She had to take Lenora back to the house.

Lenora had stayed quiet for a moment, but she knew she was still there. Did she hear me? Did Lenora have her thoughts? She couldn't tell.

She stumbled out of bed and pushed the switch on her bedside lamp. Nothing happened, no light. Bother; a fuse gone. Oh, please, not now! She couldn't cope with this. She didn't have a clue how to fix it, she didn't even know where the fuse box was. She fumbled around in the dark for the candle she knew was on the desk and lit it.

'All right, all right, Lenora. Stop! You are confusing me.'

What date was it? How long had she been away? How could she think clearly with Lenora occupying her mind? She had to get rid of her, back to the house, it was the only way. She glanced round, the cottage looked unlived in. It was cold, and she shivered as she pulled on her thick jumper. She'd hardly spent any time here. Was there any milk? The fridge smelt of cheese when she opened it. She unscrewed the top and sniffed the milk bottle. It smelt OK. What she needed was a cup of tea, but there was no electricity. She took a sip and grimaced. It was off, she spat it out. Where had she put the mobile?

'I said all right, Lenora, I'm doing my best.'

Where was it? She'd always left it in the cottage, when she went to the house, no point bringing it there. Oh yes, in the drawer of the bedside table, she pulled it out. No charge. Oh, damn! Probably had lots of messages, she hadn't checked them for days. And now she couldn't even leave the phone to charge. It couldn't be helped, she'd read them when she got back, she'd only be gone for one more night. She was due back in Bristol on the fifth. That had to be soon. If only she knew what date it was now.

'All right, Lenora. All right!' She screamed, 'For God's sake, I am hurrying!' Mustn't stay here any longer; Lenora being with her was a huge mistake, she wanted to be at Lakeside House. There must be a reason for this mix up, but she didn't know what that was.

Her car was parked on the grass verge outside the cottage, there was a thin layer of frost on the windscreen. The car parked at the cottage next to hers had a heavy coating. She must have got back in the early hours of the morning, but she'd no idea how she got here. It was a terrifying thought.

Lakeside House

Lenora took over as soon as she stepped inside the door. George stood in the hall, dressed in his heavy coat and woollen hat.

'We've been waiting for you, Miss Lenora. Gladys and the carriage are ready.'

'Go and see Molly. She'll give you a cup of tea. I'll be back directly.' Lenora made for the stairs but stopped as Edouard came into the hall.

'Where have you been? I told you we'd leave for Kendal after breakfast.'

'I'm sorry, I took a short walk down to the lake. It's such a sunny pleasant morning. I've admired the frost on the trees, they glint like silver in the sunlight. The woods are stunning and the lake takes my breath away. I had to see it. It is not to be missed.'

'Your appreciation of nature is a gift, 'Edouard smiled. 'Your description is so vivid I can see it through your eyes. Thank you, I'm glad. George told me that the roads are clear, only a dusting of snow. Now hurry, dear. I'll wait here.'

Edouard is the dearest of men, she thought, as she quickly changed into a warm but smart town dress. It would be a pleasant change to go to Kendal with him. She was excited and looked forward to it. She'd not been to the shops for a long time; she needed a new fur hat and perhaps she would get material for a dress. Edouard was a generous man and wouldn't let her spend much of the legacy her parents had left her, and it remained mostly untouched. But today she'd use some to buy his Christmas present and those for George and Molly. What about Charles? They would have to buy him a gift as well, and it would have to come from both of them. She hadn't thought of Charles all day and that pleased her; she would not do so again today.

Chapter 18

George watched as his master climbed into the carriage unaided and extended his hand to Miss Lenora, assisting her up. He held Gladys firmly; the horse was lively in anticipation of the outing and pulled impatiently at the reins. 'Easy girl, easy girl,' he soothed. He added more hay to her nose bag, just enough to give him time to tuck in the sheepskin rug around his master and young wife. George had much respect for his employer; he had worked at Lakeside House for over thirty years and he knew him to be the best of men, honourable in everything he did, a good master and someone you could trust. He remembered his devotion to his first wife and his grief when she died. Now he showed the same devotion to Miss Lenora, who had always been good to him, although Molly said that at times the mistress could be moody and impatient. Not right, she'd said, for a young girl to be shut up in this house with an old man. Molly had clicked her tongue and shaken her head. Well, Molly could be wrong. When he'd tucked in the sheepskin rug, he'd noticed his master's firm grip of his wife's gloved hand.

Since his blindness, his master had come to depend on him more and he now assisted him with personal matters. He had his trust and that made him proud. George pulled his eyebrows together: young Charles, now that was another matter. Could he be trusted? He wasn't sure.

His own marriage to Molly had been one of convenience, but it worked well. They were both happy and had grown fond of each other. They did dilly-dally in the bedroom, now and again, when it took his fancy. Molly was always obliging.

The same wasn't happening at Lakeside House, he was sure of that; he'd been long enough in the household to know. This was why Molly clicked her tongue and shook her head. Well, it was none of his business and shouldn't be of concern to Molly either.

He slowed Gladys down as they entered Kendal and he could hear Lenora's excited voice as they stopped in front of Jennings & Jennings. Known to be select, it was the town's most expensive jewellery shop, owned by two brothers. A week ago he had been sent to the shop with a letter, to give notice of their coming visit.

He watched his master and young wife enter the shop and prepared to wait until they came out with their purchase. He adjusted the nosebag with oats for Gladys and stroked her muzzle. It was a cold day, so he covered her with the horse blanket. He was warm enough himself in his woollen trousers and heavy twill jacket.

Chapter 19

Lenora held her breath and stared down at the polished mahogany counter; displayed on a tray covered with red velvet was a diamond necklace, on another lay one with diamonds and rubies, but the one which caught her attention was the necklace with sapphires. Her breath quickened: it was exquisite, a large sapphire hung in the middle and, to either side, two slightly smaller stones; on the sides of these, the stones gradually grew smaller. 'May I hold it?' She whispered.

'Certainly, Mrs Villiers, we can do better than that.' Mr Jennings beckoned to the assistant, who came forward with a mirror.

Lenora stood erect, hardly breathing, as Mr Jennings placed it around her neck. It was so beautiful, she'd never owned anything so lovely before. It would suit her blue velvet dress perfectly. She turned to her husband, 'Oh Edouard.'

'I can hear that you're delighted with this one. You shall have it.'

'It looks stunning on your wife, as if it were made for her. We do have a matching bracelet,' Mr Jennings ventured.

'Then we shall have it too.'

'Oh Edouard, are you sure? I'm perfectly happy with the necklace.'

'Nonsense! If there is a matching bracelet you shall have it. Of course.'

'But I've not even seen it…' Lenora's voice died away as the jewellery was put in front of her.

'Guard these with your life.' Edouard joked as he handed the small packages to George outside the shop.

'I will that.' George nodded knowingly as he tucked them into the inside pocket of his coat.

'Now take us to the Emporium.'

Lenora bought the fur hat she wanted: black mink and ridiculously expensive. The necklace had put her in a frivolous mood and she chose a cherry red silk for her new dress, which she intended to wear at Christmas. She reminded Edouard that he needed more of the detachable collars and cuffs for his shirts. When they passed a male mannequin dressed in an outfit with a brocade waistcoat, she persuaded him that it would be suitable for the New Year's Eve party.

Lunch followed at the Station Hotel and Lenora asked Edouard to stay in the lounge with a coffee and cognac, whilst she ventured out alone to buy his gift. He had protested, saying that he also needed to buy her a Christmas present. She had managed to assure him that the bracelet would serve as such. It was more than enough.

George brought her back to Jennings & Jennings, where she bought a pair of cufflinks in gold. Edouard had been pleased that she'd thought of a gift for Charles and they had agreed to buy him a pocket watch of good quality. Mr Jennings had bowed her out of the shop with a huge smile.

That night, Lenora prepared herself before she went to her husband's bedroom. She'd brought hot water to her room and she flannelled her body. She brushed her hair until it shone and let it flow down the back of her lace nightgown;

the prettiest of them all, she'd worn it to bed on her wedding night. She'd known where to find it; at the bottom of the chest, underneath her carefully folded wedding gown. She took the sapphire necklace out of its box, she'd wear it now. Edouard wouldn't see it, but he could feel it, and her preparations would give her the confidence she needed for what she was about to do.

Lenora found her husband sitting up in bed, a candle on his bedside table. The fire burnt well, so not to dirty her gown she carefully added more coal to it, she wanted it to last. She didn't kiss his forehead as usual but leaned forward and placed a kiss on his lips.

'My dear...!' Edouard voice was loud, his hand touched his mouth, 'You've surprised me!'

'Edouard, tonight I've come to you as your wife.' Lenora stood in front of the fire as she removed her nightgown, the shadow of her naked body sculptured against the wall. She was wearing only the sapphire necklace. The flickering flames danced across her ivory skin, sending sparks off the blue stones.

'What do you mean?'

Lenora sat on the side of his bed, 'I'm not fulfilling all my wifely duties.'

'You're a most devoted wife, I couldn't wish for more.'

Lenora took his hand and held it against the sapphire necklace. 'Feel this, I'm wearing the necklace. I've had a wonderful birthday today.'

Edouard's hand moved around the stones, feeling them one by one, his hand brushing up against her bare neck, 'It must look very beautiful on you, dearest.' His voice was low and trembling.

'Could you really not wish for more?' Lenora took his hand and moving it down, she cupped it around her bare breast.

'Lenora!' Edouard's hand moved down her body until it rested on the small mound of her stomach, 'You're naked!' He couldn't hide the astonishment in his voice and he withdrew his hand sharply. His face showed bewilderment.

'Yes, let me warm you.' She reached for his hand again, 'It's your right as my husband.'

He took her hand, steering it away from her breast, his face distorted. 'Lenora, my dear child, I've thought about you as the daughter I never had, for too long to have any other thoughts. I've failed you, this proves it. I cannot offer you what you want, even if I felt so inclined.'

Lenora knew that she'd made a terrible mistake; embarrassment welled up inside her. What had she done? 'But the necklace, you've never spent so much money on a gift for me,' she stammered.

'Oh, dear Lord, did you think that's why I gave it to you?' Edouard had tears in his eyes.

'No, not precisely, but I felt that I should repay you in some way and you did say you loved me yesterday.'

'The necklace was my way to make up for my failings, not yours and not this. I'm considerably older than you, one day you'll remarry.'

'Hush, don't speak so.' Tears were running down her cheeks.

'Please, Lenora, put your gown back on. I should have been honest with you before we married. I wish I could turn back the clock.'

How she wished that she could do so as well and that this hour had never happened. But a slow anger rose in her; it wasn't entirely her fault. There was truth in what Edouard had said, she'd done her best, and she wanted to explain.

'Yes, feel this nightgown, Edouard, it's so pretty, I wore it on our wedding night. I sat in bed and waited a long time, but you didn't come. I waited many nights, but you never came. So, I put it away. There were times when you'd been especially attentive; I would bring it out again and wait. But it has long stayed forgotten until tonight.'

'I always thought you loved me as a father.' Edouard was

deeply distressed and tried to show restraint.

'Yes, I have done so.'

'Then this would be wrong, Lenora.' His voice rose and became harsh.

'Yes, I can see that now. I'm sorry, I've made you angry.'

'No, I'm not angry with you. More so with myself. Please, go now. Leave me alone, I'm so very tired.'

Chapter 20

Oak Tree Cottage, Cumbria, 6th December 2005

Ellen opened the door to Oak Tree Cottage, it was nearly midnight, but she'd have to fix the fuse and charge her mobile before she went to bed. Automatically her hand went to the light switch and to her surprise the light came on. Strange, but wait, when she'd left in the morning it had still been dark and the streetlight had not been on, so it had not been a fuse, it had been a power cut.

Good, the heating had come on in her absence, the cottage was reasonably warm. It had been an awful day at Lakeside House. Lenora had returned to her bedroom with tears in her eyes, humiliated, but also relieved by Edouard's rejection. Her devotion to her husband had made her do what she'd thought was right. But Lenora's frustration had increased; she felt worse than ever. Was there no solution?

Ellen stopped abruptly, Lenora's twenty-ninth birthday was on the sixth of December. Today. But it was also her twenty-ninth. Was that a coincidence? How could she have forgotten her own birthday? Crazy!

Oh God, she should have gone back to Bristol yesterday, to be there today. That was why her subconscious mind had brought her back to the cottage the night before. Now she understood why this had happened. She had thought it strange at the time, she should have gone to her home instead of returning to the house. But then she remembered, she couldn't have done, she had to take Lenora back.

As soon as her mobile was charged, she found several missed calls. The first one was from Annie, who sounded rather cross: Where are you? I'd arranged a surprise party for you tonight. Your Mum and Dad came from Oxford, they are staying at your flat and only left here an hour ago. Liz and Fred were here, as were Kim and Jane, and Moira.

Ellen didn't listen to the end but carried on to the next message, it was from her mother, who sounded frantic: Your father is ready to drive up there if we don't hear from you by tomorrow.

She called back at once, 'It's me, Mum. Sorry, if you've gone to bed, and sorry about the party, but I thought I'd better...'

'Thank God! Where have you been? Why haven't you called?' Her mother interrupted.

'I couldn't. I've been walking the fells, only just got back. You and Dad should do it. It's so beautiful. But no mobile signal.'

'We've tried to contact you for days. And you can't have been walking in the dark.'

'I've been away for two nights with a group of walkers from the village. We had a meal and drinks at the pub when we came back. We've walked in places you wouldn't believe existed, so isolated. No signal.'

'That doesn't account for the rest of the time,' her mother insisted, 'what are you up to? Annie seemed cagey when she talked about your stay at the Lakes. Is there something you're not telling us?'

Ellen's thoughts raced; she had to come up with something plausible, 'Actually, I've met someone, and I've been to York with him as well, so I haven't been here much.'

'I knew it! What's his name?'

'Charles,' she answered.

'What does he look like?'

'Well,' Ellen started, 'he's two years younger than me actually.'

'Oh, so you've got a toy boy!'

'Hardly, Mum,' she sighed, typical of her mum to make fun of it. 'Anyway, he's pleasant looking, good company and he takes care of himself.'

'What does he do?'

'Nothing at the moment, Mum, he's visiting.'

It struck her that she'd no idea what Charles did in Canada. She'd never heard him talk about work. 'He comes from Canada, his father emigrated there before he was born. He'll be going back eventually, he's only here to spend time with relatives and look around the country.'

'Oh, that's a pity, if you really like him. But you could still have called, Ellen.'

'I wanted to spend my birthday with Charles, he came on the walk as well, and I forgot my mobile at the cottage.'

'Surely Charles has one?'

'Yes, but I didn't know that you were so anxious about me.'

'We had a surprise waiting for you. We were so disappointed that you weren't here, but more important that you're all right. We can't wait for you, darling, got to get back to Oxford, your dad has an early appointment Monday morning. I have watered your plants and there are quite a few letters for you, mostly birthday cards. I've put them on the sideboard. But it'll soon be Christmas and we'll see you then. Be sure to get in touch with Annie now.'

'Yes Mum, right away.'

Bristol, 7th December 2005

Ellen threw the car keys on the plate on the sideboard and glanced at two piles of letters by the side of it. She smiled, her mother had separated the birthday cards from the bills.

She hadn't called Annie the evening before but had done so from the service station on the M6. Annie had asked her over in the late afternoon: If you're not too tired, she'd said. Plenty of food left over from last night and I've saved a piece of your birthday cake.

It would have been rude to refuse, and she didn't have any food in the fridge, although she probably had a pizza in the freezer. Also, it was an opportunity to talk about the new orders they had received for Christmas.

She sank down on the settee, on the coffee table lay a parcel wrapped in birthday paper and a card from her mum and dad. She looked up at the painting of Lakeside House. What have *you* brought me? Another life? Already she felt a strong pull, she wanted to be there right now. Ellen returned her attention to the parcel and tore off the paper; it contained a large selection of her favourite brand of cosmetics. Yeah, that was OK. She would open the rest of her presents later, she had to get ready to drive over to her friends.

Ellen rang the doorbell and Annie opened the door, 'We've been worried.'

'I know,' Ellen interrupted, 'I've heard it all from Mum.'

'Shame you missed your party, but we had a good time without you. It wasn't completely wasted. Your mum was knocking them back, I think it was nerves. She was frantic with worry.' Annie's face was serious, accusing. 'She cheered up after a few,' she added, when Ellen frowned.

'So, you didn't really miss me. What was all the fuss about then?' Ellen forced a smile.

'Of course, we missed you, silly cow. Come on in. It's only Ken here. It's all ready. I thought you needed cheering up after your spell of depression.'

'What depression?' Her voice was sharp.

'Oh, I meant the break-up from Pete and what happened in the Lakes. You know, the house you saw. But that's all over now, isn't it?' Annie's eyes were probing and didn't leave hers, waiting for an answer.

Ellen made an effort to sound cheerful, but her smile was strained; Annie was still having doubts and Ellen wasn't happy that her friend had brought this up again.

'Oh, that's in the past. I'm absolutely fine. I don't believe I had depression. But the rest has done me the world of good.' She was irritated but tried not to show her annoyance, and when she saw the spread on the table her face lit up, 'Annie, you've gone to a lot of trouble. That looks good. Thank you.'

'Good enough to eat,' Ken jumped up from his armchair and hugged her, 'And it's great to see you, Ellen.'

Annie smiled at her, 'You're worth it. I asked your mum and dad to stay but they had to get back. When I told them about the party, they assumed they could stay with you. So, I gave them the spare key to your place. You don't mind, do you?'

'Of course not, they are my parents.'

'Now tell us about the new man in your life.'

'Oh, Mum has told you.'

'Yes, she called before they left this morning. To thank us for the party.'

'I see. Well it's nothing serious, he'll be going back to Canada soon.'

'You went to York with him.'

Ellen nodded. Bother! Mum hasn't left much out, she thought.

'What hotel did you stay in?' Ken asked.

'We stayed at a pub.' She was taken aback, she hadn't expected questions.

'Which one? I know York quite well,' Ken said.

'Oh,' Ellen blushed, 'I can't remember.'

'Can't remember? He must have been good,' Annie joked.

'I think it was the Red Lion,' Ellen stammered. 'We wandered around a bit, to be honest we didn't see much of York.'

‘That confirms it,’ Annie smirked.

‘I see, you didn’t visit the Viking Centre then?’ Ken asked.

‘No, I didn’t know there was one.’

‘I thought everyone knew. It’s well known. Pity, it’s worth a visit,’ Ken looked at her thoughtfully.

‘I’ll fetch what’s left of the cake.’ Annie disappeared into the kitchen.

‘Not that it’s any of my business, but I don’t think you’ve been to York. What’s up, Ellen? I know you well enough. I won’t say anything to Annie.’

Before Ellen had time to answer, Annie reappeared carrying a plate with a quarter piece of birthday cake.

It was raining when Ellen left and she ran to the car, covering her head with her coat. Ken hadn’t asked any more awkward questions and she’d enjoyed herself in spite of her friends’ curiosity. Her only regret was the lies she’d told.

At home she picked up the post, still on the sideboard, she hadn’t had time to open any letters before she rushed off to Ken and Annie’s. There were eleven birthday cards in all. With a slight flutter, she recognised the writing on one of them, it was from Pete, her ex. She tore open the envelope, it was a neutral card, he wished her a happy birthday, that was all. There were no little xxxs after his name, like there used to be.

She sighed, it was good of him to think of her, they had parted friends once the finances were sorted. She had contributed to the mortgage and bills, so after the house was sold the surplus had been shared. It had made it possible to buy this house.

She placed her cards on the mantelpiece and took a step back to look at them but instead raised her eyes to the painting and her thoughts to the people at the house. How will Lenora treat Charles when he gets back? Does he really love her? He’ll be a huge temptation now that she’s sure about Edouard's feelings. Perhaps Lenora should go for it. It would make life at Lakeside House enormously interesting and do her the world of good, she was twenty-nine and no sex in her life.

Ellen moved away from the painting. Tomorrow she'd call in at the shop and take a look at the order book. As soon as her sketches were done, she could return to the Lakes. Maison Elle closed for Christmas on the twenty-first, but if she worked hard she could leave before then. The most difficult task would be to tell her mum that she wouldn't be home for Christmas, it couldn't wait much longer, she'd have to do it at the latest next week.

'But, Ellen, you must come, what will your father say?' her mother wailed.

'I'm sorry, Mum, but my mind is made up. I'm a grown woman and make my own decisions. I want to spend Christmas at the cottage.'

'With Charles? You can bring him home.'

'No Mum, it's not that serious a relationship that I want to introduce him to the family.'

'We promise not to read anything into it.'

'It's final, Mum, please don't make me cross. Bye.' Ellen heard her mother's deep sigh as she put down the phone and it made her feel guilty. She redialled her mother's number, 'I am sorry, Mum, didn't mean to say it like that. I will drive by Oxford on my way to the Lakes. Of course, I want to see you and Dad before Christmas.'

There was a moment's silence before her mother answered, 'I am so glad, darling. We'll love to see you, and we'll give you your presents then.'

Ellen understood her parents' disappointment and she would be with them at Christmas in the future. But this year she simply had to spend it at Lakeside House.

Chapter 21

Lakeside House, December 1902

When Lenora had opened the letter to read to Edouard, her heart had taken a leap, as she had seen that it came from Charles, announcing his arrival for Christmas. In an instant, she knew that she'd missed him; he'd been gone for three weeks and she'd longed for his return.

Life had been dull at Lakeside House since he'd left, especially as Edouard had treated her differently. She resolved to improve her life.

Lenora thought back to her birthday, that was when everything had changed. She'd been hurt and humiliated by her husband's rejection, and for a few days Edouard had behaved in a formal manner towards her. Once, he had even pulled back when she had come too close, and that had never happened before. It had irritated her and made it difficult to feel the same loyalty towards him. But it pleased her that Edouard's attitude had softened and most of his warmth had returned, but for her it could not be the same.

Lenora was unable to hide her cheerfulness when she opened the front door to Charles. She could see that it surprised and pleased him, he kissed her hand and held it for too long. She made no attempt to withdraw it, her cheeks flushed, 'Welcome, Charles.'

Edouard nodded, 'Yes, indeed, I'm pleased you're here and in time to help with the tree. Lenora looks forward to decorating it. It makes her happy, she's fond of Christmas. George will bring in the trees.' He pointed to a corner of the hall, 'We'll have the tallest one over there. But we'll do that later. Now, I'm sure you want to freshen up after the journey, Charles, and lunch will be ready.'

'Yes, Uncle, it's good to be back.' But he wasn't looking at Edouard, his eyes were questioning Lenora. He wanted to confirm that what her eyes were telling him was true; he wanted to be sure of what he now believed to be possible.

'I won't take long, I'll see you soon.' His words were directed to Lenora and he turned to look at her as he walked up the stairs.

'It's not straight, George.' Lenora pointed to the angel at the top of the tree.

'Is that better, Miss Lenora?' George balanced on the ladder as he adjusted it.

'Yes, much, thank you. We still have the second tree to dress in the other room, but it's much smaller, I'm sure that Charles and I can manage.'

Charles nodded; he was holding on to the ladder whilst George climbed down. 'Shall we do it now?' he asked eagerly.

'George, please take the tree and decorations through to next door. Also ask Molly to bring tea and my husband to join us.'

'Right away, Miss Lenora.'

'More tea, dearest?' Lenora asked Edouard a short time later, after they were seated in the drawing room.

'No, thank you, I'll sit here whilst you and Charles dress the tree. You can tell me what it looks like, as you go along, as you usually do.' Edouard put his cup down.

Lenora carefully removed the delicate baubles, the candle holders and tinsel from the box and placed them on the table.

'Are you ready, Charles?'

Charles jumped up, his eyes bright. He took hold of a bundle of tinsel and stepped onto the ladder, 'Where shall I put these?' He stood on tiptoe as she instructed him and let the tinsel fall in a ripple down the sides of the tree.

'This large bauble should go at the top, I'll hand it to you.' As she reached out, his hand rested on hers for moments too long. But she didn't pull away, instead she lifted up her face to him. She saw the question in his eyes and as she passed the next one, he didn't let go of her hand. She nodded her agreement. His face was alight with excitement, his mouth soundlessly formed her name and then he quickly glanced over at his uncle.

Edouard had fallen asleep in the armchair and Charles didn't waste the moment, he bent down and took her face with both hands balancing on the ladder, he kissed her quickly but fully on the lips.

'Oh Lenora, what made you change your mind?' he whispered.

Lenora put a finger to her lips, where his kiss still burnt, and she wanted him to kiss her again, 'Too much to tell you now. Later!' She pulled away, as the door opened, and Molly came in to remove the tea tray.

This woke Edouard, who sat up; 'Have you finished the tree? I must have nodded off. By the way, Lenora, have you told Charles about the Christmas Eve service tomorrow? George will have Gladys ready and take us to church. He and Molly will come with us.'

'No, I didn't know? Do you expect me to come?' Charles asked surprised.

'It would be proper to do so,' Lenora answered.

'Yes, it's customary to accompany our servants to

church on Christmas Eve. It's a good tradition, Molly and George wouldn't be pleased if we gave it up.'

Charles tried to take her hand in front of her husband, but Lenora frowned and shook her head. For the remaining day and evening he constantly sought her eyes, in an effort to resume the intimacy from earlier, but Lenora carefully avoided any further contact.

That night when Lenora came out of Edouard's room, she found Charles waiting by the open door to her bedroom, he was wearing his night robe. At the sight of him she stopped.

'Oh Charles, why are you here?' But she could see the answer in his eyes. 'No, I didn't expect this, Charles, it's too soon,' she protested.

Without speaking, he stepped forward and swept her up in his arms, 'You're not changing your mind now,' he murmured in her ear as he dropped her onto the bed.

She tried to sit up and as she did, Charles took hold of her nightgown, instead of lifting it over her head, she heard it rip as he roughly pulled it down over her shoulders, baring her breasts. He had removed his robe and stood in front of her, she'd never seen a naked man before. Her eyes travelled down his body until, embarrassed, she averted her eyes. Charles had followed her gaze, his face glowed and with a triumphant smile he yanked her gown down over her hips and discarded it. She covered her bare breasts with her hands as he stared down, his eyes travelling the length of her body before he fell upon her.

Loosening her hands, he pinned them by her sides; his mouth found her breasts and he kissed them, one by one, his tongue circling her nipples. Unintentionally, her body shuddered, a protest died on her lips. She couldn't remember parting her legs, but at the next moment he plunged into her. With her eyes staring wildly, she cried out in pain. He was unable to penetrate and thrust into her again, she saw the puzzlement on his face.

'Lie still,' he ordered, his whisper harsh. Aware of another sharp pain, she winced, stifling her cry. Now he'll stop, she thought, he wouldn't hurt her more.

He rose on his arms and his face was strained as he pulled back and forcefully thrust into her once more. He silenced the scream that escaped her, by pressing his hand down on her mouth, 'Don't...!'

Her open eyes stared up at his tense face in panic, but she nodded, her breath came in short bursts and tears flooded her eyes. She twisted her head to remove his hand, but Charles pressed down harder. When at last he took his hand away, his slumped body was heavy on hers.

Moments later, he slid off her and propped himself up on his elbow by her side. He looked at her curiously, 'A virgin, eh! You might've told me. Do you mean the old man hasn't lain with you? What do you do in his room every night?' His fingers circled her breasts.

Lenora turned her face away; she could not look at him, this had been unbearable and not what she'd expected.

'Leave me, Charles,' she ordered and fumbled for her nightgown.

His voice changed, it was low and soft, 'I'm sorry, Lenora, this didn't give you pleasure. If you'd told me, we could have done it differently.'

'Charles, I don't want you to do it anymore.' She pulled away from him.

He silenced her protest with a kiss, which was gentler than before.

'I promise I won't hurt you again. I will not do anything you don't like, but please let me show you how much pleasure I can give you.' He gently released her fingers from the nightgown, which she was clutching in her hand. She made a feeble attempt to protest, but the words would not form.

'Please, Lenora, I will stop the second you ask me. Please, let me...' He cupped her breasts in his hands and gently let his lips brush over them, barely touching. She closed her eyes and shivered as she felt her nipples stiffen and his hand moving over her body, leaving no part untouched.

She moaned as his mouth moved down; she'd never felt pleasure like this before.

'Don't stop, Charles,' she whispered, and as he continued, a sensation filled with pleasure swept through her like fire. The pain and hurt from earlier was gone.

'Do you want me now?' His voice was throaty and his breathing fast.

'Yes, I want you.' She squirmed as his body straddled hers and he gently parted her legs. This time was different, and the fire ripped through her again as he rode her slowly and deliberately.

The weight of his body was no longer on her and she opened her eyes. Charles stood by the bedside, pulling on his robe.

'What are you doing? Are you leaving?'

He nodded.

'But why? Don't leave me now, please stay.' She didn't recognise this pleading voice as her own.

He placed a kiss on her forehead, 'Not tonight, but this is only the beginning.' He left the room, closing the door behind him noiselessly.

She stayed in bed after he'd gone; she was exhausted, and she ached, but, in the end, it had been all she could have asked for. Never had she known that her body could give her so much pleasure, she stroked her flat stomach and found her way down to where she felt the soreness. It was wet and sticky, she brought her hand back and stared at the blood, frightened she jumped out of bed. There was blood on the sheet, but she calmed herself. Somewhere she'd heard that this was normal after the first time, she wasn't dying. She removed the sheet and stuffed it and her torn gown under the bed, she couldn't give these to Molly to launder. She washed herself in the freezing room with cold water and shivered as she put on a clean gown. Could Edouard have heard her muffled screams? Worried she tiptoed to his door and leaning into the room, she could hear his steady breathing. With a sigh of relief, she returned to her bedroom.

Christmas Eve 1902

Lenora woke up the next morning, instantly aware that she felt more alive and vibrant. Her face in the mirror smiled back at her; she was a woman now, she'd experienced what she'd longed for and it had changed her. She dressed in a hurry, today was a busy day, she would be working in the kitchen helping Molly with the preparations for Christmas Day. She should dress accordingly, but she didn't want Charles to see her in an old frock after last night. Instead, she chose a dress with a low-cut neckline. The nerves in her body jingled, knowing that she would have to face him at the breakfast table. What would she say to him? How should she behave? How would he behave? This was all new and exciting but, at the same time, frightening. How could she keep this from Edouard? He mustn't suspect.

Her heart leapt as Charles came into the dining room. She straightened her shoulders and looked him fully in the eyes. Her cheeks flushed when he held out his arms to form a circle in front of him and then brought his arms close to his chest indicating an embrace. His face was open, alert and happy, and apart from saying good morning, he didn't say anything at all, but to her amazement passed a note across the table in full view of Edouard.

She reached out and slid the note towards her, flipping it open, she read, Come to my room tonight. Warmth flushed thorough her body at the memory of the previous night and she nodded her reply.

'You're both very quiet. Is everything well?' Edouard asked.

'Yes, of course, Uncle, I am concentrating on my kipper, it's particularly bony,' Charles answered with a glance at her.

'Lenora, I take it you'll be spending the day with Molly, now that the provisions have arrived. George has his cup of tea with her about this time, I'll meet you in the kitchen presently and we can give them their Christmas gifts.'

'That's a good idea, Edouard. Yes, all is in order, but we have a lot to do. I'll not have time for my morning walk, so I'll be there soon.' She noticed Charles' disappointed look.

As she ran upstairs to change into her kitchen frock, Charles followed her and caught up with her on the first-floor landing

'I must hold you, I can't miss any opportunity to do so. Not now, when you're finally mine.' He pushed her up against the wall.

Flattered by his attention, she responded by pushing closer to him as his lips found hers. When he fumbled in her bodice and pulled out her breast, she felt a rush of excitement and didn't protest, it all happened so quickly.

'I can't wait for tonight,' he mumbled.

'Someone is coming!' She adjusted her dress, arranging the lace back over her exposed nipple. Charles disappeared into his bedroom.

'Miss Lenora, is that you up there?'

'Yes, Molly, I'll be with you directly. Wait for me in the kitchen.' She heard Molly's steps fade as she retreated.

During the day, Molly and George moved about the house, carrying out their duties, and she was afraid that her new-found happiness would show itself too clearly. She wanted to shout out to the world that she was in love, she'd never felt like this before. How could she and Charles hide their feelings, so as not to raise suspicion? It would be difficult. Edouard was blind, but alert.

It was late when they returned from the church. A light supper on trays was waiting for them after the service and Edouard suggested a nightcap before bed. Charles accepted but drank his in a hurry, declining the offer of another. Lenora would be preparing to come to him.

Lenora found her husband asleep, tired after the service, when she went to wish him good night. Leaving his room, she passed her own door and entered Charles' room without knocking. He was naked, and already a roaring fire warmed the room. In an instant, he stood in front of her. With her face in his hands, he kissed her closed eyelids. He pulled the nightgown over her head and let it fall to the floor, already she'd lost herself to him. Gently, he lifted her up and carried her to the bed; limp in his arms and longing for his body, she waited.

After a moment she opened her eyes, he was by her side smiling, but made no attempt to touch her.

'Charles, what's the matter?' Was she being rejected again? Perhaps he didn't want her. She felt the colour drain from her face, she'd made another mistake.

He didn't answer but put a hand on her taut stomach and let it run the length of her body, very slowly at first, and as she relaxed under his hand he moved faster and harder, more demanding until her body jerked with pleasure, 'Please, Charles, please,' she moaned.

At last she felt his weight and he rode her until the rush of blood exploded in her head.

His hands continued to move along her body and she was surprised when he entered her again, this time his thrusts were hard until finally he groaned as he spilled into her, the sweat shining on his forehead.

'You are fulfilling my dreams, Lenora. You can't get enough. Nor can I of you.'

'You light a fire inside me, Charles,' she whispered and raised her head to receive his kiss.

For several minutes neither of them spoke. Then

Charles rested on his elbow.

'This is risky. Uncle could hear us, the noise you're making.'

She looked up at him. 'He seldom wakes at night, if so he uses the commode. But you're right, he could hear us. We can't continue like this.' She sat up in sudden alarm.

'No, I won't let you go.' Charles pushed her down, his face hard and for a moment she thought he was angry. Then he smiled, 'You want this too much to give it up. We both do. You'll have to find a solution, Lenora.' His hand slid down her leg.

Chapter 22

Christmas Day 1902

Lenora woke in her own bed, flushed with the memory of the two hours she'd spent with Charles. The thought of their lovemaking excited her, and she longed to be with him. Surely this was going to be the best Christmas ever? She dressed in a hurry to lay the breakfast table, which would be special for the occasion. Molly and George had the day off and she looked forward to cooking the goose. All the preparations were done.

Edouard was seated in the dining room. She kissed his forehead as she apologised, 'I should have been up before you, today of all days, to have breakfast ready. I will bring it directly. Happy Christmas, dearest!'

'Happy Christmas, my dear wife, you sound happy. Perhaps we should have Christmas more often, at least twice a year,' he joked.

'That would indeed be good, I wouldn't have to wait so long for it then,' she laughed.

On her way to the kitchen, she passed Charles in the doorway. His lips brushed the small envelope he held, before pressing it into her hand. As soon as she'd shut the kitchen door behind her, she opened it and read: You have made me the happiest man alive. I adore you. She kissed the note and tucked it into her bodice.

She returned to the dining room with a large tray of ham on the bone, a game pie and cheese, bread and pickles, this was served with a light ale.

After breakfast Charles took his uncle for a walk in the orchard, while Lenora cleared the table and got it ready for the lunch. She brought out the special Christmas tablecloth and the linen napkins, which she had herself embroidered with a motif of Christmas roses. When these were arranged on the table, she placed their eight-armed candelabra in the middle and two smaller ones to each side of it. They were surrounded by twigs of holly, the red berries adding to the seasonal touch. When she had finished the table looked festive with the best china and crystal glasses, dotted around were small dishes of salted almonds, walnuts and crystallized fruit.

With the dining room ready, she busied herself in the kitchen preparing the main meal of the day. The goose was in the oven and the turtle soup only needed reheating before being served.

She warmed the mulled wine, removed the cinnamon stick, the cardamoms and cloves, and added raisins and almonds. Carefully, she carried the tray with the hot beverage through to the drawing room where Edouard and Charles were waiting after their stroll.

'This is giving me a glow, hot and spicy. It was cold out there,' Edouard said as he sipped his wine.

'You should be in Canada then. That's nothing compared to the temperatures we get there.'

'I know, but this is England. It's colder than usual this year.'

'I must say, Lenora, you've decorated this room beautifully.' Charles looked around at the holly resting on the picture frames and the many Christmas cards adorning the mantelpiece. He pointed at the red and green garlands hanging across the ceiling, and the pots of polyanthus and hyacinths placed around the room on the small tables. He took hold of her hand in full view of Edouard and led her to where a sprig of mistletoe was hanging from a sconce.

Lenora realised his intention and stepped away, freeing her hand, 'Yes, George helped with these before you came.'

'But you told him where to put them. You have an artistic streak.' Charles' eyes did not leave hers.

'Well, you could be right. She plays the piano extremely well. Please, play for us now,' Edouard asked her.

'Another of her many talents.' Charles caught hold of her hand again and brought it to his lips, she blushed as she saw the desire in his eyes.

Anxious to make space between her and Charles, she agreed and sat down at the piano. It disturbed her to be near him in front of Edouard, her guilt overwhelmed her. Yet she had a longing to be close to Charles. She could not bear the turmoil of mixed feelings within her. She took a deep breath before she asked, 'What would you like me to play?'

'"Jingle bells", that's a cheerful tune,' Edouard suggested.

Lenora played, following with "Oh, little town of Bethlehem", to applause from her audience.

'Now I must see to the goose, please be seated in the dining room, I'll soon bring the soup.' She left the room.

She had just closed the door behind her when Charles came into the kitchen carrying the mistletoe.

'It's the custom, so you cannot refuse.' He held the plant over her head and pulled her close.

'Charles.' Her protest went unheeded. He pressed her up against him and kissed her with passion. She caught her breath after he released her, her voice full of joy, 'Oh Charles, I'm so happy. Your attention is making me dizzy.'

'It's about time, and I can see your eyes sparkle. You've made me happy too. I told Uncle that I'm helping you to carry the food. He thought it was a good idea,' he looked amused.

'I'll not allow you to make fun of Edouard, he's a most trusting man you should be grateful,' Lenora said suddenly serious. 'I did not want you to kiss me in front of him.'

'Sorry, but I'm so happy. From the first moment I saw you, I wanted you and now you're mine. My happiness knows no bounds.' He took her by the waist and spun her around, kissing her again before they returned to the dining room.

Although Charles' eyes constantly sought hers, she would only allow him the smallest of smiles. He reached out for her hand across the table and she was sorely tempted to take it but only shook her head. She was afraid that the abundance of happiness she felt would transmit to Edouard and she had no explanation for her sudden exhilarated behaviour. She paid little attention to Charles and directed most of her conversation to her husband.

'I do so enjoy Christmas and the festivities it brings and I'm so looking forward to our presents. I do hope you like yours, Edouard.'

'My dear, anything that you've chosen for me will be perfect. Charles, will you pass me the wine I asked you to decant earlier. It will go nicely with the richness of the goose, and I have a dessert wine to complement our plum pudding.'

'Uncle, you take such pleasure in choosing your wines. I have already acquired some knowledge since I arrived and I'm looking forward to learning more.'

'For Christmas, I have my best wines brought from the cellar and your comment tells me that you've appreciated it.' Edouard held out his glass, 'Now I want to propose a toast to my wife for the perfect Christmas meal she has produced for us to enjoy.'

The wine and the compliment made Lenora feel light-headed, even so, she allowed herself a small glass of port with the stilton cheese and after dinner she was persuaded to play the piano once more.

'Lenora, my dearest wife, I cannot tell you how delighted I am that you're playing. You haven't done this for many months. You've always said that you were not in the mood. It must be the spirit of Christmas I have to thank.'

Charles' eyes twinkled at this comment and he blinked at her, 'Yes, a powerful spirit has entered you, Aunt, if your music is anything to go by.'

She gasped, he was daring her with his words, she had no doubt that he was referring to their nights together. To return to the congenial mood of a moment ago, she played "The Blue Danube" waltz, which she knew was her husband's favourite tune.

His face lit up, 'No one has been able to match Strauss as far as this waltz goes. But surely it is time for our gifts?'

'Charles, you'll find five parcels under the tree. Will you bring them, please? As our guest, you shall open yours first,' Lenora said.

Charles held up the pocket watch, which he'd unwrapped. 'Dear Uncle and Aunt,' he paused, and his eyes locked into hers, 'this watch far surpasses the one I own. I'm delighted, thank you.'

She withdrew from his gaze and removed the paper from the box containing the sapphire bracelet. She had helped Edouard to parcel it up so that she could receive it as a gift. It was bought at the same time as the necklace, but she'd saved it for this occasion.

'How beautifully the stones sparkle in the candlelight,' Charles exclaimed.

'Indeed, they do,' she agreed, 'Edouard is most generous. Will you help me, Charles?' Lenora had placed the bracelet on her wrist.

Charles seized the moment he grasped her hand and secured the clasp, after which he covered her palm with soundless kisses, she felt the moisture on her fingertips as he gently brushed each one against his lips.

Lenora was mesmerized with a sudden desire, there was a longing in her body which she found hard to control; she wanted him. Aghast, she pulled her hand away and jerked back to reality. She turned her head sharply towards her husband. Had he heard her intake of breath? Her cheeks were blazing with anger and embarrassment, brought on by her own lust. Edouard was sensitive to mood changes, in particular hers.

'Is something the matter?'

'No, Charles had a problem with the clasp, that's all.' Had her voice betrayed her lie? There was no way of telling, as Edouard's face remained impassive. She hurried over to him and placed her gift in his hand, 'Here, open it.'

Edouard carefully let his fingers trace the sides of the gold cufflinks, 'Come close, Lenora, I want to thank you properly.' As he took her head between his hands and placed a kiss on her cheek, she wondered if he could feel the warmth that radiated from her blushing face.

Charles had bought his uncle a cigar-cutter and Lenora a brooch, set with turquoise stones.

'It's your birth stone,' he remarked.

She immediately pinned the brooch to her dress, 'I like it well. Thank you, Charles.'

For the rest of the day Lenora didn't get close to Charles and moved out of his way when he attempted to touch her.

'What have I done wrong?' he asked, when Edouard left the room.

'Surely you know?'

'No, only that I adore you.' He pulled her close, his mouth seeking hers.

'Edouard could come back at any moment.'

'Yes, but it doesn't matter. He can't see.'

'I will not show disrespect in front of my husband; I've dishonoured him enough already.' Tears showed in her eyes.

'But I love you! So, it can't be wrong.'

'Do you really love me, Charles?'

'Of course, I do.' The question seemed to surprise him.

'You've never said it before.'

'I have, Lenora. But you haven't been listening. So, I say it now. I love you, I love you.'

'Hush!' Lenora pushed him away, holding a finger to her mouth, as her husband entered. 'Good, you're back, Edouard. I am ready to roast the chestnuts.' She turned to Charles, 'We usually do that in the evening, it has become a well-loved tradition with us. Come let's gather by the fire.'

That evening after they had retired, Charles was waiting in the corridor with his door open.

'Close your eyes,' he ordered and led her into his room. 'Stand still!' His hands were on her body, and her nightgown was pulled over her head. She felt the chill in the room, but it was anticipation of what was to come that made her shudder. 'Open your eyes!'

Spread out on the bed was a nightgown, she had never seen one so sheer. Charles picked it up and carefully threaded the thin material over her head.

'Come,' he led her to the mirror.

Lenora gasped, the gown left a shimmering shadow but that was all; it showed her body in all its nakedness, her breasts were heaving.

'It's to replace the one I tore,' he smiled.

'But it's not decent. It's not proper.' The protest died on her lips, she stared at her body and it excited her.

'You're so beautiful, Lenora, I want to see all of you, even when you're wearing a nightgown.'

'Oh, Charles, you make me feel so special. But tell me, is this not a gown for a woman of easy virtue?'

'What would you know about such a woman, Lenora?'

'Very little.'

'The gown is just perfect. You're beautiful and now I shall remove it.'

Later, when she sat up in bed to leave, he pushed her back.

'You're a delight, Lenora. You don't seem to mind whatever I do.'

She opened her eyes wide, 'Why do you say that? Is what we do not proper and right? Is it not what every husband and wife do?' A wrinkle appeared on her forehead.

'You're not my wife.'

'So, you mean...' she was searching for words. Charles' grin had confused her.

He interrupted her, 'But I would like to be your husband.'

'You know that cannot be.'

'One day, when Edouard is gone, I will be.' His hand moulded her breast.

'Hush! Don't speak so. He has many years left.'

'Not necessarily,' he smiled.

'What do you mean, Charles?'

'He could become ill, he is old.'

'No, he must not. I love him as a father. The thought distresses me too much.' She sat up.

'Then we mustn't speak of it.' He pushed her back and kissed her.

'Does a husband want this every night?' she asked.

'That would please him very much.' He kissed the tip of her nose and let his hand run down her leg.

'Then you shall have me, because I also find much pleasure.'

'Lenora, do I detect a spring in your steps and happiness in your voice?' Edouard asked at the breakfast table.

'Yes, you do, dearest, and you're very poetic this morning.'

'It makes me happy when you are.'

'Yes, and we have the New Year's Eve celebrations to look forward to. It was kind of Jenny and Jonathan to invite us to their party.'

'Well, they always do. You'll be able to dance with

someone younger. I'm sure Charles will oblige.'

A shiver ran through her at the thought of stepping out onto the dance floor with Charles. No one else would know that, behind the closed door of the bedroom, she would again be in his arms. It gave her a thrill. She blushed, there would soon be another night.

The days up to New Year's Eve passed in a haze for Lenora. She floated round the house doing her best to behave normally, all the time longing for when she could be with Charles. At meal times she had no choice but to face him, but, afraid that his impulsiveness would raise suspicion, she spent the days avoiding him, only to fall into his arms at night.

This evening was no exception, but Edouard had to their surprise stayed up longer than usual. It was not often that her husband enjoyed himself, so she ignored Charles' stares. She had watched his impatience grow, but he would have to wait a little longer. Surely, he would understand? But when she caught the disapproving expression on his face as he abruptly bade them good night, she wasn't sure.

Chapter 23

Oak Tree Cottage, Cumbria, 29th December 2005

Ellen didn't know why she'd left the house to return to the cottage. Her subconscious had made the decision for her. The first thing she did was to turn on her mobile. It buzzed; it was Annie.

'Where have you been this time? You obviously haven't spent Christmas at the cottage.'

'No, Charles and I booked in somewhere.'

'Somewhere?'

'Yes, does it matter where?'

'Not as long as you had a good time.'

'We did.'

'I hope the sex was good.'

'Incredible. Every night. Never had that much before.' There was silence at the other end. 'Hello, Annie! Are you still there?'

'Yes, that shut me up.'

'Well, you did ask.'

'So I did, I'll know better another time. But why haven't you answered your mobile?'

'Because I left it here. On purpose.'

'Have it your way, Ellen, but I hope you'll be back on the fourth as arranged?'

'Sure, I will. I'm a bit tired, Annie. Do you mind if I hang up now?'

'All that sex, eh!'

'Bye, Annie.'

Ellen checked her voice-mail and e-mails, which all pretty much echoed the conversation she'd had with Annie. She would deal with her mother in the morning. Annie was right, the sex and excitement had worn her out. She fell onto her bed but couldn't sleep; Lenora was on her mind. She'd done it now, good and proper. But her inexperience had made her vulnerable, she'd accepted everything Charles had said or done to her. She was probably having sex right this minute, as seemingly she couldn't get enough. Charles must think himself the luckiest man on the planet. What was his motive? Was he in love with Lenora? He had been tender and loving, but at times cruel. Leonora was in love and Charles was taking advantage. Ellen wished that she could help in some way.

Looking on the bright side, she would have a couple of nights without sex. One could have too much of a good thing. There was a limit, after all. In two days' time she would go back for the New Year's Eve party. No doubt she'd have more then. Ellen drifted off to sleep.

When she woke she turned over and tried to sleep more, although it was late. She had hours to catch up on. The nights at Lakeside House had made her tired. Poor Lenora, she really had no idea.

Later, she stumbled out of bed and pulled on her dressing gown, as usual there wasn't any fresh food in the fridge. She had to get organised. She would eat at the pub and then find a shop.

'Ellen, where have you been hiding?' Mrs Jones greeted her as she walked into the bar. 'You haven't spent Christmas at the cottage. We haven't seen your car around much of the time.'

'No, I have friends in the area, I've been with them. Oh, I can see Albert over there.' Ellen excused herself to avoid answering more questions and walked over to him. 'May I join you?'

'Yes, you may, young lady. I hope you had a good Christmas?'

'One of the best. What about you?'

'I spent it with my daughter. Yes, they looked after me very well. Guess what? I've some news for you, probably not much but you did seem interested,' he stopped.

Ellen felt the excitement rise within her, 'Oh, is it about the house?'

'It is indeed.'

'Do tell me, you're keeping me in suspense, Albert.'

'Well, the mother of my daughter's husband was at the Christmas lunch and I happened to mention your interest in the house. She told me that her mother knew the couple that stayed on to look after the house.'

'Yes, Albert, and then?'

'Well, they never could understand why their master and missus hadn't got in touch. Something bad must have happened to them. Not at all like the master, they said, and they were worried. Early on they came to their own conclusion, but they were loyal and wouldn't say what that was. They felt sure that there was an urgent reason for them to go away, as their decision to do so was very sudden. They tried to get information from the solicitors but were told none was available. However, they stayed on for as long as they could.'

Ellen nodded, that would be typical of George and Molly devoted to the end. They were a nice couple, and Edouard and Lenora had always treated them well. Since she'd read the article in the Courier, she'd known that Edouard and Lenora would leave Lakeside House. But what had happened to make them do it and never come back? She hoped that one day she'd find out. But what Albert had told her only confirmed what she already knew.

Back at the cottage, she sat down and pondered her life at the house, reliving her experiences, trying to analyse the people she'd met. Her thoughts wandered from one person to the next, she wasn't sure about Charles, he was selfish and too full of himself, but he could be kind too. Lenora had integrity but was naive and frustrated with her life and therefore easily led. Her highest regard went to Edouard, he was a trustworthy man and someone who would stand by Lenora, no matter what. Molly and George were hard-working, loyal and decent. Ellen thought of these three as genuine people.

For two months, she had lived life at the turn of the twentieth century, at times it seemed like a dream, but it was real. It had been a fantastic experience to know how they lived life and to discover that their beliefs, their dearest wishes and thoughts were pretty much the same as today. But we had moved on since, the standard of houses, food and technology, nothing was the same. Why had she been given this unprecedented privilege?

The thought of food made her remember that she'd only had a snack at the pub. But her larder was replenished and her fridge full, she'd gone shopping after her conversation with Albert. How quick it was to empty a tin of asparagus soup into a bowl and microwave it. The turtle soup she'd eaten on Christmas Day had taken Molly hours to prepare.

Her thoughts returned to Edouard. His actions had pushed his wife into the arms of his nephew. He was an intelligent man. Ellen couldn't help wondering if he'd done so intentionally? But had he misjudged Charles' character? Edouard wouldn't do anything that would harm Lenora. Did he believe that Charles was a decent man and could offer what he could not: a different love and closeness? It wouldn't be unheard of, this sort of thing did happen.

Or was he oblivious to what was going on? That could also be a possibility. Where was this taking her and everyone at Lakeside House?

Pushing these thoughts aside, she picked up her sketch book, the fashion she'd seen had given her ideas for new designs and she spent a couple of hours drawing.

Tomorrow she'd go for a walk in the fells, she'd brought her walking boots from Bristol and providing it wasn't snowing, she would make use of them. The air in the hills would clear her head. She'd had overexposure of Lakeside House and needed to recharge her batteries.

Ellen was in luck, the morning was glorious. It wasn't too cold and the sun was shining. There was no snow on the ground and she decided to drive to Bannerdale and from there take the path which led to Angle Tarn. She'd been told it was one of the loveliest lakes in the district. Different to most tarns, it had more to offer than just scenery and isolation: it had an individuality of its own. Ellen agreed with this description when she arrived. She walked along the shoreline, far out were two small islands and above the lake, the Angle Tarn Pikes rose, with its two separate peaks.

Now and again she met other walkers and struck up conversations with them. Some were local people, but a few had come to celebrate the New Year at the Lakes.

She returned to the cottage feeling relaxed and happy. The time she'd spent in the stunning scenery had made her feel close to nature, and calm had descended on her troubled mind. It had been a good day and she had been able to forget about Lakeside House for a while.

Chapter 24

New Year's Eve 1902

On arrival at the Edmondsons' impressive mansion, they were greeted by the host and hostess with their daughter Emily by their side. Lenora caught sight of the large ruby pinned onto Jonathan's grey cravat and noted that his red waistcoat was of the same design as her husband's, although Edouard had preferred the blue colour; it suited his grey hair.

Jenny was expensively dressed in a deep purple creation. Her hair swept back over her forehead in a manner which made her look more severe than usual. But now she looked at Lenora and gave her an appreciative smile.

'You look so well, exceedingly charming.'

This surprised Lenora, as Jenny did not often compliment anyone. But Jenny was an astute woman and she had noticed the change; Lenora's new-found happiness was shining through.

The party progressed with a lavish dinner: a consommé accompanied by oyster rolls, as a second course lobster salad, followed by beef wrapped in pastry. Lenora loved the dessert – a delicious ginger ice-cream. Spread around the table in small crystal bowls were the usual bonbons, salted almonds and crystallised fruit.

Twenty guests were seated at the table, most of them

farmers and landowners from the neighbourhood. Lenora knew that, in her midnight blue velvet gown, she was perfectly dressed for the occasion. The sapphire necklace and bracelet were an excellent match for the gown. Before they left home, she had admired her appearance in the mirror and Charles had paid Edouard a compliment on his choice of jewellery.

Lenora longed for her dances with Charles and felt her face glow. However, Charles asked Emily for the first dance, she wore a gorgeous gown of a pale lilac taffeta, which rustled as she moved around the dance floor. Lenora had to admit that Emily had never looked lovelier; her blonde curls were draped up over her head, held up with a tortoiseshell comb.

Instead Lenora took to the floor with the host, glancing over her shoulder as Charles swept past with Emily firmly in his arms. He danced the second dance with Jenny, and Lenora had to be content to sit by her husband's side.

'I'm so happy you're enjoying yourself and by all accounts looking beautiful tonight.' Edouard found her hand and squeezed it. She looked at his dear face and lightly stroked the sleeve of his coat.

It was only when the music struck up for the third time that Charles' hand touched her elbow, 'May I have this dance, Aunt?'

She frowned, she didn't like to be called this and Charles knew it. It made her feel older than her years and it dampened her good mood. Charles noticed her displeasure.

'I'm sorry, but I can't show too much interest in front of all these people. It was correct of me to ask the hostess and her daughter to dance before you. Surely you know that?'

'Of course, you're right,' she murmured, but it didn't seem so to her and the joy she'd felt was gone.

'You've done your best to avoid me all week, so I assumed you wanted me to be discreet tonight. I've tried to talk to you, but you've run away from me.' His grip on her hand became uncomfortably hard.

'That's because I don't want us to be found out,' she whispered.

'Exactly, so what's the fuss?' was Charles' short answer.

At the end of the dance, she engaged Edouard in conversation and turned her back to Charles. A moment later, he asked Emily to dance and Lenora saw her cheeks flush with obvious delight.

Once more Lenora danced with Charles and remained stiff in his arms, this wasn't how she'd imagined the evening.

'Lenora, you're not engaging with me. Do try to look as if you're enjoying the dance. A little conversation wouldn't go amiss.'

'It so happens, I'm not in the mood for conversation.' She forced a smile and the dance ended with few spoken words. Throughout the evening, she observed him and took careful note that he danced with Emily five times.

At the stroke of midnight, the church bells in the surrounding villages could be heard ringing in 1903. The room erupted in cheers and wives turned to their husbands to receive the traditional kiss to welcome the New Year.

Lenora had stayed by Edouard's side all night, and now he pulled her close and kissed her cheek. He did not immediately release her, not for several moments. She was pleased by the special affection her husband showed her this evening; he had obviously decided to forget about the embarrassment she had caused on the night of her birthday. Together, they held up their champagne glasses and toasted the coming year.

Her gaze was not kept on her husband, but she continuously glanced over his shoulders, searching the room for Charles, who was nowhere to be seen.

Only after the first cheer had gone up and died away did Charles appear by her side.

'Uncle, may I give my aunt a kiss for the New Year?'

Edouard let go of her hand, which a minute ago he had brought to his lips and gently kissed. He nodded, 'You may indeed. Let's welcome 1903!'

Charles' kiss on her cheek was brief. Lenora had tried to turn her head aside and she was aware that, to anyone watching, her reaction to the kiss had been odd.

The party broke up an hour after midnight, when Jenny approached them, her eyes without warmth.

'Lenora, dearest, will you excuse us whilst we have a word in private with Edouard?'

Astonished, she nodded her consent and watched with concern as the host and hostess left the room with her husband.

Edouard returned some ten minutes later, his cheeks reddened with what she knew to be anger. He would not speak on the carriage ride home and, sensing his displeasure, both Lenora and Charles remained silent.

Lenora did not undress, she was too upset. For a long time she sat gazing at the mirror of her dressing table, where her tearful eyes stared back at her. The evening had been a huge disappointment. Why had everything gone wrong? Charles was of course right to dance with Emily and Jenny, but as a result the fun and warmth inside her had vanished. She'd been certain that his wish to hold her in his arms for a first dance together would have been strong enough to override his sense of duty. She had risked so much by falling in love with him. She couldn't help but feel rejected. And why had Edouard insisted on a word with Charles as soon as they had arrived home? She had heard both men come upstairs more than thirty minutes ago. Charles' door had banged shut after him.

Disillusioned she stood up and stepped out of her dress. At that moment, Charles entered her room. She hastily put a finger to her lips.

'It's late. Why are you here?'

'Uncle is asleep, I've checked.' His unsmiling eyes met hers. 'Undress, but keep the necklace on,' he ordered brusquely.

'Why?' Lenora's eyes widened.

'I want to see you naked wearing just the necklace. You told me, that's how you offered yourself to Edouard. Only I won't reject you.'

The colour rose on her cheeks, she regretted having told him. 'Charles, you should leave. You've been drinking.'

'Yes, I sometimes get loud. You don't want your precious husband to wake. Do you? You seem to care more about his feelings than mine.'

'Please, don't speak loudly. You will wake him. Go to your room now.'

'No, hurry up and undress.'

'I will, if you lower your voice. At least turn around, any gentleman would.'

'Perhaps I'm not one.'

Afraid that Edouard would wake she hurried, but fumbled to loosen her white satin corselet. Charles' impatience and anger grew, and he stepped forward and pulled at the laces.

'What's happened, Charles? Your mood scares me. It's not the way to start the New Year.' She let her last remaining garment fall to the floor and stood naked in front of him, wearing only her jewellery.

'But this is.' He carried her to the bed and she caught the wild look in his eyes as he flung her down and immediately entered her. He didn't caress, nor look at her.

'You're hurting me, the necklace is scratching my skin.' She struggled to shake him off.

Charles gave no sign of having heard, his lovemaking was forceful and short, his only intention was to relieve his anger and soon he pulled on his nightshirt and left without a word.

She removed her jewellery and bathed the scratch on her neck. Anxiously she examined the necklace to make sure it hadn't been damaged, before she carefully arranged it on the crème coloured velvet lining of the box.

'What have I done wrong?' Lenora whispered. That question and another thought were churning in her head and stopped her from sleeping. Does he still love me?

New Year's Day 1903

Lenora got her answer the following morning, when she sat down at the breakfast table.

Edouard looked tired, 'I'm afraid that I had to have a serious word with Charles on our return home last night. He didn't like it much. But he's in England now and must respect our way of life. I made him apologise to Jenny and Jonathan.'

'Why? What has he done?'

'He kissed Emily.'

'What! Surely not,' Lenora shouted.

'He says it was a kiss to celebrate the New Year, but Jenny happened to come upon them and she says the embrace showed that it was much more than that. Emily had to admit that it was improper and showed much distress. Who knows if she would have done, had her mother not seen them? Nevertheless, I had to severely reprimand him. In this country, you only kiss a girl after your betrothal.' Edouard stopped abruptly, a frown on his face, 'You are very quiet, Lenora. What do you have to say?'

Lenora gripped the edge of the table to stop herself from swooning, her lips opened, she tried desperately to speak but her mouth was dry and no word would come.

'Lenora!' Edouard reached out searching for her hand. 'You're as cold as ice.'

'I don't know what to say,' she stammered, having found her voice, 'I'm shocked that he should do such a thing. Excuse me, I must go.' She stood up abruptly, 'I have remembered, I have a pot on the stove.' She restrained herself from running out of the room, but she had to speak to Charles immediately. It could not wait, he must explain. Why kiss Emily, when he loved her? There must be a mistake. She ran up the stairs, stumbling on several steps, she knocked only once on his door. Charles gave her a sullen stare from his bed and looked away.

'Edouard told me. Please, tell me why?'

'It was a kiss to greet the New Year.'

'That's not what I've been told.' Tears were burning her eyes. 'If you love me, why did you do it?'

'They are making trouble out of nothing. You should believe me. Mrs Edmondson is a hysterical woman.'

'Charles, it was a lover's kiss and Emily was distraught.'

'Ha! Emily enjoyed it until her mother appeared. In fact when I embraced her she responded, which encouraged me to hold her tighter.' He met her eyes in a steady gaze.

'Charles!' She could feel the heat on her cheeks and her eyes flared, 'Don't come to my room tonight. Don't come ever again!' she choked on the words. With her hand up against her throat, she slammed the door shut as she ran from the room.

There was no need for Lenora to stay away from Charles for the rest of the day, as he avoided all contact with her and Edouard.

'Charles isn't joining us for lunch,' her husband informed her. 'I believe he resented the words I had with him. Let's give him time and he'll come round to accepting that he was wrong. He will apologise to me.'

'I'm sure you're right,' Lenora nodded.

'Do I hear a tremor in your voice? His behaviour has

upset you too. Am I correct?'

'Why do you ask?' She turned her head sharply towards Edouard. Was he suspicious? But her husband's face was calm and revealed no trace of emotion. She bit her lip, her question had come too quick and her voice had been shrill and anxious.

'He is our guest and his conduct reflects on us. You have a right to be upset.'

Edouard did not pursue the subject and she remained quiet, nervously looking around to find something else to talk about.

'Come, Edouard, let's go to the drawing room, I want to play for you. It will cheer us.'

'What a splendid idea! It will indeed. I enjoy your music.' Edouard rose from his chair, and the tapping of his cane followed her across the hall.

The music was loud and forceful to hide the many sobs, which shuddered through her chest. She took her frustration and anger out on the piano, her fingers hammering away on the keyboard, and at the end tears were running down her cheeks.

'Dearest, there's too much energy in your music and not the cheerful tune I expected.'

She didn't answer; her voice would reveal her distress. Instead, she chose a piece more suitable to lift their spirits and the notes of "When the Saints Go Marching In" filled the room. Edouard's cane tapped the floor in time with the music. She followed up with "The Blue Danube", her husband's favourite waltz.

'How Victoria and I loved this waltz.' Edouard had been leaning back with his eyes shut, but now he sat up, 'I'm so sorry, Lenora. I believe I've only danced with you on our wedding day.'

'That's correct, dearest, but don't let it worry you.' Her answer had sounded resentful, it had come out wrong and she bit her lip. It was Charles she'd wanted to dance with all night at the New Year's Eve Ball.

The rest of the afternoon was spent quietly, but Lenora's embroidery rested on her lap untouched. Her eyes stared unseeing across the room, only shifting to Edouard to answer him briefly when he spoke.

The next day Charles showed up at meal times, having offered a short apology to Edouard. Apart from that, he kept his own company. On several occasions, however, he attempted to pass an envelope to Lenora, but she refused to take it. Her time was spent in her husband's presence, which made it difficult for Charles to speak to her.

That night the door to her bedroom opened quietly and Charles crossed the room with his arms outstretched. He fell on his knees by her bed.

'Please forgive me! I cannot bear to see you angry.' His pleading eyes were filling with tears. 'My life is worthless without you. Why don't you believe me when I say the kiss was innocent? I love only you.' His head slumped on to the bed by her side.

Lenora's hand went up to stroke his hair, her resistance weakening, his tears had affected her. She had loved him, and he had made her feel happy and fulfilled. But she hesitated, her anger returned and she let her hand drop.

'You're lying, Charles.' By his own words, he had admitted that he had desired and enjoyed kissing Emily. When he'd had too much to drink, he had told the truth. No! She must not give in to him.

Before she spoke, she took a deep breath, 'You're not showing me respect and proper love. It isn't just the kiss for Emily that I object to. Your behaviour later that night, when you came to me, wasn't that of a lover. You hurt and humiliated me.'

‘I was angry with Edouard. I didn’t know what I was doing. I beg your forgiveness.’

‘No, I was weak and foolish when I gave myself to you. I regret it. I believed that I loved you. I cannot forgive you. I’ll be a better wife to Edouard. Never again will I share your bed. It was wrong. Leave me, Charles!’

Chapter 25

Oak Tree Cottage, Cumbria, January 2006

Ellen unlocked the door and leaned against the frame, it was the third of the month and she was due back in Bristol the following morning. Her head was full of Lenora, she was doing the right thing. Charles was no good for her, Ellen was sure of it. She prayed that Lenora would be strong enough to stay away. She was too inexperienced to realise that he had been taking advantage of her sexually. Mind you, the sex had been good, Ellen felt sheepish to admit it. Let's see if Lenora can resist going back to him.

Annie greeted her with open arms as she walked into the shop the next day.

'You're late, but who cares. It's good to see you! Please, Ellen, tell me you won't rush back to the cottage in a hurry. We need you.'

Ellen laughed, 'Great to see you too! Yes, I can spend more time here now. Until it warms up at the Lakes, I'll just go at weekends to see Charles, you know.' She had to look after her life in Bristol, it was precious to her.

Because of the cooled relationship between Lenora and Charles, she could relax, there was no need to spend all her time at the house. She couldn't say why she was sure of this and it intrigued her.

However she had no intention of giving up this other life in Cumbria. To be in the body and mind of another person, who had lived a hundred years ago, was extraordinarily special. Why had she been given the chance? Why was she there? She still didn't know, but she would stay on to find out. There must be a reason. Nothing could change her mind. She couldn't influence Lenora's decisions during the time she spent being her, nor did she have any sense or recollection of being Ellen. But, as Ellen, she could remember everything that had happened at Lakeside House.

At times doubt crept into her mind about the wisdom of what she was doing, but she always had the answer immediately. There was no turning back, a will stronger than her own had decided for her. In time she would know.

One day at the end of February, Ellen sat daydreaming in the shop, something she often did when there was little to do. As always, her thoughts had gone to Cumbria.

'Wakey, wakey,' Annie's cheerful voice rang out.

Ellen turned to her friend, 'I've been thinking. We should diversify. The doorbell hasn't rung once today. We've never been this quiet during January and February.'

'You mean expand our range?'

'We could start making lingerie and bathing costumes, for example,' Ellen suggested.

'Yes, more casual clothes. People don't dress up like they used to.'

'I'll start making a few sketches right now. No time to waste.'

'Wow! The bell went! I'll see to it.' Annie disappeared into the shop.

Ellen worked diligently for the next week and presented her designs to Annie.

'I'll order the material and make up a couple of these, then we'll get Moira to try them on, she's got the figure for them.' Annie pointed to several drawings of minimal bikinis.

'Thanks, I'm off to the Lakes by the way and I'll be away on Tuesday as well. Can you have them ready for when I get back?'

'Yeah, there's not much to them. But why doesn't Charles come to Bristol instead?'

'I need to check out the cottage.'

'Couldn't Charles do that for you? Ken is convinced he doesn't exist.'

'Annie!' her voice sounded appropriately disappointed. 'No, he couldn't and I'm seeing Mum and Dad on the way. It's a detour to Oxford, but it's worth it. That's why I'm not back at work until Wednesday.'

'OK, sorry!' Her friend grimaced and looked away. 'How about it, if we spend a weekend with you? We'd like to meet him.'

'Sure, but not now. There's plenty of time. It will be nicer, when it's warmer. The cottage is pretty cold.'

'If you say so,' Annie sighed.

Life at Lakeside House went along at a slow pace during Ellen's visits in the spring of 1903. Lenora still refused any advances from Charles, and Ellen admired her steadfastness. As long as the couple stayed apart, all would be well. Ellen couldn't explain how she knew that and that eventually Lenora would give in to him. But Lenora was part of her subconscious mind, so it was possible that some of her feelings were transmitted to her. By now she was convinced that Charles' affair with Lenora was the reason for her being there, and when it resumed all would become apparent. But lack of events had made her realise that this time was yet to come. Every weekend, when she returned to Lakeside House, her anticipation grew. Lenora's memory became hers, and the week's events played out for her like a TV serial.

With Lenora still rejecting him, Charles had sought his uncle's permission to take the horse and trap on outings. Two or three times a week, he spent afternoons in Kendal and Edouard had been pleased when Charles told him that he had gained a number of men friends at a gentlemen's club.

Chapter 26

Lakeside House, March 1903

'Charles, do not follow me around, and I wish you'd not write me these letters.'

'Please, Lenora!'

She dismissed him with a wave of her hand and walked briskly away. But she had accepted the envelope and tucked it inside the pocket of her woollen skirt.

As in all the other notes, he begged her forgiveness. She sighed deeply and walked across to the large wooden chest, deep inside under her wedding dress, lay a bundle, tied together with a purple ribbon. She added the letter to it.

In her head were many troubled thoughts, she had not been coping with her shame. How could she have behaved so badly towards Edouard? He had always treated her with love and respect. Her anxiety grew, and too frequently she had gone to make sure he wanted for nothing. She would always regret betraying him for a man who didn't love her.

⁂

Lenora climbed the stairs to Edouard's studio on the third floor. Although he had continued to paint after he'd lost his sight, it was now some time since he had done so. Even whilst blind, he had accomplished some interesting work. There was an unfinished painting, and she intended to encourage him to complete it. She found the one she was looking for and also came across several others in a cupboard. Most of these she had not known existed, as Edouard had worked on them before she came to the house.

Surprised, she held up a painting of Lakeside House, with it still in her arms, she sank down on the nearest chair, feeling faint, her forehead clammy. Surely it wasn't the picture that affected her? She held it out and anxiety overcame her. The lake seemed to be sucking her in, closing over her head, she became icy cold. A memory tried to push its way to her consciousness, but, although she struggled to bring it forward, it remained at the back of her mind. Disturbed, she studied the painting for several minutes, before returning it to the cupboard.

Instead she picked up the unfinished picture, but before leaving she turned and stared at the cupboard door. She shrugged her shoulders, but the feeling of unease wouldn't leave her.

She went immediately to her husband, 'Edouard, why don't you complete this one? It's one I like.'

'Do you? Remind me what it looks like.'

'You've painted it from memory, it's of the fells and sheep are roaming the field, some of them have ended up in the blue sky. In fact, one Herdy is standing on a cloud,' she laughed.

'I will if it pleases you. It's a good idea.' Edouard sounded amused.

'Excellent! I'll ask George to move your materials down to the study, so you won't have to climb the stairs.'

The move was carried out the following day and Lenora spent time with Edouard, until he found his way around his new studio. She laid the paint out in a special order, so he'd know where every colour lay, and she helped by mixing paint.

Edouard was good but not exact in his ability to determine the size of his canvas. He would run his hands over the surface and trace the sides several times before he started to paint. This could have striking results and, in some instances, produce a painting worth keeping. She often found his work highly amusing and unable to contain her merriment would laugh out loud. This never annoyed Edouard, he always asked her to describe exactly what had made her laugh, so that he could join her.

'Dearest, can I get you some refreshments? I think you've done enough for today.' She removed the brush from his hand. 'By the way, there's a painting of Lakeside House in the cupboard. When did you paint that?'

'Before you came to live here, long before I lost my sight, but I didn't think it was good enough to be displayed. Haven't you seen it before?'

'No, it's been hidden away, and I was quite surprised to see it. But now I want a drink, let's go to the drawing room. I'll ask Molly to bring tea.' She changed the subject, regretting the question. The strange effect the painting had had on her previously had returned as soon as she'd mentioned it. It disturbed her, and she preferred not to think about it.

Edouard put his cup down and Lenora fell onto her knees by his chair, resting her head in his lap, something she did often.

'Shall I play for you?'

'My dearest wife, you've done enough for me. Surely there's a task in the kitchen you can help Molly with? Come to think of it, why don't you bake me a fruit tart?' Edouard stroked her hair, her increased affection made him respond in kind.

Lenora jumped up, 'What a good idea. We'll have it with our tea tomorrow.'

As she opened the door, Charles stood in her way but stepped aside to let her pass.

'When did you come back? I thought you'd gone to Kendal.'

Lenora closed the door, 'Have you been listening, Charles?'

'With all the fuss you're making, I'm surprised Uncle hasn't guessed that you have a guilty conscience. And you have; you love me still. This is just your way of convincing yourself that you don't.'

'No, life is very comfortable, thank you. I'm at peace with myself.'

'I will do everything in my power to keep it that way. If only you'd let me,' Charles said softly.

'Then leave me be.' Lenora gave him a cold stare in return.

'My pleasure will be to bring you happiness. I will prove to you that I've changed.' Charles bowed to her, 'I love you dearly.'

Lenora swallowed hard, her chest rose as her breathing increased. For a moment she allowed herself to believe him. Oh, how much she wanted to do so. But she lowered her head to avert her eyes, clasping her hands together, she walked away with his words ringing in her head.

Lakeside House, April 1903

Life at Lakeside House continued in a period of calm as the weeks went by. Charles went to great lengths to prove that he was indeed a changed man, his manners were impeccable, and he continued to be helpful and considerate. He paid much attention to his uncle, assisting him in any way he could, on occasions carrying out errands for Edouard on his frequent trips to Kendal, where he also visited the Station Hotel, having made several acquaintances in the card room.

'Charles appears to have calmed down and learnt his lesson after the Edmondson affair. My impression is that he's become humble, and I'm pleased that his intake of alcohol is less,' Edouard said to Lenora one afternoon. 'Does he behave well towards you?'

'Yes, he is polite and I've no complaints.' It was true, she thought, his behaviour was different, and he had become most helpful in all things. Also, he had stopped pestering her with letters. She had become a good wife to Edouard and she had prayed in church every Sunday for her sins to be forgiven.

'I'll read for you now, my dearest, or shall I play?'

'You are the most attentive wife any husband could wish for, but I'm an old man and I'm tired. Although I love you playing the piano, I must admit that I miss my afternoon rest. I wish to close my eyes.'

She looked up in surprise, but she left the room and found Charles waiting in the corridor.

'Please, it's such a beautiful day, walk with me. What harm can it do?'

'No, what harm can it do? You're right, I'll walk with you,' she smiled.

The walk was pleasant, Charles kept his distance, only once did he touch her and that was to assist her over a fallen branch.

❦

'Will you walk with me today?' Charles asked the following day.

Lenora nodded, 'Yes, Edouard is asleep and I did enjoy our walk yesterday.'

'I've missed them.' A smiled played on his lips.

'I have too.' She blushed and looked away.

Charles and Lenora walked most afternoons, and she didn't pull away when he rested his hand on her elbow. He was attentive to his uncle and the atmosphere around them was always pleasant. He made an effort to lighten their days by telling them about life in Canada and reading out the letters he received from his father.

❦

Lakeside House, May 1903

Charles' persistence paid off, Lenora's attitude towards him changed, the old warmth returned, her affection for him flared up and she looked forward to every new day.

In the afternoons, she often played the piano before Edouard had his rest, and many times Charles chose to sing along.

'Charles, you're so funny,' Lenora and Edouard laughed at the animal sounds he made up, when she played "Old Mac Donald had a Farm".

When the days became warmer, Charles got the carriage out and with Gladys harnessed he took the reins. Lenora and Edouard sat in the back, with a light blanket covering their knees. They made many tours along the country lanes, where the long-horn cattle grazed behind the stone walls and the blackthorn flowered in the hedges. Edouard, to his delight, could smell the wild garlic. He didn't need his sight to enjoy these outings. He suggested various routes, which took them past farms where the fields were worked all hours weather permitting. They drove along valleys and lanes that climbed steeply before levelling out, and where Charles admired the soaring fells. Lenora pointed out the Herdys as black and white dots on the landscape above them.

In the afternoons when Edouard rested, Charles and Lenora played backgammon or cards. Although Edouard shook his head and told him not to fuss, Charles would insist on escorting him to the library to make sure that he was comfortably seated before returning to Lenora and the game.

'You're kind to your uncle. Yesterday he told me it makes him happy that you and I have got over our past difficulties.'

'Do you think me kind also?'

'More than kind, in truth, my affection for you has returned,' she blushed.

Charles knocked over the chair in his hurry to get up and fell onto his knees in front of her, 'Please, stop me immediately if you do not wish me to speak.'

Lenora remained silent.

'These few months have served to strengthen my love for you and made me realise that I love you more than ever. If you wish, I shall leave this room and not speak like this ever again. But if there's a chance that you've forgiven me…' he stopped, overcome with emotion. His pleading eyes were moist with tears, his hands were gripping hers, holding them tight.

Lenora was solemn as she answered, 'I have forgiven you. Your devotion of the last few months has proved to me that you've changed. I do believe you when you say that you love me.'

'Oh, Lenora!' Charles kissed the palms of her upturned hands, 'Will you say that you love me too?'

'You must give me time. I have Edouard to consider still.'

'But if you love me...?'

Lenora's eyes opened wide, 'Please, Charles, you're not listening! You don't hear what I'm saying.' She showed her displeasure by turning away from him. 'Let us play cards.'

He was silenced by this, his face became sullen, and he returned to his chair. Their game was further interrupted by Molly, who came in to tell Lenora that she'd finished for the day and would be early in the morning.

That night her thoughts were on Charles, she'd admitted her love for him. In her mind she relived the pleasure and excitement of their lovemaking, with his body against hers. Her hand moved to her breasts in the same way he used to, then gently slid down to her stomach touching her navel and then..., she blushed.

She shivered with excitement; she wanted him. The longing became strong and overwhelming. It no longer seemed wrong, now that she knew that his affection was genuine. She would continue to be a good wife to Edouard and protect him in every way. He must not find out and he would not be hurt. She would have Charles back. Why wait?

She slid out of bed and opened the chest by the window, hidden at the bottom was the sheer nightgown that he had bought for her. She pulled it on and walked to his room.

Charles jumped out of bed and fell to his knees in front of her, he wrapped his arms around her legs and buried his face in her gown.

'Oh Lenora,' his voice was barely audible. Without standing, he pushed her gown upwards, slowly inch by inch, covering her thighs with kisses, and he lingered... a gasp escaped her, and she shuddered with pleasure. At last he raised himself up and without another word pulled the gown over her head. She shivered in her nakedness but not from the cold. Charles' lips found hers and then he moved to her breasts.

'Please, don't make me wait.'

He carried her to his bed and then he came to her.

'Charles,' her breath came in short burst and she arched her body to meet him.

Chapter 27

Oak Tree Cottage, Cumbria, May 2006

Ellen ran into the cottage, she didn't know if she should laugh or cry. Charles' behaviour was erratic, and she didn't believe he loved Lenora. Poor girl! She flung herself onto the bed.

'Lenora, Lenora, what are you doing?' she moaned. 'Why have you changed your mind?' Yet she had known it would happen. A chill ran through her, for she sensed danger. Nothing good would come of this.

Since the beginning of the month, she had stayed in Cumbria and not returned to Bristol to work; she'd had an overwhelming feeling that going back to the house only at weekends would not be enough. Where it had come from she didn't know, but she felt it was right, and it had been a timely decision. Now that Lenora had resumed her relationship with Charles, it was imperative that Ellen spent more time at Lakeside House. Life would not be the same. Lenora was making a huge mistake. Did this spell the beginning of the end? Suddenly, she was unsure about being part of this other world.

She switched on the TV, but her thoughts wandered to Lenora time after time. Frustrated, she pressed the remote and the screen went dark. She had to occupy herself with something physical instead, so she vacuumed every corner of the cottage. A nagging doubt, which she couldn't shrug off, made her angry. It grew when she realised that she didn't want to return to the house, *not ever*. She vented her anger on the rugs, which she brought out into her small back garden and vigorously beat the dust out of. Then she admitted that she was scared.

Later in the shower, she let the cold water run down her face and body, hoping it would help to clear her mind.

The chair she was sitting on was hard and wobbled; it kept her mind alert. After an hour's soul searching, she concluded that she was compelled to go back. She had no choice. Ellen remembered the shock she'd had when she had discovered that Edouard had painted the picture of Lakeside House, not the artist she'd bought it from. It had caused her a lot of concern. She had no doubt that it was the same painting. Why had the artist lied? It didn't make sense. It had raised a new set of questions. The way Lenora had acted when she'd found the painting had been peculiar, to say the least. It suggested that the strong reaction of her own mind had been transmitted to Lenora. That meant that Lenora was subconsciously aware of her. Ellen became excited. Had she finally found a way? Might it be possible to communicate, if she concentrated really hard? Could she get inside Lenora's head? Would that change how events unfolded in the future?

She remembered that Ken and Annie would soon arrive, so these thoughts would have to be put aside for later. Her friends had not taken 'no' for an answer, despite her efforts to politely stop them from coming. They expected to meet Charles, her boyfriend from the other world. How disappointed they would be when she told them that he'd gone to York for the weekend.

'Ellen, didn't you tell him that your best friends were visiting and that we wanted to meet him?'

'Yes, but his meeting was arranged weeks before. He

couldn't change his plans. You can see him another time.' Ellen felt her face tighten and forced a smile.

'I'll believe that when I see him,' Annie muttered. 'Why are you hiding him?'

'I'm not! It's just the way things have worked out.'

'You look peaky, Ellen. Are you OK?'

'Sure, why do you ask?'

'It's your face. You've got a worried look about you. Have you had a row with Charles?' Without waiting for an answer, she continued, 'You should have told us the truth instead of making up York.'

'But it's true! He has gone to York,' Ellen protested.

'Annie, leave it, for heaven's sake!' Ken butted in. 'We're here for the weekend to enjoy ourselves. Let's go for a drive, the weather is lovely.'

'Yes, it could be raining again tomorrow. You're lucky. It's been pouring for three days and when it does the views are shrouded in mist.'

'Let's show Ken your invisible house!' Annie suggested with enthusiasm.

'No!' Ellen's voice was sharp. 'I'm not going back there. There is no house, so what's the point?'

Annie narrowed her eyes, 'OK, no need to get upset. When are you coming back to work full-time by the way? Your clients miss you.'

'I design for them from here, so why should they?'

'It's not the same; they want to talk to you in person. You've forever been telling me there is nothing like the personal touch. You know that, Ellen.'

'I'm not ready to come back yet.'

'When then?' Annie insisted.

'I don't know. Leave it.' Ellen felt her back stiffen.

'Do as she says,' Ken nodded to his wife. 'Come on, girls, this way. Your chauffeur is waiting.' He led the way out and held the car door open.

'Ellen, you have to go in the back. I get car sick, so must

sit in the front. It's only when I'm not driving,' Annie pulled the door shut.

'I didn't realise, you've never told me.'

'You don't know everything about me, do you?' Annie remained quiet for a moment, 'And I'm convinced I don't know anything at all about you and what's going on here.'

Ellen was taken aback, but she'd expected some comments from Annie about her extended stay in Cumbria. Annie might have pretended to be OK with it, but this proved that she still had doubts.

Ellen opened her mouth to answer, but Ken took over, 'That's enough you two, you'll soon have something else to think about. I want to take you through the Hardknott Pass. It's one of the most dangerous roads in England. Don't want to miss it now that we're here, the gradient is one in three. Pretty steep, I'd say.'

'Yes, I've heard the scenery is spectacular, let's do it,' Ellen agreed.

'Here, Ellen, check out the map. Which is the best way to get there?'

'OK, turn left outside the cottage to start with and I'll let you know.'

'I'm scared,' Ellen laughed nervously, holding on to her seat with both hands as Ken steered the car along the single track of the Hardknott Pass.

'Yeah, I need all my concentration,' Ken answered, keeping his eyes on the road.

'Don't talk then,' Annie piped up. 'Oh God, this is going to make me sick.'

'No, Annie, you can't. It would be a bad idea to stop here,' Ellen had caught sight of the sheer drop as they turned on a knife sharp bend. Below, other cars slowly made their way down the pass. 'Here are some tissues if you really are going to.'

Annie pressed the tissues to her mouth, her face white, 'OK, I'll be all right in a minute.'

'Look at the fantastic scenery. That'll take your mind off it,' Ken suggested.

'You're joking, I daren't take my eyes off the road, nor should you,' Annie replied.

'You don't have to, I'm driving. Don't you trust me?' Ken grimaced at his wife.

'Of course I do, darling.' Annie grimaced back.

'I am glad I'm not holding the steering wheel,' Ellen said.

'So am I.' Ken smiled at her, through the back mirror, taking his eyes off the road for a second.

As they reached the bottom of the pass, Annie removed the tissue from her mouth and turned to Ellen in the back seat.

'Phew, that was an exciting drive, and I'm feeling better now.'

'I'm glad I've done it though,' Ken said. 'And that we are taking another road back.'

'Agreed,' both girls said in unison and turned to each other, laughing.

'Let's eat at your local tonight.' Ken manoeuvred his car into the parking place outside the cottage on their return.

'No!' Ellen said it too loudly. 'I mean, I've bought steaks for tonight and they need eating.'

'I insist, my treat. The steaks will keep.'

Ellen frowned, she'd only been there on few occasions lately and she wanted to keep her friends away, in case the landlady let slip about her always being on her own.

The pub was busy, Mr Jones and his wife were running from one end of the bar to the other. Ellen introduced them and they briefly shook hands, 'Back in a sec,' the landlord promised, but it was Mrs Jones who came to take their order.

'I expect you see a lot of our friend here and Charles,' Annie piped up.

'Charles?' Mrs Jones lifted her eyebrows and turned to Ellen with a surprised stare.

Ellen was standing behind Annie and Ken. Without thinking, she gave Mrs Jones a quick nod and the landlady answered, 'Yes, a fair bit.'

Ellen sighed inwardly; Ken had raised his eyebrows, a smile on his lips. He always noticed everything, and he had turned to see the exchange between her and the landlady. Well, it couldn't be helped, and gradually she relaxed and enjoyed the evening. But soon she would have to find a plausible excuse to explain Charles' absence.

Annie and Ken left early on Monday morning and soon after, Ellen had a call from the estate agent, who had let the cottage.

'What?' she exclaimed. 'Say that again.'

'Well, don't you remember that the contract expires at the end of this month?'

'I didn't actually.'

'It's already let to somebody else.' The estate agent sounded wary anticipating a problem.

'You might've offered it to me first,' Ellen grumbled.

'I did inform you at the time of signing the contract that it is let every summer for three months to the same client.'

'I'm sorry, I do remember now, that's right,' Ellen agreed, then arranged a date for the cottage to be inspected. Probably just as well, she thought, as she ended the call. She couldn't afford the summer rent anyway, it was sky high. Perhaps she could negotiate a price to stay at the pub?

Ideas were creeping into her head, which intrigued and excited her. Could she get away with living as Lenora the whole time? How would she explain her absence to her family? Gone to Canada with Charles for three months? No, reluctantly she had to admit that it wouldn't work. It was going to be tricky, but she needed somewhere to live, and she had to find a solution. She couldn't leave Lenora at this time. She'd been sent to help her. What else? She had accepted that she was reliving a previous life. In that life, she was Lenora. This woman had been reborn in her. They were as one.

Chapter 28

Lakeside House, May 1903

Lenora walked past Charles' room and unlocked the door at the end of the corridor. Here she made her way up the stairs to the second floor; this staircase ran to the side of the house, from the kitchen up to the first floor and onto the second. This was where the servants' quarters used to be. On both floors there were doors to give the servants access to the family rooms. This staircase was no longer in use, so the doors to the landings were kept locked, including the one from the kitchen. Now, these rooms were only used for storage.

Edouard's studio had been on the opposite end of this floor to give him a view overlooking the lake. Lenora had recently arranged for all his materials to be moved to the study on the ground floor. She opened the door to the last room to this side of the corridor. The walls were painted white and it had a window on the gable overlooking the wood. This was where Molly used to stay after working late, serving at their dinner parties. But it was a long time since she'd slept here.

Lenora pressed her hand down on the bare mattress; it wasn't damp. The window was stiff, and she had to push hard on the frame to open it, it had been a long time since this room had been aired. She laid the pillows and blankets on the windowsill and made a mental note to replace the curtains, which were bleached by the sun. In the room there was a small bedside cabinet, a table, a wardrobe and a chair. On the table stood a porcelain jug and wash bowl, decorated with roses, and under the bed a chamber pot. When Molly wasn't at work, Lenora would carry water upstairs and the jug would be heavy.

She returned to the first floor to collect sheets and pillow cases from the linen cupboard. Back in the upstairs room she made the bed and before leaving, stood by the door for a moment, taking in every detail. It was cleaned and aired, and it would be warm enough to use without a fire.

Next to Charles, she never felt cold. She was in a hurry to surprise him with this room, where they could be undisturbed. Nobody came up here, she kept the only key. Molly and George had no reason to, unless she specifically sent them to the storage rooms. Satisfied she smiled, locked the door and put the key in her pocket.

Lenora playfully rubbed her nose against Charles' naked shoulder and looked up at his smiling face, 'I never dreamt that I could feel so alive.'

'I like to hear you say it.' He tapped her nose.

'Yes, as long as Edouard never finds out. I couldn't bear it. That would ruin our lives. I am so very serious about that, Charles.'

'Then we must make sure he never does.'

'We may only show our love in this room, our hideaway. Do you like it?' She nudged him anxiously, waiting for his answer.

'You've done well,' Charles kissed her.

'You must promise that, outside of this room, we must behave as if this has never happened. Promise me that!'

'I do. Here you belong to me, and that makes me happy.'

Their days continued in a pattern: as soon as Edouard had made his way to the library, Lenora would give a nod to Charles and run upstairs, knowing that minutes later his arms would be encircling her in a wild embrace.

Sinking back in bed with Charles' weight on top of her, she looked into his boyish face.

'You have changed my life,' she whispered.

'I aim to please you. Your wish is my command.' Charles kissed her.

'You respect my every wish and I love you more because of it.'

'To be here and hold you close makes me happy.'

'It's only possible when Edouard is asleep, I cannot come every day.'

Charles raised his eyebrows, 'No matter, as long as the refusals are few. I'll never question you.'

Lenora laughed, 'Why would I want to refuse you?'

Charles buried his head in her hair, 'How I wish we didn't have to hide away. If Edouard wasn't here, I would marry you tomorrow.'

'That would be impossible,' she laughed. 'I'd have to wear mourning clothes for two years. But my husband is in good health, don't talk so.'

'You'd only wear those clothes in public. No one would know.'

'George and Molly would find it objectionable.'

'They are servants. Why should you care what they think?'

'I do. I am fond of both and I believe them to be fond of me.'

'Do you think they know that I love you?'

'We're not behaving as recklessly as we did at Christmas time, I think not,' she answered.

Lenora had just put down her comb and removed a hairpin from her mouth. She had arranged her hair in a loose bun and was ready for breakfast, when Molly's panic-stricken voice reached her.

'Miss Lenora, Miss Lenora.'

She rose in alarm from the dressing table, knocking over the stool and barely missed tripping over it in her hurry. 'What's the matter?' she shouted as she ran.

When she reached the banister and looked down, she knew, Edouard was sitting on a step, at the top of the last flight of stairs clinging to the handrail with one hand, his face ashen.

Lenora hastened down, careful not to trip on the hem of her dress. George also came running and meant to pull his master to his feet, but Edouard stopped him.

'No, George, I've hurt my foot. First, I must make sure that I can stand on it.'

'Where is Charles?' Lenora called out. 'He'll help.'

At that moment he appeared. 'Did you call?' Charles took one look at his uncle and hurried to his side, 'What happened?'

He didn't stop to wait for an answer. With George's help, he carefully lowered Edouard down the stairs and sat him on the nearest chair.

Lenora fell onto her knees, embracing her husband, 'Oh dearest, are you badly hurt?'

'My foot is sore, but I think it's not broken. Let me try to stand.'

George and Charles held him up by his arms, either side, and Edouard carefully put weight on his foot, 'No, I cannot, I must rest it for a few days. I will be more careful in the future.' He looked shocked.

George and Charles carried him to his chair in the library, where Lenora tucked him in with a blanket and bathed his swollen foot.

'Shall we send George for the doctor, dearest? It would be

best to have it seen to.'

'Let's wait for the morning, if it's not better, then we will.' Edouard took her hand and brought it to his lips, 'Thank you, dearest wife.'

'I will bring your breakfast, Molly is preparing it.' She squeezed his hand.

Lenora pulled up a chair and read a book for Edouard until lunchtime. When she left him, she found Charles outside the door.

He took hold of her arm, 'I'll wait for you.'

'No, not today.'

'But I want you, Lenora.'

'How can you ask? Edouard needs me.'

'But so do I. Why do you stay with him?'

'Charles, you told me you'd understand. I have to fulfil these simple duties as a wife. If I don't, I cannot love you. You have promised to be patient. What has changed?'

'You should have time for me as well. For heaven's sake, Lenora, your face is full of guilt. You are not his servant. Uncle hasn't married you out of the goodness of his heart. He has taken advantage of you.'

Lenora shook her head; tears filled her eyes. 'You're so wrong, Charles, so wrong,' she whispered and hurried away to escape his displeasure.

'Lenora, you don't have to stay by my side every day, it must be weary for you,' Edouard said on the third day after his accident.

'I don't wish to be anywhere else.' Lenora looked up as Molly came in with the lunch tray. 'Thank you, I'll also take my supper in here with Edouard tonight. If we have it before six o'clock, you can leave earlier. I'm aware your hours are longer since my husband's accident.'

'That's all right, Miss Lenora. We want the master to get well quickly, and he will with your help.'

Lenora nodded.

'Thank you, you're so right. Can you ask George to come and see me after lunch? I have an errand for him,' Edouard said.

'I'll do that, Master.'

As Molly was leaving, Charles came into the room.

'I hope you're feeling better, Uncle?' Charles threw a glance at Lenora, who glowered at him. 'The colour is back in your face.'

'My wife is refusing to leave my side. Perhaps you can tempt her away. She's spending too much time here.'

'I would be delighted to do so. I am not sure that she'll agree,' Charles smirked.

'I am not leaving Edouard, until he's better,' Lenora confirmed and made her voice strong.

A bed had been set up in the library and for two more days, Lenora remained until Edouard's bedtime. She turned down Charles' requests to join him in their hideaway, he insisted on asking her every day and his demands irritated her. After a time, she wouldn't even answer him. At night, she prayed for her husband's recovery and forgiveness for deceiving him. His accident had resulted in an overwhelming feeling of guilt, and she had no longing or desire for Charles.

Edouard's foot improved steadily, it had been a bad sprain, and he was reluctant to stand on it too soon. He preferred a long rest as the doctor had ordered. Lenora was aware that Charles' impatience was growing. He didn't hide his annoyance and became less agreeable.

Lenora swept this aside. Charles had to accept what she was doing. For her own peace of mind, she had to do what was right. She'd made that promise, to make up for her infidelity.

‘Lenora, must you spend so much time by his side? Why not walk with me today?’ Charles implored her. He’d taken hold of her arm in a firm grip outside Edouard’s room, where he’d made a habit of waiting for her.

She pulled herself free. ‘Charles, you’re not showing much understanding. I’ve told you, this is the only way I can allow myself to be with you. It’s my duty to first look after Edouard. I don’t understand the change in you. Until this happened, you were patient and it increased my love for you.’

‘Not much sign of that love now,’ he frowned. ‘It’s a beautiful day, sunny and warm. Do come!’

Lenora looked out of the window, ‘Yes, so it is. I’ll take Edouard into the garden, the air and sun will be good for him. Will you help me to bring him out?’

Edouard was duly installed in a comfortable garden chair with a blanket pulled up to his chest.

‘Enjoy the sun, Uncle. I’m going for a walk.’

‘Why don’t you take Lenora with you? It will do her good. She has spent far too much time with me lately.’

‘Indeed, she has,’ Charles threw her a glance, a sarcastic smile on his lips.

‘Do go, Lenora, it would please me. But ask George to help me inside in half an hour.’

Lenora was unhappy about Charles’ mood, but, hoping it would improve if she accompanied him, reluctantly she agreed. She hurried inside and after talking to George, she put a shawl over her shoulders and joined Charles outside.

She didn’t speak to him, annoyed that she’d agreed to the walk, but Edouard had been so insistent. At the sight of the lilac trees at the end of the lawn, her mood improved. The lilacs were in full bloom and she inhaled their scent as they walked past.

‘I am glad you came along,’ Charles said and when they could not be seen from the house he took her hand.

Lenora didn't remove hers, instead, she pulled him along. 'Come, I want you to see my secret place, where the lily of the valley grows.' Leaving the path, she led him in amongst the trees. 'Here they are.' She fell onto her knees and picked one delicate lily, which she brought to her nose. Charles pulled her up and reaching out, she tickled his nose with the flower. 'Oh Charles, there is nothing to surpass this perfume.'

He pressed her up against him, 'You surpass it.' His voice was hoarse and impatiently he brushed away the flower, which flew out of her hand. His face was close to hers and she could smell alcohol. 'I haven't had you for days.'

Roughly, he yanked at her dress; his hands got tangled up in her underskirt, until he swore and swept it over her head. Her face was covered, she inhaled into the material, unable to see or breathe freely.

He does not know what he is doing, she thought. The look on his face had scared her. They were not far from the house and she dared not scream. The skirts hindered her, when she fought to push him away, beating with her fists against his chest. She felt him fumbling with the drawstring of her pantalets and at the next moment, she was forced up against a tree trunk; her feet momentarily left the ground as he pushed himself into her.

'Charles, you are hurting me, please stop,' she cried, but he ignored her. She had expected him to listen. 'I beg of you. I cannot bear this!' she stuttered.

'It suits me well enough,' he groaned. 'It's about time I had it my way. I've done what you've asked for too long.' After one final thrust, he stepped back and yanked her skirts down.

Her hair hung undone and she swept it out of her face, her shoulders hurt from rubbing up against the tree and she was worried that the back of her gown might be torn. Her despair was total and she had no fight left, she felt alone. Tears rose in her eyes. 'Why are you so angry?'

'Because you're spending all your time with Edouard.'

He did not meet her eyes.

'But he is unwell.'

'Not unwell enough,' he muttered.

'What do you mean?' She took hold of his shirtsleeve and shook it. 'Tell me!'

'Oh, nothing.' He buttoned his trousers as he turned away from her.

Lenora sighed, 'I love you. You must not be jealous of my husband. I will come to our room tomorrow,' she paused, 'if it makes your mood better.' What else could she do to reassure him? She could bear this no longer. All she wanted was a Charles, who understood her, the old Charles, the warm and kind man he used to be. 'Please, Charles, look at me!'

His dark mood vanished instantly, and he grinned at her sheepishly. 'I'm sorry, I should not have lost my temper. I didn't mean to hurt you, I don't know what came over me. Please, say you forgive me!' He took her by her shoulders and carefully pulled her to his chest.

'I do,' Lenora brushed away the tears, and the relief she felt to see his smiling face in front of hers made her fears melt away.

The following afternoon Charles' lovemaking was gentle and he took much care, but her thoughts were with Edouard. Her usual reluctance to leave their love nest had been replaced with an eagerness to be gone. She slid out of bed to hurry back to her husband.

Charles grabbed her wrist. 'Leave him a bit longer! Must you show him so much attention? I am your husband in all but name and one day we'll be wed.'

'You are fantasising. The only reason I came here was to please you. You will not listen to what I say, Charles.' Her rising anger had made these words slip out and hurriedly she dressed. She felt his eyes on her back, she already regretted her outburst and as she left the room her unease grew.

Chapter 29

The Caravan Park, Cumbria, early June 2006

Ellen waved and shouted, 'Good Morning,' to the occupant of the van next to hers. She had never seen him before, but he smiled and waved back. She unlocked the door to the static caravan she had rented, since leaving the cottage at the end of May. The inside felt cold and unlived in, which was her fault, as most of her time was spent at Lakeside House.

Although she had vowed to stay with Lenora as much as possible, she had to make contact with the real world and at times found herself back in the present, not quite knowing how she'd got there. Her subconscious mind had released her from this other life.

Her eyes wandered around the van. It wasn't as spacious as the cottage, but it had all the amenities: a kitchenette, shower and flushable toilet.

Mrs Jones, the pub landlady, had advised her to check out this caravan park, as she couldn't offer her a reduced rate at the pub for the summer months. The site was only two miles out of the village and to Ellen's delight there had been a cancellation. The manager hadn't been helpful to start with, protesting that there was a waiting list. She'd convinced him by offering to pay up front, for the full three months, thus covering the whole cancellation period. The rent wasn't cheap at the height of the summer period, but it compared favourably with the cost of the cottage or a room at the pub.

She opened the fridge and closed her nose with her fingers. The milk was solid, the cheese mouldy, and a bad smell came from the packet of ham. She emptied it all into a bag and carried it out to the bin. The shop on the site was reasonably well stocked with the essentials, such as bread, milk and a few meat and fish products. She'd have to make her way there.

After a brisk walk to the shop and back, Ellen made a coffee and inhaled the aroma of the bread before putting it into the toaster. She'd been lucky, the baker had just delivered and if there was one thing she loved it was fresh bread. She had a craving for it, she sighed and took another bite.

As usual, her mind settled on Lenora. She was having a time of it lately, trying to keep a balance between Edouard and Charles. Obviously, her husband's need was greater, having fallen down the stairs, and Charles' demand on her time and body was selfish, he didn't make it easy for her. Now that he had Lenora's love, he didn't want to share her with Edouard.

Ellen had come to dislike and mistrust Charles, he'd turned out to be cruel, with alcohol on his breath.

'For heaven's sake,' she muttered, 'didn't the silly woman realise that she'd been raped in the wood?' Ellen supposed that in those days it wasn't considered rape, and women just put up with it. Lenora had seemed oblivious to the fact. She'd been submissive to an extent that bordered on an apology for not making herself available. Charles satisfied his own needs, without much regard for his uncle and the woman he swore he loved.

It was possible that he did love Lenora in his own way, but it wasn't love as Ellen knew it. She shook her head and put the plate and cup into the sink, where she left it to soak in the hot water.

Chapter 30

Lakeside House, Cumberland, early June 1903

The swelling on Edouard's foot had gone down and using care, he was able to walk again, albeit with a limp. With support he could climb the stairs at night, so the temporary bed in the library was removed.

At his first meal back in the dining room, he wobbled up to the sideboard and leaned his stick against it.

'I am now holding the whisky decanter.'

'Yes, dearest, you know you are.' She sighed, guessing what he was going to say.

'George filled it up on the day of my accident and it is nearly empty,' he frowned.

'Oh, it can only be Charles.'

'Yes,' Edouard nodded, 'he has also drunk several bottles of wine. I will have a word with him.'

'That might be as well.' Lenora was relieved to hear this. If Charles took notice of Edouard's reprimand, it would benefit her too. It filled her with dread when she could smell alcohol on Charles' breath, as he was usually in a bad mood on these occasions.

After lunch, when Lenora was reading for her husband, Charles came into the room.

'It is a shame to spend this beautiful day indoors, Lenora,' he said.

Edouard, who had been leaning back with his eyes closed, sat up at once.

'I agree. You must go with Charles. You can finish this chapter later. Lenora lowered the book in her hand.

'Edouard, I would rather stay here with you.' She threw an angry glance a Charles, remembering what had taken place on their last walk.

'Then I shall go on my own.' Charles stared back at her, before slamming the door shut behind him.

'I believe my nephew's mood is changing for the worse. Perhaps there is not enough for him to do here?'

'He has not told me of any such displeasure,' she lied.

'If his behaviour doesn't change, his stay here may have to end. What do you think, dearest?' Edouard turned a serious face towards her.

She stifled a sharp intake of breath and hoped that he hadn't heard. His head was tilted to one side, eager for her reply. She had to be careful how she answered.

'Well, Lenora …?'

'It must be your decision, dearest, but do talk to him and give him a chance to improve his behaviour,' she answered at length.

'Of course, you are right. We must give him that opportunity.' Edouard nodded and his face relaxed, but his voice was firm when he spoke, 'When Charles returns, will you send him to see me at once?'

She would have to speak to Charles urgently before he saw Edouard.

'I hope the walk was long enough to cool your temper. Edouard wants to speak to you in the library. You would do well to show respect and apologise, for both our sakes,' Lenora said to Charles, when he returned a short time later.

Charles nodded, 'I'm sorry, I did behave badly. I'll see Uncle now.'

She was expected in the kitchen, but Molly would not mind if she was a little late. She had to find out what Edouard told Charles. While she waited, Lenora worked on her embroidery and saw at once, from his red face, that his anger had returned.

'The old goat!' he burst out. 'He is threatening to send me back to Canada!'

'I hope you didn't show your temper, because if you did he's sure to do that.'

'I'm not stupid. I'll outdo the old goat.'

Lenora raised her voice, 'Charles, don't speak of my husband in that manner. I'll not allow it! Never again call him that in front of me.' She could feel her cheeks burning.

Charles immediately changed his attitude; he fell onto his knees in front of her and grasping her hands in his, kissed them gently.

'I promise not to,' he whispered. 'I will make it up to you when I see you shortly. You will come to our room this afternoon, won't you?'

She nodded her reply, although not sure that she had forgiven him. Her refusal would bring on his mood swing, so she always tried to please him. Charles in a bad temper made her unhappy.

Only after he had left, did she remember that she'd promised to see Molly about the food needed for the picnic and she was already late.

Lenora climbed the stairs to the second floor; she opened the door, showing no intention of entering.

'I've come to tell you I cannot stay. I have no excuse to give Molly; she's waiting in the kitchen.'

A naked Charles jumped out of bed and forced her hand off the door handle, pulling her into the room. Her protest was silenced by a finger to her lips, 'Shush.' He kissed her and eagerly fumbled in her bodice to pull out her breasts, kissing them in turn. Lenora felt her nipples harden under his roaming tongue.

'Charles,' she moaned, 'I haven't got time to undress, I must go, please...'

Her words died away as he swept her up and put her down on the bed, 'I'm ready for you, no need to undress.' He yanked up her underskirt and pulling at the drawstring, released her undergarments. He groaned as he entered her and moments later fell upon her breathing heavily, 'You can go now.' He rolled off her, his eyes cold.

'Have I displeased you?' Lenora slid off the bed, picking up her undergarments she turned her back to Charles before putting them on.

'I don't like being rushed.'

'Surely one afternoon…why are you in such a mood? You've been tender and caring. What has changed?' She smoothed out her crumpled skirt.

'Yes, exactly. I've done everything in my power to make you happy. One would expect more,' he grimaced.

'As I have done, I have come here to please you.'

'And you do. Off you go, don't keep Molly waiting.'

Lenora left the room, biting her lip, he made her unhappy and she didn't know how to behave to quell his temper.

She made her way-down the narrow staircase to the first floor and checked that the key was hidden under the loose floorboard. Charles would lock the door when he came down. Lenora was confident that Molly and George wouldn't surprise them in their love nest. She had told Molly that between the hour of three and four she would be in her room, adding up the household accounts, and had given strict instructions not to be disturbed. Molly spent this time preparing the evening meal or baking, and the arrangement suited them both. Tomorrow morning George would be driving his wife into Kendal to pick up provisions for the yearly Grand Picnic, which was to take place in two days' time. Lenora had prepared a list, and there were still purchases she had to agree to.

She caught the quick glance Molly gave her crumpled skirt and froze, but the cook's smile was carefree when she spoke.

'Miss Lenora, shall we have the capon, as we've done in previous years and the cold beef?'

'Yes, do you have the old menu?' She took the small notebook out of Molly's hand and scanned the page. 'Let's remove the beetroot and have asparagus instead this year. Beetroot isn't suitable for picnics; it stains easily.'

'Yes, Miss Lenora, I do agree. May I suggest that we have fresh strawberries, instead of a mousse, for the same reason?'

'That's a good idea.' Again, she caught Molly glancing at her skirt. Instinctively, she bent down to smooth out any wrinkles and explained. 'I've just come from the garden, tending to some plants,' she lied and felt a blush on her cheeks.

'Yes, Miss Lenora,' Molly studied her list carefully.

'Edouard should be awake by now. You'll find me in the library should there be anything else.' She tried to hide the annoyance in her voice and regretted having made up an excuse, she shouldn't have done that.

Chapter 31

Molly put down the menu book and looked thoughtfully after Lenora as she left. Something wasn't right, and she thought she knew what it was. 'I hope I'm wrong,' she sighed. It would be too shameful. But the girl hadn't had much experience and her life had been sheltered. She didn't know if she dared to mention it to George. Molly shook her head; she couldn't keep this to herself. She had to share her suspicions with her husband. She couldn't tell anybody else.

Half an hour later, when he came in for his tea, she ventured, 'I know that Miss Lenora isn't in her room between three and four as she says. Now, where do you suppose she is then?'

'What do you mean, woman?' George looked up from his cake.

'I mean that she's lying and why is she?'

'Don't speak in riddles, woman. It's none of our business anyway.' George studied her face carefully.

'Do you see young Charles around between the same hour?'

George slammed his cup down on the saucer.

'Careful, you'll break the cup,' Molly said.

'No, I can't say that I do,' he answered slowly. 'You mean…' he left the words unspoken.

'I do, and it's a shame; she's far too good for him and it's shameful to the master.'

'I don't like the scoundrel,' George raised his voice, 'and if it's true, he should be flogged, repaying his uncle in this way. I've a good mind to tell him.'

'Steady on, we don't know it's true. It's only my suspicion.'

'I think you're right. Many things make sense now. The way they look at each other, it's too familiar,' George growled.

'You can't tell the master, it would break his heart. He adores Miss Lenora, and young Charles will be going back to Canada before long. It will be over then.'

'You're right,' he calmed down, his red cheeks returning to normal, slightly less red. 'I wouldn't have thought it of Miss Lenora, it makes me sad to think. I've always been fond of her, since she came to this house as a young girl.'

'Not entirely her fault though, George. Think of it! The master treats her as a daughter, always has done. Even a woman has her needs.' Molly blushed slightly.

George's face lit up, 'So there's a chance of a bit of dilly dallying when we get home!'

'Hush!' Molly threw a dishcloth at him, but her eyes sparkled, and she showed her teeth in a big smile.

'Just the same, I'm disappointed in Miss Lenora, it's no way for a lady to behave.' George rose from his chair, 'We'd better set off to Kendal early in the morning to get the food for the picnic. It's going to be larger than ever this year. The Clarkson family is coming and they have invited the Wilsons from Keswick.'

'Sounds like all the big families from the area will be there. I won't be pleased to see the Harpers' housekeeper. You do remember Marie, don't you? 'Course you do, she had her eyes on you. And don't shake your head, George, this is no fantasy of mine.'

But George was still shaking his head as he put his cap on, a smug smile on his face.

Chapter 32

The Grand Picnic, June 1903

'Edouard, I hope the weather will stay fine for the Grand Picnic tomorrow. It looks uncertain. We have all the provisions and Molly is making the preparations now.'

'Don't worry, dear. Nothing you can do about it, we can't change the weather,' Edouard smiled reassuringly.

'I know, but we could be left with a great deal. It's our turn to supply all the food for the Edmondson family. They did so for us last year.'

'I remember and very good it was too. Well, if it rains we'll ask them to come here instead.'

'It would be such a shame, I enjoy meeting the other families. It's only once a year. We don't see them any other time now.'

'We haven't got room for all of them. But if Jonathan cleared out their large barn, we'd all fit in there. But that takes preparation, not done in a hurry.'

'It will be a big gathering this year: the Shepherds, the Brown family, and the Harpers, to mention a few. The Burtons aren't coming as they have a wedding to attend in Edinburgh.'

'How very pleasant, it's a long time since we went to such a happy celebration.' He felt for her hand, 'I think it might have been our own, dearest.'

Her hand stiffened as he brought it to his lips. Had he noticed? Her hesitation stemmed from her own shame and guilt, only an hour ago she'd deceived him in his own home. She stared at the floor, she couldn't bear to look into his trusting eyes.

'Is everything all right, dearest? You seem tense.'

'Yes, all is well. I'm worried about the picnic tomorrow. I'd better go to Molly, she's waiting for me.' She eased her hand free and placed a kiss on his forehead.

As she made her way to the kitchen, her thought was on his question. What if he found out, could she bear it? The consequences would be unimaginable. Their world would fall apart. Was it worth it? The hurt to Edouard would be immense. He must never know.

It would mean giving up Charles and she couldn't do that. In spite of his demands, she loved him; she'd never felt like this. When they were together, she was happier than she could remember ever having been. She needed the warmth and the closeness he gave her. He made her feel beautiful and desirable. He had brought something into her life that she had never experienced before.

Lenora's thoughts changed abruptly and brought her back to reality. She rubbed her forehead; Charles had changed again, and his mood swings worried her, if only he could give up alcohol. On those occasions, she never knew how to best deal with him.

The sun shone and the sky was blue the next morning.

'Your fears were unfounded.' Edouard turned to Lenora, standing next to him on the porch. 'And I can hear the trap coming down the lane.'

Molly, George and Charles had gone ahead with the food, tables and chairs. Charles had returned to collect them. He had become an expert at handling the horse, as he often took her out on trips to Kendal and outings with Lenora and his uncle.

Charles jumped off the trap, 'Let me help.' He hurried towards them with his hand outstretched. Edouard placed his straw boater onto his head, before letting Charles assist him. When it became her turn, Lenora acknowledged with a smile, the brief kiss he placed on her hand.

The drive took them through the village and past a row of cottages. From the trap, Lenora looked into their gardens, amongst the flowers were roses and foxgloves and harebells grew on the grass verges outside. As they passed one in particular, she called out, 'Oh, Edouard, we've just passed Molly and George's cottage, and their rhododendrons are in bloom, they are beautiful.'

They had arrived where the picnic was to be held. Edouard's face lit up as he stepped down from the trap with Charles' help, 'I can smell newly cut grass.' George was waiting for them by the edge of the field. He stepped up to Gladys and took hold of the reins, leading her away.

'Yes, it was cut yesterday,' Charles said.

'Oh, it looks so pleasant, Edouard, the tables are placed differently this year. They are in rows, and we're sharing ours with the Edmondsons.' Lenora took her husband by the arm and led him forward.

'We have laid out the food on separate tables: one with savoury dishes, the other with desserts, which look delicious,' Charles said.

'I can see Jenny and Jonathan. We must join them at once.' Lenora shook Edouard's arm excitedly, 'It's all so cheerful with the different coloured canopies. You won't need your boater.'

'I think I'll keep it on just the same, the sun is hot today.' Edouard smiled, 'Your enthusiasm is catching.'

'I suggested the different layout of the tables, glad you

like it,' Charles looked pleased.

'It's definitely an improvement from last year. Well done, Charles.' Lenora nodded to him. 'Come on, let's find our place, most families have already done so.' She took Edouard's arm and led him to where the Edmondson family were waiting, Emily standing next to her mother.

'Emily, you look delightful.' Charles bowed and brushed her hand with his lips. Jenny Edmondson raised her eyebrows but didn't comment, merely nodding her head as Charles bowed to her in turn, without taking her hand.

Lenora silently agreed with Charles, the yellow dress Emily wore had a print of white daises. The sparkle in her eyes and the blush on her cheeks, as Charles paid her the compliment, did indeed make her look lovely.

The weather had lifted everyone's spirits, and people moved around, greeting their friends. More canopies were raised to give shelter from the sun.

The ladies wore bright summer dresses and hats with huge brims, decorated with bows or flowers. It was obvious that on this occasion the women tried to outshine one another. Lenora wore a floral dress, made of layers of sheer organza, and on her head, a white hat trimmed with the same material.

Jonathan Edmondson had just brought the tankard to his lips when he received a sharp jolt in his back from one of the Harpers' children, who were running out of control.

'I apologise, Jonathan, the excitement tends to make them wild.' The children's father indicated the brood of six behind him. 'I shall gather them up and get them seated, so that we can all eat in peace.'

'That's all right, Robert, let the children enjoy themselves today.' Jonathan brushed off the ale spilt on his jacket and forced a smile.

The staff enjoyed their own picnics at tables a short distance away, Lenora waved to Molly. Everyone had worked hard to get everything ready, including members of the families. But once the preparations were in place, this was a day free from work. Lenora raised her arm again to George, and he lifted up his pitcher of cider in a greeting.

The noise level rose at the tables of workers and employers alike, as the picnic progressed. Lenora was seated some distance from Charles, who sat at the far end. Jenny obviously hadn't forgotten the New Year's Eve kiss and had made sure that her daughter was by her side and as far from Charles as possible. Emily repeatedly turned her head towards him, and Lenora knew that would not please her mother.

She observed the lingering looks Emily gave Charles; holding his gaze for a moment, blushing and looking away, only to immediately seek his eyes again. Silly girl, Lenora thought, Charles is mine. Confident, she turned to Edouard and Jonathan and joined in their conversation.

'Charles,' Lenora called out to get his attention, 'it's usual for all families to share desserts, so you can help yourself to what you like at the other tables.'

'That's a splendid custom. I'll do so at once.' Charles was soon engaged in a lively discussion at the next table, where he helped himself to chocolate mousse.

'Time we did the same, Lenora; I want to speak to Harry Brown, I've not met him since last year.' Edouard rose, fumbling for his stick, which had fallen to the ground.

Lenora laughed, 'Anything to do with the fact, that his wife makes the best bread and butter pudding in Cumberland?' She handed him his stick, as she stood up to guide him from the table.

'Well, that could be part of it.'

She looped her arm around his as they walked off to meet the other families. Her heart warmed, her husband enjoyed this outing and loved to share news with neighbours they only met on this occasion. She glanced over her shoulder to locate Charles and it pleased her that he'd not moved closer to Emily.

Back at their table, Lenora observed Charles filling his

glass every time the port was passed around, his face turning red from the sun and wine. Jenny frowned deeply when he removed his jacket. However, as the day wore on, most men followed his example.

'Well, that was a successful day.' Edouard patted Lenora's hand as they sat together in the trap on their way home. George was in charge of Gladys and Molly was sharing the front seat with him.

'Don't you think so too, Charles?' he asked.

'Yes, Uncle, indeed. Such charming company and a pleasure to meet your neighbours,' he smiled.

Charles held his hand out to assist Lenora from the carriage, but George stepped in front of him and briskly pushed him out of the way, 'Allow me, Miss Lenora.'

Surprised Charles took a step back, and Lenora was amazed to see George's stony face.

What's the matter? Lenora wondered, as she watched the smile die on Charles' lips.

'It is not like George to behave like that,' she mumbled to Charles as he caught up with her on the porch.

'Lenora, I...' but nothing more was said as Molly appeared behind them, interrupting any further conversation.

Chapter 33

Charles closed the door to his room. He was annoyed with George's behaviour. It had been rude coming from a servant, but he'd long suspected that George didn't like him. Also, he'd been unable to speak to Lenora; she had remained cool towards him the whole day and it bothered him. She had only spoken to him when it had been necessary. He didn't like to be ignored. Had she noticed the exchange of glances between Emily and him? He knew when a lady found him attractive, and he remembered only too well her warm response when he'd kissed her on New Year's Eve. She had been limp in his arms and slumped towards him, with her breasts pressed up against his chest. He knew she went to Kendal every Wednesday with her maid; he would go too and hopefully arrange a rendezvous. He was confident that this lady was willing.

Charles positioned himself in the doorway of the tobacconist's shop, in the knowledge that Emily would walk past with her maid.

'Oh, Miss Emily, how delightful!' His voice was full of surprise, as he stepped out in front of the pair. 'I so regret that I was unable to speak to you at the Grand Picnic. It appears that you were well guarded… I beg your pardon, well looked after, I mean.'

'Yes, indeed,' she stuttered, taken aback by his sudden appearance, the colour rushing to her cheeks. 'Mama can be very protective,' her blush increased.

'Forgive me, for being presumptuous, but would you do me the honour of accompanying me to the tea room for refreshments? It would make me happy to think that I could in some small way make up for my previous behaviour.' For a moment he thought that she would refuse him, but her eyes lit up.

'I'll be delighted, refreshments are just what I desire at this time.' She spoke to her maid, 'Meg, wait for me here.'

Charles put his hand on her arm and felt it shake slightly as he escorted her to the tea room. Once they were seated, he dropped all pretence, leaning forward and taking both her hands in his across the table.

'Emily, you've surely no notion of how I've longed for this moment, how I've suffered, unable to be close or speak to you. I've thought of nothing else but the day I could be in your presence.'

Her face turned blood red and she glanced around the room, 'Charles, someone could see us.'

'What if they do? We're having tea!'

'But your hands...' She reluctantly pulled hers free.

'Oh, I see,' Charles smiled. 'I find it hard to control myself, when I'm close to you. Dearest, Emily, tell me now if you don't feel the same.'

'I… I…,' she stammered, 'this is not proper. My mama has forbidden me to see you.'

'But she need not know. Can you trust your maid?'

'Meg doesn't know what Mama has said. But I do not want to involve her.'

'Emily, make me the happiest man in the world and meet me alone. Tell me where and when, and I shall be there waiting for you.'

She looked down at her cake, and he could see that she

was struggling with her answer. 'I think I'd better not,' she whispered, her lips trembling.

'But would you like to? I'll wait for you, however long it takes.'

'Yes, I'm fond of you, Charles.' She raised her head and tears pooled in her eyes.

'Well then, don't deny yourself happiness.'

'But surely you do know that we cannot be alone until we're betrothed.'

Charles stared at her. Betrothed? That was not in his plans, but again he took her hands. 'How can we confirm our feelings for each other, if we're not allowed to meet?'

Emily averted her eyes. She seemed to take an interest in the far corner of the room, and a minute passed before she answered, 'I walk the woods at the back of our house every afternoon after three o'clock, weather permitting. Father has a small hunting lodge twenty minutes from the house, but for you it would take longer.'

'Emily, I would walk to Kendal for you.'

I'll give you directions,' Emily said, blushing. 'From your uncle's house, you just follow the edge of the forest. You cannot miss it.'

Charles' smile was warm, and inside he felt triumphant, 'You have made me happy, knowing that I'll soon see you again.' Charles picked up the teapot. 'Thank you, and may I refill your cup?'

Emily nodded; Charles poured the tea, and then let his hand briefly rest on hers. Emily's eyes were anxious and her smile uncertain. This woman will need much reassurance, Charles thought, as he watched her sip the tea.

'My maid will be waiting, I must leave now.' Emily abruptly put her cup down.

'So soon? Of course, I'll escort you back to your maid.'

Emily fumbled with her thin gloves. 'No, I prefer it if you don't. Tomorrow afternoon then.'

'Until tomorrow.' Charles' green eyes held hers.

Charles was on his long walk through the wood, the following afternoon, when he remembered that Lenora would be waiting in their upstairs room. He should have talked to her, but she had only herself to blame. Lately she'd been passive and hurried back to her husband, as soon as he'd made love to her. He resented that. It hadn't always been so, Lenora had been willing and often surprised him; to feel her body squirm with pleasure under his excited him. But no longer; she had developed a conscience and feelings of guilt. Well, Edouard wouldn't live forever and then she would have no need to feel guilty. Lenora and Lakeside House would belong to him. He could wait! For now, shy and lovely Emily would pass the time for him.

Charles reached the lodge only minutes before she appeared. He ran up to embrace her, but when he attempted a kiss, she pushed him away pulling the cape closer to her body.

'Have you got the key?' Charles nodded towards the lodge.

'No,' there was an edge to her voice. 'I'll walk and talk to you, but we're not going inside.'

'Why not?' he muttered.

Emily walked on and Charles followed behind. This was going to be more difficult than he'd anticipated.

Eventually the path widened enough for him to walk by her side and when he put his arm around her waist, she didn't protest. The trees got fewer and they arrived by a meadow full of clover, daisies and harebells.

'This is the perfect place.' Charles pulled her close and kissed her forehead, her eyelids and finally her lips. Emily accepted his kisses whilst she remained passive; it was only when Charles loosened the cape around her body and briefly touched her breasts that she reacted.

'Oh Charles, you must not, you should not…'

'Tell me at once and I shall stop. Shall I stop, Emily?'

She didn't answer, her eyes remained closed and she was breathing through her open mouth, the moisture glinting on her red parted lips, inviting him to seek them again. Slowly, he lowered her until her head was resting on the meadow grass. His breathing became heavy as he lifted up her gown and fumbled with the underskirt. Only then did her eyes fly open and she screamed, 'No! What are you doing, Charles? No!'

'Emily, do you not want this?' Charles mumbled, struggling to clear his voice of the desire he felt.

'No, you must not, you must not!' She was shaking as she struggled to sit up, both arms fluttering wildly in her futile attempt to push him away.

'Then I shall not.' His eyes hardened, but he pulled down her skirts and lay by her side. 'Shush... shush...,' he tried to soothe her as teardrops rolled down her cheeks. 'I'll never do what you don't want, but I want you to be mine, all of you. Let me show you affection, Emily, at least.' He kissed away the tears.

After a short time, she stopped crying, 'I'm sorry, Charles, this is not what I had intended. Why did you think that I would…? I'm not that girl…' she sobbed again.

He helped her up and held her gently, stroking her back, 'No, I'm sorry, Emily, please forgive me. Only it's so hard for me, to be this close to you…'

'Please, Charles, can you look to see if I've grass stains on my dress. If Mama were to suspect…' Emily didn't finish her sentence, but her expression was one of high anxiety, and not waiting for his answer, she twisted her body and pulled at her skirt to see for herself.

Charles' eyes widened when he realised that she was more scared of her mother than of him. He must make her overcome her fear, he thought.

'My darling, please don't fret, I will not do anything that you'll regret in front of your mother. Being in your company is all I ask. Just to hold you like this.' He closed his arm around her shoulder and pressed her towards him, rocking her gently and stroking her at the same time. 'My dear, dear, Emily,' he mumbled into her hair.

By now Emily was breathing calmly but turned a worried face up to him.

'It's not your fault, Charles, I've invited you to believe otherwise. I'm to blame. It's just that I couldn't help myself.' Her voice was apologetic and she tried to smile.

'Because you do like it when I kiss you and hold you close. Is that not so?'

Emily nodded, 'I do,' she breathed.

Charles' lips brushed hers, 'Will you meet me here again?'

'Yes, tomorrow.'

Charles smiled inwardly on his way home, he hadn't got what he'd come for, but it had nevertheless been an interesting encounter. It was more rewarding when one had to work for it. These society girls played hard to get, it had taken time to seduce Lenora, but then she was married. She'd been worth waiting for; he'd unleashed years of frustration and a passion, which had taken him a delightfully long time to satisfy.

With Emily, he'd thought it would have been easier, but it wasn't. His uncle had warned him that you don't even kiss a girl unless you're prepared to marry her. Well, Uncle was wrong and old-fashioned, he hadn't moved with the times. Charles had worked his charm on many maidens in his own country, not only those of a lesser reputation and he'd found it no different here.

At dinner Charles pushed a note across the table to Lenora and saw her grimace, she didn't like it done in front of Edouard, it showed disrespect. Charles scowled, the old goat was too stupid to suspect. He could fondle his wife's breasts in front of him and the old man would be none the wiser. But Charles had to admit that he would receive a slap in the face from a furious Lenora, should he attempt to do so.

In his note, he apologised for the afternoon and informed her that he wouldn't attend to her the next day either, as he'd found shooting rabbits so entirely to his satisfaction that he would be doing so most afternoons this week.

After a few moments Lenora left the room and he guessed she'd gone to read his letter, which she wouldn't do in front of her husband. He smirked, considering what else they got up to, he couldn't see why.

When she returned, the anger on her face was clear to see, her furious eyes were seeking his. When he didn't acknowledge her, she ignored him and directed all her attention to Edouard.

The following afternoon, Charles brought a blanket in his rucksack and at the meadow he spread it out for Emily. As promised, he did nothing more than softly kiss her lips, and they talked. He told her about life in Canada and she suddenly sat up with a scared expression on her face, 'Oh Charles! Will you be going back? Oh, I shouldn't like it.'

'Emily, and leave you? I think not,' he answered.

'If only Mama could get to know you, she would like you.' She dropped back onto the blanket.

'Tell me about your mama. What can I do to charm her? Is she always strict?' He rested on his elbow by her side.

Emily let the pink tip of her tongue play on her moist lips. She had a habit of doing this and he found it irresistible. Without waiting for an answer, he took it between his teeth and nibbled gently. Her response was unexpected and immediate; she pulled his face close, pressing her lips hard against his. A surge of excitement flooded his body and his hands went to her hips. She went rigid at the touch. Charles sat up and looked around for a way to break the tension. He snatched at a daisy growing by her head, and smiling, tickled her nose with it.

For a week, Charles and Emily spent every afternoon in this way, although Charles was growing impatient, he didn't show it. Emily picked daisies in the meadow and he tied them into crowns for her hair. She vowed that she'd keep every single one forever.

'Charles,' she said a week later, 'we've met like this for two weeks and Mama is asking why my walks are so long now. I'll have to return home sooner or Mama will suspect.'

'Then we mustn't waste time. Come here and let me kiss you.' He spread out the blanket for her to sit beside him.

'You are right, we must make the most of the short time we have each day. Charles, you may fondle me more. I should like it. Like this.' She placed his hand on her breast and closed her eyes.

Charles lowered her down and slowly untied the ribbons holding her bodice together; his hand slid under the material and let it rest for a moment, feeling the mound of her breast and the softness of her bare skin. He pushed the dress off her shoulders, careful not to rush, baring her small breasts. They were round and firm with pink nipples.

'Oh Emily,' he groaned, 'may I kiss them?' his voice strained. She nodded and when he felt her nipples go stiff as he circled them with his tongue, she moaned.

'Emily, may I go further?' His hand rested on her leg.

'Oh no, Charles, we can't.'

'Why not, Emily?' He knew that his voice betrayed him, but at that moment he didn't care. This had been going on long enough. He sat up and ran his hand through his hair. 'It must be time for you to hurry home,' he said, not looking at her.

'Tomorrow I'll try to stay longer, I promise.' Emily's eyes were pleading and her face anxious.

'I'm not sure I can come tomorrow, better leave it for a day.' His voice was flat and uninterested.

'I'll be there, Charles. Please, say you'll be waiting for me?'

Emily was already at the lodge when Charles arrived two days later. She ran up to embrace him, 'Oh, I was afraid you wouldn't come.'

'Why shouldn't I, Emily?'

'You seemed displeased, I was afraid that I'd offended you. But look what I have here.' Emily held up a large iron key.

Charles pulled her close and kissed her, 'The key to the lodge?'

'Yes!' Emily laughed. 'Come, I'll show you.'

The lodge was sparsely furnished; there was a table with an oil lantern and six chairs, to one side a small bed was attached to the wall. A large fireplace with logs in a basket stood to the side of it. Deer antlers hung from the timbered walls. Two small windows let in some light to either side, but the lodge remained in semi-darkness. He walked over and lit the oil lamp, which spread a yellow light across the room.

'Shall I light the fire?' he asked.

'Better not; it isn't cold, and the smoke could be seen.' She took his arm and led him to several sheepskins arranged on the floor. She lay down and slowly raised her skirts.

'Emily!' Charles fell onto his knees beside her. 'Emily!' he repeated. 'What does this mean?'

'I love you,' she answered, a blush appearing on her cheeks, and closed her eyes.

'I want to undress you first.'

'No, hurry!'

Charles undid his breeches and kicked them off. He didn't see a flickering shadow across the small window pane as he fell upon her.

Chapter 34

Lakeside House, Cumberland, 1st July 1903

'Charles, you're quiet this lunchtime. Far, far away in your thoughts.' Edouard's voice was soft, as if he didn't want to intrude.

Charles' head jerked up, 'Sorry, Uncle, I'm looking forward to this afternoon's shooting, my mind was on that.'

'Was yesterday's successful?'

'Indeed, it was my most successful day.' Charles smiled at the memory of Emily's blond curls spread out on the sheepskin rug.

'Tell me, what did you shoot?' Edouard poured himself another glass of ale.

Charles hesitated, 'I… a hare,' he lied after a moment.

'One hare only?' Edouard raised his eyebrows.

'In fact two, that's why it was such a good day.' He hadn't expected the question; he should have done and been prepared. In fact, he hadn't fired a shot all day.

'Excellent, we can look forward to Molly's jugged hare.'

Charles' quick mind soon had an answer, 'I'm afraid I lost them. I hung them on a branch to pick up later and couldn't find them. I was in a part of the wood, which I'm not familiar with.'

'Well, the rabbit stew we had last week was delicious.

We'll have to be content with that,' Edouard laughed. 'No doubt you'll shoot a hare again. I'm glad you've taken it up, it seems to suit you. Don't you agree, Lenora?'

'Yes, I do agree.' Her face remained serious and she continued to stare at him.

Did she know that he was lying? Suddenly he remembered, she had seen him walk off with the gun over his shoulder, but he had forgotten his cartridge bag in the hall. She knew, and she'd kept that information to herself.

'Dearest, is all well? You have hardly spoken a word.'

'I have much to think about.' Lenora held Charles' eyes as she spoke.

'What would that be?' Edouard asked.

'It's the first of July. Molly and I do the inventory every year. We also restack the china and freshen up the linen,' she answered.

'Yes, of course. Victoria's idea, she started it.'

Charles half listened to the conversation. His thoughts were again on the lovely Emily; the shy and timid bud of a girl had opened up into a rose in full bloom. He briefly closed his eyes and longed to cup his hands on the two silken white mounds that had heaved so tantalizing in response to her breathing. The transformation within her was so visible that anyone who knew her would wonder... and ask what had happened.

Charles frowned. It would spell trouble if her mother became suspicious, but he was sure that Emily was too scared to admit to anything. No, he had more pressing matters to attend to, his money was running short. He had asked his father for more, but there was no mention of this in the reply he had received today. So, he must write urgently and renew his request. His visits to bars and dining rooms in Kendal and Keswick were costing money, which he did not have, and after a long spell winning at cards, he had recently been losing badly. Since his uncle had locked the wine cellar, his consumption of alcohol had been dramatically reduced; he had to pay for it elsewhere. He became aware that Lenora was staring at him, her face set in stone.

He rose and left the room. 'Excuse me, I also have much on my mind. I must retire to pen a reply to my father's letter.'

Chapter 35

Lenora sat upright, her eyes on the door for several moments after Charles had closed it. His note saying that he preferred shooting rabbits, rather than bedding her, had made her furious. For several afternoons she had stayed away from their little room. But when she realised that he hadn't missed her, she had become concerned. Charles had seemed absent-minded on the few afternoons they had spent together, his thoughts elsewhere and his lovemaking hurried, his shooting breeches and gun waiting on the chair by the bedside. This had suited her at first. The flush of excitement and desire she had felt in his arms had diminished.

Now, he was even tempered; the shooting gave him fresh air and exercise and it benefited him. She was beginning to miss his company and his embraces, and she was afraid that he had tired of her.

A moment later, she excused herself to Edouard, 'I must join Molly to do the linen.' As she walked passed Charles' open door, she saw him by the writing desk and further along the corridor Molly was waiting by the linen cupboard, 'You have made a start, I see.'

'Yes, Miss Lenora, I have counted the bed linen several times and make it short. There are many items missing.'

'Oh,' Lenora felt the colour rise on her cheeks, she had meant to do the sheet and pillowcase section herself.

She knew there would be a discrepancy, but she had an explanation at hand. 'Yes, I can account for the missing items. I've had a clear-out and have given them to the needy. I forgot to tell you.' To avoid looking at Molly, she busied herself by straightening piles of pillowcases, which didn't need the attention.

'Then I'll enter these figures as correct,' Molly held out a small note book for Lenora to see.

'Yes,' Lenora nodded somewhat impatiently. 'Well, if you're done here, we have finished this inventory, another job completed for this year. Next, it's the china. By the way, has Charles brought you any rabbits lately?'

'No, Miss Lenora, I don't think it's going too well. He comes back without anything most afternoons.'

'I see, thank you, Molly.' Lenora pinched her mouth.

'But George brought a couple of woodcocks. He'd seen them near the lodge on Edmondsons' land and that's where he shot them.'

Late that night, after she had finished reading for Edouard and left his room, Lenora hesitated in front of her own door and after a moment's pause, continued to Charles' room. She entered without knocking. He was in bed and looked up at her in surprise.

'Do you still love me?' She stood in the middle of the floor, some distance from the bed.

'Of course, I do.' He yawned.

'Well then, show me!'

'Not tonight, Lenora.'

'Why not? What has changed?'

'Nothing.'

'Why did you lie to Edouard about the shooting? If you didn't shoot, what did you do?'

'I couldn't shoot without cartridges, so I just walked. Good night, Lenora.'

She pulled off her gown and stood naked in front of him, her full breasts heaving as her breathing increased.

'Lenora…' He sprang out of bed, 'I had almost forgotten how beautiful you are,' he whispered and carried her off to the bed.

Alone in her room, she slipped off her nightgown again and stood in front of her full-length mirror. Her body gleamed in the candlelight; her skin was pale and without flaws. She was pleased with what she saw. Her breasts had become fuller and were rounder and firmer to the touch, she cupped them with her hands. She could still feel his caresses from moments ago and she knew that he loved her still.

Lenora woke late the following morning and found her husband and Charles discussing shooting at the breakfast table.

'I'm glad you get along with my twelve bore. You're welcome to keep it. No use to me anymore,' Edouard was saying as she bent down to kiss his forehead.

'I am so grateful, Uncle, and thank you for arranging permission to shoot over Edmondsons' land.'

'It has given you more ground to cover. Jonathan isn't worried about what happened at the party, he has accepted that it was in the spirit of the New Year. But he had to support his wife. Jenny is overly protective of her daughter. Anyhow, my woods are not big enough. George also has permission to shoot his land. I'll have a word and ask him to accompany you one afternoon. He will be able to teach you a thing or two, and he knows his way around.'

'That would be splendid, Uncle.' Charles frowned. He turned to Lenora, 'May I pay you a compliment, Aunt? You look so well this morning.' His eyes told her that he was thinking about the previous night.

Chapter 36

A second letter had arrived from Charles' father that morning, and he hadn't even finished his reply to the first – it was still half-written on his desk; there was no point in sending that one now. He crumpled the letter in his hand and letting it drop onto the floor, he banged his fist on the writing desk. What was his father thinking? He picked up the sheet of paper and smoothed it out to read it again, *time to come home*, he read, *only enough money for the journey will be sent.* His father implied that asking for more money meant that he was spending too much. Furthermore, he must not overstay his welcome: one year was long enough. He crumpled it up once more and threw it in the fireplace. He was not leaving. He had other plans. Father didn't know it, but he was determined to marry Lenora.

He put both hands on his forehead, he had a headache. What could he do for money? He had little left and he already owed his uncle some, which he couldn't pay back, even when his father's money arrived. He needed that for himself and certainly would not use it for a ticket home.

He dressed in shooting breeches and tweed jacket. He must not show his bad mood to Emily. He would soon meet her and see her loving face and adoring smile. He was attracted to her innocence and longed to have her again. He would enjoy it so much more the second time. He hurried across the wood, the gun over his shoulder. As soon as he reached the lodge, he knew that something was terribly wrong.

Emily stood on the porch, a brown cloak covered her dress to the ground, her head slumped down and her arms were folded on her chest. When she heard him approach, she raised her tear-stained face.

'Emily!' He dropped the gun to the ground and ran to her, taking her in his arms.

'Oh Charles,' she cried, 'I cannot stay. Mama has found out that you're shooting in our wood. Papa happened to mention it this morning, and she has forbidden me to walk here. Because my walks are longer than usual, she believes that I am meeting you.' She sobbed, 'Papa would kill you if he finds out what has happened, so I lied to Mama and told her I'm not seeing you. Charles, I love you so! What can we do?' She cried so hard, her head shook on his shoulders.

Charles held her close, 'Calm, calm, Emily. We must think of a plan.'

'But I cannot stay much longer.'

'It is clear that we cannot see each other for a time. It will be hard for me not to be near you, dear Emily. Let me make love to you once more before we part, to show you how much I love you.' He held her close. 'I must have you, I ache for you.'

'Oh no!' Emily's eyes widened in alarm, 'Meg, my maid, is waiting for me not far from here. I am not allowed to go out alone. I'm not sure how well I can trust her. It was hard to persuade her to let me wander off, even for a short while. I only came here to tell you this.'

She tore herself free, 'Goodbye, my love.' Her eyes were brimming with tears as she swept her cloak off the ground and ran towards the forest. Then she swivelled round and with a flowing gesture she brought both her hands to her lips and threw him a kiss.

Charles stared after her; that was that. He was annoyed that what had taken him weeks to achieve should have come to such an abrupt end. He had no intention of pursuing her further. That would be too dangerous and doomed to failure. As long as she didn't confess to her parents, he had little to fear. Pity, as he had been growing fond of the lovely Emily. But he still had Lenora, he was pleased that he had reassured her the previous night.

Charles made his way back to Lakeside House and shot two pigeons on the way, tossing them into the bag. He'd give them to Molly, who would make a pie. He hurried his steps, now he would be able to spend more afternoons with Lenora.

Chapter 37

Lenora's face glowed; her visit to Charles' room had worked. As a result, he had promised to give up most afternoons' shooting to spend time with her again. Where was he? She longed for him, and she couldn't bear waiting for him a moment longer. Her clothes were draped over the chair; she knew that her naked body aroused him.

Charles unbuttoned his trousers and fell fully clothed on top of her, the rough material chafing against her bare thighs, 'Charles, have you been drinking Edouard's whisky?'

'Yes, so what? I walked past and it was left unlocked. Can you blame me? It serves the old goat right.'

She pushed hard on his chest, 'Stop. Charles, stop! I don't want you like this. You must not...'

'What's the matter?' he sneered but slid off the bed without touching her.

'Leave me,' she burst out crying, 'I'm not well and you distress me.'

The door banged shut after him and she dragged herself out of bed, she was weary. He was drinking again. She dried her tears and dressed. In the mirror, her red eyes stared back at her. She rinsed them with cold water and made her way to the kitchen, hoping that Molly wouldn't notice her tear-stained face.

George met her in the hall, hastily removing his cap

before handing her a mauve envelope, 'Miss Lenora, this has just come from Mrs Edmondson.'

She immediately recognised the strong fragrance of Jenny's perfume as she unfolded the paper, her forehead wrinkled, and she read the note again. 'Please, get Gladys ready. The trap will do.' George nodded in reply.

Lenora made her way to the library, 'Edouard, dearest, Jenny regrets but they cannot come to our luncheon party on Sunday. Emily is not well. I hope it's not serious. I've asked George to take me there.'

'Of course, you must go. Please give my best wishes to the family and we'll arrange another date as soon as Emily is better.' Edouard turned up his mild face to receive the kiss on his forehead, which he was accustomed to.

When they arrived by the front door of the Edmondsons' magnificent stone mansion, George parked the trap behind that of the local physician, Dr Weston.

'Oh dear,' Lenora said. 'It must be serious.' She looked up to the second-floor window, where she knew Emily's room was located.

The door was opened by a maid and Jenny greeted her in the large hall, her face strained. 'How kind of you to come, the doctor is with her now. I don't know if it is possible for you to see her. Please, take a seat in the drawing room and I'll find out.' Gathering up her skirt, she proceeded to climb the stairs.

'I'll wait here, if that's all right,' Lenora called after her and sat down to admire the huge tapestry on the opposite wall. It was a work of art; it depicted a scene of a medieval castle and the surrounding countryside; the colours were subdued and somewhat faded. Lenora knew that the castle had once belonged to Jenny's ancestors.

'The doctor says it is a severe attack of vapours,' Jenny said as she returned. 'Just what I said, but her father insisted on sending for Donald. Emily is highly strung and not a strong girl,' she paused, forcing a smile. 'I'm afraid you can't see her; Donald says she needs to rest. Will you take tea with me?'

Lenora saw the impatience on her face and realised that her visit was inconvenient. 'No, thank you, it is kind of you, but I'll come back another day. Please tell Emily that I called.'

Jenny nodded and moved towards the front door, which she held open for her.

'Please, tell me how Emily is; I hope the dear child is not too unwell?' Edouard asked at the precise moment Charles entered the dining room.

'Donald was attending, when I arrived. Unfortunately, I was unable to see her,' Lenora answered with a sigh. She caught the alarm in Charles' eyes as he pulled out his chair.

'Emily...,' he paused to recover his voice, 'what's wrong with Emily?' His voice was clipped, as if every word was difficult.

Lenora's eyes bored into his. Why was he so affected? He hadn't seen Emily since the Grand Picnic, yet he was clearly shocked. Was it possible...? No, she dismissed the thought.

Charles drained the glass of claret and smiled nervously. He'd obviously realised that he had shown too much interest.

'Edouard, please pass the decanter; Charles needs a refill.' Her face felt taut, and she knew her eyes were cold as she took the decanter.

'Charles, I am pleased that you appreciate the claret. However, I find it more enjoyable to sip it slowly.'

'Sorry, Uncle, of course you're right. More satisfying.'

'Quite so,' Edouard replied.

Lenora noticed that the line above her husband's eyebrows had deepened. This was a sure sign of his displeasure. Most of the meal was taken in silence, and Charles made his excuse to leave before the dessert was served.

'Edouard, I can tell that you're unhappy with Charles,' she said, as soon as the door had closed behind him.

'I am, my dear. This afternoon he asked me for money. He tells me that he hasn't received Henry's allowance yet. Charles says he will return it to me, when it arrives. But he hasn't yet returned the money borrowed months ago.'

'Oh, Edouard, I didn't know.'

'I didn't want to ask you, but now I fear I must. Has he asked you for money?'

'No, he has not.' She was glad that she was able to tell the truth.

'You would tell me, wouldn't you? Does he always behave with respect towards you? This is extremely important, Lenora.'

Cold sweat broke out on her forehead and feeling unwell, she placed her head in her hands. Before she looked up, she made an effort to calm her agitation and her fists were clenched when she answered, 'Yes, dear, at all times.'

Was her lie a little hollow?

Lenora expected Edouard to question her further; she tensed – she had not sounded convincing after all – and swallowed hard.

There was a long silence before Edouard put his cheese knife down, and she waited for him to speak. His face betrayed none of his thoughts and at no time did his unseeing eyes look away from her before he spoke, 'Good, good, then all is as it should be.'

Chapter 38

'George, please have Gladys waiting by the porch in an hour. I'm going to Kendal.'

'Certainly, Miss Lenora. We'll be ready.'

'Our first stop will be the dressmaker's store; I need materials for a new dress. After that, I'll take tea and have a stroll down the High Street. Who knows what I might find?' Lenora made an effort to sound happy and carefree. She wanted to put the memory of last night's dinner out of her mind and was rewarded by a big smile on George's face.

One hour and thirty minutes later, George pulled Gladys up in front of the store, 'Williams it is, Miss Lenora.'

'Thank you, please pick me up in two hours' time.'

'Will do, Miss.' George touched his cap and drove off.

It took Lenora twenty minutes to search through the many rolls of material to find the right one, a watery soft rose-coloured silk. She arranged for the parcel to be picked up later and walked down the High Street to the teashop. In front of Jennings & Jennings jewellery shop, a pair of sapphire drop-earrings set in gold caught her eye. She took a deep breath; they would match her necklace perfectly. Delighted, she pushed at the shop door, which was opened from the inside by a young shop assistant.

Mr Jennings nodded to the assistant, 'Thank you, Miss Mason.' With a smile, he approached Lenora. 'Mrs Villiers, I'm so pleased to see you, I was becoming concerned. I expect that you've come for your sapphire necklace. I'll fetch it directly, it's in the safe. Mr Villiers' nephew assured me that it would be collected within the month and now it's already six weeks.'

Mr Jennings stopped abruptly. He appeared to be acutely embarrassed. Lenora was staring at him incomprehensively.

'My necklace…?' she stammered.

'Yes, Mrs Villiers.' The jeweller had difficulty finding his voice and the right words, 'Your nephew said that you'd sent him to keep the matter discreet and that you didn't want your husband to know. You needed the money to help out a friend in desperate need. I was surprised, of course, as it was an unusual request and not one that I have encountered before. But I've known your husband for many years, so I was happy to oblige.'

His words came through a thick fog. What was he talking about? Slowly, her brain registered what had been said, and she sank down on the nearest chair.

'I am so sorry, Mrs Villiers, this has come as a shock. I assumed that you knew.'

Her mind was in turmoil, but it didn't take long to comprehend the seriousness of Charles' action. She could not be part of this deception and pretend that she did. 'No, no, I did not. I am sorry, I feel faint.'

'Miss Mason, please fetch a drink for Mrs Villiers.' The assistant quickly returned with a glass of water.

'Thank you.' Lenora sipped the water slowly; thoughts swirled in her head, while Mr Jennings regarded her anxiously. At length she spoke, 'Please, may we have some privacy?'

'Of course, come with me to the office.'

Lenora was unsure that her legs would carry her, but shortly she was seated in a comfortable armchair at the back of the shop.

'Now, please, tell me again.'

Mr Jennings removed a handkerchief from his pocket and wiped his brow.

'Mr Charles Villiers deposited the necklace here in exchange for the sum of one hundred pounds; that's what he said you required. Of course, that is not the full worth of the necklace, as you know. The rest I have told you. He assured me that he would collect it within a month. I have his signature here.'

Lenora felt her face go clammy; her mouth was so dry she was unable to speak, and she reached for the water glass. 'Please, may I see?' Mr Jennings handed her the signed copy of the transaction, where Charles' signature could clearly be seen. 'Mr Jennings, it is imperative that I have your absolute co-operation and discretion in this matter. My husband must never find out. He knows nothing of this. It is a serious misconduct on my nephew's part, and I will discuss it with him. This must remain private. Do you understand?'

'I assumed that when you came into the shop, it was to collect the necklace,' Mr Jennings said. 'I thought it strange at the time; but it was difficult for me to question your nephew's authority. I thought about writing to you in the next few weeks; I'm glad now that it's not necessary.'

'Quite so. Please have the necklace ready for me and the sapphire earrings displayed in the window. I will come back directly.' She left the shop, pleased that the bank was across the road, as her legs barely supported her.

'Miss Lenora, what is the matter? You look as if you've seen a ghost.' George took her arm to assist her into the carriage.

'It's the heat. I'm not good with it. Have you collected my purchase from Williams?'

'Yes, Miss,' George looked hard at her. 'Are you sure all is well, Miss Lenora?'

'Yes,' her voice was short, 'I did say so.' She clutched the parcel from the jeweller close to her chest. 'Please, hurry home.'

George turned to glance at her several times on the journey but didn't raise any further concern.

In her room she lay down on her bed, still holding the small parcel tightly, staring unseeing at the ceiling. How could Charles have done this to her? She wiped away the tears running down her cheeks and felt anger rise in her chest. What if Edouard were to find out? Unthinkable!

After a time, she walked over to the dresser, in the third drawer down lay two leather cases, now she knew that one was empty. She held her breath, as she picked up and opened the smaller case, the bracelet was still there. Carefully, she placed the necklace back in its box and let her fingers run over the gleaming precious stones resting on the crème velvet. She'd only worn the necklace on special occasions and had not missed it. How could she face Charles? What would she say to him? At the thought of him, she clenched her fists.

Edouard and Charles were already seated when she entered the dining room. She had dressed carefully that evening. In the mirror on the opposite wall, above the sideboard, she could see the sapphires sparkle in the candlelight, bouncing off the stones onto her pale skin. It pleased her and gave a feeling of achievement, but it did nothing to quell the anger and resentment she felt. Her bosom heaved rapidly in anticipation of Charles' reaction, when he saw the necklace.

Charles had been in conversation with Edouard; now he

stopped abruptly in mid-sentence. His eyes were transfixed on the necklace, and his face turned deadly white. He appeared a person paralyzed with shock. At last, he lifted his eyes to meet Lenora's icy stare. His lips moved but no sound came. For some moments there was silence.

'Charles...?' Edouard raised his voice, 'Charles...?'

Suddenly Charles' body jerked, and he stumbled out of his chair, 'Sorry, Uncle, I must leave the room,' he stuttered.

'What is wrong with Charles?'

'I believe he's gone to clear his throat, Edouard. He appeared to be choking. Perhaps he swallowed his bread the wrong way,' Lenora suggested, pulling her lips into a crooked smile.

Charles returned minutes later, seemingly calmer, but he refused to look at Lenora as he addressed his uncle, 'Sorry, if I alarmed you.'

'Leonora tells me you choked on a piece of bread. That is very uncomfortable.'

'Yes, Uncle, so it was, but I'm fine now.'

It was hard for Lenora to keep her anger from showing. She maintained a polite conversation throughout dinner, but she avoided addressing Charles directly, only answering when eventually he spoke to her. She made her eyes hard as she stared at him, causing Charles to avert his.

Edouard was extremely sensitive to tension in a room. He had noticed, of this she was certain. His face had taken on the thoughtful expression he always had, when he sensed a problem.

Later that night, after she had read for Edouard and she stood by his bedroom door ready to leave, he called out her name, only to hesitate and shake his head, 'Oh nothing. It's nothing. Good night, dearest.'

She was about to undo her dress when there was a soft knock on her door, which opened before she had answered.

'Charles, what are you doing here?' She spat out the words.

'Lenora, I can explain. Please, listen to me!'

'Then explain!' Her voice was ice cold.

'I would have put it back.'

'When? You were already two weeks overdue. I might never have found out if you had.'

'That's what I intended. I had debts in Kendal. Father's money hasn't come yet.'

'What do you spend this money on? I know there's a group of men meeting to gamble at the Station Hotel. Are you taking part?'

'It's none of your business.'

'It is, when you steal my necklace. Edouard has also lent you money. It's unforgivable.'

'I only borrowed your necklace. Let me make it up to you,' Charles strode forward and embraced her.

'Let go of me this minute. I cannot forgive you for this.' She pushed hard at his chest, struggling to free herself.

'I do love you, Lenora.' His eyes filled with tears.

'Love me? Do you? Leave this room!' The anger in her voice could not be mistaken, although she kept her voice low.

Charles backed out of the room. 'Please,' he began, but after one look at her face he left.

Lenora was shaking with anger and frustration; her legs would not carry her, and she slumped to the floor.

Chapter 39

'Edouard, let me take you for a walk through the orchard after breakfast. It's such a beautiful day.'

'I would like that. I haven't been to the orchard for a while. Is the fruit looking promising?'

'Yes, dear, it'll be a good year. And this plum jam is delicious, I must compliment Molly.' She licked her lips and replaced the lid on the pot.

'I'm surprised, you don't normally eat anything sweet.'

'I have changed my taste, just fancied some today.'

Edouard inclined his head, 'It seems Charles isn't joining us again. He's increasingly restless and short of temper. Perhaps there's not enough for him to do here?'

'You could be right.' She was pleased that Charles had stayed away. The previous night she had not been ready to speak to him about the necklace, she had been too angry. Today, she intended to seek him out to severely reprimand him and have clarity in the matter.

In haste she rose from the table, a hand in front of her mouth, 'The jam didn't agree with me after all.' She only got as far as the hall when she was sick, and she hurried into the kitchen to dispose of her soiled napkin.

'Miss Lenora, you don't look at all well! Sit down and I'll get you a glass of water. Your forehead is wet with sweat.' Molly fussed around her.

'I'm all right, just need to rinse my face. I don't know what came over me. Please don't fuss!' But she accepted the glass of water and regretted her harsh words. 'I'm sorry, I know you mean well. Take no notice, but it's so unusual for me to feel this way.'

Molly's anxious face broke into a smile, as she handed her a cloth to dry her face. 'Don't worry, Miss Lenora, I've known you too long to take offence.'

'Thank you, I must go back to Edouard, I've promised to walk with him in the orchard.'

'It's a while since you walked together, the master will like that…' Molly stopped abruptly and turned to busy herself, realising that she had spoken out of turn.

Lenora felt a stab of guilt. Molly was right.

'I think we should send for Donald. You've felt unwell for a day or two,' Edouard said as she sat down beside him.

'I'm sure it's nothing, I'll see him if it continues. Are you ready?'

She walked behind her husband as he expertly negotiated his way out and down the steps of the porch, where he offered her his arm. They walked side by side to the back of the house and into the orchard, through the arch-shaped opening in the hedge.

'This is so enjoyable.' Edouard put a slight pressure on her arm, 'Tell me what you see, dearest.'

'Well, the cherries are over. You've been eating lots of them. Mind you, the birds have had their fair share. The apples are doing well, and we'll have plenty of pears this year. Maybe a few trees are too old. Perhaps they will have to come down. I'll have a word with George.'

Edouard laughed, 'Can you smell the air? I can smell summer.'

This lifted Lenora's mood. 'I have neglected you recently. We must do this more often.'

'You could never neglect me, Lenora. You're a good wife.'

Guilt stabbed at her again, and her chest tightened. A good wife she was not. She had committed the worst sin of all, by deceiving him in his own home. A shiver went down her back.

Suddenly the sun disappeared behind a black cloud, which loomed overhead. She stared up at it. A dark sky had appeared out of nowhere. It scared her. Was it a bad omen? Would she have to pay for her sin?

'Edouard, there's a thundercloud right above us. And a flash of lightning! Come, hurry! It's starting to rain.'

'Yes, I can feel that,' Edouard laughed, still in a good mood, despite the weather.

Lenora took a firm hold of his arm and hurried her steps, leading him quickly to the porch. By the time they entered the hall, the rain was coming down heavily; a thunderclap followed a bright flash of lightning. Edouard brushed the rain off his shoulders and arms, 'You know I felt pressure in my head earlier. I can usually tell in advance when it's going to thunder. But I've enjoyed the experience of being out in a storm.'

'Yes, I find thunder and lightning exciting,' Lenora answered, 'but we'd better go and change our wet clothes.'

After Lenora had put on a dry dress, she found Charles waiting in the corridor.

'I want a word with you,' she said.

'Yes, that's why I am here too. Can I come in?' His eyes searched her face for clues as to her mood.

'Now is not a good time,' Lenora said flatly and pointed towards her husband's room. 'I'll see you upstairs at three-thirty.'

Charles' face lit up. 'Oh, Lenora…' he began, but she interrupted with a finger to her lips as Edouard's door opened.

'Lenora? Is that you?' Edouard made his way across the

landing towards the stairs.

'Yes, and Charles, we're on our way down too.'

'Let me assist you, Uncle.' Charles offered his arm.

'You have been here long enough to know that I don't need help. I know my way around this house as if I were sighted. Don't make me feel like an invalid.'

'Of course, Uncle, I thought…' he faltered.

'But thank you just the same.' Edouard followed Lenora as she made her way down, her taffeta skirt rustling on every step.

Later, when it was time to meet Charles, she made her way to the second floor, full of apprehension. As she entered the room, she found him naked on the bed.

'Get dressed, Charles,' she ordered, her face tight, 'I'm here only to talk.' Because of her anger, she felt no shame as her gaze wandered down his naked muscular body, and she saw that he was ready for her. A shiver of excitement rippled through her stomach and involuntarily she took a step forward.

'No, take your clothes off or I'll do it for you.'

'No, Charles.' But already her voice was fading.

He sprang out of bed and swiftly pulled down the lace of her bodice. He gripped both breasts and held them firmly, one in each hand, while his tongue encircled her nipples, hungrily moving from one breast to the other. There was a determination in his movements, which made her attempt to protest futile. Lenora moaned and succumbed immediately, she allowed her legs to go limp and he carried her to the bed. Hurriedly, he undressed her and her body ached for him under his hands.

He kissed her with a fervour she'd not known and whispered, 'I love you.' He placed a finger on her lips as if to silence protests that were not forthcoming. 'I couldn't bear to lose you,' he mumbled in her hair, 'I want you now.'

'Yes, yes,' she urged.

And as he held her, she melted into him and became fluid, unreal. She could feel that he made love to her with his entire being, and she accepted him with every fibre of hers. A feeling as strong as this he couldn't fake. This was real. All thoughts about the necklace and the reason that had brought her to this room were forgotten.

But as she lay snuggled up in his arms, the unease returned, 'Charles, the necklace, why did you do it? Where has the money gone?'

Instead of answering, Charles kissed her and moved his body onto hers again and when she tried to speak, his mouth silenced her.

Later still, Lenora sighed, 'I feel happier now, Charles, whatever you've done, I know you love me. That's all that matters.' She covered her breasts with the sheet as she sat up, 'I was sick again this morning, Edouard was worried. He said I should see the doctor. But I'm sure it will pass.'

Charles heaved himself up and stumbled out of bed, fumbling as he hurriedly pulled on his trousers, his voice loud, 'You've been sick? Several times?'

'Yes, but there's no need to be so alarmed, Charles.'

'Not be alarmed! Lenora, has it not occurred to you that you might be with child?' He paced the floor, his face ashen.

Her world fell apart. Her head swooned; she felt her skin go clammy and with a small scream, she fainted.

She woke moments later to Charles gently slapping her face, 'For how long have you had this sickness?'

'Only for a couple of weeks,' she could barely utter the words.

'And have you bled?'

'Bled?' she looked startled, not understanding at first, then she coloured, 'Oh, Lord, I can't remember if I bled last month. If not, it should be soon.'

'When?' Charles stopped pacing the floor, his question urgent.

'Oh, I'm not sure. I don't count the days, perhaps next week.'

'Think, Lenora, think! It's important.' He grabbed her shoulders.

She fell back onto the pillow; she wanted no part of this. 'It must be about seven or eight weeks now,' she whispered, a sob escaping after each breath.

What would she not give for the bleed to start? This could not be true, it could not happen to her. A child? She'd never given it a thought. Why on earth not? Cold crept into her body and she shook uncontrollably.

'Oh, my Lord, what will become of us? What shall we do? It will break Edouard's heart. I never meant for this to happen,' her voice was distorted by sobbing.

'It might not be necessary to tell Edouard.' Charles shook her gently.

'Not necessary?' Momentarily, she stopped crying, 'I don't understand.'

'You might not be with child. And if you are, many women lose it before it's born.'

'I am strong and healthy. There's no reason why I should lose this child.' With an effort, Lenora pulled herself together. 'I'll have to pay for my sin. But where will we go? I have some money, but you have none.'

'I'll marry you and we shall live here at Lakeside House.'

'You cannot marry me; I'm married to Edouard.'

'Shush, shush, stop crying.' Charles cradled her head against his chest, 'We'll think of something.' His voice suddenly became strong, 'I will think of something!' He sounded sure of what he was saying.

Chapter 40

'Lenora, have you not got something you want to tell me?' Edouard asked.

The tea tray fell out of her hands onto the table and two cups rolled off the side, smashing into each other on the hard mahogany surface; one broke in half. After the clatter of china, a moment's silence followed. Her hand shook as she bent down to pick a teaspoon off the carpet.

'How clumsy of me,' she mumbled, her voice barely audible.

'What happened?' Edouard had his arm outstretched as if to offer his help.

'Oh, it's the tray. One cup broken. I'm afraid it's the Crown Derby, one of our better sets.' She'd always admired the intense blue colour of this china. 'I'm so sorry, Edouard, this set was a wedding present from your old friend, Clifford.' Lenora held the two pieces up against each other; the rough sides grated as they met and fell apart again as she put them back onto the table. The broken cup was a small mishap but enough to make her feel that her world was falling apart. Her thoughts were all over the place; she couldn't stop shaking. Everything was going wrong. Edouard had turned a concerned face towards her and attempted to raise himself out of the chair.

With an effort, she asked, 'What do you mean? I don't

understand.' But she knew that her voice revealed the strain she was under.

'Lenora, it's only a teacup, was it the Derby Lily?'

'Yes, I'm afraid so.'

'Why does it upset you so much? We can replace it. Molly told me that you've talked over a menu with her. If we're having a party, shouldn't you have discussed it with me first?'

'Oh, that!' Relief flooded over her and gratefully she sank down onto the sofa. 'I wanted to know if Molly was free to work, before I mentioned it. Also, I've picked a menu, which isn't easy. I had to be sure she was comfortable with it.'

'I think it's an excellent idea. Molly and George will be available; they have never refused.' Edouard said.

'Yes, but let's not make definite arrangements yet. I had planned it for the last weekend of August.' Her face was clammy.

A party won't be feasible, not if I am with child, she thought. How could she plan anything, now that her mind was full of these other thoughts? The possibility that she was with child overshadowed everything. She stood up abruptly, faintness overcame her and she had to leave the room, 'Excuse me, I will fetch another cup and I've forgotten the milk.'

In the hall she met Molly, 'You're as white as a sheet, Miss Lenora! Whatever is the matter?'

'I'll be fine, thank you. I am going for air.' She could feel Molly's eyes on her back, as she hurried towards the garden door.

When Lenora returned five minutes later, Edouard said, 'I poured myself tea, whilst you were out and the milk jug was here all along, I felt it on the tray.'

'Yes, so I see.' She quelled the nausea that was once again overwhelming her.

'Charles is taking me for a ride in the trap later.' Edouard held out his cup for a refill.

'Why the trap?' Her hand shook as she poured the tea. 'Won't you be more comfortable in the carriage?'

'His choice.' Edouard turned towards the door, 'Oh, here he is now.'

Charles hadn't knocked but coughed discreetly, as he entered.

'Are you ready, Uncle? Gladys is waiting, raring to go.'

'Indeed I am.' Edouard hoisted himself out of the chair, leaving his tea untouched, and followed his nephew.

Lenora stared after them thoughtfully and suddenly her body crumbled; a sob escaped her. Oh, dear Lord, what would she do if she were with child? She could not be! Yet, there was the sickness and she had not bled. No, it must not be so! She had done wrong and it would not happen again. If she wasn't with child, she must make sure that she would never be. She would not allow Charles to come close to her ever again.

She stood up resolutely, straightened her shoulders and smoothed down her skirt. Everything would be all right. He had to go back to Canada. Had his father not mentioned it in a letter to Edouard? She would tell him that she agreed. Then she and Edouard could have their lives back, as it had been before he had turned up.

Lenora hoped that she had imagined the inquisitive look she'd seen on Molly's thin face as she walked into the kitchen.

'Miss Lenora, I'm pleased, you look much better.'

'Thank you. What's for dinner? Charles and Edouard have gone for a drive and I'm not sure when they'll be back.'

'A steak pie, I can set it back by half an hour.'

'Excellent, Molly, make it an hour just in case.'

Molly's mouth drooped but Lenora ignored it. It would give her time to change into another dress. It was going to be a fresh start, and to look her best tonight would give her the confidence she needed.

Her blue velvet gown was worn for special occasions only, but to Lenora this was such a day: it was the start of her new life. From now on, it would be different. She had chosen not to wear the sapphire necklace as it reminded her of Charles' deceit. She sat down in the drawing room to await their return. When she heard the trap, she walked into the hall to meet them.

'You look lovely tonight, Aunt,' Charles said in a surprisingly cheerful tone. Amazed, she wondered what had brought it on. He couldn't possibly be pleased at the prospect of becoming a father. No, most likely he had come to the same conclusion that she had: she was not with child. That was why he was in a good mood.

She looked at him in a way she'd never done before, studying him carefully with fresh eyes. Why had she been so enthralled by his boyish face? Now, she felt only disdain. In fact, it would solve her problem if he vanished in front of her at this moment. There would be no more secret meetings. There would be no more Charles in her life. The way she scrutinized him brought a concerned frown to his face, and his smile faded.

'Thank you, Charles, but you shouldn't have kept Edouard out for so long. The afternoon has gone quite chilly. He might have caught a cold, the trap is too open. Why didn't you use the carriage?' She didn't smile back.

With a stinging glance at him, she hurried across to her husband, 'Edouard, you're frozen. Let me take your coat and I'll bring your warm jacket.'

'Thank you, dearest, but don't fuss. I'm well.' Edouard waved a hand to dismiss her.

'Edouard can experience the scenery more in the open trap,' Charles answered curtly.

'The scenery?' Lenora began.

'He's quite right,' Edouard interrupted, 'although I can't

see, I can hear and feel the wind and the air on my face. It tells its own story. The trap is better than the carriage and Charles will take me out again. Tomorrow, we'll travel across the high pass.'

'Oh no, that could be dangerous! There are many narrow and steep bends. Ask George to drive!' Lenora spoke up sharply.

'Am I not good enough, is that what you think?'

'Frankly I do. It takes a lifetime of experience to negotiate the passes.'

'Lenora, your concern is touching, but I'm confident Charles will manage. He would not choose a pass he could not.' Edouard raised his hand to bring the conversation to a close.

After dinner, Lenora played the piano and played well, as if her new found confidence had expanded her talent.

'I am tired, it must have been the fresh air. I'll go to bed early. No need to read for me tonight, Lenora. You and Charles must stay and enjoy the rest of the evening.'

Don't go! She wanted to shout after him. Don't leave me alone with Charles. But instead, she kissed his cheek and wished him good night.

As the door closed behind her husband, Charles took her in his arms, 'We'll be together, Lenora, I will marry you one day.'

Lenora gasped; she pulled herself free and took a step back, 'No, it's over. Charles, I am not with child. I cannot be and I never will be.'

'What are you saying?'

'You heard me. I want you to go back to Canada.'

Charles forcefully pulled her back into his arms, 'You don't mean that.' He tried to kiss her, but she struggled so violently that he let her go. 'Lenora, have you taken leave of your senses?'

'Go! Leave me! Leave me alone.' She slumped onto the sofa, her body trembling uncontrollably.

'But in your situation, you need me,' Charles protested.

'I'm not, I'm not.' Lenora sobbed hysterically; her new-found confidence had vanished in seconds. Deep inside her, a new voice said that it could be right – she was with child – and she was scared. With her hands covering her chest, she tried to hold back the sobs; her breathing came in short uneven bursts.

Charles slammed the door shut behind him, but she didn't even notice. She was full of remorse and regret. She was not with child, and from now on she would be a good wife. Edouard deserved it. In church this coming Sunday, she would go down on her knees to pray for forgiveness and renew her promise. With this in mind, she calmed down. Everything would be fine, as long as Charles returned to Canada.

During the coming days, Charles would often fix his eyes on her and smile reassuringly, but she looked away and remained on guard.

So, Charles gave his attention to her husband instead. He took him out in the trap and eased himself into small tasks, which Lenora usually carried out. Suspicious of his motives, she decided to speak to her husband.

'Dearest, you mentioned that Charles' father is expecting him back. You haven't replied to his letter. Let's do it now. I have pen and paper in my hand; tell me what you want to say. You do agree with Henry, you said so.'

Edouard looked up, startled, 'What now? Have you had a change of heart? Will you not miss his company?'

'Yes, it's been nice having him around, but I realise that he'll have to return one day. I think that day has come.'

'Do I detect your displeasure? Has he misbehaved, Lenora? If so, you must tell me. I cannot impress enough how important it is that I know.'

Lenora was taken aback and hesitated before she answered, 'No, but to be honest I want the life we had before Charles came. He has upset you by borrowing money and you cannot go on supporting him.'

'You tell me that he has not caused you distress, which would have given you reason to change your mind, Lenora, so I must believe you. Therefore, you must let me decide when it's time. He has always behaved with politeness to us both. And I am sure the money matter will be taken care of by his father.'

You don't know, my dear husband, what he has called you behind your back, Lenora thought, and in response she spoke in earnest, 'But can you not see that, by making himself useful, he has found a way of securing his stay?'

'He might think that he has, but I have given it much consideration. I will tell him shortly that it is time for him to leave. But I want him to go back to Canada with pleasant memories of his stay at Lakeside House and to tell my brother that he's been well received and treated here.'

'I see,' Lenora sighed with relief, pleased that Edouard had agreed to speak to Charles, it couldn't happen too soon for her. She prayed he would not delay.

But her anxiety flared up a few days later when she brought up the subject of Charles' return to Canada. Edouard dismissed it with a wave of his hand.

'In time, in time,' he answered.

Chapter 41

The Caravan Park, Cumbria, late July 2006

Ellen sat down with a cup of black coffee, her thoughts on Lenora. She was always on her mind, so that was not surprising. But more so now, if that were possible. As a matter of fact, she concluded, *she's inside my mind.*

Lenora was pregnant. The silly girl had not understood that sex often resulted in pregnancy. For the hundredth time, what could she do to help her? What purpose did she serve being at Lakeside House?

In the hope that she could invade Lenora's mind, she had on a previous visit to the van recited a mantra, in which she pushed Charles away. Could she make Lenora believe these thoughts were her own? Had it already worked? She was after all demanding that Charles should go back to Canada.

Ellen prayed that Lenora would stay strong and not sleep with him again, but she'd changed her mind many times. When he'd forced himself on her, she had not thought of it as rape. It probably didn't count as such in those days.

But Lenora was behaving differently. Had she influenced her? There was no way of knowing. She leaned back on the sofa and closed her eyes; over and over she mumbled, 'Lenora, rid yourself of Charles forever.'

Her mobile was ringing, she ignored it and continued to

repeat the mantra for five more minutes.

Her thoughts wandered to Edouard; she was certain that his devotion to Lenora was unbreakable; he would forgive her. Lenora should confess to him. If he declared that the child was his, a scandal would be avoided. He was her husband and he would know that this was the best option, but would Lenora see it this way? But now she wanted to forget about Lenora and when the mobile rang again she answered. It was her mother, as usual, she asked all the same questions and Ellen surprised herself by answering them differently, 'The summer is soon over, Mum. I won't be staying much longer.'

After she put down the phone, she wondered how she'd reached this conclusion, she didn't know. But she felt that it could be right. Had the time come? Was life at Lakeside House reaching its final chapter?

Ellen picked up her drawings, she was especially pleased with some of the sketches and finished them off in a hurry. Living at Lakeside House had given her ideas and inspiration for new dress designs. She was about to mail them to Annie when she decided to surprise her friend and deliver them in person. A change of scenery would do her good and help to clear her head. She needed a break and a few days at her house in Bristol.

Once she'd made up her mind, she was keen to leave; she couldn't bear the thought of spending the night in the van and this made her hurry. If she got in the car right away, she'd be able to deliver the sketches to Annie before closing.

'Ellen, is that really you? I wasn't expecting you.' Annie's face lit up as she walked into the shop.

'It was a spur of the moment decision. Thought I'd surprise you.' She dropped the folder with the sketches onto the desk, 'with these.'

Annie picked them up and quickly looked at each one in

turn, 'They are good! Your work has improved, must be the air in the Lakes. Or is love doing this to you?'

'Neither,' Ellen laughed. 'Are you saying that my designs were no good before?'

'No, of course not! It's just that now they have a certain edge to them. This one is fabulous!' Annie held up the sketch of a short red dress.

'I knew you'd like that one. Red is your favourite colour and that is one of my best designs.'

'Yes, it's striking,' Annie nodded. 'I wouldn't mind making it up for myself, but then it wouldn't be an exclusive.'

'You can have it, a token of my appreciation, for being so understanding. About me staying away from the shop, I mean.'

'Ellen, thank you, I'll love wearing it. But come on,' Annie smirked, 'it's got to be love keeping you there. How is Charles?'

'Oh, he's good, but he'll go back to Canada soon. That's fine by me, we're not serious.'

'You're saying that, but you wouldn't hang on if it wasn't.'

'OK, have it your way.' Ellen sighed. The thought of Charles leaving pleased her. Lenora would be better off without him. Although she'd enjoyed the novelty of virtual sex, it had become too frequent and had lost its appeal. Charles was far too demanding. No wonder he'd made Lenora pregnant, it had only been a matter of time.

Ellen turned to the clothes dummy by Annie's side, 'I see you're working on the grey silk.'

'Yes, this is the sketch you sent me weeks back.' Annie made a small tuck in the material and secured it with a pin. 'I'll put the kettle on you must be gasping. Did you come straight here?'

'Yeah, I wanted to catch you before you shut up shop.'

'I've kept an eye on your plants. I've been meaning to go more often. You know how it is. I hope they're still alive.'

'Don't worry and thanks.'

'Ellen, you don't seem yourself. Is everything all right?'

'Why do you ask?' Ellen bit her lip, she'd done her best to appear relaxed, but it hadn't worked. Annie knew her too well...

'You seem a bit tense.'

'Really? You'll be the first one to know,' she lied.

'Hmm,' Annie pulled a face, 'I'm not too sure about that. Look, why don't you come for dinner tomorrow evening? We've invited a work colleague of Ken's. He's a really nice guy only just started. You'll like him. You're staying, aren't you?'

'Tomorrow, yes, but I'm going back on Sunday.'

'Really?' Annie frowned and looked away, 'so soon?'

'Yes, really, but I'll come. Thanks for the invite.'

Ellen dropped the bags onto the floor in her bedroom, not bothering to unpack. She ran a hot bath and had a long soak. This is heaven, she thought, it was one of the amenities she missed most. At the van she did have a shower, of course, but it wasn't quite the same as a bath. The bathing facilities at Lakeside House were cumbersome and involved a lot of work. Certainly not a task Lenora performed daily. Most of the time, she washed herself with a flannel. Ellen sighed and sank deeper to let the water cover her shoulders.

Afterwards, she dressed in an old pair of trousers and a baggy top and poured a glass of wine, she was going to have a relaxing evening watching TV.

Her eyes strayed to the painting of Lakeside House. Oh no, she thought, not this time. She unhooked the picture and carried it through to the spare room, where she put it down facing the wall. She left with a satisfied smile. She'd done it: she had won.

She walked around the sitting room, dipping her finger into the pot plants all needed watering and the Hibiscus plant was dead. Shame, it was one of her favourite flowers, so beautiful, but fragile. Still, she couldn't complain, it was good of Annie to keep an eye on the place and it had been exceptionally hot recently.

That night, she had the best sleep for weeks and woke refreshed. There was no need to go to work. Saturday was early closing and no one had expected her back, so the shop was fully staffed. She had plenty to occupy herself with; she had neglected her home in her long periods of absence. For the first time she wished she could stay longer, but the thought didn't linger it was swept out of her mind. She knew that she had to go back to Lakeside House.

She dressed carefully for dinner that evening. It felt good to pamper herself and be Ellen for a change. She put her hair up in a loose bun but took it down again. It made her look like Lenora and that was the last thing she wanted. Instead, she let it hang down over her shoulders. She picked a blue dress, the colour matched her eyes.

What would Ken's friend be like? Annie had told her his name was Daniel and that he'd recently moved to Bristol, they didn't know much more about him. The invitation was to make him feel welcome in his new job.

Ken opened the door closely followed by Annie, who reached for the bunch of flowers in Ellen's hand.

'Thank you, these are lovely. I'll just put them in water.' Ken carried Ellen's other offering, a bottle of red wine, through to the sitting room holding it up like a trophy.

Ellen stopped dumbstruck at the sight of the man in front of her, his tanned face glowed back at her and his brown eyes twinkled.

'Dan!' A surge of excitement swept through her.

'Ellen.' Dan stepped forward and his arms encircled her, holding her close. They remained like this for several moments, not speaking.

Ken stood in the middle of the floor, his mouth hanging open, 'You know each other!'

Ellen pulled free from Dan's embrace, but they were still holding hands, 'Yes, a hundred years ago, so it seems. Before Pete,' she added. 'Where have you been, Dan?'

'I've worked in the States.' He wouldn't let go of her gaze.

'Are you going back?' Ellen held her breath waiting for his answer.

'No, here for good.'

'Pleased to hear it.' And she was, she felt a blush on her face.

'Well, don't mind me, three is a crowd.' Ken shrugged his shoulders and disappeared into the kitchen with the wine bottle.

'You know each other,' Annie echoed as she came into the room carrying a bowl of olives, a big grin on her face. 'Well, I never would have guessed. But you'll have to let go of his hand unless you want to lead him to the table.'

'Oh, that's not a bad idea, I'll do just that,' Ellen laughed, but she loosened her grip on Dan's hand. 'It's so wonderful to meet up with old friends.'

'Seems like more than old friend to me. Come on tell me, I'm dying to know.' Annie laughed.

'Honestly, not much to tell. I was nineteen when I met Dan, a long time ago.'

Ken came into the room and placed the opened bottle on the table. He'd heard Ellen's remark, 'Well, they say the first love never dies. Could it be true then? This is a turn up for the books. I'm pleased you know each other.'

'Come on, sit down, food is ready and you can tell us all about it. Where did you meet and when? And for how long were you two together?' Annie was asking all the questions.

'We met at college,' Ellen laughed.

'What happened, why did you break up?'

'Annie, don't be so nosy,' Ken said.

'It's OK, Ellen dumped me for Pete.'

'Well, actually you moved to Nottingham and it kind of fizzled out. Yes, then I met Pete,' Ellen corrected.

The dinner passed in a light atmosphere. Dan told them about his work in the States and then turned to Ellen, 'What about Cumbria? What are you doing there?'

As she was about to answer, she caught the glance Annie gave Ken. 'The break up from Pete was upsetting. I needed a change of scenery.'

'Well, you have plenty to keep you in the Lakes,' Ken joked. 'Scenery, I mean,' he explained, when Ellen turned a surprised face towards him.

Annie's eyebrows shot up and she opened her mouth to speak but thought better of it when she caught the warning look from Ken.

'You've stayed for some time, I understand.' Dan said.

'Yes, I got to like it. I wanted to see if I l should make a permanent move to Cumbria,' she lied.

'You never told me that.' Annie looked astonished.

'Oh, didn't I?' Ellen cleverly avoided further questions by asking Daniel several of her own. Continuously smiling at Dan, she wasn't really taking in his answers, because as he spoke he didn't take his eyes off hers. She loved what she could read in them.

'That was an excellent dinner. And thank you both for bringing Ellen back into my life,' Daniel addressed the hosts, more than four hours later.

'Ken, let's leave these two lovebirds alone for a minute. Help me out with the plates.' As the hosts disappeared into the kitchen, Dan reached out and took her hand in his.

Ken winked, when he and Annie returned. 'Perhaps we'll see more of her now, as you've heard, she spends most of her time in Cumbria.'

'It's possible I'll soon be back for good,' Ellen smiled.

'Don't you know? Isn't that for you to decide?' Annie asked.

She didn't answer. What had made her say this? Instead, she said, 'Dan has offered to see me home. I'm ready now.'

Dan took the key out of her hand and unlocked the door to her terraced house. Inside, Ellen leaned against the door as he kissed her. She fumbled to undo two buttons on his shirt, enough to put her hand inside, the other moved down to his belt. She shivered in anticipation when Dan found the zip of her dress.

Ellen stretched out, feeling good when she woke the next morning. Dan was asleep by her side. She sighed; she hadn't had sex for a long time, not since Pete. Not counting Charles of course, but he'd had sex with Lenora not with her. She turned over and kissed Dan's shoulder; his reaction was instantaneous. He swivelled around and the next moment his naked body pressed down on hers.

'Nice place you have here,' Dan said as he followed her into the sitting room later. 'So far I've only seen the bedroom.' His eyes twinkled as he kissed her nose, 'Not that I'm complaining. Let me take you out for lunch. I can't let you go so easily, now that I've found you again.'

'I could be persuaded, to stay longer…' the words died on her lips and her legs buckled underneath her.

Dan grabbed hold of her as she stumbled, 'What's the matter, Ellen?'

'Have you been in my spare room?' her voice shrill.

'Spare room? No, I've slept by your side all night.' He looked astonished.

'The picture! It was in the other room.' Ellen pointed to the wall above the fireplace. 'The picture, did you hang it back?' To her dismay, she sounded angry.

Dan stared, dumbfounded, at the painting of Lakeside

House and then quickly turned to her with a puzzled look in his eyes.

She stumbled on her words, 'I'm sorry, Dan, I forgot. Of course, you haven't moved the painting. I put it back there yesterday. How very silly of me.' She looked away from Dan's bewildered face and felt the blush on her cheeks as she stammered, 'But I've just remembered I've promised to meet a friend for lunch. I'm really sorry. I'd love to see you again.' She pulled his head towards her and placed a kiss on his lips, 'It's meeting you, it has made me so happy, I'm forgetting everything else.' She kissed him once more, longer this time.

Had she ruined her chances with Dan? On her drive to the Lakes, Ellen tried to keep hold of her new-found happiness. Her explanation had been rushed and she swore silently, when she remembered that she'd contradicted herself at least once. Dan had not looked convinced but he had kissed her back, although some of the warmth had gone out of his smile. If he talked to Annie, she might tell him about the house and her strange behaviour. Then surely he'd stay away from her? Ellen calmed down, she had promised to call Dan when she arrived at the van, and she would tell him how happy she was that they had met again.

The incident with the painting had shaken her to the core and she had to return to Lakeside House immediately. She had not put it back above the fireplace. Unless she'd been sleep walking? But she'd never done that in her life and she would have woken Dan. Had he put it back? Why should he move a painting, he didn't know existed, in the middle of the night? Of course not. As soon as she got back to Bristol, she would return it to the guest room that's where it would stay from now on.

Ellen pressed hard on the accelerator on the motorway, risking a speeding fine. With her nerves on edge, she fidgeted with the radio changing channels and not finding any music that suited her anxious mood. She wouldn't stop off at the caravan, instead she'd drive straight to the house. There was no time to waste. The painting was forcing her back. It was urgent. For every mile she covered, she became more convinced that she was right. An icy cold feeling engulfed her.

It was only much later she realised that, in her hurry to return to the house, she had forgotten to call Dan.

Chapter 42

Lakeside House, August 1903

Lenora rested the embroidery on her lap. The sun was low, and Charles and Edouard had not yet returned from their drive.

There was a loud rap and the door was flung open, George hurried into the room followed by Jenny Edmondson, correctly dressed for a day out in a summer cape and matching bonnet. She appeared not to have noticed that the ribbon holding her bonnet had come undone, resulting in it sitting askew. Her cheeks were flushed and her hands were fluttering nervously. She tried to contain her agitation.

'Lenora, dear, there's been an accident. Edouard and Charles are at the hospital in Kendal. We must go! Our carriage is outside. Do hurry, dear!'

Lenora stood up, feeling the colour drain from her face. 'What news do you have of Edouard?'

Molly rushed in at that moment, 'Miss Lenora, I have your cloak here.' She was wringing her hands, 'Oh, I hope the master isn't...' When she saw Lenora's face, she stopped, 'Oh, I'm sorry I didn't mean…'

'It's all right, Molly.' She flung the cloak over her shoulders and turned back to Jenny. 'What's happened?'

'By chance, we passed shortly after the accident. Charles

was standing by the roadside, he was dazed but appeared unhurt. Edouard – I'm afraid, I don't know. He was still breathing but…' Jenny stopped. 'Anton Wilson and Jonathan went with them to the hospital. We have been out with the Wilsons and were using two carriages.'

Lenora's legs gave way and George ran forward to catch her.

'Molly, bring the smelling salts.'

But Lenora struggled up, waving him away, 'No, we must hurry. I want you to come with me, George.'

As she was about to step into the carriage, she asked, 'Gladys? Is she all right?' George didn't answer, as he took his seat next to the Edmondsons' coachman.

Lenora took this as a bad omen and didn't repeat the question. Pale and shaken, she sat next to Jenny on the journey to Kendal. A thousand thoughts whirled around her head.

Jonathan met them in the hospital corridor, he hurried to Lenora and took both her hands in his, 'Lenora, you must be brave.'

'Oh Lord, is he…?'

'Edouard is unconscious. He's had a bad knock to the head, a very bad knock,' he added. 'The doctor is with him now. I'm afraid you can't see him immediately.'

'Where's Charles?'

'I'm here.' Charles was sitting on a chair not far away. He had not been noticed by the party as they entered. He got up and limped towards Lenora, 'I was lucky, just badly shaken and I jarred my foot a little.' His face showed discomfort and his eyes flicked from her to Jonathan but avoided Jenny, who was glaring at him. Lenora caught a glimpse of contempt in her eyes and this puzzled her. Surely, she didn't still have New Year's Eve in mind? It was a long time ago and should have been forgotten.

Jonathan turned to her, 'We'll leave as soon as we have news of Edouard's condition. Anton is waiting outside, he'll take us home. You may have the use of our carriage for as long as you need it, so George can drive you both home.'

The door to the sickroom opened. 'Who is Mrs Villiers?' the doctor asked.

'I am.' Lenora came forward.

'You may see your husband, he is unconscious. We don't expect him to wake for some time. Please, don't be alarmed, he has bruising to his face that will heal.'

'But will he?' Lenora pleaded.

'It's too soon to say, and I am sorry but there's not much you can do here. Tomorrow we'll know more.' The doctor rested a hand on her arm.

'I will sit with him for a while, if I may?'

The doctor nodded his consent.

'I will stay with you,' Charles offered.

'No, Charles, please wait outside.' Lenora's voice was sharp. Charles blushed and stepped back.

Although prepared, Lenora was shocked to see the dark blue discoloration, which covered Edouard's face and swollen eyes. His head and both arms were bandaged. As she leant forward and brushed her lips against his forehead, she mumbled, 'Oh Lord.'

On the way to Lakeside House, she sat quietly by Charles' side. She silenced every attempt he made to speak, 'No, tell me at dinner this evening. I am too distraught to listen to you.'

'If only you'd let me, there's not much to say. Gladys was spooked by a flock of birds.'

'A flock of birds!' Lenora echoed, surprised.

'Gladys took off and the carriage overturned, close to the ravine. It was sheer luck it didn't go over. I jumped clear. Edouard was thrown out; if he'd gone on the other side…' he left the words unsaid.

'What about Gladys?'

Charles looked away, a grimace on his face. 'I am sorry,

it was instantaneous, she didn't suffer. It will be of comfort to you to know that.'

'Dear, gentle old Gladys.' Tears trickled down her cheeks, 'I loved that horse. We shall need a new horse then,' she said tonelessly.

'And a new trap,' Charles added, 'I fear it's been damaged beyond repair.'

'Good neighbours in time of need are worth their weight in gold,' George said, as Lenora climbed into the carriage next morning.

'Yes, they are,' she agreed, 'and with horse and carriage to spare, which we can use until we have replaced Gladys.' Lenora's voice broke as she remembered the lost horse. Edouard would have to be much recovered before she could tell him. He had bought Gladys as a young mare.

If he recovered…? The thought hit her with force. Of course he would, she convinced herself.

Lenora spent a fraught day by her husband's side, pacing the floor, holding his hand and whispering encouragements into his ear. Edouard didn't stir. The nurse came and went, and each time Lenora asked if there had been an improvement. The nurse only shook her head and gave a sympathetic smile. By the time George came to bring her home there had been no change.

That night, Lenora was on her knees by her bed, praying for Edouard's recovery, when the door opened. She glanced over her shoulder and saw Charles standing there, his face blank. He averted his eyes and left without a word, closing the door silently.

Chapter 43

Lenora was at Edouard's bedside the next morning, anxiously waiting for a sign of improvement but none came. She rested her forehead on his hand, hoping to feel a twitch or slight movement. The doctor spoke to her reassuringly but left grim-faced and Lenora feared the worst.

At the end of the day, she was exhausted and slumped down in the carriage as George drove her to Lakeside House in time for supper. Molly fussed around her and announced that she'd braised a cockerel. She knew Lenora was fond of this dish.

Charles had kept discretely in the background, but he was seated in the dining room when she entered. She barely glanced at him. He hurriedly got up and moved round the table, her shoulders tensed as he placed his hands on them.

'I didn't think you'd take this so badly. Why?'

Lenora turned to face him, her eyes burning, 'You ask why? Edouard is my husband.'

'You treat him as a father.'

'Don't you love your father with all your heart?'

'Yes, I suppose I do.'

'Well, I love Edouard.'

'Lenora,' Charles placed a kiss on top of her head, 'surely you can see what this means? If my uncle doesn't pull through, we'll be free to marry. It would solve all our problems. We could live here…'

She struggled to stand, shaking off his hands. 'How dare you?' she breathed, her face hot with anger. She pushed past him as the door opened and Molly came in carrying a dish.

'I'm not hungry, Charles will dine alone tonight.'

'Poor lamb,' Molly stared after her, 'she's so upset. I pray the master will live.'

'We all do, Molly. It was a terrible accident,' Charles answered.

'You said that Gladys was spooked.'

'Yes, a flock of birds.'

'I see,' Molly looked thoughtful. 'Well, I'll take a tray to Miss Lenora before I leave. She ought to eat something.'

Lenora didn't go to her room, instead she sat down at Edouard's desk in the library. The desk was placed in front of the window, which overlooked the back garden. It was just possible to see the archway in the hedge leading into the orchard. Mahogany bookcases were attached to three of the walls, reaching the ceiling. Every shelf was covered with leather-bound books of various genres by Edgar Allen Poe, Priestly, Herman Melville, Dickens, Scott, Defoe and many more.

Edouard had been an avid reader before losing his sight. Now, he depended on her to do so for him. This was his favourite room; she felt close to him here. She sighed and dabbed her eyes. She glanced up at the image of herself, the portrait, which Edouard had painted of her as a twenty-one-year-old: smiling, young and carefree. He had insisted on it being hung in the library where he spent most of his time. Tears sprang to her eyes again.

What Charles had said disturbed her. If Edouard died, and he must not, would Charles' father inherit Lakeside House? And quite possibly pass it on to Charles?

Or was there a will in her favour? It was something that Edouard had never discussed with her, although he must have thought about this. Was that why he'd allowed Charles to remain, in spite of his behaviour? Charles could be well-mannered and polite when he made the effort, the past weeks had proved it. But she'd seen too much of his ugly side to know that his newly created image wasn't genuine. He had demonstrated this to her this very evening. She could no longer love him.

Lenora was pleased when Molly brought her the supper tray, 'Thank you, Molly. I admit I'm hungry.'

'It's not too much, just a taste of the broiled cockerel you like. If you're going to spend tomorrow at the hospital, you must keep your strength up for the master,' she said.

'You're kind and looking after me well. Yes, I'll be leaving first thing in the morning.'

'I know, George told me. I'll say good night then and I'll pray for the master.'

'We both will,' Lenora said.

Sometime later Charles entered her room without knocking, 'We must talk…'

Lenora interrupted, 'Where are your manners? You're not welcome. Please, leave.'

'So, I need to knock now? You're upset, but it will pass. This is a blessing in disguise. We can be together.'

'Go away, I don't love you.'

'But what will you say to Edouard, if he lives? When are you going to tell him about the child?'

'I'm not with child, I'm not,' she could feel the hysteria welling up inside her.

'You're distraught, but you must accept that you could be with child. I will take care of you both. You will love me! Everything will be like it was before.'

'Get out,' she hissed, 'before I scream.'

'There's no one to hear you, if you do. But I'll leave.'

Lenora sighed with relief when the door closed behind him. Soon she would know if she were with child. Within the next few days she must bleed; if not, she'd have to come to terms with the fact. Until then, she refused to believe it.

⁂

The following day Edouard's condition had worsened; his pulse was weak and he showed no sign of coming out of his coma. This distressed her so much she was unable to speak calmly to reassure him. After three hours by his bedside, with tears burning her eyes, she was overcome with such emotion the nurse urged her to leave the room. To clear her head, she walked the hospital grounds.

Back by his side, she steeled herself to steady her voice. It would do Edouard good to hear her talk and she'd grown tired of the silence. She told him that everyone at Lakeside House was waiting for his return. He must hurry and get well, because she missed and loved him very much. She made her voice strong, although it took a huge effort. She also told him that Charles had escaped the accident with only a slight limp, so he mustn't worry. This she added after some thought, as it was possible that he could hear her and Edouard would have been concerned about Charles. It gave her comfort to speak and improved her mood. When George arrived she was reluctant to leave, but knew she must as she was exhausted.

In the evening she asked Molly to bring meals to her room until further notice. Molly opened her mouth but closed it.

Good, Lenora thought, she was not in the mood to answer questions. From now on, she'd keep away from Charles.

⁂

It was a grey morning as she stepped out on the porch. George was waiting by the side of the carriage, holding onto the reins of a restless black horse, impatient to move on. Lenora had been too distracted to take notice of the horse.

But this morning she'd fetched a carrot from the kitchen and now she held it out to him. He immediately calmed and took it carefully from her hand. It occurred to her she didn't even know his name.

'What a beautiful animal. It was kind of Jonathan to lend him to us. What's his name?'

'It's Belinda, Miss Lenora,' George laughed.

'Oh, so it is. The black colour must have made me believe differently. I don't know why. Shame we can't keep her forever. We must find a new horse, George.'

'Yes, but the master would want to come with me to choose.'

'But you're the expert. He listens to your advice. We can't wait for my husband to get well; it will take time.'

'I see. I'll put my ear to the ground. I'll find a good replacement for old Gladys, bless her soul. There was no horse quite like her and it was unusual for her to spook.' George shook his head.

'I miss her. She was so good tempered…' Lenora's voice broke.

'Ay, Miss Lenora, don't fret. Don't upset yourself and think of it now. Not with the master ill and all.'

At the hospital Lenora found that Edouard's condition was unchanged. The bandage around his head had been replaced by a large pad, this was the only improvement. She was grateful that at least he was not worse. The monotony of the day was broken by a gentle knock on the door.

'We have visitors for Mr Villiers. The doctor will allow a few minutes.'

'Who is it?'

'It's me, Lenora.' Jonathan Edmondson put his head around the door. 'Jenny and Emily are also here. We won't come in all at once.'

'Oh please, do come in all of you. Edouard cannot be

disturbed, he's still unconscious and I'm so glad to see you.'

Emily rushed forward with outstretched arms, embracing Lenora, tears showing in her eyes. 'Oh, Lenora,' she whispered, 'this is too awful.'

Jenny also embraced her and she received a warm handshake from Jonathan, after which they stood by Edouard's bedside, their faces distraught at the sight of his bruised and sunken face.

'Jenny and I will stay with Edouard so that you may have a rest. Emily will walk with you,' Jonathan said.

Lenora accepted gracefully, it would be a pleasant change to have her company. She had not seen Emily since she'd been sickly and thought that she still looked frail and had lost weight.

Emily already had her hand on the door handle, eager to leave the room. Outside, she immediately took Lenora's arm, her face flushed, 'Please, tell me, how is Charles? Is he hurt? Mama tells me not, but she refuses to speak further about him.'

'He is well enough, amazingly. He jumped before the trap turned over, only a slight sprain to his ankle.'

'Oh, good!' Emily's voice betrayed her relief and her face lit up.

Lenora looked at her curiously. Charles had obviously told the truth when he'd said that Emily responded to his kiss on New Year's Eve, but it was a long time since then. It appeared that Emily still cherished the memory. As far as Lenora knew, he hadn't seen her since the Grand Picnic.

Lenora took Emily's arm and they walked side by side in the pleasant but small hospital park. Worried about Emily's pale complexion, she asked, 'Are you quite well, Emily?'

'Yes, I've lost weight but otherwise I'm well, thank you! Can we meet in Kendal, just the two of us? I would like to speak to you.'

'You can speak to me now.'

'No, it's not suitable, not with Edouard ill. We must wait

until he's better. I want to speak about a matter close to my heart.'

'You've made me curious, but you're right. When Edouard is better, we'll have a special day together. I am so looking forward to it already. Let's turn round now I must go back to him,' Lenora said.

The Edmondson family took their leave when Lenora and Emily returned to the sickroom. The visit had lifted Lenora's spirits, and it didn't seem long before George knocked on the door.

Charles was waiting in the hall on their return, 'How is Uncle?'

'Four days and no change,' Lenora's voice was curt. George' couldn't fail to notice the dislike she showed Charles, but she was too tired to pretend otherwise. He wouldn't be surprised though, as Molly had most likely told him about the meal arrangement. They probably believed that she blamed him for the accident.

She had intended to brush past Charles, but the thought hit her hard and with such force that she stopped abruptly. Did she blame him? She hadn't done so up to now. Why not? What if he'd been careless? Taken risks? It was possible. Her face became taut, she pressed her lips down hard and stared intently at him.

Charles averted his eyes and took several nervous steps away from her. He fumbled for his handkerchief and wiped his forehead.

Without a word she left him standing there whilst George retreated outside, closing the door softly behind him.

Chapter 44

Lenora buried her head in the pillow and cried. It was one week since the accident and Edouard showed no sign of waking up. Matters were made worse by the uncertainty of her own condition. She believed it to be two months since she had bled, and she had felt a change within her. There was no one she could confide in; she felt utterly alone. Edouard was at death's door and she most likely carried Charles' child.

'What will become of me?' she whispered. She staggered out of bed, wishing that she could have stayed. She didn't feel able to cope with the day ahead. She wanted to give up, never to face the world again. But she had to, for Edouard's sake.

The only person she could speak to was Charles and she hated that thought, but at this, her weakest moment, she would not refuse his company. Was she a bad person? Perhaps not bad, but she knew she was not strong-willed. If she didn't speak to someone soon, she would lose her mind.

Since the accident, Charles had done his best to be supportive and assist in any way he could, reluctantly, she had to give him credit. In the last few days, she'd been too exhausted in body and mind to openly show her dislike. Instead, she had ignored him. She hoped that he would not take this as a sign that she had forgiven him.

That night, Charles came to her room. Lenora was woken by a hand on her shoulder and as he leaned over her, she smelled alcohol on his breath. She angrily twisted her head sideways, but he held it, his fingers digging into the flesh of her cheeks. Forcefully, he made her face him.

'Look at me! Tell me you want me! I know you do, why pretend otherwise?'

She fought him, to sit up but he held her down, 'Charles, go away. You've been drinking.'

'I've come to claim what is mine. You and the child. When Edouard is gone, you'll be pleased to have me.' His face was close to hers.

Lenora pushed back into the pillow, 'Not like this, Charles,' she moaned.

'All this will be ours, we won't have to hide anymore.'

'But I don't love you. How can I, when you behave like this?' her voice broke.

Charles stared at her and abruptly pulled away, the anger left him and his face took on a sullen look. Unsteadily he left the room, the door open behind him.

She got up to shut it, but it was a long time before she slept.

The next morning, she used all her willpower to be ready in time for George to drive her to the hospital, she felt her strength gone and her legs barely obeyed her. She asked George to assist her into the carriage and then did not answer, when he spoke to her. She registered that he looked at her anxiously, but oddly enough this did not concern her, and it pleased her when he didn't repeat his question.

Without thoughts about anything and without much feeling, Lenora spent another day by her husband's side; it was as if nothing mattered anymore. There was no change in Edouard's condition. Lenora hardly noticed the day passing and looked up in surprise when George called for her. During the journey to Lakeside House, she sat silently on the back seat.

She took her dinner in her room to avoid Charles. She noticed the worried side glances from Molly as she put the tray on the table, taking longer than usual and hesitating by the door before leaving the room.

Lenora had spent several evenings counting the days since she had last bled, she'd recounted and this evening did so again. She tried to remember with some certainty but couldn't, she sighed deeply, her head slumped onto her chest in resignation.

That night, she finally admitted that she was with child. Kneeling by her bed, she prayed that her husband would recover, so that she could unburden herself and ask his forgiveness. Only then would she know which direction her life would take. Not feeling the cold, she repeated this prayer again and again, her eyes swollen with tears, until she stumbled into her bed frozen and exhausted, sobbing uncontrollably.

Moments later Charles found her like this, he ran across the floor and took her shaking body in his arms, 'Oh Lenora, don't cry. I'm here for you, I'll look after you.' He held up her face and wiped away the tears, 'I'll make you love me again and in time you'll forgive. Perhaps you already have?'

To this, Lenora managed to shake her head.

'But you will, my darling, you will.' He stroked her hair and face, all the while holding her close, rocking to and fro. 'I came to apologise for last night, I was drunk.'

'Charles, I know I am with child now.' Her sobs intensified.

He held her at a distance, his hands on her shoulders, 'Our child,' he smiled. 'I will comfort you. You'll forget your distress.' His hands moved over her breasts.

Lenora registered the warmth on her skin, she was so very cold. In the fog that clouded her mind, she remembered that she had not lit the fire.

Through her tears she saw him remove his clothes, and

she watched unresponsive as he got into the bed beside her. His body was warm and comforting on hers, and she was so cold. Charles would make her warm again.

Next morning, when Lenora was ready to leave for the hospital, Charles was dressed in his overcoat and waiting in the hall. He walked towards her to take her in his arms.

'I'm coming with you to see Uncle.'

'I think not!' her answer was curt and her hand went out to stop him.

'After last night, how can you refuse me?' His eyes had lost their warmth.

'Last night was a mistake. You took advantage of me, I was distraught.' She kept her voice cold.

'But you were not when I left you. You slept as a child and you loved me back. Don't deny it!' Charles pressed his lips together.

'I do!' Lenora said furiously. But he was right, she had wanted him, her whole body had welcomed him and he knew it.

'When my uncle dies, your life will be with me. He's an old man, it would be best if he dies now. It would suit us very well. He should have died at the accident.'

'How can you talk like that?'

'That's what I thought would happen...' Charles stopped abruptly.

'What do you mean? Do you wish him dead?' Lenora felt the blood drain from her face.

'I mean, I thought he was dead. He didn't move, and his head was bleeding.'

'Oh, stop it, Charles! I can't bear it.'

He grabbed her wrist to pull her closer but let go when the front door pushed open and George entered.

Lenora turned away to hide her distress, 'I'm ready. Charles has dressed for a walk. He's not coming with us. I'll be out in a minute, you go ahead.'

George nodded, his eyes downcast. 'I'll be outside then, Miss Lenora.'

As soon as the door was shut behind him, she turned to Charles, 'Don't come near me again.'

Charles nodded, but the flash of anger in his eyes scared her and she was careful not to slam the door behind her.

At the hospital Lenora received news of an improvement in Edouard's condition, his pulse was stronger. She greeted this information with an overwhelming feeling of gratitude, her prayers had been answered and it gave her renewed energy. The nurse said there was a strong possibility that he could hear her. It made her happy to think that it would give him comfort, so she talked about the garden, the fruit trees and Molly's cooking. She was about to tell him that Jonathan had agreed to sell them Belinda as a replacement for Gladys but stopped in time. This she could not tell him yet.

Before she left, the doctor told her that Edouard was on the road to recovery but would spend weeks in hospital once he regained consciousness.

Two days later Edouard came out of his coma and if Charles was disappointed he hid it well. Lenora joined him in the dining room that evening, the first for a long time.

She was elated, 'We must celebrate, Charles. Fetch a bottle of our best wine and I shall ask Molly and George to join us. We deserve it and this news will make us feel much better.'

Molly and George entered the dining room in high spirits. Molly wiped her tears away with a tea towel she'd tucked into her apron. George toasted his master at the same time praising the Lord that their prayers had been heard.

Lenora had become aware that Charles joined in the

celebration with genuine warmth, so when they were left alone she held out her glass to him, 'I'm glad, I see that you're happy too.'

'Of course, the beef stew was one of the best Molly has ever made, the claret excellent, and you look radiant when you're happy. Let me pour you more wine, I can see it's relaxing you. You've been under a lot of strain.' Charles had opened a second bottle of Edouard's excellent Bordeaux and refilled her glass.

Lenora drank too quickly, 'I'm not used to drinking this much, but you're right it's warming and doing me good. I must go to my room, before I become unsteady on my feet.'

'I'll see you to your room, my darling.'

'Don't call me that. Thank you, but I can manage on my own.' Lenora left, her smile replaced by an anxious frown.

'It does seem a shame to waste this wine.' Charles filled his glass again.

It was an hour later that she was woken by the presence of Charles in her bed, his naked body pressing down on hers and his hands fumbling with her nightdress. Her protests were silenced by his mouth on her lips. She tried to push him off, but his weight was too much and his arms pinned her down...

Chapter 45

The following day Edouard merely whispered a few unintelligible words and gave her a weak smile before drifting back to sleep. For several hours Lenora refused to leave his bedside, watching him intently until at last his eyelids fluttered and he spoke to her.

'Lenora, my dear wife, I will be well now. Don't worry any more, you're making yourself ill. I can see the shadows under your eyes.'

She squeezed his hand gently, 'Hush, don't tire yourself. Don't speak too much.'

'I have been aware of your presence for a long time. It has been of much comfort to me. I couldn't wish for a better wife.'

His words tore at her heart. She wished that he hadn't spoken them. Soon she would have to tell him about Charles and the child. His world would fall apart. 'Don't talk. Rest now.' She was gnawing at her bottom lip, as the guilt rose in her and she suppressed a sob.

'Nonsense! *I will speak.* I've stayed quiet for too long. I have much to say. I've known for some time that you're troubled. I wish that I had talked to you before the accident...'

'Hush, Edouard, don't upset yourself.'

'Let me speak! Whatever it is, all will be well. I'll do anything to put things right. Absolutely anything.' He tried to raise himself up.

'Edouard!'

'I'm tired. Soon you'll tell me.' Edouard closed his eyes; his breath became shallow and he fell back. When she gently rocked his shoulder, he showed no sign of awareness.

She rushed into the corridor shouting for the nurse, who came running. Lenora pulled at her arm, 'Please, hurry. My husband is worse. I think he's unconscious.'

The nurse put a hand on his forehead and checked his pulse, 'What happened? It appears he has exerted himself.'

'He was emotional, he talked. I asked him not to. Is he unconscious?' A sob escaped her.

'No, but the effort was too much for him. He mustn't speak more than a few words. I will ask the doctor to come and see him.'

Lenora brought his hand to her lips and kissed it gently before lowering it back onto the folded sheet. Quietly, she left the room. Outside, she leant against the wall and wept silently.

That evening she faced Charles across the dining table. Her husband's words had given her courage, 'Edouard will recover and I want the life we had before you came. You should leave before he comes home. It wouldn't be appropriate if you're here.'

'So, you will tell him?'

'Yes, I'll take my chance and tell him the truth. I know he'll forgive me. Better if you're not here, you should leave.'

'You want me gone so that he'll hear only your side of the story. He needs to know how you willingly came to my bed and that you prepared our little love nest in his house.'

'You wouldn't dare. He would despise you and send you away.'

'Is that not your aim in any case? He will find out that you have given yourself to me, while he's been unconscious in hospital. Will he forgive you? Or are you going to say that I've forced myself on you?'

'You have done so in the past week.'

'I haven't heard you protest much.'

'I have tried to, Charles.'

'Uncle will know the truth from me.'

'Yes, Charles, he will, but it must wait. *It cannot be done until he is better.* He must have total rest and not be upset under any circumstances. Is that understood? When the time is right, *I will speak to him.* Let us think of other matters now.'

Charles nodded reluctantly and pulled a letter from his pocket, 'Do you remember Wilfred – my distant cousin? I went to see him in Edinburgh.'

Lenora nodded.

'He wants to visit, and I've told him that he is welcome.'

'You should have consulted me.'

'You're spending all day at the hospital, so he won't be in your way. I didn't think you'd mind.'

'Molly will have to cook for another person. When will he arrive?'

'The day after tomorrow.'

'Too late to change it now. Not a good time with Edouard in hospital, but I suppose it'll be alright. That's what Edouard would have said if he were here. Yes, let Wilfred come. Shame Edouard won't be able to see him.'

'We can visit him one day, that'll give you a rest.'

'I don't need a rest, thank you, but it's kind of you to offer.'

The afternoon of Wilfred's arrival Lenora stepped out onto the porch to greet him. She watched him climb out of the coach in a clumsy manner, his huge frame making it difficult for him. He wiped his sweaty brow as he waddled over to where she stood. She took an instant dislike to his plump and arrogant face but held out her hand.

'Welcome to Lakeside House, Wilfred. It's always pleasant to meet one of Edouard's relatives. I hope you'll enjoy your stay.'

Wilfred bowed, his damp lips brushing her hand, 'Indeed I will. We've just come from the hospital. It was a most unfortunate accident, I must say. Such bad luck. We weren't allowed to stay long, but it's been good to meet my father's cousin. If only circumstances had been different.'

'Thank you, Edouard is recovering and he'll soon be home.' As she spoke, she looked over his shoulder at Charles, who approached carrying two small cases. She raised her voice for him to hear and nodded towards the cases, 'George will take those.'

'No, I'll show Wilfred to his room. I've asked George to see to Belinda.'

'Good looking horse, you have, I know a bit about them.'

'I'm glad you approve, Wilfred, but I miss Gladys, we lost her in the accident.' Lenora turned and walked into the house. 'I will see you at dinner.'

'Lenora,' Charles said during the evening meal, 'Why don't I take you to the hospital tomorrow morning? While you visit Edouard, I can take Wilfred for a sight-seeing trip in the area.'

'Yes, this is a splendid idea, and do come for me in the afternoon. It will give George an uninterrupted day to carry on with his chores here.'

'I'm glad you approve, Aunt.' Charles winked at her.

Wilfred had noticed the wink and turned a rosy face to her, 'Yes, Charles tells me his stay here is most agreeable. I hear you've made him very welcome indeed.'

Lenora sat up ramrod straight at the suggestive undertone of his voice, her shoulders stiff. What did he mean? Surely not? She dismissed the thought as ridiculous. Charles had faults, but he wouldn't stoop that low. She tried to catch his attention as he opened a second bottle of wine. Since Edouard's hospital stay, Charles had full access to the wine cellar.

He avoided her eyes and pulled the cork with a flourish,

'This is one of the best. Uncle knows his wines. I'm sure you've never drunk one better.'

Wilfred lifted his glass and drained it, wiping his mouth with his hand, 'Excellent!'

What a waste of good wine, Lenora thought, but said nothing. Edouard had taught her that his wines should be handled with care and allowed to breathe before drinking. Judging by Wilfred's red nose, it was just another wine wasted.

By now, both men were quite loud. Molly had frowned disapprovingly when she brought in the dessert, a frown which had deepened by the time she put the cheeseboard down.

Lenora had struggled to keep a smile on her face; she could do so no longer. She rose from the table, 'Please, excuse me. I will retire. Do enjoy the port.' The sarcastic tone of her voice was wasted on Wilfred.

But Charles jumped up, 'Don't leave us now!'

'I feel I must. I have a headache.' She nodded curtly at Wilfred and left the room.

A pale-faced Charles joined her at the breakfast table, 'I am sorry about last night.'

'You had too much wine. Molly wasn't happy with the state of the table this morning. Isn't two bottles of wine enough? Anyhow, where is Wilfred?'

'I looked in on him, he's asleep. I left him, it'll do him good to sleep it off.'

'But you'll need to be ready in an hour.'

'We will be. I've asked Molly to take him breakfast in his room.'

'She won't like that. You're taking advantage. And be careful with the wine tonight. How do we explain the missing bottles to Edouard?'

'But he can't see that they are gone.'

'No, but he can count. Sometimes he does it himself. We

take stock once a year of the cellar. I help him.'

'Well then, surely, Aunt, you can count a few bottles more...,' he stopped. 'No perhaps not.'

Lenora's felt her face go tight and she threw him a furious glance, 'I'll be waiting for you and Wilfred in the hall, an hour from now. Be ready.'

Edouard showed signs of further improvement, but the nurse warned that her visit had to be limited. Further, she must not let him speak more than a few words. His head injury had been serious.

As she sat down by his bedside, he opened his eyes, 'Lenora, is that you?'

'Yes, dearest.' She rose to gently kiss his forehead and took his hand.

'I'm better now,' he whispered.

'Yes, you'll soon be able to come home. But hush! You should rest, don't speak.'

'Charles and Wilfred came to see me yesterday. That was good of them. What's Wilfred like?'

'I've only just met him. It's too early to say. Hush, don't speak now.'

'I know you, Lenora. That means you don't like him.' But Edouard closed his eyes and remained silent, so she didn't answer him.

There was a discreet knock on the door and Jenny Edmondson's head appeared, 'We're all here. May we say hello to Edouard?'

He opened his eyes and nodded.

'I'll ask the nurse, I've had strict instructions,' Lenora said.

'Never mind asking the nurse,' Edouard's face lit up.

However, Lenora didn't dare to go against the rules, and when the nurse saw her patient's happy face she agreed to their visits. One by one, they were allowed to enter for a few minutes.

While Emily's parents were in the room, Lenora spent the time in the corridor with her and they agreed to meet in Kendal the following week.

'Mrs Villiers.' The nurse approached her, 'This has been pleasant for your husband but tiring. It would be best if you leave now as well.'

'We'll drop you off, I insist,' Jonathan said at once. 'No need to wait for George. No trouble at all.'

'Oh, but Charles is coming to fetch me later. I've no way of informing him otherwise.' She noticed the effect Charles' name had on Emily, her cheeks flushed and she looked down. Lenora turned to the nurse, 'Can you inform my nephew, Charles Villiers, when he arrives, that I have been taken home by my friends, the Edmondsons?'

'Of course, Mrs Villiers.' The nurse nodded her agreement.

On the drive to Lakeside House, Lenora realised how much she'd missed the company of other people. During the journey Jonathan asked if she was pleased with their purchase of Belinda.

'It was most kind of you to sell her to us. We couldn't have found a better horse anywhere. You must miss her.'

'She's a good horse, but we can manage without her. Have you told Edouard yet?'

Lenora shook her head, 'No, it's too soon. He must not be told anything that will upset him. He was fond of Gladys. I would like to shorten his stay in Kendal and bring him home. I want to nurse him myself.'

'It's a small hospital – not many beds and they need them. I believe they will let you do that, if at all possible.' Jenny put a reassuring arm around her shoulders.

Emily remained quiet, she had a weak smile on her lips and appeared withdrawn. This puzzled and worried Lenora. What did Emily have on her mind that troubled her so? Perhaps she'd be told next week.

Chapter 46

'I'll serve dinner tonight, so you can go early. You have had extra cleaning this morning.' Molly had not been happy with last night's experience and Lenora didn't want to upset her further. She had expected her to protest but her face lit up.

'Thank you, Miss Lenora. How long is your guest staying?'

'He's here for four days. It'll pass quickly. Do I detect your disapproval?'

'It's not for me to say,' Molly sniffed.

'Please, have dinner ready at seven and then you can leave. I'll see to the rest.'

Molly nodded.

Lenora was thoughtful, she'd been right to save Molly from an evening like last night. She would have a serious word with Charles. Their drunken behaviour must not be repeated. It had been a disgrace.

To avoid a repetition, she had suggested that to decant one bottle would be enough, but Charles ignored her. During dinner, a second bottle of wine disappeared down their gullets and their voices grew louder. She attempted to keep up a conversation and maintain a cheerful mood. To her alarm, Charles began to address her in a too familiar manner. Wilfred raised his eyebrows and looked at her with interest after which he winked. She ignored him.

'Gentlemen,' she began and frowned inwardly: gentlemen they were not. 'Excuse me, but I shall retire. Please, Charles, help me to the kitchen with these.' She picked up a few plates.

As soon as the kitchen door had closed, she turned to Charles with such fury in her voice that he stumbled backwards in his drunkenness, 'Show me respect. Wilfred doesn't know about us and it must remain that way.' The sheepish look on his face betrayed his embarrassment and not wanting to hear his answer, she hurried out of the kitchen, the door banging shut behind her.

Lenora climbed into bed and sank back into her pillows. She had found the evening unbearable and she was unusually tired. The effort to be polite to Wilfred and their disturbing behaviour had been draining. She couldn't have stayed in their company a moment longer. She slept.

Aware of the cold, she woke sometime later. Her bolster was missing, and she made a semi-conscious movement to pull it up. The room wasn't totally dark, her bedroom door had been left wide open and the dim light from the corridor was seeping in. Startled, she could make out the shadow of a man by her bedside. Her first thought was Charles. But this wasn't him. This man was stocky and he was stumbling from side to side, as he pulled off his trousers.

Lenora was mesmerized; she watched, too stunned to react. The next moment, he fell heavily upon her. His massive body pushed the air out of her chest and his weight pinned her down. Her scream was silenced by his mouth, reeking of alcohol. His hands pawed her breasts and letting go, he moved down to pull at her nightgown, pushing it up and roughly prising her legs apart.

With her fists as tight balls, she hit the bulging soft flesh on his back, again and again, but with no impact. To stop her, he grabbed her wrists and held them down above her head. With the other hand she could feel him trying to enter her, guiding his limp manhood. Lenora fought back screaming and able to yank one arm free, she slapped him fully across the face.

'Why are you fighting?' he slurred. 'You can't get enough. Trollop! At it like rabbits. It's my turn,' his voice was hoarse. Again, his mouth came down on hers and the bile rising in her throat choked her. For a time he grunted and panted, as his hand fumbled in another effort to enter her.

Suddenly, his body went limp and he slumped down onto her. At the next second, to her disbelief, he snored. The sounds escaping her were a mixture of erratic screams and sobs, tears flooding her face. She fought to push him off and at that moment Charles ran into the room.

'Lenora!' He stopped abruptly, stunned by what he was seeing, unable to move.

'Get him off me, get him off me!' Her screams were hysterical.

Now Charles rushed forward, his face flushed with anger, as he tore at Wilfred's huge frame. With a vicious shove, he managed to heave him onto the floor, where he lay collapsed, a fat naked belly hanging out from underneath his crumpled shirt.

Charles furiously shook Wilfred's shoulders and he sat up dazed, holding his head. Lenora saw a flash of Charles' arm as he drove a hard fist into his chin, 'You blundering idiot,' he shouted. 'Get out.'

Wilfred stumbled out of the room, rubbing his face. Charles threw his trousers after him and he stooped unsteadily to pick them up, without a glance at either of them.

Charles fell onto his knees by her bed, totally sober, 'Oh Lord, Lenora, I'm so sorry. I'm so sorry. Did he...?' he was unable to complete his question.

Lenora's chest was heaving. She leaned over the side of the bed, holding back the vomit, as she fumbled underneath. Charles reached for the chamber pot and held it as she spewed.

He sat still, waiting for her to be calm, his eyes full of remorse. He attempted to pull her close, but she pushed him away.

Finally, she looked at him, 'He was too drunk. Now get out of here and out of my life, Charles.' She didn't recognise her own voice, it was full of venom.

'Don't look at me like that, Lenora. Your eyes scare me. I know you're upset, but I didn't know this was going to happen.'

'Didn't you? Could you not imagine it?'

'No! How could I?'

'You told him. You told him about us. How could you?'

Charles looked aghast and lowered his eyes, 'I might have said something. I'd had too much to drink, I didn't mean for this...'

'You let him believe that it was possible. *I will never forgive you.*'

'Lenora, please let me explain.'

'Get out! Tomorrow morning, Wilfred must be gone. I do not want to set eyes on him.'

Charles left and Lenora crawled out of bed, she was sore and her body ached from the assault. Even though she was crying with anger and shivering from cold, she changed the bed. She couldn't bring herself to sleep in sheets that had been in touch with Wilfred's flabby fat. The water in her basin was freezing, but she flannelled her breasts and moved downwards, following the movement of his hands to where his smell could linger, and she winced when the flannel touched places where his fingernails had scratched her.

The rest of the night was spent between awareness of being awake and restless slumber. When morning came, she was exhausted and unable to leave her bed.

'Miss Lenora, are you not well?' Molly's worried face peeped round the door.

'No, I'm not, Molly, and I won't visit Edouard today. Please, ask George to take a message to my husband and tell him not to worry. I'm just a little tired after a restless night. I'll see him tomorrow.'

'I will do that, Miss Lenora, and I'll bring you a breakfast tray. I see that our guest has left. Master Charles took him to Kendal this morning. He hasn't returned yet.' Molly's tone of voice left a question hanging in the air.

'Yes, he had to leave sooner than expected,' she didn't offer any other explanation. Molly sniffed, her lips firmly pressed together. Lenora knew that she had seen the wine bottles and drawn her own conclusion. This kind of behaviour wasn't tolerated in this house and would never have taken place in Edouard's presence. She should have been able to stop it but had failed miserably. She'd no control over Charles; she had lost her authority, he didn't respect her. What had happened in the night was still raw and the shame rose in her. Tears welled up and she turned her back to Molly, but her shoulders shook involuntarily as a sob escaped her.

In an instant, Molly's hand was on her arm, 'Whatever is the matter?'

'I'll be fine as soon as I get some rest.'

'No wonder. It's been too much for you. You've had a lot of upset with the master in hospital. The travelling every day has tired you. It'll be easier when he's home with us.'

'You're right, we need him here. Ask George to bring a bed to the library. Edouard will sleep there. The stairs will be too much for him. You've helped me to make up my mind. I'll bring him home tomorrow.'

'Good, but you are awfully pale. Shall I send for the doctor?'

'Oh no!' Both hands flew up in a dismissive gesture, 'No doctor, absolutely not.' The thought was horrifying. A doctor would discover her pregnancy. It was out of the question.

'If you say so.' Molly stopped at the door and hesitated, 'I really think...,' she saw Lenora's determined face and said no more but left the room with a shake of her head.

Lenora placed a hand on her stomach. Did it show? No, not yet; her breasts were fuller, but that was all. Had she made Molly suspicious? How long would it be before she was forced to tell Edouard?

The bile rose in her throat, and it wasn't caused by the unborn child, the memory of last night flooded back. She ran over to the wash bowl, retching and retching until the sweat broke out on her forehead. The sweat turned clammy and cold and she returned to bed, she didn't want to be in it, this was where it had happened but she had no choice, she had to get warm.

The door opened, it was Charles, 'I'm so sorry, Lenora. You know I am. Let me comfort you, you're not well.'

'Get out! Immediately. You're adding to my distress.'

Charles said nothing. He turned to leave but stopped for a moment by the door, his eyes dark with concern.

Molly found her shivering when she returned with the tray. Hurriedly, she dumped it on the nearby table and rushed over to the bed, 'I shall send George for the doctor.'

Lenora sat up with a jerk, 'No!' she shouted. 'Sorry, I didn't mean to shout. I've caught a chill and I'll be well in the morning. I want to bring Edouard home from the hospital. Nothing must come in the way of that. Nothing!' She sank back into the pillows, the outburst had drained her. She nodded to emphasize her words and managed a weak smile for Molly.

'If you say so, Miss Lenora.'

Chapter 47

The next morning, Lenora was indeed better, she'd regained much of her strength through sheer determination. When she entered the dining room, Charles leapt from his chair and attempted to take both her hands in his, but she pulled them out of his reach.

'Please, forgive me. You must believe that I didn't want this. Nor could I have foreseen it.'

'I don't agree. Your loose talk brought it on.'

'I will do anything you ask to make amends. Anything!'

'Including leaving this house?'

'Anything, except that.' Charles' eyes lost their pleading look. He was no longer asking for forgiveness. 'Your condition and state of mind don't allow you to think clearly. You and I and the child belong together. When you come to your senses, you'll know that I'm right.'

'I hate you, Charles.' Her voice held no emotion and was matter-of-fact.

'You don't hate me. You love me.'

Lenora shook her head in despair and pulled away. But she needed his help right now and he had offered it, 'I would like you to come with George and me to the hospital. I am bringing Edouard home today and you'll be able to assist.'

'Of course, but isn't it too soon? It would be better if

he stays longer, better for him.' He did nothing to hide his displeasure.

'Better for him? Are you sure that's what you mean? No, he's coming home. I'll nurse him myself. I'm sure it will speed his recovery.'

It was late afternoon by the time they returned to Lakeside House with Edouard. The doctors had been reluctant and, before agreeing to discharge him, had insisted on giving him a thorough examination. Once this was done and the formalities were over, they were at last allowed to leave. This decision had been strengthened by Edouard, who had taken Lenora's hand and brought it to his lips, 'Dearest, you're so right. I'm ready to go home. The thought of it makes me feel better already.'

Lenora received strict instructions as to his care: he was to remain in bed and only allowed a few minutes each day in an armchair by his bedside. His surroundings had to be peaceful and nothing must upset him. His head injury had been serious. Molly had made up the bed in the library, everything was in place for his homecoming.

A week went by whilst everyone in the household tiptoed around Edouard, who rewarded them by showing a marked improvement. At the end of the week, he insisted that he would be able to walk, 'Here, Lenora, help me to stand.' He was already lowering his legs over the side of the bed.

Lenora put her arms around him, startled at how thin he was. 'I don't think this will work, even though you've lost a lot of weight. I'm not strong enough.'

Edouard's legs buckled underneath him, 'Fetch Charles,' he demanded. 'With him on one side and you on the other to support me, I will learn to regain the use of my legs.'

During the coming days Charles and Lenora walked Edouard around the room, increasing the time by a few minutes every day. She was grateful for Charles' help. In front of his uncle, he was the doting nephew, eager to assist. She still felt a deep resentment towards him. He had humiliated her in the worst manner possible and it was festering within her. But she was careful not to show her dislike in front of her husband; such behaviour would have been difficult to explain.

She had to link arms with Charles and be close to him when they walked around the room to support Edouard. A shiver went through her when the familiar smell of his body touched her nostrils. Charles removed his jacket and cravat, unbuttoning the top buttons of his shirt to free his movements when lifting his uncle. It unsettled her. She'd felt a stirring in her stomach. Memories that made her blush flooded back and aroused her. Memories of him undoing the remaining buttons, stripping off his shirt and standing bare-chested in front of her, with his lithe and muscular body and his hands moving to undo his belt...

Lenora turned her head away as her cheeks burnt. Charles' power over her was strong and she hated it.

In time, Edouard was able to walk unaided and to sit outside, a blanket wrapped around him, the fresh air beneficial. Lenora relaxed, as she was no longer forced to be in bodily contact with Charles during her husband's walks. That, combined with Edouard's rapid improvement had put her in a better mood. Her manners towards Charles eased.

There was a soft knock on her bedroom door. Without waiting for an answer, Charles entered.

Lenora sat at her dressing table, wearing only her night-gown. To hide her body, she jumped into bed and pulled the cover up to her chin. 'You're no longer welcome here.'

Charles ignored her and sat down on the bed, 'We must talk. We belong together. Only Edouard stands in our way.

You love me. It's only your sense of gratitude to him that makes you act the way you do. Can't you see that?'

'No, you're wrong. I hate you for what Wilfred did to me. It was your fault. Please, go away!' Nervously, she sat upright, her shoulders tense. She was weak, if he touched her, she would succumb; her body wanted him.

'Let me love you. It will remove the memory of Wilfred.' As she shrank away, pressing up against the headboard, Charles leaned forward and released her fingers from the cover, pulling it down. Under the sheer material of her gown, her nipples stiffened between his fingers, as his hands moulded her breasts.

Why didn't she protest? But she did not. She hated herself for it. She remained silent. His hands sent a ripple down her body and she closed her eyes.

Charles placed his hand on her stomach, 'Our child,' he whispered.

Tears sprang to her eyes and a manifold of emotions tore through her. Her anger rose because of the hold he had over her and shame that she couldn't resist him. She should protest and push him away, order him out of the room. But she longed for what he could give her at this moment.

Oh Lord, she had missed him so much.

Remember. This is Charles, you detest him. You hate him. Don't let him.

Just once more. He'll be leaving soon. Please, just once more. Then never again.

Charles had pulled up her gown and his hand rested on her stomach; she was ready for him now. She wanted his body. But he didn't come to her.

She opened her eyes and he was looking down on her, his expression watchful, and it puzzled her.

'Do you want me, Lenora?' His hand eased its way to her groin, where it rested.

She nodded.

'Say it! Say, "I want you Charles".'

She gazed back at him through half-closed eyelids. She wanted to hit him, but she quelled her rising anger, for she could not deny her body. Her skin already burning, this had gone too far. She answered, 'I want you, Charles.' And, as he lowered himself, her body arched up to meet him.

Afterwards, Charles showered her with kisses, 'I was right. You do love me. This proves it.'

She didn't answer; she'd already regretted giving in. She hated him; she was weak and should be ashamed for allowing him to do what he did. How many times had he humiliated her? And now he had done so again.

At last she looked at him, 'You must leave. Go back to Canada. I don't want you here when I tell Edouard. It wouldn't be appropriate.'

Charles' eyes flew open, 'After this? After what we've just done?'

'Yes, Edouard will forgive me, I'll tell him soon. He's well enough to hear the truth. Surely you can see that it would be most uncomfortable for you to be here, when I do?'

'You can't be serious; you love me. Your love-making just now has proved it. I'll find a solution.'

'I do mean it, Charles. I have to tell Eduard, you do know that. He must be told.'

'How soon?'

'Soon. You'd better pack and make arrangements.'

'I won't leave, Lenora. You can rest assured of that.'

'Edouard will ask you to leave.'

'You're crazy. You prefer the old man over me?' He spat out the words and swept his arms around the room, 'All this could be ours. Just you and me.'

Lenora turned her back to him, 'Go now, Charles.' Her voice was toneless.

'If you think it will be that easy, you're wrong,' Charles hurriedly left the room, his face red with anger.

Chapter 48

Ellen was angry with Lenora. My God, this woman was sex mad. She became putty in his hands, as soon as he touched her. How many times would she let Charles humiliate her? Lenora wanted him gone, so why did she sleep with him? This wasn't the way to put things right with Edouard, if she was desperate to return to the life they had had before. Heavens knows what she would do if Charles refused to leave.

But still her heart went out to Lenora; one couldn't help but feel compassion for her, she was immature and impulsive. She was right to put her faith in Edouard. He loved her and, that apart, he would want to avoid a scandal. He would say the baby was his and if anyone suspected Charles to be the father, nobody would ever voice this opinion. One had to remember this was 1903.

Ellen hated and loathed Lenora's sex life; she found it hard to endure; Charles used and degraded her. Now that Daniel was back in her life, he was all she wanted.

During the past weeks, it had become increasingly difficult to explain her whereabouts to him. She was afraid to lose him. It had been her saving grace that he had several business trips abroad. Every time he told her he was off on a new trip, she drew a sigh of relief. Had he noticed? Their arrangement wasn't working for him and she was running out of excuses. She hated the fact that she was lying to him.

One night she returned late and found Daniel asleep in his car outside the caravan.

'Where have you been, Ellen? I've tried to contact you,' he looked hurt. 'I came to tell you I'm off to Singapore and will be gone for a week.'

'To York to visit an aunt,' she lied, walking up to him with her arms outstretched. Ellen was too surprised to think of a better excuse. Why do I always use York in my lies? she wondered.

'I didn't know you had an aunt. And why didn't you tell me you'd be away?'

'I'm sorry,' she blinked. She didn't have an aunt and hoped that he'd never find out. She raised herself up onto her toes and kissed him, 'I've missed you like crazy.'

Dan's face lit up, 'Come on, woman, open up this van. I'm cold and my neck is stiff from sleeping in the car.' Once inside, he frowned, 'How long did you say you've been away? This van needs airing.'

'I didn't say, Dan.' She answered and steered him towards the bedroom.

Daniel had to leave early on the Monday morning, to get ready for his trip to Singapore, and it pleased her. It meant she could return to the house immediately. But another longing took hold: for the first time, she would have been content to return with him to Bristol. She'd begun to wish that Lakeside House would give up its secret and give her an answer. Let it be soon or she would lose Daniel.

Chapter 49

Lenora had been unable to keep her promise to meet Emily for afternoon tea, due to Edouard's early discharge from the hospital. But this day they were meeting at Polly's teashop in Kendal.

'Emily, I am sorry you've had to wait so long for this meeting, but with Edouard ill, it's been difficult.'

Emily interrupted, 'I do understand. We're all so pleased that he's doing well. As Papa said, a head injury isn't to be ignored. Edouard is lucky to be alive.'

'Quite,' Lenora nodded. 'I'm glad that you're looking better. Are you fully recovered?'

'Yes, I have come to terms with my unfortunate circumstance and the reason for being unwell. I think there's a solution to my dilemma.' Emily stopped as the waitress approached their table. The two women watched in silence as the girl placed the teapot, followed by daintily cut cucumber sandwiches, scones, jam and clotted cream, on the table. A moment later, she returned with a pyramid of small cakes.

'I need to unburden myself and ask for advice and your help. I think that you'll understand.' Emily lowered her eyes and her cheeks blushed, 'Especially as you know him well.'

This could only mean Charles. Lenora paled and put a hand on her stomach; she was carrying his child. She'd long suspected that he was part of Emily's problem, but she couldn't understand in what way. He hadn't seen her since the Grand Picnic and they hadn't got close enough to speak. Yes, she'd seen her glance over to Charles several times. Surely, she couldn't still be enthralled by a New Year's Eve kiss?

'Are you sure, Emily, that you want to tell me this?' Lenora half wished that she wouldn't; the other half desperately wanted to know.

'It's about Charles,' Emily said.

'Yes, what about Charles?' Lenora held her breath.

'I love him, and he loves me,' Emily blushed.

'Has he told you this?' The words came out in a whisper, as the blood rushed to her head. She stared at Emily, as if she had suddenly turned into a ghost.

Emily was so concerned about what she was going to say that she didn't notice, 'Yes, many times, when we were together.'

As her words sank in, the colour drained from Lenora's face and she felt very cold as a chill ran through her body, 'You have been meeting him? When?' Her voice was shrill, and she looked around the room; nobody had taken any notice. 'Do forgive me, I didn't mean to raise my voice, but I was so very surprised.'

'Oh, I understand completely. We've kept it a secret.'

'Are you seeing him now?'

'No, that's why I wanted to see you. It was when Charles had permission to shoot on Papa's land. Well, that was just an excuse – although he did shoot a rabbit now and again to avoid suspicion – but he was meeting me in the forest.' Emily sighed deeply, 'But Mama found out, and forbade me to see him ever again. Meg, my maid, was instructed to never leave my side or she'd be dismissed without a reference.'

Lenora nodded, unable to speak; the bile was rising in her throat. June? July? She was trying to remember. That was when Charles had distanced himself from her, not wanting her. She had missed him and she had been unhappy. Why? She had asked. What had she done wrong? Now she knew, he had been meeting Emily. Had he bedded her? She was soon to find out.

'Well, Mama has relaxed the rules, so I'll be able to see him again.'

'Has Charles been in contact with you?' Lenora's voice trembled.

'No, I'm a little surprised, but he has abided by my wishes. I made him swear to do so.'

Lenora remained quiet, crumbling a scone to small pieces between her fingers. You don't know Charles, my dear Emily, she thought. Your mama wouldn't stop him from seeing you, had he wanted to. No, there had to be another reason.

Emily took Lenora's silence as disapproval, 'I can see that you're shocked. Oh, you think I'm an awful person, bad and wicked, to give myself to him before we're wed. But I do love him so very much. Now I can't marry anyone else, but it won't matter when Charles and I are wed. Do you think badly of me?' Emily stopped and stared at Lenora, 'Oh you do! You despise me. Your face has gone awfully pale.'

'No, no, Emily, I do not! Please don't think that. But you should take my advice and forget him.'

'Forget him? Why? I don't believe I've heard you right.' In spite of Emily's distress, Lenora put her head in her hands and would not answer. 'Oh, Lenora, my behaviour has made you so very upset.'

How could she tell her? She could not. Poor Emily. Lenora sat upright as a thought struck her, 'Emily, are you with child?'

'Oh, heavens no.' A deep blush spread over her face, 'it only happened once. But I'll tell you, Lenora, it was wonderful.'

Lenora wanted to scream at her, You silly girl! Instead, she reached out and took her hand, 'I don't know how to break this news to you.' She paused as Emily visibly tensed and her blue eyes filled with dread.

'Tell me what? Oh, please, tell me. Is it Charles? Is he not well?'

Lenora took a deep breath, 'Charles is due to return to Canada in a few days' time.'

The effect was immediate, Emily crumpled in her seat, 'Help me, the salts!'

Lenora searched Emily's bag for the small blue bottle and waved it under her nose. The girl inhaled deeply and after a moment had regained her composure.

'He can't be. He can't intend to leave me without a word. It's not possible.'

'I'm afraid it is. Please trust me when I say that Charles isn't what you believe him to be. Your mama was right.'

'No, how can you say that? If you were not my friend, I would be angry.' Emily continued in a hurry, 'I must see him. I've written a letter, which I hoped you'd deliver to him. Now I must give him another. But I've nothing to write on.'

'If I do as you ask, I'll be breaking your mama's trust.'

But you're my friend, more than Mama's. You can't refuse me.'

'No,' she sighed, seeing that Emily was intent on her action. 'There's writing material at the reception of the Station Hotel. Let's go there.'

Emily rose from her chair, unsteady on her legs, she gratefully accepted Lenora's arm.

Standing by the fireplace in her bedroom, Lenora unfolded Emily's note,

My darling, darling Charles,

How I have missed you! I am writing to tell you that we can soon be together again, as Mama is no longer having me watched. My heart nearly stopped when I heard the news that you are planning to leave. Because of me? Is your heart broken, like mine, until I can be in your arms? I know that when you hear my news you will stay! I blame myself for not writing to you sooner and, because of that, you have given up hope. I will meet you by the lodge tomorrow at four and I will bring the key. We will be able to experience the joy of being in each other's arms again. I will count the minutes, my darling.

Yours for ever,

Emily.

Lenora read the note once more, she'd no idea that Emily could be so romantic and poetic in her writing. Well, Charles wouldn't be there, this was a note he would never read. The lodge, she frowned, so that was where they had been meeting. She felt calm and detached as she crumpled the note and watched the flames turn it black and the fragments fall apart. At that moment, she decided that Charles had to be punished.

Chapter 50

'Miss Lenora!' Coming through the door the next morning, Molly wiped the tears from her face. 'George and me, we've had bad news. The neighbour's boy has been with a message. It's my sister, she's in a bad way. I'll have to go over to Keswick and George best come with me. Can we take a few days off?'

'Of course, Molly.'

'Is there anything we can do before we go?'

'No, we'll manage. Tell George that you can both leave at once. Where is he?'

'Oh, he's by the lake getting the boat ready for Charles to take the master out.'

'Onto the lake? A boat trip for Edouard? Why wasn't I informed? He shouldn't go out in the boat.'

'That's what I thought too, Miss Lenora, but the master knows his own mind and he's set on going. Seems he thinks the air and wind will do him good.'

'He's stubborn when his mind is made up. I had better go with them.'

'Right you are, Miss Lenora, but you'd better hurry or they'll be gone. George and I will be back early on Monday morning.'

'Don't worry. If you need to stay longer, you should.'

'Thank you, if that's necessary, I'll send George back and he can fetch me home later.'

'If you so wish, do what's best for you. Now I must hurry.' Her mind was racing. What was Charles up to?

She snatched her cape and scarf from the chair in the hall and also a warm jacket off the coat stand for her husband. He had probably not taken one. She swung the cape over her shoulders and ran down to the lake.

'Wait for me!' she called as she got closer.

Charles was about to push the boat out and her concern grew as he turned an irritated face towards her, 'What are you doing here?' his voice was hard.

'I'm coming with you.'

'I'd rather you didn't.' Charles heaved at the boat.

Lenora saw Edouard become alert, seemingly surprised at Charles' answer and tone of voice.

'I'm not sure that Edouard should venture out onto the lake yet.'

'Lenora, I'm looking forward to feeling the breeze in my face. Charles was careful when he helped me into the boat and of course you must come.'

'Why wasn't I told?'

'I sent Charles to tell you, dearest, but he couldn't find you.'

Lenora was dumbstruck. Charles had known where she was all along. It was obvious that he didn't want her there. A feeling of dread grew in her and took hold, 'I am coming.' Her voice was firm.

Charles glowered at her, 'Suit yourself, but it's windy out there.' He reached out to help her on board and she sat down next to her husband.

'Edouard, I knew you would come away without your coat. Here, let me help you with this one.' She struggled to get the coat over Edouard's shoulders without him standing up, as Charles had already started to row, the oars digging deep into the water.

What was he up to? He rowed fast, not as on a leisurely boat trip. She held onto the side of the boat and became increasingly concerned. Charles was in a hurry, he bowed his head, avoiding her eyes. When he raised his head, she saw a look she'd never seen before.

Lenora quelled her panic, she must not alarm Edouard. She took hold of his hand and he responded by giving hers a gentle squeeze, 'Tell me what you see, Lenora.'

'Yes, I will.' In spite of the dread she felt, she tried to be strong, 'The sun is making the water shimmer like streaks of silver. If we were to turn to the left, we would come to the Edmondsons' moorings.' A sob broke her voice but the wind had swallowed her last words and Edouard hadn't noticed. 'I can see a pleasure boat far in the distance.' She was aware that she was rambling and slowed down, 'We're a long way out.'

Nervously, she gripped the side of the boat. 'All the trees look quite small.' She stopped suddenly, 'Is this not far enough, Charles? I think we should turn back.' A chill went down her spine when he didn't answer.

Lifting his head, he stared back at her with a crazed and wild expression on his face, 'You insisted on coming…' he continued his rambling and as she listened, the hysteria rose in her to a high pitch.

Charles shifted his gaze to Edouard, his voice distorted with fury, 'It's time you know that I intend to marry Lenora, she loves me and is carrying my child.'

Lenora covered her ears to block out his words and a sob escaped her. How could he be so cruel? In panic she stood up in the boat, 'What you're saying is wrong. I'll never marry you! I hate you,' she screamed at Charles.

Then she stared at Edouard in horror. His face had turned grey with shock, 'What are you saying, Charles? In the name of the Lord, Lenora, tell me…'

Chapter 51

An uneasy stillness descended on Lenora and Edouard that afternoon as they sat in front of the fire in the drawing room. Lenora had lit it after their return; both had been frozen, and Edouard had a blanket wrapped around him. Still he shivered. They had spent more time on the lake than had been their intention. Such had been their distress at the events of the day, neither had any appetite for food.

Edouard was slumped back in his armchair, motionless, his eyes staring at the wall in front of him. He did not react when Lenora fell onto her knees and placed her hands on his.

With her tear-swollen face raised to him, she begged him again for forgiveness. 'There is a pain in my heart, which will never go away. The memory of today will remain with me for the rest of my life and I will have to live with what I have done. Charles behaved like a man possessed, he terrified me, and I could see that you were equally affected and shocked. He didn't know what he was doing and saying. But if you cannot forgive me, I'll understand.' She waited for his reply but dared not prompt him.

Edouard's face had regained none of its colour. It was ashen, and his hands were shaking. 'What has happened has made this the worst day of my entire life. It will take some time to come to terms with it,' he answered at length.

'Of course, but I must explain. I wanted to tell you myself.

He shouted it out in the worst manner possible; it was cruel. Charles pursued me from the moment he arrived. I found his attention flattering but also disturbing. I resisted him for a long time. Then I fell in love and he assured me of his love. What we did was unforgivable. We deceived you in your own home.' She shook his arm gently as he appeared not to be listening.

At last Edouard stirred, but his face wasn't turned towards her, 'You're having his child.' It was a statement. His voice trembled.

'Yes, I carry his child. When I realised, the awful truth became clear to me: I didn't love Charles. I have no feelings for this child, I don't want it. I decided to tell you and suffer the consequences. But Charles would have none of it. He wanted to marry me and live here at Lakeside House after you were gone. I came to despise him. Never could I have lived with him, but he wouldn't believe me.'

Edouard said nothing, his head still turned away from her.

A slight sob escaped her, as she continued, 'I think that I must go away until the child is born and if you wish, I will not return. I cannot bring this shame on you.'

'How can I believe anything you say? Charles said that you shared his bed less than a week ago. Is it true?'

Lenora hung her head; she had never seen him so defeated. She could lie to spare him, but no more lies. Charles was gone. 'It's true.'

She heard Edouard's sharp intake of breath and continued, 'I know, and I hate myself for being weak. He had power over me and he threatened to tell you. I wanted you to know but only when the time was right.'

'Please, bring me a cognac, a large one. I need to blot out the memory of this day.'

Lenora brought him the drink and he sipped it slowly, lost in thought. When he didn't speak, she stayed quiet.

'Get me another.' It was more of a command and she ran

off to come back with the decanter. Edouard seldom spoke to her like this.

'You haven't eaten anything today. Perhaps you shouldn't drink,' Lenora protested, when he reached for the decanter a third time. But his face silenced her. She'd never seen such anguish.

'I will leave you now. I'm very tired.' Edouard struggled to stand.

'I'll come to help you undress tonight.'

'No, don't do that. I can manage. I must be alone with my thoughts. Although I would prefer never to speak about this day again, I fear that we must. We'll talk tomorrow.'

'I am glad that Charles…,' she stopped and with some difficulty continued, 'is gone. It's for the best.'

'I agree, Lenora. I only wish the dreadful circumstances could have been avoided.'

Lenora shuddered at the memory, 'Yes, it shouldn't have happened in this way. I pray that you'll forgive me. My fate is in your hands.'

It was gone midnight when Lenora thought she heard the door to Charles' room opening and closing, and she was gripped by fear. It couldn't be... No, Charles would never come back. Horrified, she felt compelled to tiptoe down the corridor and with every nerve in her body on edge, she pushed the door open; the room was empty. Afterwards, she paced the floor of her bedroom, sobbing, only stopping for a moment or two to listen for the sound again. Frightened, she wanted to go to her husband but changed her mind when she remembered his demeanour earlier that evening. What would become of them? Edouard had previously said that he'd forgive her anything. Even this?

To her surprise, Edouard knocked on her door the next morning; this rarely happened. He was already dressed, 'I will wait for you in the dining room. Do come directly.' He turned and walked away, without waiting for her answer.

'I will bring your breakfast,' she called out after him.

'No, don't. Later. We must talk first.' Edouard sounded tired, but his voice was firm. Lenora stared at her husband's back. She didn't know him. He had changed, and she was to blame.

She dressed in a hurry. Inside the door of the dining room, she hesitated, 'I am here, Edouard.'

'Come and sit next to me. I haven't had much sleep, instead, I've made plans. We will go away, both of us. I cannot let you go on your own. We'll tell George and Molly that we're going to visit my family in France for a few months. Furthermore, I'll arrange for Holden & Son to take care of the money matters. George and Molly will look after the house.' He paused and hesitated before carrying on, 'You told me that you don't want the child, but you must think carefully about this. You might change your mind once it's born. If you do, I will treat the child as my own.'

'Oh, Edouard, dearest, you're the kindest man.'

'Let me continue. George and Molly will be back tomorrow. Well, George should be at least. He will take me to Kendal to make arrangements. I cannot let you be punished for this, when it is as much my fault. Any father would do the same.'

Lenora fell on her knees and laid her head in his lap, 'I don't deserve you,' she sobbed quietly. When she lifted her swollen face to him, he appeared to be somewhere far away. His had a look of peace, a change from his troubled face.

'How can you be so calm, Edouard? I've sinned, and I should be punished.'

'Lenora, only by marriage could you inherit Lakeside

House. I wanted to give you that protection, so I asked you to become my wife. But by so doing, I've put you in a gilded cage. No, we should share the punishment. Also, we must think of the child.'

Chapter 52

Early the next morning, Edouard set off to Kendal with George. Molly's sister had shown some improvement, so Molly had returned with her husband.

She was preparing vegetables in the kitchen when Lenora joined her, 'So Master Charles is gone then,' it was a statement. 'A bit sudden, not that it's any of my business,' she sniffed.

Lenora shuddered at the mention of his name and swallowed hard, 'Yes, as Edouard told you, he's on his way back to Canada. But he will stop by in London, as he has never been there. His father wrote and asked him to come home. His mother is unwell. Nothing too serious but she wants him home.' Lenora turned away from Molly, so as not to show her face; she wasn't a good liar.

'I'd better do his room then,' Molly said.

'Thank you, Molly, you might as well. I'm glad your sister is better.'

'Yes, she's turned the corner but some way to go yet. Not much I could do there by staying. But you don't look too well, Miss Lenora. Hope you don't mind me saying. You're pale today.'

'I didn't sleep well, that's all.'

They were interrupted by George, 'Well, we're back, and the master would like to see you in the library, Miss Lenora.'

She hurried to her husband, who was pacing the floor,

'What do you have to tell me?' she asked eagerly.

'Mr Holden said that it could take up to a couple of weeks to draw up the necessary documents, but, to his consternation, I told him that wouldn't do. I must have them within days, I said. He did ask why, and I told him that it was family matters and left it at that. He had the sense not to question me further.'

'Must we hurry so?'

'Yes, you do know why, surely? If you don't keep the child, it's essential that nobody here knows about your condition. I cannot see, Lenora, but others can. No doubt it will soon show.'

'You're right, of course,' she blushed.

'I'll have to go back to Holden & Son in three days' time and then I will also finalise the arrangements for the journey.'

'You have thought this out thoroughly.'

'We mustn't leave anything to chance. We don't know for how long we'll be gone. Can you please ask George and Molly to come in? I'll tell them about our travel plans; for this to succeed, they must agree to what I intend to ask them.'

'You mean to look after Lakeside House?'

'Precisely that.'

George and Molly came into the room, looking around nervously. They knew that something was afoot. George twirled his cap in his hands and Molly was pulling at her apron. 'Is anything the matter, Master?' George ventured to ask. 'I thought with the visit to Kendal this morning...'

'No, nothing is the matter, on the contrary. Now that Charles has left, we are planning a trip abroad to visit my relatives in France. We intend to stay for several months. I want you both to move into Lakeside House. Well, at least one of you, until we come back.'

Lenora saw the astonished look on Molly's face as Edouard continued, 'I hope you'll agree. It's a big favour to ask, I know.'

George looked at Molly, who nodded, 'Can't see much

of a problem with that, Master. You said you'll be gone for months?'

'Yes, I have wanted to do this journey for a long time. Lenora and I haven't travelled and now we will. While it's still possible.'

'I see. Will that be all?' George asked.

'No, I have arranged that once a month, George, you will visit Holden & Son. Mr Holden will give you a sum of money, which will pay for the upkeep of Lakeside House and your wages.'

'Right, Master, and when will you be gone?'

'As soon as the arrangements are in place. In two weeks' time.'

Molly drew a sharp breath, and George's face showed bewilderment. Edouard's voice was reassuring, 'I expect you're surprised. But now that we've made up our mind, there no point waiting longer.'

'Right, Master,' George said, but on his way out his steps were hesitant and slow. Molly followed closely behind her husband without a word, her face betraying her confusion.

Chapter 53

'What's all this about then?' Molly asked, as soon as the door closed behind them, 'A bit sudden. Isn't it?'

'I agree, but the master knows what's for the best, always has done. We shouldn't question his decision.'

'Do you think it's got something to do with Charles? There was no hint of him leaving. I've had my suspicions for a while.'

'About what?'

'Well, them carrying on.'

'We don't know that for certain.'

'What if the master found out and sent him packing? I've seen the change in Miss Lenora. Women notice these things.'

'Hush, woman. I pray to the Lord that you're wrong. Best keep these thoughts to yourself.'

'Oh yes, I will that. I'd never let the master down or Miss Lenora for that matter. Even if she has done wrong. The master must have forgiven her. Like you said, he knows what's for the best.'

'Let's leave it at that.'

Molly nodded, 'Yes, and we can live like gentry. I'll be lording it in Miss Lenora's bedroom as soon as she's gone.'

'You'll be doing no such thing. You'll be sleeping right next to me. But I do think we can use Master Charles' bedroom. I'm sure that will be all right.'

‘Or perhaps not. She might want us to sleep in the old servants’ quarter. I’ll ask her.’

‘I hadn’t thought of that.’ George stroked his chin, ‘Hasn’t been used for years though.’

‘I’m not too sure about that,’ Molly frowned.

‘What? Do you mean that…?’

‘Yes, where else?’

‘I feel for the master, if what you say is true. Don’t know how he can tolerate it. Don’t let it give you any ideas.’

‘He shouldn’t have wed her, if he wasn’t prepared to bed her. Like I said, it’s not only the men folk who have their needs.’

‘I shall hold you to that when we get home, woman. But the master has always thought of her as his daughter, he’s too honourable to bed her. It wouldn’t have been right.’

‘Well, he’s truly doing the honourable thing now, that’s for sure. But come on, let’s put the kettle on. We’ve got much to mull over.’

Chapter 54

When Edouard returned from Kendal, Lenora met him in the hall, 'Let me help you off with the coat.' She dropped it onto the armchair and turned to her husband. 'I worry that the preparations for the journey are too much for you. Neither of us has slept much in the past week.' Racked by guilt, she was eager to please her husband and she dreaded the nights, when she would wake from nightmares and be terrified of seeing Charles' contorted face in front of her.

'Nonsense, I'm fully recovered. In fact, it's doing me good to be busy. All the arrangements are completed, and we leave in five days' time. I have seen to the business side and you will sort out the packing with Molly's help.'

'I have already started. We're going to need winter clothes, as well as summer. We'll have to buy more trunks as we have extra luggage.'

'Yes, but we mustn't overload ourselves with too much baggage. If necessary, we'll buy new. You're going to need new clothes soon: a larger size, I take it.'

Lenora blushed, 'You think of everything, Edouard.' Instinctively, she put her hands to her waistline; there was a noticeable rounding on her stomach, which didn't show under the folds of her dress. She never let any thoughts about the child linger but immediately pushed them out of her mind. She didn't want to acknowledge it and for a long time, had denied its existence. It had been easier to forget, once her morning sickness had passed and that hadn't lasted for long. Soon she'd have to face the fact, as Edouard had just reminded her. She was brought out of her thoughts by the tapping of his cane, as he made his way to the drawing room.

On the day of departure, Molly stood on the porch, dabbing her eyes with a corner of her apron. At the station in Kendal, George bade them goodbye with a tremor in his voice. His shoulders slumped as he walked back to where he'd tethered the horse.

He stroked her head as he talked to her, 'Somehow this doesn't seem right, Belinda.'

Chapter 55

When Edouard and Lenora left Lakeside House on their way to the station and Ireland, Ellen found herself in her car on the way back to the caravan. Their departure had made it clear to her that she shouldn't follow. Her time as Lenora was over.

She returned to her caravan home much traumatised by the memory of what had happened on the lake. Needing to calm her nerves, she poured a large glass of red wine, but she doubted that would be enough. Ellen didn't want to remember, but whenever she closed her eyes, she saw Charles' face contorted with rage. It was the face of a madman. The Charles she knew was unrecognisable. With his action and words, he'd been intent on hurting Edouard beyond words. His anger had been a threat to the stability of the boat, which had rocked violently. Lenora had begged him to come to his senses. Ice ran down the core of Ellen's back and she shuddered.

She felt so sorry for Edouard. Poor man, he had been dumbfounded and bewildered: it had been so sudden. He had slumped down in the boat, his face ashen, *Is Charles speaking the truth?* His voice had been a mere whisper. He had been met by silence. Impatient to get an answer and make himself heard, he had regained strength and shouted, *In the name of the Lord, Lenora. Tell me!*

She had confirmed it to be true.

At last Edouard knew the truth, Ellen thought. It had to happen sometime. His decision to take Lenora away from Lakeside House was right, considering the circumstances.

But Ellen was disappointed. Was it meant to end like this? After a year at the house, she still didn't know the purpose of her stay.

Now what? She was confused, angry and scared. In frustration, she picked up her hairbrush and hit the table by her side. The brush broke in half. 'Damnation, my best brush.' Irritated, she threw the bits into the bin. Her only option was to leave Cumbria and push the memory of what had happened to the back of her mind. If that was possible.

Never to tell anyone. Not even Daniel, least of all him.

But Bristol was good, that was where she wanted to go: back to Daniel and her own life. She'd finished with this place, but she regretted not having had the answer she had sought for so long.

In the morning Ellen packed her belongings into the car. She handed in the keys at the site office and told the receptionist that she wouldn't be back, even though she'd extended her stay and paid to the end of September. Daniel was waiting and she missed him.

It was only when she turned off the main road that she realised to her consternation that she was on her way to the house. She was going back to see if it was there. Surely it would be gone? She had to make sure. And she was right: there was no house.

Ellen turned the car round and headed for the motorway. She drove fast, exceeding the speed limit and hoped there were no cameras. She wished that she'd sent Daniel a text, but she'd been in a hurry to get home. Just as well, she wanted to shower and wash her hair before she saw him.

Ellen dumped the bags on the floor of her hall as the mobile buzzed. It was Daniel.

'When can I see you? Are you coming home soon?'

'I am back...'

'You're back? When? Why didn't you tell me?'

'I only got back this minute. I was going to call you.'

'I'll be right over.'

'No, give me an hour, make it two. I'm desperate for a shower. I want to look my best for you. Smell nice, you know.'

Daniel sounded put out and disappointed. She hadn't meant to be dismissive but that's how he'd seen it. Why did she always get it wrong with him? He had asked questions which he never got answers to, because she couldn't give him any. He had been patient. He had found out about Charles, but she'd assured him that it was over. Why then did she stay in the Lakes? She had been evasive in her answer.

On the phone, Daniel had asked to take her out, but she was tired and preferred an evening at home, so he'd offered to bring a Chinese takeaway.

'Hmm, you smell good.' Ellen buried her head in his shirt, as soon as he'd put the food bags down in the kitchen.

'You too. Good enough to eat.' He held her at arm's length.

'Why don't you?'

'I will, but food first, and I'll have you for dessert.'

An hour later Ellen turned over in bed, 'I've a surprise for you. You'll like it.'

'You've finished with the Lakes?'

'How did you know?'

'Know what?'

'That I'm finished, I'm never going back.'

'I saw the bags in the hall. But do you mean it? Honestly.'

'Yes, honestly.'

'You promise?'

'I promise. I'll never, never go back.'

'Hmm.' Dan turned over and pulled her close, 'We must celebrate that.'

In the week to come, Ellen had trouble sleeping; she had one recurring nightmare: the boat trip. She couldn't forget it. Back on the lake, she saw Charles's distorted face, as he stood up in the boat: a man possessed by the devil, his mouth twisted and his eyes black with madness.

One night when Daniel had stayed over he woke her, by gently shaking her shoulder.

'Ellen, you're dreaming. What kind of a guy was this Charles? You shouted out his name and sounded terrified. Has he treated you badly? You'd tell me, wouldn't you?'

She sat up in a daze, rubbing her forehead, 'Oh God no, nothing like that. It's just that he had an accident and it scared me. He's fine now, I don't see him anymore.'

Ellen was happy to be back at the shop. She made use of the fashion she'd seen a hundred years ago, making alterations to suit today's taste.

Her mind would drift back to Lakeside House. It wasn't easy to shake off the memories, good and bad, of life there. What had happened to Edouard and Lenora?

Ken and Annie were pleased that they had been instrumental in bringing Ellen and Daniel together. Annie let slip that she and Ken never liked Charles, although they had not met him, 'It's the way he came across when you mentioned him,' she said.

'Really?'

'Yes, are you sure you liked him? We did think it strange.'

Ellen was astonished; she realised that she had been unable to hide her true feelings about Charles.

Daniel arrived, dressed and ready for the evening; he had invited Ellen to a party in connection with his work, a grand affair for one of the directors.

He held up the vodka bottle, 'I'll fix us a drink, while you make yourself even more beautiful.'

'Good, I won't be long.' Ellen disappeared into the bedroom.

'I've booked a taxi. It'll be here in forty-five minutes,' he called out by the door.

Half an hour later, she made an entrance, wearing a black dress, especially designed for the evening. She knew she looked good. Daniel gaped at her, 'Ellen you are stunning!'

Her cheeks glowed at his compliment and she reached out for the drink. She brought it to her lips and froze... Leaving it untouched, she whispered, 'It's not possible.' The ice in the glass rattled as she put it down with a shaking hand.

'What's not possible?' Dan pulled his eyebrows together, his eyes searching hers, 'I don't understand.'

'The picture! It's back,' she stammered and pointed. The painting of Lakeside House hung above the fireplace.

'Yeah, it was there when I got here. What's the fuss?'

'I didn't put it there,' she raised her voice in protest, 'it's been in the guest room for weeks now.'

'Oh, come on, Ellen, what is your obsession with this painting? I asked Annie, as you wouldn't tell me. I thought it was over?'

'So did I.' But that wasn't true. Deep inside, she'd known that it wasn't. She had been waiting for this moment. She covered her face with her hands, 'Sorry, I'm feeling faint.'

'Ellen, you are terrified. Are you unwell again?'

'What do you mean: "unwell again"?'

'Well, Annie told me you'd gone to live in Cumbria to

recover from a breakdown.' He stopped.

'She's wrong,' Ellen shrieked.

'Calm down, Ellen. But then why did you spend all that time there? It seemed like a reasonable explanation to me...'

'Annie had no business telling you anything,' Ellen interrupted, her voice rising again. 'But, yes, initially I did go for a change of scenery, and then I got to like it. Absolutely no breakdown. Of course, I'm fine. It's nothing! Really it's nothing.'

'Doesn't seem like nothing to me. You're trying too hard to convince me.'

'Who do you choose to believe? Me or Annie?'

'Don't shout, Ellen.'

'I'm not shouting.'

'Yes, you are. Just now you implied that the picture has moved to the fireplace on its own. It's not the first time either, according to you.'

Ellen lowered her voice in an effort to calm down. 'I remember, I did move it,' she lied, biting her lip. It *had* moved on its own once before and she had returned it to the guest room, but here it was again. She felt numb, her thoughts racing. Last time there had been an emergency at Lakeside House: Edouard had ended up in hospital after the accident. She had to go at once; she'd been called back.

'I'm sorry. Dan, I can't come with you tonight.'

'You're not serious.' He looked flabbergasted, 'You're leaving me to go on my own?'

'I am. Please leave now. Ken and Annie will be there.'

'Not quite the same, Ellen. For heaven's sake, I didn't mean to upset you. I was concerned. I didn't mean to start a row.'

'I know, Dan.' She lowered her head, rubbing her temples, not meeting his gaze, 'Please, go.'

'Are you not giving me an explanation?' Dan shook his head in disbelief.

‘I can’t, not now.’

Dan put down his unfinished drink and left without a word and without looking back. She knew that she had upset him terribly. The party had been important and she’d let him down.

Chapter 56

It was late when she arrived at the Lakes, and she was too scared to go to the house in the dark. Why had she been called back? Lenora and Edouard had left, so what could be in store for her and why? Perhaps she had overreacted? Perhaps nobody would be there. She'd been an idiot to rush off, leaving Daniel in the lurch. And yet...

She booked into a pub where they didn't know her. She couldn't give Mrs Jones a good explanation for her return, and she didn't have it in her heart to lie to her again.

Ellen was first to arrive in the dining room for breakfast and she checked out as soon as it got light. Would Lakeside House be waiting for her? There had been no house last time. Had she been right in believing she had unfinished business there?

The house stood at the top of the slope, derelict like the first time she had seen it. Ellen covered her face with shaking hands, her heart hammering. Slowly, she removed her hands and stared at it again. A chill ran down her back; this was the end. At last she would know.

As she stepped out of the car, she narrowed her eyes, not taking them off the house. Her hand shook as she banged the car door shut behind her and then jumped at the noise it created. Now she was about to find out why she'd been compelled to spend a year of her life here. The answer was waiting inside.

The house had been vibrant and lived in, the home of Edouard and Lenora. Now she was in the past, but long after they had gone to live abroad in 1903. What year was this? She had no idea. By the state of the house, she guessed that she could be in 1935: the year it was pulled down.

Lenora and Edouard had left suddenly, and she knew they had never returned. For a short time she had gone back to her life in Bristol, taking with her a memory which haunted her.

Annie had encouraged her to get rid of the painting, but that would have been wrong; she had moved it to the guest room. Her subconscious mind had told her that she would return.

This house was ready to let her go. The time had come, and she was scared.

What was waiting for her? Her steps were hesitant, her nerves on edge and her breathing fast. On the porch she paused, before pushing the door open. As she took in the scene of the hall, she grimaced; the splendour was gone.

A sense of sadness enveloped her. Dear Edouard, he'd been an honest man, upright in everything he did. Once he had broken that rule and made a momentous exception, which must have shattered the beliefs he held and destroyed his self-esteem. It had been for Lenora's sake. He had stood by her in all her wrongdoings. He had forgiven her everything. How could you not feel respect for such a man? As Lenora, she had felt love and gratitude towards him. Lenora's love for him as a father had, in the end, proved stronger than her misguided love for Charles.

The real reason why she'd been called to the house was about to be revealed.

In the drawing room, the red velvet chair stood in the same corner as the first time she'd seen it. She touched the stain on the chair and was overcome with emotion. Edouard had spilt hot chocolate, and Molly had rubbed the stain so vigorously that it had left a permanent mark. Even though tense, Ellen smiled: she'd enjoyed happy times living with the people in this house. But there had been a darker side...'

She stood by the window overlooking the orchard; it had once been beautiful, now there was nothing left.

At that moment, she felt a slight tap on her arm and her panic was extreme. She stood rigid with fear, her breath still in her chest. For a fraction of a second time stopped, and then a hand on each shoulder guided her to turn around.

'I am sorry to frighten you.'

The panic rose to a pitch and engulfed her. She gasped for air, until she thought she could no longer breathe. A memory from the back of her mind stirred: the man in front of her seemed vaguely familiar. She frantically searched her brain but there was only emptiness. The blood rushed to her head and she leant against the window frame to stop herself from falling.

'Lenora,' the man said, 'we meet at last.' His face was serious and his eyes hard; he appeared calm, but she could see the pulse beating on his temples. Where had she seen these eyes before?

Ellen shook her head, 'I'm not Lenora, I'm not,' she stammered. 'Who are you?'

'Don't you recognise me?'

'No, no! Have we met?' Tears were trickling down her cheeks. Then she remembered the stone-coloured eyes, which had disturbed her so much, and was overcome by confusion. 'You're the artist! The painting...,' she'd realised that her voice was shrill, and she stopped abruptly.

'Yes, I've waited a long time for this moment and now it has come.'

'You're Henry Allen. But why? What do you want from me?' She was unable to stop her body from trembling.

'No, not Henry Allen,' he paused. 'I am Henry Villiers, Charles' father.'

The room spun, her legs buckled underneath her. She grabbed hold of his arm as she fell towards him, 'Please, help me,' she mumbled before she was swallowed up by darkness.

Chapter 57

When Ellen came to, she was sitting on the red velvet chair, supported by Henry Villiers. She shrank back from him in fright. Her face felt distorted in an awful way: it was hard, paralysed, and she found it difficult to form the words she wanted to speak.

'You can't be. It's impossible.' But she knew it was true. She could see a resemblance with Edouard: the eyes were the same stony grey, only Edouard's were kind, his brother's hard and cold.

'I've made this possible.' Henry Villiers made a half-circular sweep of his hand around the room, 'I devoted the rest of my life to studying life after death, so that when the time came I could return. I've worked hard and waited many, many years to bring you back, Lenora.'

'I am not Lenora,' Ellen protested. 'What do you want from me?'

'You're going to tell me what happened to my son. Charles never returned to Canada.'

There was so much pain on his face that Ellen dropped her eyes and bit her lip. This was unbelievable. Good God! How could she tell him?

'I came here to look for Charles. Your servants told me that my son left for Canada in rather a hurry. I told them that he had not returned home. This made them confused and disturbed. Soon after his departure, you and Edouard went to France. The servants remained tight-lipped and would not tell me much. I made many enquiries and couldn't find any news about Charles after he'd gone from here. No ticket was booked on the steamer in his name. Nothing! I paid several visits to Edouard's solicitors but was told the information as to your whereabouts was confidential. They were not at liberty to disclose it. However much I threatened, they would not move in the slightest degree.' He paused, 'I decided to follow you to France. I assumed you'd gone to visit our relatives. But as you know, they hadn't set eyes on you. Where did you go, Lenora?'

Ellen stared back at him. *To Ireland*, she thought but remained silent.

Henry Villiers continued, 'I returned to Canada, but I couldn't let it rest. I came back, hoping you had returned. Your servants were still looking after the house, but by then they were restless. I believed that they had their own thoughts as to what had happened but wouldn't tell me out of loyalty to my brother. I noticed the glances they exchanged. Now, I was convinced that your absence had something to do with my son.' His eyes bored into hers, 'I will have my answer, Lenora.'

Ellen shook her head, 'I am not her, not anymore. Stop calling me by her name. Why me? Why involve me? Why did you sell the painting to me?'

'You know by now, of course, that Edouard painted it. I found it at the house, when I came back to dispose of the furniture. I kept it. Now the house belonged to me.'

He stopped briefly, his face strained. 'Always, my love for my son brought me back many times. I had to know his fate. I cannot rest until I do. It became an obsession. I studied ancient texts, the Greek, and Buddhism's belief in rebirth; punarbhava.' He paused to explain, 'It means "renewed becoming".' After another short delay, he continued, 'Also pre-Socratics and even the Celtic druids' beliefs. It was about reincarnation, rebirth and the wheel of existence. Through endless meditation, I was able to concentrate and control my mind. I accumulated karma and samsara, the concept of the cycle of birth and death. To achieve this state of mind took decades of dedication.' His eyes narrowed, 'Now listen carefully. You are indeed Lenora. I had to wait until she was reborn in you and you reached the age of twenty-eight years, exactly the same age as Lenora when Charles arrived. I sent you back to live here so that you can tell me what happened to my son. You are the key, without you, it couldn't be done.'

Ellen gasped, 'You're not real. All this is not real.' In frustration she shouted, 'And I am not Lenora!'

'Ah, but it is real. In the time we are now. Look at the rings on your hand. Is one of them not the wedding ring Edouard gave you? Have you not noticed your dress?'

Stunned, Ellen stared at the heavy gold band on her finger and put her hand down to touch the green taffeta dress. Lenora was back. But it was different; this time Lenora didn't yet have control of her mind.

'You seduced my son. Don't deny it. I have the letters to prove it. It was careless of you to leave them under the floorboard. I was here, in spirit, when you found them. Later I took them from your room at the inn.'

'I intended to burn them before we left, but the hurried events at the last minute made that impossible. I put them there. I prayed they would never be found. So, it was you.' A voice inside her head had pushed to the forefront and she was answering as Lenora.

He nodded, a satisfied smile played on his lips; he knew that *she* had taken control.

Lenora continued, 'It was Charles, who seduced me. Your son was not a good person, or a gentleman. You didn't teach him well, Mr Villiers.' His grey eyes darkened, and alarmed at the look on his face, she stopped.

He took her roughly by the shoulders, 'You will tell me. We will not leave this place until you do. I have worked too hard and too long. I will not let this go.' His eyes flashed.

Lenora crumbled in front of him; her head fell, her shoulders hunched, and she visibly shrank. It was several minutes before she spoke. She nodded, her voice was tired and resigned, 'Charles was taking Edouard out in the boat, he said, to give him a taste of the air across the lake. He insisted that I should stay behind, but I refused. In front of Edouard, he had to agree to let me come, but it made him angry. I was suspicious of his motive.'

She stopped, 'I do not want to carry on. I will not tell you.' She stared at him defiantly.

Henry Villiers shook her shoulders hard, his grip menacing, 'You will speak.'

Lenora pulled herself up and continued, 'He rowed the boat out into the middle of the lake, and I'll never forget the look in his eyes when he addressed me. "*You insisted on coming, I wish you had not, I didn't want you to see this. I am not going to fail this time. I intended to tell you that Edouard had fallen overboard and drowned; for this is the moment I'll set you free to marry me.*"

I stared at him, unable to speak. I find it impossible to describe Edouard's face. His shock was immense, his face turned grey with disbelief. He called out, "*What are you saying Charles? Lenora, tell me...*" and then he stopped, incapable of carrying on.

Without mercy, Charles continued, "*It means that she loves me, she's carrying my child and you're in our way.*"

It was horrible; I shouted at him to stop, several times I shouted to stop. "*What you are saying is wrong,*" I screamed. "*I don't love you and I want no part of this. I'll never marry you.*" I shouted all this at Charles, but he just stared back at me. He looked deranged. He had a wild look about him.'

Lenora lowered her head, feeling a blush appear on her cheeks. 'And then he said in a hateful voice, "*You can't deny that I was in your bed a few nights ago? Will he believe you now?*"'. Lenora paused and looked straight into Henry Villiers' eyes, 'That made me very angry. He shouldn't have said that.' She put her hands over her eyes, 'I find it hard to tell you more.'

'But you must.' He had not loosened his grip on her shoulders, and his fingers dug into her skin.

Reluctantly, Lenora nodded, 'After that, it was all so sudden. I heard Edouard's sharp intake of breath as Charles flung himself onto him and started to heave him overboard. I couldn't let him do that. Although the boat was rocking and the waves washing over the side, I managed to take hold of one oar and found the strength to swing it at Charles' head. I don't think he was dead and I could have stopped. I could have stopped,' she repeated and looked at Henry Villiers as if she wanted to be sure that he'd heard. His eyes darkened, and she spoke again, 'But I swung the oar once more, and again, and I think perhaps once more. After that, he was quite still. I wanted to kill him. I knew what I was doing. I couldn't let him kill Edouard. My love for him was stronger than my love for your son had ever been. I had none left for him. I hated him, for what he'd done to Edouard, to me and Emily.' Lenora halted, expecting a reaction from the man in front of her, but none came. 'Charles is out there, at the bottom of the lake. That's why I could never return to Lakeside House.'

Words were forming on Henry Villiers' lips, but she put a hand out, 'No, let me speak. This was the third time your son tried to kill your brother. This is the truth. I had been suspicious, but I refused to believe it, until we were on the lake; then his action made it clear. He had planned to do so several times.'

'You're lying. My son might not have been perfect, but he was no murderer.'

Lenora ignored his remark, 'Edouard was extremely shaken. "*In the name of the Lord, Lenora, tell me! What has happened?*" he begged.

I told him, "*Charles tried to kill you. You heard him.*"

"*Yes, yes,*" he answered, "*where is he now?*"

"He is dead. I killed him."

Edouard didn't believe me. He insisted we should hurry ashore and find a doctor for Charles. I told him it was too late. In time the hysteria in my voice convinced him that this was true. I said to Edouard, "*Can you hear him talk? Can you?*"

Edouard answered, "*No, but...*"

"*That's because he is dead, he is dead,*" I said. "*We have to inform the constabulary.*"

Edouard reached out. "*Please, Lenora, give me your hands, I must hold them.*" We sat like this in the boat, I don't know for how long. Neither of us spoke, and we were getting wet. It had started to rain, but we didn't seem to notice.'

She paused for breath. 'At length Edouard said that he was partly to blame, and he couldn't let me hang. So, we decided to send your son's body to the bottom of the lake. I was about to heave him overboard, when Edouard stopped me. He told me the body would float, so I rowed back to shore.' Lenora grimaced, 'It wasn't easy with Charles lying there in front of me. His eyes were open and they had that astonished look I saw, when I swung the oar at his head. I fetched the heavy anchor from the boathouse and struggled to carry it to the boat. Then I roped it to the body, tugging at the knots to make them secure, and I rowed all the way out again. I don't know where I found the strength...,' her voice faltered.

She remained silent for several minutes and only spoke when Henry Villiers shook her shoulders. Her voice was toneless, 'I heaved him overboard and watched him sink. Edouard stayed with me throughout.'

Henry Villiers' face was tense, his lips pulled back, baring his teeth. He looked as if he were about to strike her. Lenora shuddered and pulled away.

'Shall I continue?'

'Yes, I want to hear it all.' The look in his grey eyes sent shivers down her back.

'I rowed us to shore. Edouard didn't say a word. At home, we changed our wet clothes and sat by the fire in the drawing room and, there, I went down on my knees and begged his forgiveness. I told him about my infidelity, how I had willingly let myself be seduced. I had loved Charles and I had been happy. It was true that I was carrying his child, and that had made me realise the madness in what we were doing. I had regrets. But Charles wouldn't let me go. He insisted that I loved him. With Edouard gone, he said, we could marry and live at Lakeside House.' Lenora paused for a moment.

'Charles also seduced Emily, the daughter of our neighbour. I explained it all to Edouard. He just sat there, still as a statue and didn't ask any questions. When I had finished, he went to his room, saying he was tired, his face drawn and his shoulders slumped. I didn't see him until the next morning. I had left out the most humiliating; what I couldn't bear to tell him. Because of Charles' loose talk, I was degraded by another member of your family. I wanted to spare him the pain of this knowledge.'

Lenora waited for a reaction, but none came, 'Do you not wish to know who it was?'

Henry Villiers shrugged, 'No, continue.'

'I spent the night pacing the floor. I wanted to go to Edouard and again ask for his forgiveness, to explain more. But the ashen look I had seen on his face and his silence scared me. In the morning, he told me that he hadn't slept that night, but he'd made plans. He would make arrangements with Holden & Son, whose owner knew him and had served him well. They would take care of the money matters. We would live in Ireland until we could be certain that Charles' body wouldn't return from the deep. He asked if I had securely tied the rope with the anchor around the body. I had spent most of the night asking myself that question. I had been extremely distressed. Only the passage of time would tell if this crime would be discovered: a crime that would take me to the gallows. Edouard told me that the lake was deep, which I knew. To his knowledge, nothing had ever come back from its depths. We would be able to return once we were sure. However, Molly and George were to be told that we were going to France, to spend a few months with his relatives. Edouard had decided to accept the child as his own. He forgave me everything, even killing Charles. He'd encouraged me to spend time with Charles. He believed that he'd pushed me into the arms of your son, and blamed himself for what had happened. Your brother was very forgiving; perhaps you should learn from him.'

She paused to see what effect her words had had on Charles' father, but his face betrayed no emotion.

She continued, 'Edouard's plan was good, it worked well. I had packed all Charles' belongings, and his cases were hidden in larger ones we'd bought. I had made sure there was nothing that could identify them as belonging to him. In Ireland, we left them standing by the quayside.

Your granddaughter was born in Ireland. She had Charles' good looks. I had not wanted this child. I had no longing and felt no emotion or happiness when I thought about this unborn child, only regrets. But when she was born and I saw her, I loved her. She grew up to be a beautiful young woman and married well. She was a constant reminder of Charles but gave me much comfort. He did bring me happiness, after all. She never learnt about her background, always believing that Edouard was her father.'

Henry Villiers interrupted her, 'Please, tell me my granddaughter's name.'

'We named her Victoria, after Edouard's first love and yours, I believe.' Lenora saw his eyes soften for a moment but quickly regain their hardness.

'Thank you, please continue.'

She nodded, 'Edouard loved her, but he had been unwell since we left Cumberland, and Victoria was a sickly infant. We had to delay our return to England. When Victoria was six months old, he caught pneumonia and died. So, you see, I was severely punished for my sins. I was left on my own in the small cottage we'd rented on this large estate. I had no wish to return here.

Eventually, I married the landowner's youngest son. I had some money of my own, and Edouard had brought with him a considerable sum, but I was left with no other income after he died. I didn't contact his solicitors; my decision to stay in Ireland stood firm. I had left Lakeside House forever. I couldn't live here, knowing that Charles was in the lake.'

Henry Villiers let go of her shoulders, 'After my passing from this world, I had to roam in twilight between life and death, day and night, until you were reborn in this other woman. It was a long time. Only then could I return. It was for her to relive Charles' year at Lakeside House and to tell me what had happened to my son. My power was able to take me back thus far in time, but no further.'

'Your powers are extremely impressive, to achieve what you've done; I acknowledge that I cannot fight you.'

'It pleases me that you know this. It will make it easier for both of us. You do understand that I'll have to punish you?'

'I have lived with what I did to Charles and the immense pain I caused Edouard. Even so, he was much comforted by the knowledge that he'd saved me from the gallows. It was remarkable that he blamed himself. We lived in the shadow of what had happened, and we never recovered our old contentment. He was not the same man; I believe he lost the will to live. I have been punished, as I've told you.'

'It's not enough for me.'

'No, I know, but I stopped Charles from becoming a murderer.'

'How do I know this is true? You lured Charles out in the boat and killed him in cold blood, to stop him from telling Edouard.'

'That is not how it happened; your mind is distorted. Charles was a killer. He was responsible for Edouard's fall down the stairs and the accident with the horse.'

'What accident?'

'You see, you don't know everything. I have no proof, but....'

'Be silent! You're lying. I've waited years for this. Nothing you say will change my mind. I must achieve nirvana, and only retribution can give me that.'

'I am also Ellen. You can't let her suffer for my crime.'

That's absolutely right, Ellen wanted to scream, but, with Lenora in control, she couldn't speak. Ellen struggled to push her own mind forward, she felt that she was close. Perhaps with more effort she could reach her...

'No, I blame only you, Lenora. You must show me where my son is. We need this other woman to do that. I shall take you both to the lake.' Henry's voice was firm.

Oh no, not there, Ellen panicked, her mind racing; she had to stop this happening. The pain in her head reached a pitch, as her mind struggled to come to the forefront. She heard a voice she barely recognised as her own, but it was decisive.

'I will not go there.' She was elated; she'd managed to push Lenora out of her mind.

She froze as Lenora returned, 'But we must, Ellen, you'll have to come. I am in your body. I have to follow him.'

'Why? Why do you want to punish me for what you've done?' Ellen pleaded.

Lenora answered, 'Because it's the only way I'll find peace. It's what I want. I have no choice, nor have you.'

'Listen, for heaven's sake. Listen! I should have a choice,' Ellen choked; this was madness beyond words; two voices were coming from her body.

Henry Villiers spoke, 'Ellen, you're two now, with two minds, and hers is stronger. She can't release you, because I won't let her. You can try to fight her, but she'll fight you back. She wants peace and when she finds it, we'll both have it. There's one precise moment when she can let you go. If she misses that, you'll be lost too.'

‘Lenora, please don’t do this. I’ve tried to help. I really have.’

‘I know, but I need you.’

Henry Villiers took hold of Lenora’s arm and led her towards the door, ‘Come, it’s time.’

‘No!’ Ellen protested. Her head ached with a pain she’d never experienced before.

‘I’m taking Lenora for a boat ride.’

‘I will not. I forbid you to go, Lenora.’ Ellen’s voice was strong.

‘I am not sure I can come...’ Lenora stopped abruptly, ‘she is holding me back.’ She pulled her arm free of Henry’s grip.

‘I can do it! I am succeeding,’ Ellen cried out. ‘I want no further part of this, Henry Villiers. I have a strong will too. You’ll have to let me go.’ But Ellen felt the pain in her head drain away and with it her new-found strength. The other voice inside her head wanted to be heard.

‘I believe Lenora is in charge again,’ Henry said in a matter-of-fact way.

‘Yes, I am. I will come with you. Let’s not linger.’

Henry’s eyes showed a flicker of satisfaction but quickly turned cold and determined. He led Lenora out of the house and down to the lake.

Ellen knew that Lenora had full control and wouldn’t let her speak, and she tried to push her mind to the forefront: to escape. This was crazy, and she felt that she was truly going mad.

As they reached the lake, Lenora showed no outward signs of distress. She pulled the shawl closer around her body, before she lifted her skirt to climb into the boat, accepting a helping hand from Henry.

He rowed with strong purposeful strokes, not taking his eyes off her until she nodded. He let the oars drop, ‘Is this where my son was murdered?’

Lenora turned sideways and seemed to study the water, ‘About here,’ her voice was emotionless. ‘It was a long time ago.' When she raised her head, she didn't focus on him but stared over his shoulder with a distant look on her face.

'What is on your mind?' he asked.

'That Charles has won in the end.'

'In what way?'

'He said, "*I shall have you, you will belong to me.*" And soon I will.'

'I have no choice.'

'I had no choice. I couldn't have spent the rest of my life with Charles, knowing that he'd killed Edouard.'

'This is the only way that I can leave this world. And you must come with me. You understand that, don't you?'

'Yes, I do,' Lenora answered.

Oh God, he intends to drown us both. Is this how my life will end? Ellen was about to lose hope.

'Stand up!' Henry pinned Lenora's arms down by her sides and folded his arms around her body.

The next moment they were in the lake. Lenora's skirt floated up above them, ensnaring them, covering her face as she gasped for breath, her chest hurting. Henry's grip remained strong as their water-logged clothes pulled them down. The shock of the cold sharpened Ellen's senses.

With one last effort, she pushed her mind forward, her thoughts intense. Lenora, let me go! You don't want to take another life, I know you. You don't want to kill me. In her half-conscious mind, Ellen heard her reply; *You're right. I never intended to. I don't need you now. I'm on my way. You're free.*

Suddenly, Henry's grip fell away. Ellen was shooting upwards; glancing down, she saw the bodies of Henry and Lenora disappear out of view. Above her, a light appeared, and she broke the surface, gasping for air. Where was the boat? Her head moved wildly from side to side; she had to get to it or she was doomed. She saw it floating a few metres away. Her clothes made swimming difficult, and she reached the boat exhausted. For a minute she clung to the side, before starting to pull herself up. She failed and cried in frustration. The lake wanted to pull her back into the deep, not to let her go.

Mustering all her strength, she made a last successful attempt; she had to get out before hypothermia set in. Her body shook with cold as she fell into the boat and scrambled onto her knees. Her hands were blue and painful when she tried to rub them warm. She could only row slowly, it was difficult to grip the oars. Her clothes clung to her, but the movement of rowing brought some warmth back into her freezing body. She reached the shore and heaved herself out of the boat, then struggled to secure it to its moorings.

Dazed, she walked towards her car she should hurry, but there was pain in her legs and arms from the cold and the effort of rowing. The suitcase felt as if it weighed a ton as she brought it out of the boot, although she knew it wasn't heavy. She was barely able to lift her arms to pull off her wet shirt and put on a warm jumper and dry jeans.

In the car she sat with the engine running and gradually her body responded. Her thoughts went to Daniel. Would he have her back? She was a murderer. Could she tell him that she'd killed in a previous life? Would he feel unsafe? Did he still think that she'd had a breakdown? If she told him the truth, would he believe that now she was having another?

Was it her fault that Lenora had killed Charles? In her mantra, she had repeatedly asked her to get rid of him forever. Perhaps she had changed events, perhaps a hundred years ago, Charles had left for London on his way back to Canada and mysteriously disappeared. Perhaps...

When she was warm, she walked down to the shore. This was the last time she would see the lake. For several minutes she stared out over the water; it was no longer threatening. She looked up the slope, she knew that Lakeside House had disappeared and would never come back. Lenora had joined Charles at the bottom of the lake. Henry Villiers had sought justice for his son and achieved it. This had been her reason for being at Lakeside House. She had been instrumental in making this possible for him. He was reunited with his son.

Glancing sideways, she let her eyes follow the water line to an area overgrown with sea grasses and algae. There was no boathouse to be seen, or moorings, nor the boat which had brought her to the shore.